REDEEMING SLATER - DISCREET

SHANDI BOYES

Edited by
MOUNTAINS WANTED PUBLISHING

Illustrated by
SSB COVERS AND DESIGN

ALSO BY SHANDI BOYES

Denotes Standalone Books

Perception Series

Saving Noah *

Fighting Jacob *

Taming Nick *

Redeeming Slater *

Saving Emily

Wrapped Up with Rise Up

Protecting Nicole *

Enigma

Enigma

Unraveling an Enigma

Enigma The Mystery Unmasked

Enigma: The Final Chapter

Beneath The Secrets

Beneath The Sheets

Spy Thy Neighbor *

The Opposite Effect *

I Married a Mob Boss *

Second Shot *

The Way We Are

The Way We Were

Sugar and Spice *

Lady In Waiting

Man in Queue

Couple on Hold

Enigma: The Wedding

Silent Vigilante

Hushed Guardian

Quiet Protector

Enigma: An Isaac Retelling

Twisted Lies *

Bound Series

Chains

Links

Bound

Restrain

The Misfits *

Nanny Dispute *

Russian Mob Chronicles

Nikolai: A Mafia Prince Romance

Nikolai: Taking Back What's Mine

Nikolai: What's Left of Me

Nikolai: Mine to Protect

Asher: My Russian Revenge *

Nikolai: Through the Devil's Eyes

<u>Trey</u> *

The Italian Cartel

Dimitri

Roxanne

Reign

Mafia Ties (Novella)

Maddox

Demi

Ox

Rocco *

Clover *

Smith *

RomCom Standalones

Just Playin' *

Ain't Happenin' *

The Drop Zone *

Very Unlikely *

False Start *

Short Stories - Newsletter Downloads

Christmas Trio *

Falling For A Stranger *

One Night Only Series

Hotshot Boss *

Hotshot Neighbor *

<u>The Bobrov Bratva Series</u>

Wicked Intentions *

Sinful Intentions *

Devious Intentions *

Deadly Intentions *

<u>Coming Soon</u>

Nanny Dispute *

Protecting Nicole (December 26) *

WANT TO STAY IN TOUCH?

Facebook: facebook.com/authorshandi

Instagram: instagram.com/authorshandi

Email: authorshandi@gmail.com

Reader's Group: bit.ly/ShandiBookBabes

Website: authorshandi.com

Newsletter: https://www.subscribepage.com/AuthorShandi

COPYRIGHT

No part of this eBook may be reproduced or transmitted in any form or by any means, electronic or mechanical, including photocopying, recording or by any information storage and retrieval system, without written permission from the author.
This is a work of fiction. Any names or characters, businesses or places, events or incidents, are fictitious. Any resemblance to actual persons, living or dead, or actual events is purely coincidental.
Editing: Mountains Wanted Publishing
Cover: SSB Designs
Some photo edits were made to the photograph.

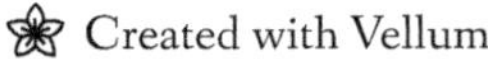 Created with Vellum

DEDICATED TO:

Kym, my number one fan.

Thanks for all your words of inspiration.
Your words mean the world to me.

From, your writer girl.

CHAPTER ONE

SLATER

Pure adrenaline. That's what surges through my blood when I'm behind my Tama Starphonic drum kit. Then, not long later, exhaustion kicks in. If you've ever heard someone say being a drummer is easy, be assured they've never played the drums in their life. Being a drummer is hard work—it sucks the life right out of me. Some concerts take me days to recover from.

By the time I reach the end of a set, I feel like I've run a marathon; my hands burn as if I placed them directly on the sun, and my clothes are soaked with sweat. And don't get me started on the pesky drumsticks. Those slippery fuckers escape my grip at the most inappropriate times. I'm lucky I can maintain the tempo of the song while scrambling for another set.

Don't misconstrue—I'm not complaining. Nothing in the world competes with this—not one single fucking thing. Tonight, we're playing to a crowd of over forty thousand people at Safeco Field, home of the Seattle Mariners. The roar of fans requesting an encore is almost deafening. It's an electric energy that makes me both agitated and reckless. Not because I hate what I'm doing, but because I'm afraid nothing will ever replicate the high I get while performing.

Only once has something spurred this much hype from me. It wasn't really a thing—more a her. A real pretty "her" with freckles and wild hair and a smell that made me think of fields upon fields of sunflowers. She wasn't a groupie I lost myself in. She was before the fame. Before the notoriety. She saw me as just me—*until she didn't.*

I'm drawn from my thoughts when Nick picks up the water bottle he stores behind my drum kit. "Every night." He nudges his head to the crowd surging toward the pitch-black stage. "Never grows old, though."

I laugh. "No, it doesn't."

The band does the same routine at every concert. We wait for our fans' screams to reach an eardrum-damaging level before giving them one last song—the final hurrah of the show. While waiting for that to happen, I run a towel over my sweat-drenched head and hands. I've gone through four pairs of sticks already tonight. I don't want to add more to my tally. For one, they're not cheap. And two, every pair I lose I have to sign at the end of the night since Nick kicks them into the crowd as souvenirs.

Upon noticing Noah's beaming bright smile, our signal that it's time to perform, Nick stuffs his water bottle back behind my drums before resuming his position on the right-hand side of the stage. Once everyone is in place, I tap my sticks over my head, counting in the beat. The instant they hit my snare drum, the lights on the stage illuminate, and the crowd's screams intensify even more. This is what I love, right here, right now. Pure. Addiction. There's no drug stronger than this.

My muscles flex, and sweat dribbles down my back as Rise Up gives the crowd what they paid for. We perform our hearts out, providing them the encore they so desperately crave. Our music will thrum in their veins for hours to come. It's like sex, just more addictive, and they gobble up every tingle we give them.

By the time our hit single "Tastefully Despised" comes to an end, my lungs are void of oxygen. Mercifully, the buzz of performing will run through my system like morphine for hours to come—much longer than the drugs that used to feed my high.

I'm clean now, have been coming up on two years. The road to sobriety wasn't pretty, but I did it; I survived rehab and came out with my insanity intact—*for the most part*. My veins are clear of drugs; I just feed my obsession in other ways now. Groupies. Alcohol. The buzz of an overhyped crowd who'll never quit requesting an encore no matter how many we play.

At the start, the band got so excited they loved our shows, we did encore after encore after encore. Thank fuck we soon caught on that their requests would never end. Now, they get one last song, then Maddie and Jasper are brought onto the stage, signaling it's the end of our show.

Once Maddie finishes wooing the crowd with her chubby cheeks and toothless grin, she bolts for Jasper, who's using his daddy's thigh to hide from the crowd. After standing from my drum kit, I throw my sticks into the crowd. Whoever catches them will be given an all-inclusive backstage pass to have their stick autographed by me. We've had a few people try and sneak backstage with sticks they brought from home. It did them no good. My sticks are custom-made. They also have my signature engraved on them, making them impossible to replicate.

Emily thought it would drum up good publicity, no pun intended. Unlike her predecessor, she ensures the band as a whole is included in any press junkets involving Rise Up. When our debut album rocketed up the charts, most interview requests were only addressed to Noah. Their mistake cost them dearly. Not only did Noah refuse their invitations, but he snubs the offending journalists during the conferences we hold in each state we visit.

People think we're just a bunch of guys who play music. We're not. We're a band of brothers, and as much as this kills me to admit, that statement also includes Nick.

Rise Up's debut album, *Beginning,* became one of the highest-selling albums of all time. It rocketed us to superstardom, and lined our pockets with more money than we'll ever need. But, even with us being filthy rich, the band has remained humble. That might have something to do with the fact we travel with two babies in tow. That would soften even the hardest group. It's lucky Jasper and Maddie are cute. It's also lucky I travel on my motorbike between towns.

A tour bus takes the band to each location. Once we arrive where we're touring, we're put up in fancy-schmancy five-star hotel with all the bells and whistles, and we don't pay a cent for it. It's all compliments of the record label. I used to travel in the tour bus with the band, but there's no such thing as peace with two toddlers running around.

I had my bike, a custom Harley Davidson Fatboy with twelve-inch ape hangers, shipped to Los Angeles. Now, I travel behind the bus. Cormack shit bricks when I arrived in San Francisco on my bike. He said it was unsafe for me to travel alone. I assured him a protective detail wasn't needed. I have my trusty baseball bat in my saddle bag. What more protection do I need?

I can't say I don't understand Cormack's worry. Life has become crazy the past two years. I can't even shit without the public being updated on its length and texture. Every event we do is splashed onto the gossip pages the very next day. Even the most mundane task is treated as if it's front page news. You realize how fucked-up the world is when it's more important to know what Noah Taylor had for dinner last night than worrying about the millions of children in the world starving every day.

While shrugging off the eccentricity of life, my eyes stray to Nick. He's hobbling off the stage since Jasper is wrapped around his leg. Jasper's personality is a stark contradiction to his father's. He's been running onto the stage at every concert since he could walk, yet he's still shit-scared.

With a growl, I scoop Jasper off Nick's leg before blowing a raspberry on his t-shirt-covered belly. He giggles loudly, sending baby spit flying in all directions.

"Again, Uncle."

I assume that's what he saying since I don't understand a word of baby talk. When I blow on his belly again, and he giggles even louder than before, it's safe to say that's what he was requesting.

When I enter the wings of the stage, I hand a giggling and red-faced Jasper to Jenni. She smiles at our banter, her cheeks blushing to match her son's. She's not reddening in amusement. It's from catching sight of Nick over my shoulder. For some fucked-up reason, she has it bad for him.

Gagging, I join Marcus in our shared dressing room, happy to leave Noah and Nick to make out with their flustered baby mommas. Before we were famous, Noah and Nick were all about the groupies. Now nothing but their horny housewives are on their minds. I swear Emily practically humps Noah's leg the instant he exits the stage.

I jerk up my chin to greet the security officer standing guard at my door. He's paid to protect us, but in reality, he fought tooth and nail for his placement. Since Marcus and I are single, we have to pick up the slack of our taken counterparts. With that number constantly higher than two men can handle, our roadies and the men paid to protect us greatly benefit from the deficit.

When Marcus notices my arrival, he sets down our concert schedule for this week. "Beer?"

"Sounds good."

My eyes stray to the itinerary he set down. We're booked to do four gigs while in Seattle. Our first was tonight, then we have a four-day break before kicking it off again on Friday. After toeing off my boots, I slump onto one of the three sofas in the room that is bigger than the entire floorplan of my first house. It's only fair Marcus and I get the biggest room since we have to share.

There are only four dressing rooms in the stadium. The largest is ours, Noah and Nick have one each, and the remaining one was given to our supporting act Big Halo. They're a new age pop group who are signed to the same record label as Rise Up. Cormack thought they'd suit our fan base. They have a similar sound to Rise Up, but half of their band are girls. Hot girls. *Smoking* hot girls. The bassist, Miranda, has drool-worthy looks. Her thick, luscious brown hair hangs halfway down her back; her eyes are green and big, and her lips are the plumpest I've ever seen.

Her only downfall is that she likes girls as much as I do.

My eyes float up from my shoes when Marcus hands me a recently popped open bottle of beer. We thought the perks at Mavericks were good. Half our pay there was supplied with unlimited beer. Now we get anything we request. We could even have our M&M's color-coordinated if we wanted. Our roadies and assistants should thank their lucky stars that we aren't assholes. For the most part, we keep our requests to a minimum.

"Cheers, fucker."

When I clink my bottle of beer against Marcus's, he smiles against the rim before taking a generous swig. Marcus is the quiet one of our group. Other than when Noah was in a coma, I don't recall hearing a swear word seep from his lips. He drinks beer, plays the bass guitar like he was born to do it, and is a kick ass friend; however, I know there's more to him than he's letting on. My dad always says, "It's the quiet ones you need to watch." Marcus is the very definition of that saying.

We couldn't be any more different if we tried. My arms are covered with tattoos, where he doesn't have one. I wear jeans, motorcycle boots, and t-shirts. He wears trousers, button-up shirts, and polished dress shoes. I have long blond dreadlocks and a stubble-covered chin, whereas he's clean-shaven all over, including his hair. Despite our differences, we're the best of friends. He's my brother from another mother, and do you know what brought us together? Music.

Marcus's grandma lived next door to my parents. I'd heard him play around with the instruments in her garage many times during his weekly visits. Most of the time, it sounded as if he was preparing for a church solo, so you can imagine my shock when one Sunday afternoon I heard the distinctive sound of Breaking Benjamin's song "Diary of Jane" blaring out of his garage.

I bolted to his house, expecting to see Benjamin Burley because the person singing matched his voice to perfection. I was shocked when I discovered a scrawny teenage boy belting out the lyrics. He would have been around thirteen at the time, but his voice was a lot more mature. When Marcus fiddled with computer equipment at the side of the room, drums, guitar and a keyboard boomed out of the speakers behind him. I watched them in awe, knowing without a doubt that the boy singing would become one of the world's greatest performers because Marcus's production skills would ensure it.

Once the song ended, the teen threw the microphone stand like a true rock star before raising his hands in the air. When his head flopped back, I couldn't help but clap. They were musical prodigies. My loud clap startled both Marcus and the singer when it echoed around the small, dingy garage, but their shock didn't stop me from saying, "That was fucking brilliant."

The young dark-haired boy grinned a mega-watt smile. You could see he was in his element. At that point in his life, nothing but music mattered.

"Thanks," he replied humbly.

And that, ladies and gentlemen, is how I met Noah Taylor and Marcus Everett, two of the world's greatest musicians. That afternoon, I found out they met at a music store in town. Marcus's grandma was there to sell her vintage 1955 Esquire White Guard Fender. When they got to talking about all things music, Marcus invited Noah to see the studio his grandma had set up in her garage for his mom when she was in a band.

I'm three years older than Marcus and Noah, but that didn't stop me from pursuing a music career with them when they said they were starting a band. I just needed to learn how to play an instrument. Marcus said if I was dedicated, he was more than willing to teach me.

During our first rehearsal, I cockily strolled to an electric guitar leaning against an amp, certain I had the makings of a skilled guitarist. When I strummed the strings, it sounded like someone scratching their nails down a chalkboard. Noah laughed at my lack of a musical bone; however, Marcus continued encouraging me. Over the next two hours, he handed me a range of instruments to test out. Only one showcased my talent in a favorable light. It was the silver triangle they give every untalented kid when they join the school band.

I was on the verge of giving up when Marcus pulled a bedsheet off a drum kit. As dust filtered around the room, my heart rate soared. That was it, staring right at me. Love at first sight does exist, because I loved that drum kit from the moment I saw it.

And as they say, the rest is history.

Marcus visited his grandmother's house every weekend, so every weekend we practiced from sunup until sundown. A year later, when Marcus moved into his grandmother's house permanently, we added weekday rehearsals into our schedule as well. Now, ten years later, we're at the pinnacle of success. Our concerts are sold out within hours, and we do press junkets and meet and greets after each show. Life couldn't be more perfect—I'm just missing the final piece of my puzzle.

Refusing to let my past dampen my mood, I jump up to my feet. "I'm gonna take a quick shower."

I slap Marcus on the shoulder two times before entering the bathroom attached to our dressing room. It's nearly the same size with a double-headed shower, a wall of mirrors, and a counter covered with a range of products advertising execs are praying we'll endorse.

I always shower before the fan meet and greet. I don't want sweaty pits scaring away our fans. I'm not joking when I say my clothes are drenched with sweat after each performance. Well, my jeans are. I don't wear a shirt while performing. What's the use? I can't remove it halfway through a set. Drummers don't prance around the stage like guitarists and singers do. My body is constantly moving, meaning there's no time to whip off a shirt, so I don't bother starting our gig with one.

Once I've showered and changed into jeans and a short-sleeve black shirt, I make my way to the room Emily sets up after every concert for our fan meet and greet. The band used to sit at one long desk, but it was a pain in the ass when we tried to interact with our fans, so Emily arranged for four individual tables—kick ass tables. She had them designed to match our musical instruments. Nick's is an electric guitar. Marcus's is a bass guitar. Mine is obviously a drum, and Noah's is....

I don't know what the fuck Noah's is. I think it's supposed to be a mic stand, but the microphone sticking out the middle of it makes it seem as if he's holding a press conference every time he sits down. I've seen him push the mic out the way any time Emily leaves the room. I've told him many times to grow some balls and tell Emily he hates his table, but he swears until he's blue in the face that he loves it. His lie ensures I make whipping noises at him as often as possible. He's so fucking pussy-whipped.

The buzz sizzling in my veins grows as more fans trickle into the room. To ensure they get their money's worth, only a handful of people are permitted to enter at one time. It gives them a chance to truly meet their idols instead of it appearing like a cattle drive. We sign autographs and pose for pictures with a select few who either paid top dollar to meet us or won the opportunity.

My eyes hover up from the CD I'm signing when the pretty blonde in front of me murmurs, "You know my friend."

"Is that so?"

While she nods, I scan her body. She's cute—actually, she's pretty hot—my tastes just lean more toward brunettes. This girl's platinum blonde locks are cut into a fierce bob; her eyes are the color of an ocean, and her plaid button-up shirt is tied in the middle of her stomach. Her tiny denim shorts show a nice amount of skin, and she has a real playful vibe about her, which is revealed in full detail when she notices my prolonged perusal of her body.

After cocking her hip out, she raises her brow high into her hairline. "Sorry, I don't do vanilla." Her lust-riddled eyes stray to Marcus, who's sitting next to me. "I only like chocolate ice cream."

When I chuckle, Marcus stops signing a photograph to peer at me. Realizing she's secured his attention, the blonde strikes a pose, looking prepared to walk the catwalk in a Victoria's Secret fashion show.

After flashing the envious fan a grin, Marcus interacts with the fan at his table, and the blonde's focus shifts back to me. "The things I could teach that boy," she murmurs under her breath while handing me one of the drumsticks I threw out earlier tonight.

Now everything makes sense. Since she didn't pay for the privilege to meet us, she can't visit the bandmember she really wants to visit. It's for the best. Marcus has no issues with the ladies, but he's very particular about whom he allows to warm his sheets. Nothing against this blonde bombshell, but she doesn't seem like Marcus's type. She's too wild for him. He likes them tame and meek—somewhat submissive.

I scribble my name along the stick in a black permanent marker before handing it back to her. "Thanks." She smiles a beaming grin while stuffing it into her oversized handbag. "My friend can add it to the collection of sticks she already has from you."

"So your friend is a fan of vanilla?"

She pulls a face like she just vomited. "She's as vanilla as they come, and I mean that in more ways than one."

When she jingles her phone in the air, I move to the other side of my table to take a quick selfie with her. My pulse spikes as high as my brow when her hand gets friendly with my backside. "How the hell did she ever give that up?"

After taking over a dozen photos, she scrolls through them, explaining to me that she wants to ensure she got at least one decent picture before she leaves my table. "The last thing I want to do is wrangle those bunch of crazies again. She nudges her head to two giggling brunettes waiting to meet me next.

"We good?"

She purses her lips. "Yeah, I think so."

Just as I'm about to walk back to my seat, I catch one of her photos in the corner of my eye. It doesn't just halt my retreat, it freezes my heart as well.

No way. That couldn't be her.

"Scroll back." I plaster my body to the blonde's back so I can peer over her shoulder. I don't even care if she can feel my raging heart. Maybe if she feels the urgency of my request, she'll hurry the fuck up.

"You look great. Me, on the other hand..."

Her words trail off when I flick through the thousands of photos in her album at the speed of a bullet being dislodged from a gun. She's taking too long, and my patience is stretched thin.

"Holy fuck."

The blonde peers at me curiously at the same time my heart stops beating. The person I thought I saw is right. It's her—Kylie. I haven't seen her in years, but I'd never forget her face. Not only is it burned into my retinas, but I memorized every tiny freckle that adorns her beautiful nose.

When the blonde notices my shocked expression, she rolls her eyes. "I said you knew my friend."

She did, but I thought she meant a *friend* friend, like a groupie friend, a casual hook up. Not the girl I used to love—the one who stole my heart and never returned it.

"She caught your stick but asked me to get it signed for her—"

My eyes snap to the blonde so fast, my head gets a rush of dizziness. "She's here?!" Kylie lives on the other side of the country, so it's highly doubtful she's in Seattle.

I'm proven wrong when Kylie's friend nods. "Yep." The "p" pops from her red-painted lips. "She's right over there."

When she points to the other side of the room, my head flings to the side so fast I give myself whiplash. It's got nothing on the dead hum my heart tries to break out when my eyes land on Kylie for the first time in nearly two years.

She was the only girl I ever loved.

The only girl I would have risked everything for.

And the only girl who broke my heart into a million pieces.

Maybe we weren't meant to last forever, but it shouldn't have ended how it did, either.

CHAPTER TWO

KYLIE

When Slater's eyes skim down my body, a tingling sensation builds between my legs. It's the same buzz that made me feel alive years ago, a teasing, familiar vibration that reveals I'm once again falling under his spell.

The noose is wrapped halfway around my neck when the eyes that were staring at me in wonderment only seconds ago narrow into thin slits. Slater glares at me, his greeting less than welcoming. His response is unwanted but understandable.

Nearly two years have passed since we last saw each other, yet guilt still eats away my insides. The horrid, black slosh swishing in my stomach is the reason I fought Melanie tooth and nail not to come to tonight's concert. I knew the instant I saw Slater again, guilt would resurface, not to mention the feelings I try to deny every day.

However, Melanie wouldn't take no for an answer, and I soon caved—like I always do. I bet she wishes she weren't so stubborn now. Slater's scowl is so white-hot, anyone caught in the crossfire is on the brink of being singed. Since Melanie is closest to him, she's feeling his wrath just as intensely as me.

Incapable of withstanding his glare for a second longer, I peel my heart off the floor before darting for the corridor. I already look like a blubbering fool, so I refuse to add more idiocy to our reunion by letting strangers witness my tears.

Just as I'm about to exit, I bump into someone taking the corner too quickly. "Sorry." Our collision wasn't my fault, but I'm so desperate to get away, I'll take the blame.

I'm partway out the door when a voice I don't immediately recognize calls my name. When my eyes lift from the polished concrete floor, I instantly identify the light blue pair staring back at me. "Hi, Jenni."

Jenni shoves me one step closer to coronary failure when she squeals an ear-piercing scream before wrapping me up in a firm hug. Even in the tense circumstances, I relish her embrace. It's heartfelt enough to thaw even the iciest of stares—like the one Slater is still directing at me. I can't see him, but I can feel his eyes on me. Who knew hate ran so cold?

After a final squeeze, Jenni inches back to peer into my eyes. "I haven't seen you since the cabin..." Her reply falls short when her eyes zoom in on the moisture brimming in mine. "Are you okay?"

When my watering eyes stray to the handful of Rise Up fans who witnessed my exchange with Slater, Jenni tugs me into the hall, not only saving me from Slater's wrathful glare, but from being booted out for creating a fire hazard as well.

"What's going on? You seem upset."

I shoo away her worry with a wave of my hand. "I'm fine. The smoke machines during the concert muck up my sinuses. I'm just grateful the mess is coming out of my eyes and not my nose. That would have been awkward." *Like things aren't already a hot mess.*

As I dab at the moisture pooling in the corner of my eyes, I plaster my best fake smile onto my face. Jenni's pursed lips reveal she isn't buying my act, but mercifully, she doesn't push me.

"The smoke can be a little overdone at times."

Our conversation is interrupted by a little blond-haired boy wrapping his arms around Jenni's leg. Laughing, Jenni bends down to pick him up. My heart beats in an unnatural rhythm when my eyes run over his adorable face. Nick would never be able to deny this little boy is his. He's the spitting image of his father in every way, except for his strawberry blond hair.

With my heart not up for more shredding, I avoided entertainment programs and gossip magazines the past two years. Other than hearing the occasional Rise Up song on the radio, I'm clueless about anything in their private lives.

My head cranks to the side when a gentleman I'd guess to be early forties stops to stand next to us. "I'm sorry, you know what he's like when he wants his mom."

The stranger's blond hair is clipped close at the sides, but the top is a little messy. He has striking blue eyes, and a fit and enticing body. Although he's a few years older than me, I doubt he has any problems attracting the ladies. He's gorgeous.

"It's fine, Harrison, I was about to come grab him anyway." Jenni's voice is as sickly sweet as her personality.

After tickling the boy's tummy, Harrison walks down a long black corridor.

"Jasper." Jenni bobs up and down, striving to steal the boy's attention away from blowing kisses at Harrison. She achieves the seemingly unachievable when Harrison enters a room at the end of the corridor. "Jasper, can you say hello to Kylie?"

Jasper either lacks social skills, or he communicates via spit. Not only does his raspberry cover my face and arms with baby slobber, it coats the wall next to my head as well.

"I'm so sorry."

The giggle bubbling in my chest erupts when Jenni attempts to wipe away the spit careening down my cheek with the cuff of her shirt.

I step back from the firing zone. "It's fine—really." Spit is a perfect excuse for the wetness my cheeks are close to holding.

When Jasper peers at me from beneath long lashes, I glance into his big blue eyes before making a monkey face. When he smiles a toothy grin, I drag my index finger down his screwed-up nose. "Hi Jasper. I'm Kylie. It's a pleasure to meet you."

He awards my friendliness by holding out his arms for me.

"Can I hold him?" I ask Jenni, my eyes shooting to hers.

Smiling, she passes him to me. I melt into a gooey puddle when he bands his tiny arms around my neck before snuggling his head into my chest. Now the moisture in my eyes is there for an entirely different reason. I've only ever had one boy immediately smitten with me. He's the same man I hurt beyond repair almost two years ago.

When Jenni spots the tears pooling in my eyes, she slaps my arm. "Don't. If you cry, I'll cry, then I won't stop."

"I'm not going to cry. I'm just..." I stop, having no plausible excuse. You can't deny you're on the brink of a sob-fest when every syllable you release cracks upon delivery.

Within minutes, Jasper's faint snores overtake my thumping heart. I'm not surprised. I'm tired, and I'm not a toddler. When Jenni hears Jasper's lengthened breaths, she motions for me to follow her. We head for the door Harrison walked through not long ago. Upon entering, I spot a white crib set up in the corner of the vast space.

Jenni carefully transfers Jasper from my chest to his crib. Once she has him settled, she shifts on her feet to face Harrison. He nods, answering her plea. After we tiptoe out of the dressing room big enough for a marching band to rehearse in, I lock my eyes with Jenni's. "He's adorable."

The hem of her dress swishes around her slim thighs when she twists on the spot. "Thanks, I think so too."

When I pivot on my heels to retrace my steps, I spot Melanie halfway down the hall. Her eyes are wide and panicked as she flicks them up and down the packed space. Relief skates across her tear-shaped face when I increase my five-foot-eight height half an inch by balancing on the balls of my feet to wave her down. She darts between dozens of knee-clanging girls so eager to meet Rise Up, they appear seconds from peeing their pants.

"Jesus, I thought I lost you." Her voice is unlike anything I've heard before—panicked, yet hopeful. But she's not the least bit worried. "I was panicked a roadie was having his way with you in the broom closet, and I was missing out on the action." She bumps me with her hip, her smile playful. "Don't worry, Voyeur Theresa is here to save the day! Where's the hot hunk of man-meat you couldn't keep your mitts off until I arrived?"

It takes Jenni laughing at her theatrics for Melanie to realize we have company. Ignorance is nothing new for Melanie. If there's a hot guy within a five-mile radius, she won't pay you any attention.

"Holy shit." Melanie grabs my arm to squeeze it, her lips circling more the longer she stares at Jenni. "You're Nick Holt's wife!"

Jenni's nose screws up. "His fiancée—"

"Same fucking thing."

"Melanie, language!" I scold, horrified by her bluntness.

Melanie rolls her eyes like it's no big deal. To someone who has no filter, it may not be, but not all of us are rainbow, bubblegum, hot fudge, sprinkled sundaes with cherries on the top. Some people are just straight up vanilla ice cream that's been in the freezer so long that it's starting to turn yellow. With how many ogling eyes Slater had on him earlier, I bet he's offered more than one flavor of ice cream tonight—and I doubt any of them will be plain old vanilla like me.

Hating the bitterness scorching my throat, I return my focus to the present. "Jenni, this is my potty-mouthed friend Melanie." I wave my hand to Melanie, who appears pleased by her nickname. "Melanie, this is Jenni."

Instead of peppering my introduction with a handshake or a quick, none-stalkerish hug, Melanie asks, "How the fuck do you two know each other?"

She stops thrusting her perfectly manicured finger between Jenni and me when I say, "We've met previously... *only once.*" I force out my last two words in a hurry when the suspicion on Melanie's face switches to anger. "We stayed at a cabin together two years ago when Rise Up got together for one last hurrah before their debut album dropped."

A brick lodges in my throat when Melanie's bouncing eyes lock on mine. They're bristling with unbridled anger. "Let me get this straight..." She pauses to take in a brain-sucking breath. "...The entire time I've known you, you failed to mention you've met Rise Up previously?"

Despite being mere seconds from death, I nod.

"*All* of them?"

"Only once," I retort, attempting to pacify her anger.

Melanie has a slight obsession with Marcus, the bassist of Rise Up. By slight, I mean a full-on, *he most likely has a restraining order against her* obsession. She swears he's her future baby's daddy; it's just no one has informed Marcus of that yet.

"Excluding Slater. You guys—" I cut Jenni off with a *please shut up* glare. It might have worked if she had met me more than once many moons ago. "You were his girlfriend for almost six months, weren't you?"

After extracting the truth from Jenni's frank eyes, Melanie's bugged out ones drift to me. "You lying little witch!" Her high-pitched squeal booms down the hall. "You said it was a couple of dates!"

When her shriek gains us attention I don't want, I plead for her to be quiet. I'll even get down on my hands and knees if I have to, that's how desperate I am for us to have this conversation anywhere but outside the room Rise Up is holding their fan meet and greet.

Before a single pathetic beg can escape my lips, Melanie's attention is diverted from glaring at me to gazing at Nick. He strolls into the corridor, smirking at his screaming fans. They might be awarded his smile, but they'll never gain his focus. He has eyes for only one person in the room. That person is his fiancée.

Once Nick kisses Jenni on the forehead and nods a greeting to me, I introduce him to the bursting-at-the-seams Melanie.

"I tried to get in your line, but..." Melanie's starstruck gaze turns to the long line of mostly girls that goes down the hall and around the corner. "...I like you and all, but that shit is crazy."

When she hooks her thumb to Nick's adoring fans making gaga faces at him, Nick chuckles. Melanie was able to jump the queue since I caught Slater's drumstick at the end of the concert. I really shouldn't say caught. It more hit me in the head before landing in my lap. I still have a headache from where it struck me on my left temple.

Anyone who catches Slater's sticks or Nick or Marcus's guitar straps gets to skip the line for the fan meet and greet. Since I was reasonably sure Slater would deny my request for a signature if I arrived at his table, I was hoping Melanie would agree to go back to our hotel with an unsigned stick.

Silly me. Even considering that for a second was foolish. Melanie wanted to go backstage even more than she wished she hadn't given Devon Cooper her virginity. And when Melanie wants to do something, we do it—hence our unplanned trip to Seattle.

I try not to eavesdrop on Jenni and Nick's conversation when he brushes his lips against the shell of her ear, but I can't help it. There are over three dozen people gawking at Nick, yet it's as if there's no one else in the room when he stares at his fiancée. That could have been me if I didn't foolishly throw everything away.

I drag my thumb under my eyes to ensure they're dry as Jenni says, "Everyone is getting ready to head to the after party. You two should come."

Her offer barely leaves her lips when Melanie shouts, "Yes!" at the top of her lungs.

My reply is a lot more reserved. "Thank you for the offer, but it's very late, so we better call it a night."

Melanie stomps her feet like a five-year-old at the same time Jenni brings out the big guns—her light blue puppy dog eyes. "You have to come. Emily will be there, and she'd love to see you again." She stares up at me with her bottom lip dropped and her eyes begging. "Please..."

I shoot my eyes up to Nick, seeking his thoughts. He shrugs, leaving all the burden on my shoulders. I don't need to seek Melanie's opinion. I can feel her pleading eyes burning a hole in the side of my head.

"Are you sure it won't cause any issues?" Nerves jangle on my vocal cords, making the country twang in my tone more noticeable.

When Jenni shakes her head, I pretend I can't feel butterflies in my stomach. "Okay, but only for ten minutes."

Melanie squeals so loud, my ears will ring for a week.

I can only hope that's the worst thing that will occur tonight.

CHAPTER THREE

SLATER

"What's taking them so long?"

Marcus's eyes shift from the window of the stretch Hummer we're sitting in to me. When he shrugs, curse words roll off my tongue like lyrics. We've been waiting for our bandmates for nearly an hour, and my patience is hanging on by a very thin thread.

Every concert series is kicked off the same way. We have an elaborate, all-expenses-paid afterparty at one of the hottest nightclubs in town. Roped-off VIP section, endless women, and unlimited booze. Usually, I veer toward the women. Tonight, my focus will be on the booze. I need to get *her* out of my fucking head. You'd think radio silence for two years would have clued my brain in to the fact that she's enemy number one, but nope, one look at her pretty little face and tight-ass body, and my cock overruled all rational thinking. And don't get me started on my head.

"Do they know we're waiting for them?"

Marcus shrugs again. His dislike for tardiness is visible all over his face.

"Fuck it, I'll go get them."

Just as I'm about to slide out the open side door, Jenni slips inside. "Sorry," she mumbles, noticing my glare. "I can't just throw on jeans and show up. This takes time."

When she runs her hand down her body, my eyes follow its descent. I still don't understand why it took her an hour to get ready. She's wearing a dress. Simple—you throw it over your head. Shoes would take, what, two minutes to put on? Her face isn't even coated in makeup, so what the fuck has she been doing?

The truth smacks into me when my eyes drink in the pink hue on her neck. I'm about to give her the *what for?* when Nick enters the limousine. His smug smirk and damp-at-the-tips shaggy locks confirm what I suspected.

Marcus chokes on his drink when I growl, "Can you save your fucking for when we're not waiting?"

Nick's shit-eating grin brightens the flush on Jenni's cheeks. When Emily and Noah *finally* arrive, I signal for the driver to go. With the delay, I could have walked to the venue by now.

When I step out of the limousine ten minutes later, I'm blinded by paparazzi lights. They're so fucking bright, I can't see two feet in front of me. I'm pretty much walking blind, praying I'm heading in the right direction. When the paps request that I lower my arm, I act ignorant. I like my vision, which means I have to shield my eyes.

Once we're ushered inside the club by studio-assigned body-guards, we're swamped by fans and groupies. Do you know how to tell the difference between a fan and a groupie? Fans ask before touching. Groupies touch, grab, poke, and manhandle you as often as they want. Fans buy tickets to attend our shows. Groupies expect them for free. Well, not technically for free – they're willing to do sexual favors for them. Either way, no money is exchanged for their ticket.

It's the fans who make a band successful and the groupies who bring it crashing down. Does that mean I don't take advantage of the groupies? Hell no. They're part of the entertainment industry, and I take all the perks I can get—groupies included.

When our fame began to rocket, we hung out in the regular area of any nightclub we visited. Noah didn't want us to appear self-entitled, but it soon became apparent we couldn't move in the regular areas because we were overwhelmed by zealous fans. Now we have no choice but to sit in the VIP section. It's not all bad. Our booze is free, and the VIP section always has the best views of the club.

Tonight's VIP area is on the second floor. When you stand at the black iron balcony, you can see the entire dance floor below. Cue Ball is packed to the brim with partygoers being served by waiters in matching outfits: tight black shorts, tucked-in white blouses, and black top hats. Mercifully, the boys' shorts are a longer than the girls'—not by much, but it could be worse.

A cute brunette smiles a blinding grin while serving me a whiskey off a silver tray. Because she's bending over, her blouse dips, revealing her ample cleavage. When she notices my appreciative gawk, she flashes me a frisky wink before sauntering back to the bar. While nursing my beverage of choice, I pace to the balcony to watch a swarm of bodies dance in sync to the music blaring out of the speakers.

It doesn't take me long to spot Nick amongst the crowd. He's a Fred Astaire prodigy—always fucking dancing. I don't mind getting on the dance floor, but I don't dance like Nick does. A couple of years ago, he would've been juggling multiple dance partners. Now, he only has one: his fiancée, Jenni. I still keep my eye on him, though. One step out of line and the warning I delivered two years ago will be issued full force.

I tried to steer Jenni away from him. Some days, I still wish she had listened to me. She loves Nick, but associating with him brings a whole lot of trouble into play. The shit that happened with Megan is a prime example. Jenni is lucky to have a sturdy backbone, because that mess would usually bring down the strongest couple.

I'm often accused of being too protective of Jenni. I can't help it. When we met four years ago, all I could see when I looked at her was my baby sister, Serena. Jenni has her big light blue eyes, strawberry blonde hair, and tiny facial features.

Nick's interest in Jenni was as obvious as the sun shining in the sky; it fucking beamed out of him. Since there was no way in hell I'd *ever* allow my sister to date a guy like him, I tried to keep Jenni away from him. I thought my ruse was working... until she announced she was pregnant with his baby. I was suspicious a few months before then, but by that stage, I'd met Kylie, and my interests were on more pressing matters.

Kylie and I met under pretty unique circumstances. At the time, I thought it was the right time, right place bullshit. Now I wish I had never pulled into that old country bar on the side of the highway...

On this day, every single year, I just ride. Some days, I ride for ten hours straight before turning around and going home. Others, it may only be an hour or two. Today, I've been riding for a little over four hours before making my first stop. I don't pay attention to street signs, town markings or anything specific. I ride to escape my memories, to clear my mind of thoughts. Once I've achieved that, the GPS on my phone shows me the way home.

I pull into an old bar on the outskirts of town to use the pump at the front since I'm sitting on empty. When I scan the space, I feel like I've been transported back in time. Tumbleweeds are blowing across the road; an old timer sits in a rocking chair at the front, and the parking lot is full of big old trucks like Noah's, but they're still rusty.

After filling my tank, I walk up to the elderly gentleman in the rocking chair. He continues rocking as his eyes roam over my denim jeans, tight white tank top, and black leather vest. My sleeves of tattoos are proudly on display. My jaw ticks when he spits a wad of black, tar-filled tobacco on the ground next to me, narrowly missing my boot. When my gaze lifts from my boot to him, my eyes narrow, and my nostrils flare. Old timer or not, he's lucky he missed.

He smiles a toothless grin, loving that he sparked a reaction out of me. "You pay in the bar."

Nodding, I step over the tobacco to make my way inside. When I push the wooden door open, a banjo shrieks through my ears. I'll listen to any genre of music—except country. That shit is as lame as it comes.

The inside of the bar matches the outside: wooden, rusty, and old. The floors, walls, and even the roof are done with wood panels. I make a beeline to the peanut shell-coated bar, eager to pay for my gas and leave before my ears are subjected to more torture.

An elderly barmaid with a wonky smile and too much rack on display peers up at me when I stop to stand in front of her. I don't know if she can smell gasoline on my hands, or if she's reading my eagerness to leave, but she figures out the reason for my visit without me speaking. "How many gallons did you pump?"

I shrug. I don't check that type of shit. I just fill up and pay. "Aren't your pumps computerized?" I ask a mere second before noticing even the cash register looks like it belongs in the sixties.

Pissed, I stomp back outside to read the total off the pump, and that's when I spot her: an angel in a blue cotton dress and a cropped denim jacket. She's walking toward the bar with an eclectic mix of guys and girls. The way the wind blows up the hem of her dress teases me, but it's her smile I'm paying attention to the most. It makes me want to fall to my fucking knees.

When she notices my gawk, she stops walking before appraising my body like I did hers. I'm a little dirty from my hours on the road, but I've got plenty of qualities girls like. Thick biceps, decent height, bumps in my midsection, dozens of tattoos, and a face more than just a mother would love. If you can look past my rough and rugged exterior, you'll also see my big motherfucking heart.

Once the brunette's eyes return to my face, she smiles so big, it could be seen from space. I'm nothing like the men in her group, but she doesn't seem to mind, not in the slightest.

I step forward, preparing to introduce myself. Before I can, a country bumpkin hick slaps her bottom before curling his arm around her shoulders, forcing her to start walking again. Just before they break through the warped wood door of the bar, her eyes turn back to me. When she winks, I know I'm not going anywhere.

After reading my total off the pump, I reenter the bar, noticing the brunette and her friends are setting up music equipment on a small stage squashed against the back wall. I pay for my gas before ordering a beer, confident the brunette's smile more than makes up for her poor choice in music.

Once their equipment is set up, the brunette heads for the bar, then, not long later, country music filters through the air. "Vodka cranberry, please?" The twang in her voice rings out in the empty bar.

Once the bartender sets down her drink, she turns to face the stage. She acts like she hasn't noticed my watchful eye. It's all a ploy. Her lips rose against the rim of her glass the instant she spotted me.

I watch her for several long minutes, more fascinated by the thud of her pulse than the horrid music blaring from portable amps. I slant my head and flash her my big-headed grin when she murmurs, "Don't you know it's rude to stare?"

If she wants me to believe she's angry, she needs to quit smiling. Seeing this as my cue to approach her, I plant my backside on the empty barstool next to her. From this vantage point, I can see the adorable freckles that adorn her beautiful face. Her smell reminds me of wildflowers, which isn't surprising since we're surrounded by countryside, and she has the slightest sliver of hay entangled in her kinked hair. We couldn't be more opposite if we tried.. She screams country, where I scream...non-country?

"Why aren't you up there with your friends?" I jerk my head to the stage before signaling to the bartender that I need another beer.

Her face screws up. "The idea of standing up in front of a crowd petrifies me."

I laugh loudly—the bar would be lucky to have ten people inside. My chuckle startles her so much, she jumps, spilling her drink down the front of her dress.

"Oh, fuck, sorry." I grab a wad of napkins to dab up the liquid. I swipe at her chest three times before my brain realizes why my cock is straining against my zipper. I'm all up in her business—by "business," I mean I'm touching her breasts without permission.

My eyes dart up to her face. She's surprised by my feel-up but still smiling. I hand her the wad of napkins so she can finish cleaning her spill. While she does that, I battle to keep my eyes on her face. Let me tell you, it's a fucking hard feat. From the little grab I had, I'm confident in declaring her boobs mighty enticing.

"I guess I should introduce myself since you've already felt my boobs." She freezes before shock morphs onto her face. "I'm sorry, I shouldn't have said that."

I grin, loving the heat creeping across her cheeks.. "I'm Slater. It's nice to meet you... and your boobs."

Marcus slaps me on the back, interrupting me from my thoughts. "You coming down?"

"Yeah, in a minute." I swish my whiskey in the glass before downing the generous nip in one gulp. "I need a bit more liquid courage first."

The whiskey burns on the way down, but it also helps stop my stomach from swirling from the memories of Kylie filtering through my head. When my eyes drop to the dance floor, my brows furrow. Jenni is sprinting toward the bathroom with her hand clamped over her mouth.

My concerned gaze seeks Nick. I find him not even a second later standing in the middle of the dance floor. He has a dumbfounded look on his face, but he's also smiling. *Freak.*

He snaps back to the present when a blonde, attractive, lady attempts to dance with him. I'm pleased to advise he sidesteps her before her backside gets within an inch of his crotch. He races in the direction Jenni fled. I should probably start giving him more leeway, but I've been burnt in the past, so I'm cautious about giving him the benefit of the doubt. Even when you love someone, it doesn't stop them from deceiving you.

I found that out the hard way—more than once!

When the perky brunette waitress notices my glass is empty, she makes her way to me with another double shot of whiskey. This time, since she doesn't need to bend over to serve me my beverage, she keeps her lust-riddled eyes locked with mine. My cock twitches when she teasingly licks her top lip. She's a sexpot, and she knows how to work it.

When I remove my whiskey from the tray, only sneaking a small peek at her generous breasts, she purrs, "Your napkin, sir." She hands me the napkin that was under my glass, winks, then saunters to the bar.

Once I've finished my perusal of her swinging hips, my eyes lower to the napkin she was adamant I have. "VIP bathroom in ten minutes," I read off the gold-etched paper.

When my eyes flick up to the bar she walked to, I find her smiling face and nod. In ten minutes, any thoughts of Kylie plaguing my mind will be a distant memory.

"Cheers to the girls that break your heart," I murmur to myself before downing the double shot of whiskey and heading to the bathroom to hook up with the horny waitress.

CHAPTER FOUR

KYLIE

I spent the last hour begging Melanie to skip the afterparty. I did as she requested. I dressed in one of her dresses; I put makeup on my face, and I watched the guy I still love perform on stage. I did everything she requested, yet she's still forcing me to attend the afterparty against my wishes.

It was only when her blue eyes pleaded did I cave. Tonight is her night. We're only in Seattle at her request, so I may as well suck it up for a little longer. The smile plastered on her face when we walk into the nightclub is worth being stabbed in the heart with tiny invisible knives. The instant we enter the bursting-at-the-seams space, I spot Slater on the second level. Tonight he matches his surroundings a lot better than the night we met. . .

"I'm Slater. It's nice to meet you and your boobs."

I smile, loving his playfulness. He's different than the guys I usually hang out with, but he has an aura I can't help but be drawn to. His piercing brown eyes and lickable tattoos made me want to offer up an immediate introduction when I busted him checking me out at the front of the Bar N Barrel, but Dylan stopped me—just as he's doing now.

He stands between Slater and me, blocking Slater from my view. He pretends to order a beer from Darla, but I know him. He's marking his territory—territory that doesn't belong to him. Dylan has been my friend since we were in diapers, but for the past three years, he's been trying to alter our status.

I like him, but I'll never see him as anything more than a friend. His presence doesn't make my pulse spike like Slater's did when my eyes landed on him. His slap to my backside didn't create one tenth of the throb that surged through my pussy when I calculated how many ways I could explore the tattoos on Slater's thick-veined arms— starting with my tongue, and don't get me started on the mess my panties were hit with when Slater's big, callused hands scraped my breasts. I've never believed in instant love, but instant lust is a different story, and Slater has my interests immensely piqued.

Once Darla hands Dylan his beer, he spins around, wraps his arm around my shoulders, then drags me toward our regular table. I shrug out of his embrace before spinning around to face Slater. "I'm Kylie, and the pleasure was all mine."

Cringing, I spin back around, ensuring he won't see the mortified expression crossing my face. That was the second worst pick up line in my life.

Within an hour, the bar fills with townsfolk wanting to enjoy their Saturday night. I feel Slater's eyes on me when I'm dancing with friends, but he never approaches me. When I catch his gaze, I motion for him to join us. His plump lips curl into a heart-stuttering smile before he shakes his head. I guess boot scooting isn't his thing?

A short time later, feeling parched from so much dancing, I head to the bar to order another drink. I may also be hoping to reignite my conversation with Slater. This time, I sit next to him instead of waiting for him to come to me. "Not a fan of boot scooting?"

He chuckles while gesturing for me to look at him. I'm more than willing to fulfill his request. He couldn't be more different than the guys in my hometown. They're clean-shaven, and most of the hair on their heads is covered by wide-brimmed hats. They wear jeans with big belt buckles, button-up cotton shirts, and riding boots. Slater also wears jeans, but his belt buckle is a biker buckle. His hair is blond, long, and in dreadlocks, and his tight white tank top shows off the impressive ridges of his abdomen. He's also wearing boots, but his are motorcycle boots.

"You have the boots for it."

He chuckles again, sending loud vibrations through to my womb.

With corny introductions out of the way, we chat for the next thirty minutes. To say he has a sense of humor would be a major understatement. I have tears in my eyes from laughter.

When the bar quiets, Slater peers down to the black leather watch circling his wrist, then his brows furrow. "It's not even nine," he informs me, like I'm unaware of the time.

Things in my hometown are obviously different than what he's used to. Here, we rise early, usually before the sun is even up, so a lot of the townsfolk are normally in bed by now. If you own a ranch, there's no Monday-to-Friday routine. The livestock and horses don't care if it's Sunday or not; they want to be fed every day.

When I explain that to Slater, he nods before flashing me a huge, cheeky grin. "So you're about to tuck yourself into bed?"

A peppering of goosebumps follow the trail his eyes travel when he drags them down my body. When his eyes return to my face, I arch a brow, advising him I caught his prolonged gawk, and I'm not the least bit threatened by it. I'm the complete opposite.

"Most townsfolk are usually in bed by now, but I didn't say I was most townsfolk."

I'm home for spring break, currently in my second year of college. I chose to attend one as far away from my hometown as possible. Not because I don't love my family, but because I want to experience life. I was raised on my family ranch, so I went to the same school with the same friends, and we had the same routine every day for the first eighteen years of our lives. To me that isn't living. It's a hamster in a wheel— boring and predictable. I want to experience life to its fullest, to have an adventure, to live the best life

I can. Maybe that's why I'm attracted to someone like Slater? He seems full of fun and adventure, like he'd ride the crazy-ass roller coaster of life with me with his arms in the air, not the teeniest bit scared.

Eager to test a theory, I set down my vodka cranberry and turn to face Slater head on. "Will you take me for a ride on your bike?"

I've never been on the back of a motorcycle, so I'd love to tick it off my bucket list of things I want to achieve before I die.

Slater smiles a heart-fluttering grin while nodding.

"Now?"

Not waiting for him to reply, I attempt to drag him toward the entrance of the bar. I say "attempt" because he weighs a ton. After laughing at my eagerness, he downs the remainder of his beer before following me outside. Once we're next to his bike, butterflies flutter in my stomach.

They become a full-blown epidemic when Slater snags a black helmet out of his saddlebag to place on my head, ensuring he tightens the straps securely under my chin. After throwing his leg over his bike and flipping up the stand, he assists me onto the back. I flatten my torso against his back before curling my arms around his waist. His six-pack feels as mouthwatering as it looks. When he kicks over the bike, the vibrations of his engine add to the crackling energy teeming between us.

"Hold on," Slater says a mere second before we rocket out of the lot.

Squealing, I look back at the dust cloud we left behind. Just as we make it onto the freeway, Dylan rushes out of the bar. Even from a distance, I can see the anxious fury settling in his eyes. He has no need to be worried. I feel the safest and most protected I've ever felt.

After waving goodbye at him, I reattach my tight death grip around Slater's ridged stomach. . .

"There he is!" Melanie's squeal already drags me back to the present, so the addition of her French tip nails digging into my arm isn't needed. "If you introduce me, I'll love you forever."

Her eyes stray to Marcus, who's making his way onto the dance floor with Emily and Noah following closely behind him.

"I'll try, but he may not remember me. I only met him once."

After clamping my hand around hers, we make our way to Emily, Noah, and Marcus. It isn't an easy feat with how many people are vying for their attention. This is one rare occasion were Melanie's aggressiveness comes in handy. She barges people out of our way without the slightest bit of remorse, meaning we reach the trio long before I've settled my sky-high heart rate from reminiscing about Slater.

I tap Emily on the shoulder. Forever polite, she cranks her neck back to face me. "Hello."

When her eyes land on mine, she bursts my eardrums with an excited scream before throwing her arms around my neck. I want to say poor hearing is the least of my worries, but if the expression on Noah's face when Emily screams is anything to go by, I'm seconds from having my intestines removed via my nasal cavities. Mercifully, Noah recognizes my hazel eyes as quickly as Emily, saving me from an operation with a blunt instrument.

After inching back, Emily locks her light brown eyes with mine. "What are you doing in Seattle?"

"Only attending the concert of the world's greatest band," Melanie answers on my behalf.

Emily smiles proudly. "I should have known."

When I introduce Emily and Noah to Melanie, I'm surprised she maintains a cool, calm composure. I can't say the same thing when Marcus joins us. Her eyes bulge out of her head as her grip on my hand turns deadly.

"Hi Kylie." When Marcus greets me with a kiss on my cheek, Melanie sighs. Don't ask me if she's swooning or mad. Her good and bad sighs sound the same.

"Marcus, this is my friend, Melanie."

Marcus greets Melanie with a dip of his chin before offering his hand to shake. When she remains still, staring at him, unable to move or speak, I pry her fingernails out of my palm before placing her hand into Marcus's.

His hand curling around her sweaty one snaps her back to reality. "Sorry, I was just imagining what our children will look like."

Noah laughs, loving her enthusiasm, but Marcus looks genuinely petrified. "Nice seeing you again, Kylie."

Noah waits for Marcus to reach the stairwell guarded by two big, burly bouncers before devoting his attention back to Melanie. "I think the baby talk scared him away."

Melanie slaps his chest like they're lifelong friends. "He'll get used to the idea... *eventually*. We'll make beautiful caramel babies."

CHAPTER FIVE

SLATER

An hour after arriving, my band members have hung up their dancing shoes and returned to the VIP section of the club, and I'm thoroughly satisfied. I never had any troubles hooking up before I was famous, but now the women are endless. It is, at times, a little too easy. I can snap my fingers, and I'd have several companions vying for my attention.

As I make my way to the red leather booths they're occupying, I ensure the zipper in my jeans is up. I've been busted with my pants down before. I don't want that social media catastrophe for the fifth time in my limited rock career.

When my gaze lifts, the first set of eyes I notice belong to Kylie. Her hazel eyes are locked on the zipper I just fixed into place. She stares at my crotch long enough for my cock to act if it wasn't drained of cum before her eyes drift to the waitress who followed me out of the bathroom. Her lipstick is no longer in existence, and her hair is ruffled from the tight grip I had on it to ensure she gave head the way I like. I could have fucked her in the bathroom, but since neither of us had protection, and I sure as hell ain't going down the parenthood route like Noah and Nick, we didn't. I don't care if the chick assures me she's on the pill, I refuse to have sex without a condom.

When Kylie's eyes return to mine, tears gather in them, making me hesitant to join my bandmates. I've always been a sucker for her tears, but they shouldn't have the same hold over me they once had.

My idiocy doesn't linger for that. That's *my* band. They're *my* friends. And I'm not the one who fucked up what we *once* had. She's on *my* turf, so if anyone should feel like an intruder, it isn't me.

While making a beeline for Marcus, I signal for the waitress to bring me another whiskey. When I plop into the empty seat next to Marcus, his eyes stray to me. "Who invited her?"

"Who?" He sounds as if he has no idea who I'm talking about. I have no fucking clue why. If anyone knows the shit Kylie put me through, it is him.

When I jerk my chin to Kylie and her blonde friend, he shrugs. "All I know is that Emily invited them to sit with us." His green eyes bounce between mine, his expression coy. "I'm the blonde's baby daddy."

I'd choke on my drink if the waitress was as eager to quench my thirst as she was to suck my dick.

When Marcus waggles his brows, I realize he's joking. My slow uptake can be easily excused. He isn't known for comedy. His humor is usually as dry as my throat feels.

Even though the blonde appears deep in conversation with Emily and Kylie, her eyes constantly dart to Marcus. "Are you going to tap that?"

Marcus doesn't answer my question, but his smirk reveals he's considering the idea. When the waitress finally arrives with my drink, I flash her a flirty wink, hoping it'll have her jumping to my command a little faster next time. She licks her recently repainted lips while twirling her freshly brushed hair around her finger. When she saunters back to the bar with an extra bounce in her step, my eyes return to Kylie. Hers are no longer filled with the tears they had minutes ago. They're narrowed into tiny slits, and her lips are hard-lined. I hit her with the same wink I just give the waitress. Her reply is nowhere near as frisky. She rolls her eyes before heading to the bar with her blonde friend trailing closely behind her.

I can't help but run my eyes over her tight body. Her hair is shorter than it was when we were dating, her long, mousy brown locks replaced with a rich chocolate bob that sits two inches past her chin. A heavy coating of makeup hides her adorable freckles, and her tight black strapless dress seems out of the ordinary for her, but when I reach her feet, I realize the Kylie I know is hiding under there somewhere because she's wearing cropped cowboy boots.

She and her friend seem to be having a heated discussion. How do I know this? From how many times the blonde's hand continually gestures to me. When Kylie gets frustrated by whatever she's yelling, she folds her arms under her chest, hoisting her fantastic breasts up higher in her dress. I'm not the only one noticing her improved cleavage. The bartender's eyes zoom straight to her alluring display.

After smashing my back molars together, I glare at him. When my daggers hit their mark, he scurries away to serve other patrons waiting for his service. He's smarter than he looks, saving another part of my body from becoming friendly with a Cue Ball waiter for the second time tonight. By friendly, I mean my fist was about to become chummy with his face.

When my focus shifts back to Kylie, I can't hear a word she's saying, but her friend's huffs can't be missed. She gives Kylie a disappointed look before storming down the wooden stairs in a hurry. Kylie sucks in numerous big breaths before she paces back to Emily and Jenni. She says a few words to them before focusing her attention on Marcus and me. "It was nice seeing you both again." Her twang is less noticeable compared to the night we met.

Marcus hugs her goodbye. I remain seated, my gaze seeking anything but hers. When Marcus inches back, he inconspicuously nudges his head to Kylie, suggesting I say goodbye so we don't again part ways with words unspoken.

Forever stubborn, I shake my head before my eyes drift to the dance floor. Kylie brushes it away quickly, but I don't miss the tear sliding down her pale cheek. I may be a coldhearted bastard, but I wasn't always this way.

Feeling bad that I've made her cry, my gaze lifts and locks with hers. I don't get a chance to issue her a halfhearted farewell smirk. She spins on her heels and darts down the stairs before my lips reach half their potential.

I realize I'm not the only one who spotted Kylie's tears. She bursts past the bouncers manning the VIP entrance at the same time Jenni's questioning eyes stray to mine. Her face is marred with confusion and a slight hint of anger. Nick defuses her angry glare by running the back of his hand down her flushed cheek, but nothing can defuse the interrogation bomb she plans to hit me with.

Any plans to spend the rest of my night enjoying the company of my friends and unlimited alcohol while I battle to forget the girl I hope to never see again are lost when Jenni fills the seat next to me. "What happened between you and Kylie?"

I slouch into the booth with a groan before signaling for the waiter to bring me another whiskey. When Jenni's head comes to rest on my shoulder, her giggles fan the cropped hairs covering my jaw. "I really liked her."

"You weren't the only one."

I loved Kylie. She was the first girl I dated since Nikki, but she gutted me, convincing me that relationships aren't for me. I never intend to be in one ever again.

"She told me how you wouldn't boot scoot with her." Jenni angles her head so our eyes collide. "I've seen you dance; you could have worked it."

My laugh rumbles over the bass blaring from the speakers. I was mortified when Kylie suggested I join her on the dance floor that day. They weren't dancing. They were *line* dancing, like full-on cowboy shit. I was getting enough odd looks as it was, so imagine how out of place I would have looked while boot scooting?

"That's not how I like to tap boots."

Jenni laughs again. When it switches to a yawn, I glance down at my watch. I'm taken aback when I see it's nearly 1 AM. I'm stunned for the second time when Jenni peers up at me. Her light blue eyes are an exact replica of my sister's. Even without similar facial features and matching hair color, I could pretend I was looking at Serena. That's how similar they are.

Serena and I were only eleven months apart. When our mom took us into town, people often mistook us for twins. We didn't have the sibling rivalry everyone else experiences. She was my very best friend in the whole world, and I miss her every single day.

When Jenni notices the sullen look on my face, she nuzzles in closer. People think our friendship is odd—even Kylie was jealous at one stage, but they soon catch on that I treat Jenni as if she's my sister, nothing more. She isn't Serena, but I can't help but treat her as if she is.

"Why were you running to the bathroom before?" My tone relays my concern. Jenni looks okay now, but she didn't look so hot earlier.

This time, when her eyes flick up, her cheeks are bright pink, and her pupils are massive. When her eyes dart to Nick, he smirks and winks before nodding. "I'm pregnant," she informs me after returning her focus to me.

"Again? Didn't you learn after the first one?" When her bottom lip drops into a pout, I twang it. "I'm joking. Congratulations."

I am joking. Jasper is one of the best kids I've ever met, solely because he has his mother's personality—thank fuck.

Nick must have shared the baby news with Emily and Noah at the same time Jenni told me. Emily squeals before rushing over to engulf Jenni in a huge hug. They crash into the booth, spilling my glass of whiskey on my jeans.

Great, now tomorrow's headlines will scream "Rise Up Drummer Slater Scott Pisses His Pants," or something along those lines.

CHAPTER SIX

KYLIE

When I walk into the small, overpriced hotel room Melanie and I are staying in, I flop onto the bed. Melanie giggles, loving my dramatics. I'm glad she's forgiven me about our earlier fight. We're only in Seattle for her, and we're supposed to be having the time of our lives, not arguing about old boyfriends.

Our spat couldn't be helped. Tonight ended worse than even my overly negative imagination could have conjured. Not only did I have to witness Slater returning from the bathroom with a lipstick-smeared, lusty eyed waitress trailing behind him, but I had to turn down an opportunity I need more than my next breath.

After mentioning to Emily I had just finished my studies in media relations and was seeking an internship, she offered me a position as her personal assistant. I was shocked. As far as I was aware, she was still attending college, so why did she need a PA?

When I worked up the courage to ask her that, Noah laughed while Emily explained that she's the publicist for Rise Up and Big Halo, and that Cormack was pressing to add more bands to her already crammed schedule. "It isn't glamorous, but until you find something else, it could help us both out," she said earlier tonight.

I was on the verge of accepting her much-needed offer when I caught sight of Slater returning to our gathering. It didn't take long to realize where he'd been the past half hour. His zipper was down, and the waitress shadowing him had ruffled hair and kiss-swollen lips.

I had been actively seeking a position the past six months, and on the cusp of being homeless, so I considered approaching Slater to seek his approval on me accepting Emily's offer, but lost the chance when the waitress sauntered up to him with a glass of whiskey on a silver tray. When he winked at her a mere second before hitting me with the same wink, proving I'm no more special to him than a random hookup, I knew I'd never survive working alongside him, no matter how desperately I needed the job.

That's why Melanie and I had a very public spat next to the VIP bar. She was pissed I was giving up an opportunity to better myself all because Slater "can't keep his dick in his pants for an hour."

I understood her argument, but since it was fueled by half-truths, I couldn't side with it. I haven't told anyone what happened between Slater and me, so most assume he went on to bigger and better things after leaving the poor country girl to mope at home.

In reality, it was me who left him.

And I've regretted it every day since.

The next morning, the disaster of last night has been set aside, and Melanie and I are beaming with excitement about the activities we've planned. The first thing on our to-do list is the Fifty Shades of Grey tour. Melanie and I read the series during her last hospital stay, and we're huge fans of both the series and the author. Because of our modest budget, I printed out maps so we can use public transport instead of hiring a tour company to take us around.

Melanie's smile beams out of her as we make our way to the elevator. "I heard a rumor Jamie Dornan is back in town. We may have missed him filming here, but my imagination has always been wonderful." She jabs the elevator button three times, her excitement unmissable. "He can be my backup baby daddy in case things with Marcus don't work out."

I giggle, adoring her eagerness. "Would you call him Mr. Dornan or Mr. Grey?"

She gives me a look as if to say, *don't be silly. Jamie is Christian.*

Seattle in May is breathtakingly beautiful. It was a gloriously bright blue-sky day, and the temperature was sitting at a warm eighty degrees. We visited all the locations on our map except the Heathman hotel. It was a little too far off the radar. So were some of the locations the cast filmed in Vancouver. Neither Melanie nor I have passports, so that adventure will remain on our list for another day.

By the time we walk back into our hotel, we're deliriously tired but incredibly happy. Even seeing Slater standing in the elevator can't wipe the smile off my face. I'm not surprised he's staying at this hotel. It's the closest one to the stadium Rise Up is playing at. That's why I chose to stay here as well. It was pricey, but since we didn't need to Uber it to the concert, we splurged.

Slater seems put-off when he notices me approaching the elevator banks, but he holds the elevator open for us to enter.

"Thank you." I doubt he heard my praise, but it felt good giving it. Seeing him with the waitress hurt last night, but I'm not naïve. I know he hasn't been pining over me the past two years. I'm the only idiot who's been craving what we had in the past.

My lips twitch into a smirk when Slater's delicious scent engulfs my senses. His manly palette still has the slight aroma of oil, which is odd considering we're in the city. When he coughs a little, my eyes snap up to him. He has a suspicious smirk etched on his face, his brows arched. He relieves my curious smirk by dropping his eyes down low. When I follow his gaze, I inwardly curse. In an attempt to get a better whiff of his intoxicating scent, I leaned in close. Half an inch closer and I'd be humping his leg.

"Sorry." I inch back, mortified as hell.

Fortunately, when the elevator dings, it opens on the floor Melanie and I are staying on. I usher Melanie into the hallway, embarrassed Slater busted me sniffing him, while also grateful Melanie was too busy scanning the photos on her phone to pay attention to anything that just transpired.

Regrettably, the snapped-shut doors don't stop me from hearing Slater's deep, pussy-clenching chuckle. I'm glad he's entertained, because I'm never leaving my hotel room again.

Melanie and I spend the remainder of our night drinking margaritas we mixed in the wine cooler bucket in our room. We don't have fancy glasses, so we use the paper cups the hotel supplies in the bathroom instead. Our lack of fancy accessories doesn't dampen our night. We dance, laugh and cry the night away. It's one of the most memorable days we've had.

The next morning, I head down to the lobby to finalize our bill. Today is our last day in Seattle. I'm fighting the hardest battle to maintain a brave front. I've only known Melanie for two years, but she's my family, so I'm going to miss her very much.

"Put thirty dollars on the AmEx, forty on the MasterCard, and the remainder of the balance on the Visa, please."

From the way the hotel clerk's eyes narrow, anyone would swear I'm paying my bill with pennies.

"Oh no, put forty dollars on the AmEx," I instruct after double-checking my online balance. I only have thirty-one dollars left on my MasterCard, so I don't want to risk an overdrawn fee.

My heart freezes when a deep voice to my left says, "Pay her bill with this."

When a platinum credit card is thrust over my shoulder, I attempt to snatch it out of the hotel clerk's grasp. "No, it's fine."

The stern middle-aged lady raises the card out of my reach. With her pointed-up nose looking down at me, she runs it through the machine, ignoring my request not to.

"Thank you, sir," she replies almost robotically before handing the card and my receipt to the man standing behind me.

Heat creeps across my cheeks. I'm utterly mortified. I don't think I've ever been more embarrassed.

I'm proven a liar when I spin on my heels to discover Emily, Noah, and Marcus standing next to Slater. The concerned gleam in their eyes reveals they witnessed my embarrassing exchange, but to save face, they smile at me like nothing happened.

I can only wish Slater would take a page out of their books. He paid my hotel bill without permission, yet he's the one who looks like he's about to blow his top.

Incapable of standing his wrath for a second longer, I mumble an incoherent, "Thanks," before dashing to the elevator banks. I make it through the doors at a record-setting pace, sighing when they commence closing with only me inside. I'd hate to add being a teary, blubbering idiot to my accomplishments today.

My reprieve doesn't last long. Just before the elevator doors fully snap shut, a tattooed arm forces them back open. My heart stops beating when Slater steps inside the car. I keep my gaze fixed on the elevator dashboard and my tears on the down low. I will not cry in front of this man.

Slater's glare adds heat to my already blushing cheeks. "Why didn't you accept Emily's job offer if you need the money so badly?"

"I have money... I... just...umm..." I try to think of an excuse for why I needed to use three maxed out credit cards to pay my hotel bill, but my mind is blank. I've never been a good liar. That's why I left Slater the way I did.

My budget was on track until I paid for us to take a taxi to the nightclub last night, then the excessive cover charge pushed my budget to its absolute limit. I would have sold my left lung on the black market if it was the only way I could fund this weekend with Melanie, though. It was our final hoorah, and I wouldn't have missed it for anything in the world.

"Why come all the way to Seattle if you're fucking poor?!" Slater's roar rumbles around the interior of the elevator, slapping my already damaged ego.

An appreciative sigh spills from my lips when the elevator arrives at my floor. I mutter a quick goodbye to Slater before fleeing to my hotel room, not bothering to answer his question. I've never felt the need to explain myself before, so I won't start now.

I don't need to turn around to know Slater is following me. If the stomping of his boots isn't obvious enough, the looks on the elderly ladies' faces walking past me are all the indication I need.

Melanie's eyes shoot up from her suitcase when I slam our hotel room door shut before leaning my back against it. My heart is racing so fast, it feels like I ran up the stairs instead of taking the elevator. Within seconds, loud knocking bellows into our room.

Melanie stands from her suitcase and saunters toward me. Her face is marred with confusion.

"Open the door, Kylie." Slater's loud voice vibrates through the white melamine door, both exciting and petrifying me.

As Melanie's manicured brows shoot up high into her hairline, she motions for me to open the door. I shake my head, my gaze shifting to look at anything but her squinted eyes.

With the strength of a tigress, Melanie yanks me away from the door, surprising me with her strength since she's ten pounds lighter than me and four inches shorter. Once she opens the door wide enough for Slater to enter, he strolls into the room, his eyes darting in all directions, seeking me.

His lips firm when he spots me hiding like a coward behind the door. "Do you need a job?"

The brisk shake of my head stops when concern flashes across Melanie's face. She peers at me from behind Slater's shoulder with tear-filled eyes and quivering lips. She encourages me to admit defeat with the grit I can only hope to emulate one day.

After biting on the inside of my cheek, I change my head shake to a nod. My ego takes a severe beating in the process, but at the end of the day, I *am* in desperate need of employment.

Slater's eyes bore into mine. I can't tell if he's angry or relieved. He's giving off both signs at the moment. "You start tomorrow morning."

Unable to form any words to express my gratitude that he's giving me this opportunity after everything I did to him, I offer my thanks with a shaky smile. Melanie's ear-piercing squeal startles Slater so much, he jumps out of his skin. When she engulfs me in a tight hug that sends us toppling to the floor, Slater slips into the corridor.

"Promise me you'll keep the skanks away from my future husband," Melanie requests with pleading, puppy dog eyes.

Laughing, I nod. "But only after you promise I'll come out of this alive."

CHAPTER SEVEN

SLATER

"**D**id you see the new chick?"

Sonny nudges his head to Kylie and Emily, who are standing in the corner of the room. I noticed Kylie the instant she stepped into the wings of the stage, but I'll never admit that to Sonny. Sonny is the lead roadie who sets up the band's equipment at each concert. He's a year older than me and currently the highest-ranking groupie fucker out of the two dozen roadies who travel with us.

Yes, they keep a tally. It's displayed in the roadie's tour bus. They follow us to each location but travel in their own bus. Unlike the band, their bus is also their hotel room on wheels.

"She's fucking hot." Sonny grabs at his crotch as his eyes roam Kylie's alluring body.

I keep my gaze planted on my drum kit. We're in the process of working out the mess another crew left my kit in. They dismantled it for a concert during the week, and when they re-assembled it, they got the angle wrong. The entire set up is out of whack. People assume I just show up and play on any drum kit. In reality, that's far from the truth. The setup of a drum kit is just as important as tuning a guitar.

Nick wouldn't perform with a guitar that wasn't tuned any more than I'd play on a drum kit set up incorrectly.

My eyes flick up from my drums when Sonny groans, "She looks sexy and innocent at the same time." He's eye-fucking Kylie from across the room, his hands rubbing together as he rocks from heel to toe.

"I haven't noticed her," I lie.

Although Kylie looks different than the girl I used to date, my cock still stands to attention when she enters the room. When she strolled into the elevator the other day, the smile on her face was so bright, I nearly fell to my fucking knees. Then, when she leaned in to smell me, I wanted to pretend she was the nice country girl I met at the bar two and a half years ago. If only I could forget what she did to me, then I wouldn't despise her as much as I do.

"How could you not notice her? She's fine." Mark adjusts my middle tom-tom drum to the angle I prefer before his eyes stray back to Kylie. "No ring either."

Half the road crew used to follow Emily around like a bunch of dogs in heat. That all stopped when Noah caught on. It took him firing two and knocking one of them out before they got the hint to leave his wife alone. Now they reserve their chasing for girls without rings on their fingers. That doesn't mean they don't enjoy the visual stimulation Emily and Jenni bring to the table. They've just learned to keep their dirty thoughts in their heads instead of sharing them out loud. I guess they figure Kylie is a prime target since she doesn't have a ring on her finger, not even the one I gave her for her birthday.

"Those lips wrapped around my coc—"

"Shut the fuck up," I interrupt, my voice a vicious snarl.

When I stand from my stool behind my drum kit, Mark's eyes drift to Sonny. Sonny shrugs, apparently confused as to why I've suddenly grown a second head. Usually, I'm more than happy to hear stories from the roadies about the groupies they've hooked up with— I've even shared a few myself—but if he doesn't shut his mouth about Kylie, I'll fucking shut it for him.

"No dibs, Slater, you know the rules." Sonny acts as if he's talking about a piece of meat and not an actual person. Furthermore, I don't think groupie rules should apply when they're talking about a girl I used to love.

Upon noticing our intense stares, Kylie's pretty eyes stray our way. When she smiles and waves, Sonny, forever a pompous prick, waves back. Kylie smirks at him before her eyes dart away. Sonny chuckles, wrongly believing Kylie is shy. Not many people know she has a wild side hidden underneath her country girl appearance.

Once Kylie leaves the room, I lock my furious gaze with Sonny and Mark. "If either of you touch her, I'll cut your fucking balls off and feed them to you."

Sonny smirks, pleased he sparked a reaction out of me. Mark is on the other end of the spectrum. He swallows harshly before nodding.

"Now do your fucking job and fix my drums," I instruct before storming to my dressing room.

I tried to convince myself earlier this week that I only offered Kylie a job to help Emily. I'm full of shit. I agreed solely to help Kylie. I thought she was the girl of my dreams. We had a good, stable relationship. The six months we had together were some of the best months of my life. Then, the day we visited the cabin, it was all over. No explanation, no reason, she just vanished.

The first week I was panicked out of my mind. When I returned from doing the radio tour on the West Coast, I rode five hours straight to her family ranch. I even went back to the Bar N Barrel. Everyone was as clueless as to Kylie's whereabouts as I was. She appeared to have vanished off the face of the earth. I was so desperate, I lodged a missing person report at the local police station that same weekend.

My panic receded a few days later when I received a text message from her. The instant I read the message, my panic turned into anger.

Kylie: *I'm sorry. Please stop looking for me.*

That was the last time I heard from her. It has been nearly two years since that text. Even though I'm pissed at the way she left, I hated that she couldn't afford her hotel bill. Neither Kylie or I had money when we dated, but that didn't stop us from having adventurous month after adventurous month. I hoped she left me for bigger and better things, but seeing her struggle to pay for a crappy hotel room makes me realize she didn't.

Kylie has been working with Emily for the past three days, but I've barely seen her. It isn't that I'm avoiding her. Other than doing press conferences and meet and greets at the end of our shows, I don't have much interaction with Emily, which means I hardly see Kylie. Half of me wants to ask her why she took the coward's way out by vanishing without saying goodbye, whereas the other half tries to pretend I don't give a fucking shit.

I loved her as much as I could, but only after she left me did I realize you never love someone as much as you miss them once they're gone. Serena's death was already proof of this. Kylie's betrayal merely sealed the deal.

CHAPTER EIGHT

KYLIE

The past three days I've been working with Emily have been surreal. I've learned so much about the industry and have used some of my university studies. Emily took me under her wing, and even though I'm technically her assistant, she treats me as her equal. She even allowed me to write up the press release about the band's upcoming concert in Los Angeles.

For the most part, I've only seen Slater in passing. He's too preoccupied by other stuff to pay me any attention. But today, I felt his intense, heated gaze scanning my body. I smiled at him and waved. He didn't wave back. When the blond on his right did, my eyes snapped back to Emily. The blond is cute. His body type is similar to Slater's, a well-formed muscular physique, and his lips would put Mick Jagger's to shame, but I'm not looking for a relationship, let alone one with a guy who looks like he wants to eat me alive.

As we pace toward the dressing rooms, Emily continues giving me a rundown on the routine she enforces on concert days. Before going on stage tomorrow, the band will talk to the press backstage. They'll then complete a two-hour gig after their supporting act Big Halo finishes their half-hour set. The band then has a one-hour break to recuperate before the fan meet and greet. She explains how the fans will line up at the side of the stage, and how I'll be responsible for ensuring only the backstage pass holders are given access past that point.

"Don't panic; you'll have two security guys with you at all times," she assures me when she notices the concerned expression on my face.

I was in the process of working out how I'd stop Rise Up's persistent fans from barging past me, so her assurance was perfect timing.

When Emily notices the relieved look on my face, she giggles. "The fans aren't the ones you need to worry about." She screws up her pointed nose. "It's the groupies who are the most trouble."

I laugh when she gags, but it's pushed aside for a dramatic *aww* when I follow her into Noah's dressing room. Noah is asleep on a large sofa in the middle of the room, and their daughter Maddie is snuggled on his chest, her snores barely audible.

Maddie is only eleven months old, but there's no stopping her. She can already walk and has the band members and their crew tightly wrapped around her little finger. Emily and Noah travel with a nanny, but they're very hands-on parents to their adorable little girl. I've seen Maddie more with them than her nanny the past three days, or should I call him a "manny," since he's a male nanny?

Noah's eyes pop open the instant Emily paces toward him. His lips curl into his panty-dropping smile when she gently removes Maddie from his chest to place her in her crib next to the sofa. Once Maddie snuggles into her stuffed bunny, Noah pulls Emily down until she's straddling his lap.

When I quickly—and a little awkwardly—avert my eyes, Noah chuckles. "I'm going to... umm... go!"

I dash out of their room like my backside is on fire, closing the door behind me. I learned pretty fast the past three days that the entertainment industry is different than a standard nine-to-five job. Here, there's no real routine. If Emily needs me, she texts me. Other than that, I have plenty of free time.

Most of my work is done while the band performs. I'll set up the press room, the meet and greet area, then make sure the dressing rooms are supplied with anything the band members request. I was surprised when Emily handed me a list of their requirements. Most were the standard stuff you'd expect any rock star to want: bottles of water, snacks, and diapers, but one list was more extravagant. Some of the items listed I hadn't heard of before.

Realizing I most likely have some time before Emily needs me again, I go ask Marcus what the items on his list are, then I can ensure they'll be delivered before he goes on stage tomorrow night.

Upon entering Marcus's dressing room, I hear a shower running in the bathroom. "Would you like me to come back later?" I just averted my eyes from one uncomfortable situation; I really don't want another one if he has someone in the shower waiting for him.

Marcus smiles a heart-fluttering grin before gesturing for me to sit on a blue chair in the corner of the room. "No it's fine. What do you need?"

I pace toward the chair. "Emily gave me the list of supplies you require before tomorrow night. There are a few items I haven't heard of before."

Marcus stops rifling through sheet music so he can give me a curious stare, only stopping when the shower faucet turns off. "What items haven't you heard of before?" he asks, his voice deeper than it was previously.

Just as I'm about to read the first item off the list, Slater strolls into the room wearing nothing but a teeny tiny towel. My pussy tingles as I drink in every inch of his god-crafted body. When a droplet of water rolls over his tattooed torso before careening down his impressive V muscle, I eyeball it with envy. Who knew a blob of water could cause such a vehement, jealous response?

Slater's eyes lock with Marcus, his chin jerking up. "Me and you, strip club tonight."

I hope he's unaware I'm in the room—because those words ripped my heart to shreds.

When Marcus's eyes dart to mine, I avert my gaze, pretending to scrutinize the document in front of me. I don't need to look up to know Slater has realized he has company. I can feel his intense gaze burning into me.

"Be ready by ten," he instructs Marcus before dropping the towel off his hips, like I'm not even in the room.

I don't care if you're one hundred years old and have one foot in the grave, when you have a male specimen like Slater standing in front of you naked, you're going to look. Even if he isn't your type, you're going to look, and my eyes do what any other eyes would do in this situation: they look, and they devour every delicious inch of him.

"Unless there's someone here willing to give me some action for free?"

As my inner vixen screams, "Me, me, pick me!" at the top of her lungs, I lift my eyes to Slater, taking in the scrumptious parts of his body I missed during my first hundred scans. He sees something in my eyes I hoped he wouldn't see. He sees my every want, need, and desire, and how they're all focused on him.

"Not good enough to say goodbye to, but good enough to fuck, eh?"

There's the cold bucket of water I needed to dampen my rampant horniness. My eyes shoot down to the document in my hand as my stomach churns.

"Be in the limo by ten, Marcus, or I'll come and find you."

Slater walks back into the bathroom, slamming the door behind him. I jump out of my skin when its loud bang ricochets throughout the room. While I suck in numerous big breaths, Marcus moves across the room and crouches down in front of me, but no words escape his lips. What could he possibly say? I'm sure he knows what I did to Slater, and I'm sure it looks like I'm a gold-digging whore who's only turning up now because he's famous, but that isn't the case. I fell in love with Slater before he was famous, and I left him just as his infamy started to rise. If I only wanted him for his money, wouldn't I have stayed back then?

"I'll take care of this." Marcus removes the paper from my hand before standing. "Why don't you have an early night? I'll let Emily know you're at the hotel if she needs you."

I nod, accepting his offer. An early night sounds like a godsend, although I doubt even twelve hours of sleep could lighten the weight on my chest.

After tossing and turning for two hours solid, I give up on my early night. Dressed in a pair of jeans and a t-shirt, I head down to the hotel lobby in search of a warm beverage. Since it's nearly midnight, the lobby is deserted. Only a handful of staff are milling around. I'm not surprised, only disheartened to discover the café inside the hotel is closed.

"There's a Starbucks around the corner," advises a male voice behind me.

Spinning on my heels, I spot the guy who smiled at me earlier today. He's with another man who has long brown hair and a curious crinkle popping between his brow. They're holding Styrofoam coffee cups in their hands, both drenched from their shoulders up.

"I'm not *that* desperate for a hot chocolate," I reply, noticing it's pouring rain outside.

When the blond takes a sip of his beverage, a moan escapes his lips. "Are you sure? They're good," When his tongue darts out to lick a smidgen of foam from his top lip, it hides half his smile.

After swallowing the lump in my throat, I reply, "I'm sure."

Up close, this guy is hotter than first perceived. His blue eyes have flecks of black through them, and they're a lighter blue near the pupil. They're entrancing, and I can see how women become quickly trapped by their allure. Doesn't mean I can't spot a player from a mile out, though.

"How do you know Slater?" the other guy questions, breaking the hypnotic trance of the blond's eyes.

"He's an old friend."

When I head to the elevators, they follow closely behind me. "Hmm, interesting." The dark-haired man hits the button for the elevator as the blond's brows scrunch.

Upon entering the elevator car, I select the button for the tenth floor before shifting on my feet to face them since they followed me inside. "What floor?"

When the blond leans across me to select floor twenty-two, my nose hairs tingle. He has a very strong pine scent that becomes considerably more noticeable when his forearm brushes my side boob.

"He wasn't acting like an old friend earlier tonight," the brown-haired guy continues, eager to keep our conversation going.

I'm about to reply, but the blond beats me. "Don't be stupid, Mark. They were more than friends." His eyes burn into mine, making me hot all over. "That's why he warned everyone to stay away from her." Some may construe the smirk on his face as callous. I see him more as a man with no filter.

It means what he says next will hurt, but it's straight-up honest. "He doesn't want her, but no one else can have her either."

CHAPTER NINE

SLATER

I do a double take when I walk past Kylie while entering the press conference room. I thought she looked different the past four days, but today she's barely recognizable. Her makeup is heavy, her mousy brown locks are black, and a purple streak runs down one side. She's wearing tiny denim shorts, black knee-high "fuck me" boots, and a white lace shirt that shows her dark purple bra underneath.

I stride to the empty seat next to Marcus and plop down, unable to pry my eyes away from Kylie. When she bends over to collect paperwork from a briefcase on the ground, my cock turns to stone.

"Holy fuck," I mumble under my breath.

Marcus laughs when I adjust myself, but I don't have time to reprimand him. I'm not the only one eyeballing Kylie's new appearance. When Noah sees her, he stops frozen in the doorway. He gives her a curious glance before shaking his head. Jenni squeals before throwing her arms around Kylie's neck to tell her how hot she looks, and the road crew keeps sauntering by the press conference room door, their pace slowing when they spot Kylie inside.

Noah's ass fills the seat next to me. "What did you do?"

My eyes flick up to his, confusion evident on my face.

"To piss Kylie off?" he explains while smiling a beaming white grin.

"I didn't do anything." You can't miss the arrogance in my tone.

Noah leans forward so he can lock his eyes with Marcus. "What did he do?"

"Strippers—"

Marcus's words are cut off when my fist lands in his gut. Air hisses between his teeth before it shifts into a chuckle. While rubbing his stomach, he shrugs like it's no big deal he's ratting me out to the rest of the band.

"Strippers? Fuck, Slater." Noah chuckles while shaking his head. "You'll feel her wrath no matter what—there's no fury like a woman scorned."

Nick nods, agreeing with Noah's statement.

"Whatever, we aren't dating." That wasn't by my choice either, but I'll never admit that out loud.

Nick's brow cocks before he joins our conversation. "Dating or not, you'll feel the wrath of her jealousy."

My eyes shift between my three bandmates, who are gawking at me with amusement. The mirth on their faces pisses me the fuck off. I'm not the one who left without saying goodbye. I'm not the one who broke her heart, so why am I the one who has to alter my life because she's re-entered it?

"Whatever, the strippers were totally worth it..."

My sneer has barely left my mouth when a sheet of paper is thrust onto the desk in front of me. Lifting my gaze, I'm stung by the angry glare of a pretty pair of hazel eyes. I swallow harshly as Kylie moves down the desk, handing sheets of paper to the rest of the band.

Once she saunters back to the table she was initially standing by, my band members' eyes return to me. When they spot my shocked expression, they chuckle in sync.

"You just dug your hole even deeper," Noah says between breathless laughs.

"Shut the fuck up." I hit him with a stern finger point before Emily joins us. Her presence brings them back into line. Bunch of pussies.

This is one part of my job I hate. Why do we need to talk to the press? Even when we tell them something until we're blue in the face, they still run a story full of half-truths. Half the shit I read on the gossip sites is fabricated. I had my fair share of negative stories printed when the band first rose to fame, but I've worked hard the past year to clean up my image. Not just for the band's sake, but also for Serena's. But even if I go to church every Sunday and never fuck another groupie again, I'll always be portrayed as the bad boy of Rise Up.

You do one stint in rehab, and you never live it down.

Not long after Kylie vanished, the band hit it big. Since my mind was preoccupied with everything going on, I didn't have a chance to work out what the fuck happened between us. When Noah had his accident, my life spiraled out of control. *Sex, drugs, and rock 'n roll* is exactly how it sounds. Once Noah recovered from his accident, I dabbled in it all.

Nick and Jenni had Jasper to keep them grounded. Noah and Emily were getting married and expecting their first baby in a few weeks' time. Excluding the occasional visit from Marcus, I was left twiddling my fucking thumbs. For years, the band practiced every weekday and performed every weekend. Then suddenly, nothing but static. When you're used to constant buzzing, deafening silence unravels the strongest person.

When I was home alone, memories of Kylie filtered through my brain. I couldn't figure out what I had done to make her leave without saying goodbye. Wanting to escape my memories, I went to have a beer at Mavericks. When I arrived unannounced, I was treated like a god by our old fans. Soon, the hype and praise overruled my moral compass, and I got swept away by the rock star lifestyle.

The women and the booze were endless, but within weeks, it wasn't enough. It only took Marcus visiting me once to know something wasn't right. When he showed up the next day with my dad in tow, I didn't have a chance in hell of not going to rehab. My dad would have kicked my ass all the way there if he needed to. Then, when I saw the disappointed look on my mom's face when she visited me after my first week, I knew I'd never touch drugs again. I was the only child she had left, and I refused to put her through the pain of losing another child.

My little sister Serena passed away six days after her thirteenth birthday. She fought as hard as she could and was strong until the very end. Even the most aggressive treatments couldn't wipe the smile off her face. Although her disease beat her, her strength and determination not to let it dampen her quality of life inspired me to improve mine.

I haven't touched a drug since the day I went to rehab, but the gossip sites consistently run stories about my booze, crack, and hooker weekends. I've never paid anyone to have sex with me, and just because they're strippers doesn't make them prostitutes. The crack was never true, but there's a slight amount of truth about the booze side of the story. I can drink any of the roadies under the table without getting a hangover the next day.

Once our press conference is over, I head to my dressing room to get ready to perform. Big Halo kicks off our show with a thirty-minute set, then we're on stage for two hours straight. I always eat something decent before we begin because I need enough food in my stomach to last me the entire two hours.

Upon entering my dressing room, I spot the back of Kylie removing containers of takeout from a delivery bag to place them on a table Marcus and I have in our dressing room. When she hears the door creak, her neck cranks to face me. She smiles shyly before she continues serving the food.

"They didn't have the chicken marsala you requested, so I got you the chicken mermaid instead, but I asked them to leave off the cashew cream sauce," she advises me, surprising me that she remembers I hate any type of nuts.

Once the items are set up, she pivots around. When I glance into her eyes, I picture the girl I met over two years ago; she's just hiding under a heavy coating of makeup and skimpy clothes.

"Why are you wearing that?" She's naturally beautiful, so she doesn't need to hide under layers of makeup.

"Because this is what *normal* people do." Her voice is cold and distant compared to a few seconds ago. "Unlike strippers, most people wear clothes to work."

Her snide comment confirms what Noah and Nick suspected. She's pissed I went to a strip club last night.

"What do you want me to do, Kylie? Stop my lifestyle because you suddenly turn up again?"

She remains quiet as her hazel eyes bounce between mine. Their wetness should house my scorn for another day, but the slight part of her lips has me stepping up to the plate I should have stood at years ago.

"This is me. This is my life now. I go to strip clubs; I fuck groupies, and I don't answer to anyone." A single tear drips down her face, but now that my anger is uncorked , I can't reel it back in. "Let me live my life, and you go live yours." My eyes roam over her heavily coated face and scantily clad body. "Your *real* life, not what you *assume* people want."

With that, I pivot on my heels and storm into the bathroom, needing distance before one of the knives her tears directed at my heart hits its target. Kylie has no fucking clue I would have picked the girl I met two years ago over any stripper or groupie. She would have always been my first choice. But *she* was the one who left without saying goodbye. *She* chose to end our relationship, so now *she* must live with the consequences of her actions.

CHAPTER TEN

KYLIE

I angrily wipe mascara tear stains off my face in the women's bathroom located backstage. This is the last time I'll ever listen to advice from Melanie. I called her last night after my one-sided conversation with Sonny and Mark. She convinced me Slater must still have feelings for me since he warned others to stay away from me. I stupidly let her words get my hopes up, which in turn, resulted in me giving myself a mini confidence boost.

My mousy brown hair, freckled nose, and cropped boots don't fit in with the music industry, so I took a portion of my first paycheck to the salon on the ground floor of my hotel and asked them to give me a "rock star" look.

When the stylist spun me around to face the mirror, my jaw fell open. Right then and there, I felt rejuvenated, and perhaps even a little bit sexy. I skipped back to my room with a new-found spring in my step, my smile unstoppable as I dressed in clothing Melanie had left behind in case I needed it. Once I finished getting ready, I peered at myself in the mirror. For the first time in years, I felt sexy.

When I arrived at the stadium, the first person I saw was Emily. Her eyes popped opened as her squeal shredded the eardrums of anyone within a five-mile radius. "Kylie, you look hot!" My confidence soared even more when her hand slid down my recently straightened locks. "You've always been beautiful, but now you look like your naughty twin."

Now I just feel like the stupid rejected twin. I never expected Slater to wait around for me, and I'm not stupid; I know he's taking *full* advantage of his rock star lifestyle, but it hurt like a million bee stings having him tell me that so harshly. The only good thing that came out of our exchange is that I'm now certain he isn't harboring any old feelings for me. He's moved on, and now it's time for me to do the same.

After taking a few more minutes to gather my composure, I walk back to the wings of the stage. I only have four more hours to survive, then my working day will be over. As I stand behind Emily and Jenni, I can't help but feel envious. They're bouncing their adorable children on their hips while watching the men they love perform. Once again, that could have been me if I weren't dealt the shittiest hand you could possibly imagine.

Since I am unable to see Slater from my position, I take a giant step to my right. Now that I'm standing next to the thick red curtains, I swear I can hear someone whispering my name. Unsure if I'm hearing things, I tilt toward the ruffled fabric. When a loud "Boo!" roars out of the curtain, I jump in the air like a cat thrown into bathwater.

"Sorry," I apologize when Jenni and Emily spin around to face me. My squeal scared them as much as my mischievous greeter made me poop my pants. Once their attention diverts back to the stage, I hunt down the person responsible for my skyrocketing heart rate.

It takes me ruffling through the deep curtain for several minutes before I spot the amused face of Sonny. "You scared the living shit out of me."

His smile grows when I slap his chest. "Sorry. You looked bored. Figured I could offer up some entertainment."

I assume he means my near coronary, but I'm proven wrong

when he guides me to the very back of the stage. A handful of roadies are using old amps as chairs and a lopsided card table holds their drinks and a stack of cards.

After a frisky wink that reveals he is as devilish as he is handsome, Sonny guides me closer to the group. Most of the men appear to be around my age—somewhere between their early to mid-twenties. Their black polo shirts have "Rise Up Roadies" written in blue on a pocket, and they're all wearing blue jeans.

"You met Mark last night." Sonny points to Mark sitting at our left. "This is Pierre, David, and Jeffrey." He points to each member of the crew.

I remove my hand from Sonny's sweaty grip to accept the handshakes each offers.

"They're twins," Mark informs me when he notices my curious gaze drifting between David and Jeffrey.

They must be identical twins because they have the same green eyes, dimpled chins, near invisible bottom lip, and blond hair. Except Jeffery's hair sits at his shoulders, and David's is clipped close to his scalp. Pierre has brown eyes and gorgeous olive skin. With his jet black hair and alluring features, I'm assuming he has Italian heritage. My suspicions are confirmed when Mark refers to him as the Italian Stallion once their game starts up again.

My curiosity piques when they lick a card before sticking it to their forehead. "What game are they playing?"

Sonny smiles a blinding grin. "It's a drinking game. You have to guess what your card is. Each wrong guess means you have to take a shot."

Laughter echoes around the room when Mark roars, "You bastards better not be cheating!" before swallowing a generous nip of brown liquor.

"Do you want to play?" Excitement dangles on Sonny's vocal cords.

I shake my head. I used to hold my own when Slater and I played drinking games, but I haven't drunk hard liquor in over a year, so I'm reasonably sure it will only take a few sips to get me drunk.

"I'm still working." I swing my gaze back to the wings where I see Emily and Jenni's legs peeking out beneath the curtain.

"So are we—"

David throws a pile of cards at Mark's head, shutting him up. It hits him under his right eye so hard, he'll most likely wake up with a black eye tomorrow morning.

"Don't tell anyone."

The slur of Mark's words has me wondering if the other guys are cheating. The band only went on a few minutes ago, yet he's already well intoxicated.

I cross my heart. "It'll remain our little secret."

Mark grins before twisting his lips with his fingers. After waving goodbye, I stroll to the curtain. Just as I'm about to enter the wings, Sonny calls my name. "If you change your mind, you know where to find me."

His bold wink makes me doubt he's still referring to the card game. Although I'm not looking for anything permanent, Slater's rejection is still fresh in my mind, so I nod at the innuendo in Sonny's tone before reentering the wings, unsure which performance will be my most damning tonight.

After the band's encore, the atmosphere behind the scenes goes crazy. There are hundreds of fans lined up requesting access for the fan meet and greet. It takes a bodyguard screaming at them to calm down or risk being kicked out before their eagerness dampens enough to give the instructions on how the meet and greet works.

Once I have the fans lucky enough to catch Slater's drumsticks, Marcus and Nick's guitar straps, and the personalized pick Noah uses when performing the acoustic version of "Surrender Me," I hand them to Emily. The rest of the crowd has to select the band member they want to meet. Because of the number of fans and limited time, they can only request one of their idols.

———

I'm pleased to advise after much shuffling and over a hundred complaints, the lines are even for each band member, and the meet and greet begins without a hiccup.

———

By the time we're down to the last two fans requesting to meet Noah, over two hours have ticked by, and I'm beyond exhausted.

"You did an excellent job tonight, Kylie. Thank you so much for your help."

Even exhausted, I smile broadly. Emily's praised wasn't needed, but it's nice to hear.

After gesturing for the final two fans to follow her, Emily cranks her neck back to peer at me. "You're good to head off. I'll see you tomorrow afternoon."

I love that even though they've been waiting hours to meet their idol, the fans' excitement is still evident on their faces.

With my curiosity still piqued, I head toward the wings of the stage instead of the big illuminated exit sign on my right. I doubt the roadies are still playing their game, but I'm not ready for bed just yet.

As I break through the thick curtain, someone yanks me back out. "You don't want to go in there."

A vein in Sonny's neck beats out a funky tune as he peers down at me.

"Why?"

I'm reasonably sure I know why, but I want him to spell it out for me. When he remains quiet, I follow the direction of his gaze. Two pairs of legs are sticking out beneath the curtain. One is clad in jeans and black motorcycle boots, whereas the other has smooth beige legs and is wearing a pair of altitude-defying stilettos.

The bile in my stomach races to my throat when the female of the duo kneels in front of the jean-covered legs. "Is that Slater?" My heart is racing so fast, my question comes out in a tremble.

Not a word seeps from Sonny's lips. He just bands his arm around my shoulders before forcefully walking me away from the exhibition tearing me in two.

The further we walk, the more my hurt morphs to anger. Even though I have no claim to Slater, it takes all my strength not to pull the groupie slut off him by the strands of her no doubt abhorrent head!

Actually, correct that. It takes all of *Sonny's* strength for me not to turn around. If he didn't carry me into the closest dressing room, I'd be up in Slater's face right now giving him a piece of my mind.

Over the next several minutes, I pace back and forth, cursing and mumbling incoherently under my breath in an attempt to rein my anger in.

After a beat, Sonny leaves his protective post at the door to stand in front of me. "Do you feel better?"

I shake my head. My fists are still clenched, and I feel seconds from detonation.

"Bourbon or vodka?"

As the ice inside of me freezes my heart, my eyes stray to Sonny. "Can I have both?"

A huge smile notches his lips high as he gestures his hand to the door he forced me through ten minutes ago. "Lead the way, Sugar Cup."

CHAPTER ELEVEN

SLATER

When I walk into the lobby of my hotel, Kylie's faint giggle jingles into my ears. It takes me scanning the vast space three times before I spot her in the only establishment still open at two in the morning. I consider joining her for a nightcap before remembering what I said to her earlier. I asked her to let me live my life how I wanted, and she's free to live hers how she sees fit. Besides, she handles her liquor better than most guys, so I'm confident she won't get in any trouble.

As I turn toward the elevator banks, I catch sight of who Kylie is liaising with. Sonny swoops down low to plant a kiss on the edge of her mouth, laughing when her nose screws up from his scruff tickling her chin.

I clench my fists into tight balls, pissed as fuck. I told Sonny to stay away from Kylie, yet here he is drinking with her in the bar of *my* hotel. Not only is he denying my request, he's doing it right under my fucking nose.

I stomp toward them, eager to teach that fucker a lesson about what happens when you break *my* rules. Sonny is saved from being ripped a new asshole when Kylie slips off her barstool and heads toward the elevator banks. She walks straight past me, not paying me an ounce of attention. She doesn't need my eyes on her. She's already got every set of male eyes in the room.

Once she reaches the elevator banks, Sonny takes his eyes off her ass and heads for the hotel exit. I wait for him to disappear through the revolving doors before joining Kylie. She ignores me, but I know she's spotted me because she tilts closer to me before her breaths grow heavier.

When she enters, she pushes the button for the tenth floor before moving to stand in the far back corner, impressing me with only the slightest fumble of her steps. I press the button for the twenty-second floor before moving to the opposite side of her. Even in the city, her wildflower smell is still prominent, although tonight it's complemented by the staunch scent of bourbon.

She remains quiet as the elevator ascends, only facing me once we reach the eighth floor. As her chest heaves, her heavy-lidded eyes drink in my body. She saunters my way, seducing me with an alluring swing of her hips. Due to her tall height and the decent heel on her boots, her beautiful hazel eyes stare straight into mine when she stops in front of me. Her breaths flutter against my hungry lips with an intoxicating mix of bourbon and mint, and nothing but rampant hunger reflects from her eyes.

No longer capable of ignoring the attraction bristling between us, my cock hardens. She purrs like a fucking kitty when she notices my body's response to her closeness. Her nipples strain against her thin shirt as heat creeps up her neck. When she inches closer to me, bringing the lips I fantasize about to within touching distance of my mouth, I close my eyes in preparation for our kiss.

I can't wait to taste her again.

Not even three seconds later, air wafts between us. I pop my eyes open, startled to discover Kylie on the other side of the elevator doors —the same set of doors that are rapidly closing. I charge for them, striving to dart between them before they shut. I don't make it in enough time. Kylie is on the other side, and I'm jabbing the open door button as if it's my only lifeline.

"Maybe next time...?" Kylie murmurs through the closed elevator doors.

Only when entering my suite do I understand what Kylie's cock tease was about. I have a giant lipstick smear on the collar of my shirt. Kylie never shied away from showing her claws when we dated. She has a jealous streak a mile long.

I wouldn't have a ruined shirt if groupies remembered the rules. You'd think since I only have one, it wouldn't be hard to follow. No kissing on the lips—ever! I don't care if they have naked lips, Mick Jagger lips, or lips of an angel, no part of their mouth is to touch mine.

Yeah, yeah, I know what you're thinking, I was about to kiss Kylie, but she's different. For one, she isn't a groupie, and two, she's the reason I created the rule.

Our first kiss was the most epic kiss I've ever had. It happened the night we met. I can still recall her ear-piercing squeals when we darted out of the gravel lot at the front of the Bar N Barrel. For the first few miles, she maintained her tight grip around my waist. Then, as our trip continued, she relaxed a little. First, she raised her right hand in the air, then once we were ten miles out, her other hand loosened its hold on my waist. Once she had both arms in the air, she squealed so loud, I couldn't help the smile that formed on my face. I grinned so wide, I ate bugs for a week. It was still worth it.

Around two miles before we reached the bar, without warning, she slipped under my arm and spun herself around so she was wrapped around the front of my body instead of the back. While peering past her glowing eyes, I slowed down, ensuring I didn't kill us both. Once my speed hit twenty miles an hour, her lips landed on mine.

Fuck me, you wouldn't believe how good she tasted.

The vodka cranberries she had been downing all night featured in our kiss, but she still tasted like pure fucking heaven. It killed me not being able to close my eyes to relish her taste, but I needed to keep them on the road.

Once I pulled over, I returned her kiss with as much passion as she was giving. It was a blur of lashing, playful bites, and the sweet movements of a set of heavenly plump lips. It was an awe-inspiring kiss, one I'll never attempt to replicate.

From then on, we were inseparable. We spent every weekend together doing adrenaline-producing activities. But even going white-water rafting, skydiving, and bungee jumping didn't come close to the thrill I got kissing Kylie for the first time.

I was forever ruined by her lips, and since I knew no kiss would ever compete with it, I refuse to give anyone the opportunity to disappoint me.

***

The next two concerts follow a similar routine. Kylie still wears skimpy clothes and heavy makeup, and my cock stiffens every time I see her. The only difference between the past two days and Friday night is the fact Kylie hasn't spoken a word to me. Not a single fucking one.

Don't think I haven't tried to force her to interact with me. I've used every lame excuse I can find, but she doesn't take any of my bait. My fishing skills suck in general, which is why I was surprised I snagged her the first time, but I still expected her to take a little bite.

I haven't been able to get her out of my head since she teased me in the elevator, so it's annoying the fuck out of me that she won't talk to me. I was harsh when I told her I fuck groupies and go to strip clubs, but I was angry, and since she was the source of my anger, I took it out on her. Sue me.

I was so desperate to spark a reaction from her, tonight I ordered a meal riddled with nuts. Marcus pissed himself laughing when my dinner arrived with every ingredient removed but the nuts. It was an assortment of nuts covered in black bean sauce. Now, I'm not just angry, I'm starving.

When Kylie enters the room to advise Marcus that *he* has ten minutes until *he's* due on stage, I try one last tactic to force her to speak to me. "Hey Kylie, we're heading to a strip club later; wanna come?"

I weave, barely missing the drumstick Marcus pegs at my head. After giving him the stink eye, I turn my attention back to Kylie. She's frozen halfway out the door, her hand gripping the handle for dear life. When she spins back around, she's smiles, but her angry eyes give away her true intentions.

"Thanks for the offer." Her voice is extra sugary, using her country twang to her advantage.

I smirk, smug as fuck that I forced her to talk to me.

My smile is wiped off my face when she adds, "But I'm going out with Sonny, so I'll have to give it a pass. *Sorry.*" She winks before making her way out of my dressing room, her hips swinging in a way that should be illegal.

When I glare at Marcus, whose laughter is vibrating in my chest, he gives me a halfhearted apology, "Sorry, but you deserved that."

I'm surprised I didn't put my sticks through my drum kit with how hard I hit it while performing. All I've been imagining the past four hours is Kylie lying in Sonny's bed with her smile directed at him and her eyes staring lovingly into his. If that isn't bad enough, the worst image by far was her lips touching his. I pounded the living shit out of my kit, and by the end of our set, I was the most exhausted I've ever been.

Even the groupie who's been eye-fucking me the past thirty minutes of the fan meet and greet isn't enough to pull me out of my slump. I'm a fucking wreck, and more than ready to give Seattle a one-finger salute farewell. My dour mood isn't Seattle's fault, but since I can't shift my frustration onto the person responsible, Seattle is getting the brunt of it.

Once I finish scribbling my name across a bunch of photographs, I make my way to the stage to grab the drumsticks I left behind. The roadies will dismantle my kit tonight in preparation to transport it to San Francisco for our next set of concerts, but I take my custom-made sticks with me to save them from getting lost during transport. My head was a little clouded after tonight's performance so I left them behind instead of taking them with me.

After gathering my sticks, I stride toward the back entrance of the stadium. My quick pace slows when I hear murmured voices coming through the velvet curtains on the wings of the stage. I've previously used heavy stage curtains as a hook-up point with groupies, so my interests are piqued as to who else uses them.

When I break through the thick velvet curtain, I pace toward people talking and laughing. Upon turning the corner, the first person I spot is Kylie. She has a King of Hearts playing card stuck to her forehead and is sitting around a table with a group of male road-ies. They also have playing cards stuck to their heads.

Kylie bites down on her bottom lip before her bloodshot eyes shoot up to the ceiling, no doubt trying to read the card on her head. "King of Spades?"

The S of spades is barely out of her mouth when the roadies shout loudly. With a grin of a man who looks like he's about to cream his pants, Sonny fills a shot glass with bourbon before sliding it to Kylie.

"Y'all better not be cheating."

When they assure her they aren't, she downs the shot of bourbon in one hit before her tongue delves into the glass to ensure she didn't miss a drop. I can't help but smile when she acts unaffected by the burning sensation most girls hate from hard liquor sliding down their throats.

From the corner of the room, I watch them go another round.

Each member of the crew has to down a nip since they guessed wrong.

Now, it's Kylie's turn again.

She taps her index finger on her pouty lips, her face showing her pure concentration. "King of Hearts?"

My jaw ticks when the roadies holler again like she guessed wrong. When Sonny slides her another shot of bourbon, I head their way. Kylie's heavy-lidded eyes lift to mine when I stop next to her. She looks neither scared or worried.

Snarling, I remove the card from her head and throw it on the table. She takes in the card with a playful glint in her eyes before they drift between the guys playing. With a wink that reveals she'll always be a wild child, she swallows her second shot of bourbon more eagerly than she did the first. The road crew cheers and claps, encouraging her defiance. My response is the complete opposite.

My jaw spasms as my nostrils flare—even more so when Kylie says, "I'm living my life."

The bad slur of her words reveals she's drunker than I thought. She's the only one, too. Other than Mark, none of the other roadies' eyes are as glazed over as Kylie's.

"You're done for the night." I nod my head to the exit, demanding she follow me out. When she crosses her arms under her ample chest, my eyes narrow into tiny slits. "I'm not requesting, Kylie. I'm telling. Move your ass, now."

When Sonny stands from his seat, I point to the amp he's using as a chair. "Sit *the fuck* down." My tone tells him I'll place him in the chair myself if he doesn't comply with my request.

Once Sonny takes a seat, I turn my furious eyes back to Kylie. She licks a card from the deck, then sticks it to her head. "Why don't you join us?" She jerks her chin to an empty amp a few spots up. "The next game is strip poker, isn't it, boys?" Her words are barely comprehensible in her drunken state.

Growling, I pluck her from the speaker box she's sitting on, throw her over my shoulder, then storm out of the room. Her hair swishes back and forth, matching the rhythm at which her arms are hitting my back. I'm just about to exit the stadium when it dawns on me that the paparazzi will photograph me carrying her over my shoulder if I turn up to our hotel like this. I hardly know her dad, but I'm reasonably sure he wouldn't appreciate having his drunken daughter slashed over the morning newspapers.

After a few seconds of deliberation, I head toward our tour bus. Because it sits in a secure lot, the driver doesn't bother locking it.

As I make my way to the back of the bus, Kylie mutters several soft curse words under her breath.

Once I enter the bedroom and set her on her feet, her words turn into a full blown rant. "Why did you do that?" When she throws her arms in the air, she sways like a leaf in a hot summer breeze. "I could've drunk them under the table." She leans against the bedroom wall, stabilizing her sways. "Are we moving?" I would laugh if she weren't dead serious.

I go fetch her a glass of water and some Advil from the kitchen. "You need to sleep it off."

I'm only gone for thirty seconds, but she removes her shoes and shirt in that small amount of time. She's drunk, but I can't help but drink in her jiggling breasts when she wrangles her jeans down her thighs. She mumbles to herself while undressing. It doesn't make any sense, but one point is featured throughout her slurs: "You don't want me, but no one else can have me either."

Once her jeans are removed, she stands before me in nothing but a silky bra and matching panties. When I get busted gliding my eyes over her enticing body, her lips curve into a seductive grin.

"Is this how you want me?" She paces so close to me, her erect nipples scrape my chest with every breath she takes. "Then take me."

Knowing there's no way in hell I can control myself having her standing in front of me half-naked, I pull off my shirt and place it over her head, effectively breaking the spell she's attempting to cast on me.

The lust in her eyes switches to anger. "Oh, that's right! You don't want me, but nobody else can have me either!"

When she jerks away from me, she trips over her jeans left lying on the floor. I grimace when she lands on her knees with a thud. When I assist her off the ground, her tear-filled eyes lock with mine. "Why don't you want me?"

"I did want you, remember? It was you who didn't want *me*."

She shakes her head, sending tears flinging off her cheeks. "I wanted you. I loved you." She scrambles to her feet so her glazed-over eyes can dance between mine. "I still love you."

"Then why did you leave?" My roar startles her, but I'm done reining in my anger. "Why were you a fucking coward who left without saying goodbye?"

When Kylie's eyes dart away, no longer able to maintain my eye contact, I return them to my face via her chin, wanting to ensure she hears the words I should have spoken years ago. "I loved you," I growl in an angry whisper. "And you fucking destroyed me."

I storm out of the room, down the long hallway of the bus, and out into a parking lot that's as empty as my heart felt when she left me two years ago today.

CHAPTER TWELVE

KYLIE

Someone please kill me. My brain is attempting to escape my skull through my eye sockets. My throat is dry and raw, and my stomach is swirling like a washing machine has been inserted in its place.

My eyes sluggishly open when something cool is placed against my forearm. Turning my gaze, I find Slater sitting on the bed next to me. His bloodshot brown eyes are staring down at me, full to brim with concern. I gingerly scoot up in the bed, lean my back against the black leather headboard, then accept the glass of water and tablets he's offering.

"Drink it all," he requests, his voice rough like he's just woken up.

I finish the glass of water before handing it back to him. As my dry eyes scan the room, I rack my brain as to where I am. The room is done in black wooden cabinets and drawers. A glass frosted door is at one side and another black door in the middle. I'm fairly sure I'm not at a hotel because this room is smaller than any I've stayed in previously, and I've stayed in some tiny hotel rooms. Although this room is fancy in detailing, it's the size of most walk-in closets.

"You're on the tour bus." When Slater pulls open a small section of blacked-out curtains, the sun shining through the crack adds to the thump of my skull. We must be moving, or I'm still drunk, because the trees lining the road's edge are flicking past us.

"Where are we going?" My throat burns with every syllable I speak. It feels like I haven't had a drink in a month.

"San Francisco." My pounding head gets instant relief when he closes the curtain. "I arranged for someone to pack your stuff at the hotel. It should arrive in San Francisco not long after us."

The next several minutes pass in silence. I don't mind. It gives me time to study all the details of his face I've missed so much the past two years. He's still very much the man I fell in love with. His dreads are a little bit longer, and the scruff on his chin could only be more devastating if it were tickling the sticky mess between my thighs.

When I scissor my legs together to dampen the buzz roaring through my veins, I realize I'm not wearing any pants. I'm wearing nothing but Slater's shirt.

Holy shit! Does that mean...? Did we...?

My eyes rocket to Slater's as my excitement turns catastrophic. I search his face for answers to the questions my mouth is failing to ask. He watches me just as intently, seemingly confused. I try to ease it by nudging my head to my bare legs.

He catches on to my silent grilling rather quickly. "Fuck me, Kylie! Is that what you think I've become? A man who takes home drunk women to fuck them?!"

His angry voice vibrates through to my stomach, curdling the mess to a point I can no longer ignore. With my hand clamped over my mouth, I dart out of bed, praying the vomit surging up my throat waits until I reach a bathroom.

Slater curses under his breath before he assists me into the bathroom, which, for future reference, is the black frosted glass door. While I vomit the glass of water I just drank into the porcelain toilet, Slater holds my hair out of my face. I'd die a thousand deaths of embarrassment if I didn't already have one foot in the grave. This is horrific. I've never felt more ill—*except those other times.*

Once my stomach is void of liquid, Slater scoops me into his arms before returning me to bed. I crawl toward him, wanting to rest my head on his chest.

When he balks, I beg, "Just for a minute, please." My head is thumping so much, the beat of his heart will make it more bearable. "You can go back to hating me tomorrow. I just need..." I try to think of a better word than "you," but when I fail to find one, I go with it. "You. I need you, Slater. *Please.*"

When he nods, I rest my ear over his heart. His familiar scent floods my eyes with moisture, but it also helps me fall back into peaceful, uninterrupted sleep.

The next time I wake up, I'm the only person in the room. My head isn't thumping as badly, and my stomach's growls are more from hunger than being hungover. As I cautiously slide on my jeans from last night, a hum of laughter sounds through the wooden door. I make my way to the bathroom to run my fingers through my hair, trying to settle down the frazzled pieces before wetting some toilet paper to remove the make-up smeared on my face. When I locate a tube of toothpaste in the top drawer, I use my index finger as if it's a toothbrush.

Although I look like shit, I feel better than I did ten minutes ago.

Once I'm half-presentable, I hesitantly open the wooden door and enter the hub of the tour bus, embarrassed I made a fool out of myself in front of my employer. The first person I spot while gliding down the aisle flanked by bunks is Slater. He's sitting on a reclining swivel chair, perusing a biker magazine. When he smiles at me, Jenni follows the direction of his gaze. Also smiling, she bridges the gap between us.

"How are you feeling?" Her questions make it seem as if my sickness wasn't self-induced.

"I'm okay," I cringe, praying she didn't hear me vomiting in the bathroom earlier. The tour bus is large in size, but at the end of the day, it's still a bus.

"I bet." She rubs my arm in a soothing manner. "Food poisoning is terrible."

My confused eyes dance between hers. "Food poisoning?"

"Yeah, food poisoning. I'm just glad you refused to share your meal, or I would have been hugging the toilet with you." This confession doesn't come from Jenni. It came from Slater, who's smirking at me from behind his magazine.

"You and me both. Although I'm sure it won't be too much longer before my bowl-hugging starts all over again." After pulling a face like she's about to be sick, Jenni saunters away.

When I walk past Slater, I bump him with my knee, wordlessly thanking him for saving me from an extremely embarrassing situation.

I spend the next hour staring at a darkened sky while trying to work out the events of last night. I remember playing the drinking card game with the road crew. I have vague memories of being carried over Slater's shoulder, but other than that, the rest of my night is a blur.

I knew the road crew was cheating from the very beginning. I was just upset Slater goaded me about going to a strip club, I no longer cared. I wanted to break free from the dull, depressing life I've been living the past two years. I guess I should thank Slater for not just looking after me while I was sick, but for also stopping me from making a huge mistake.

Sonny's interests in me have been as obvious as the sun hanging in the sky. I've explained to him on many occasions that the spark of attraction will never be reciprocated. He just has a hard time understanding the word "no." His pursuit has been relentless, and last night, he caught me in a moment of weakness.

It's lucky Slater came by when he did, or who knows whose bed I may have woken in this morning. The thought alone makes me cringe. Not just at Sonny, but myself as well. I'm not a child, but last night I certainly acted like one.

When my gaze shifts away from the window, I spot Emily's concerned face. She doesn't say anything; her eyes just dance over my face. Remorse washes over me when tears well in her eyes. I'm just about to ask if she's okay, but Noah beats me to her. He pulls her onto his lap, his concern doubling when she burrows her head into the crook of his neck so she can sob without witnesses.

After locking my eyes with Marcus, I jerk my chin to Emily, wordlessly asking if he knows what's going on. He shakes his head, as clueless as me. Wanting to give Noah and Emily privacy, I return to the room at the back of the bus, passing Jenni on the way by. She's standing near a set of bunk beds Maddie and Jasper are sleeping on. She rubs my arm reassuringly before nudging her head to the door at the end of the aisle. "I think he's asleep."

I knock softly to confirm her suspicions. When I don't get a reply, I hesitantly open it. As Jenni suspected, Slater is sprawled on the bed, the rhythm of his breaths showing he's asleep. He's lying on his stomach, wearing nothing but a pair of jeans. One pillow is cradled under his chest, and his head is resting on another. Although he's just as deserving of privacy as Emily and Noah, I quietly slip into the room and close the door behind me. He comforted me when I needed it, so shouldn't I do the same?

After tiptoeing to the other side of the room, I slip between the sheets, where I spend the next several minutes watching him sleep. Because he's removed his shirt, I can take in the differences I missed last time. He's added even more tattoos to his already vast collection, and his body is bulkier with a healthy smattering of muscles, but by looking at him, I could forget the last two years happened. The guy sleeping next to me is the same man I fell instantly in love with. The same man I still love.

Bus brakes squeaking interrupts his peaceful slumber. When he sluggishly opens his eyes, he catches my stalker watch. He seems surprised I'm lying next to him, but doesn't say anything. He just lifts his head off the pillow so he can study my face without anything in the way.

"How are you feeling?"

I wait for him to stop scrubbing his tired eyes before answering, "I'm good."

Smirking, he rolls onto his hip, mimicking my position to perfection.

"Although, I'm never drinking bourbon *ever* again."

He chuckles a breathy laugh that sets my pulse racing. "I don't think I'll touch it again either."

When he gags, I slap him on his chest, mortified he saw me like that, while also loving his playful banter. *God, I've missed his laugh.*

Once he finishes chuckling, his face takes on a more serious appearance. "What do you remember about last night?"

I bare teeth while cringing. "To be honest, I don't recall much."

"So you don't remember declaring your undying love to me?"

I freeze as my pupils widen. I've always been a talkative, affectionate drunk, but I thought I was sick enough last night that my ramblings would have been kept to a bare minimum. Furthermore, although I'd never deny loving him, I hate that he had to hear it while I was drunk.

Slater's shoulders shake, and his eyes get a cheeky sparkle as his lips curve upwards. When I spot the whites of his teeth, I punch him in the bicep. He releases the chuckle he's struggling to hold in. He's always been a stirrer, but I'm usually all over his pranks, so I'm shocked I just fell for the oldest one in the book.

When three brief taps hit the bedroom door, our heads crank to the side in sync.

"Slater, we're in San Francisco." Even with needing to project her voice through a door, Jenni's nerves can't be missed. "Umm.... is Kylie still in there with you?"

After rolling off the bed, Slater tugs a shirt over his head before opening the door Jenni is standing behind. When she spots me lying on one side of the rumbled bed, a vast grin etches across her flushed face.

"Sorry to interrupt." Her cheeks bloom even more. "I just wanted to let you know we're in San Francisco." Her eyes stray from Slater to me. "And Emily asked me to tell you she needs to see you in her hotel room ASAP."

The urgency in her tone makes me leap out of bed too quickly for someone with a woozy head. After stabilizing my footing, I drag my fingers through my fluffy hair before straightening my creased clothes. I'd prefer to get changed before our meeting, but what I'm wearing will have to do since I don't have access to my suitcase.

I offer Slater my thanks with a smile as I pad past him. Just as I'm about to exit, his hand darts out to seize my wrist. My heart squeezes when I peer up into his gorgeous brown eyes. So many things are said without a single word escaping our lips. His sorrow for the cruel words we've shared since I started working with Emily. Mine for the horrid things I still have to explain. But the most important of all is the promise that we'll work through our differences until we come to an amicable solution for us both.

Nodding, I press my lips to the edge of his plump mouth. "Thank you."

My heart races when he smiles. I may not be able to fix the mistakes I've made, but that doesn't mean I can't start fresh to create something better.

CHAPTER THIRTEEN

SLATER

"Thank fuck," I breathe out heavily when my baby arrives in San Francisco in one piece.

It killed me asking Sonny to ride my bike, but he's the only member of the road crew who has a motorcycle license. Normally, I wouldn't let my bike out of my sight, but Kylie was ill all night long, so I had to pick between looking after her or riding my bike.

I chose her. I'll always choose her.

Once I got my anger under control, I headed back onto the bus to discover Kylie huddled in a ball in the middle of the bed. Big angry tears were flooding her cheeks, leaving black smears on her face. She was sobbing so hard, her whole body was shuddering. It tore my heart in half seeing her so broken.

After sitting on the bed, I pulled her to my chest. She cradled in close before apology after apology spilled from her lips. Hardly anything she said made sense, but the word sorry was used continually, so it didn't take a genius to realize she was apologizing.

By the time she finished crying, my chest was saturated with her tears, and she was both physically and emotionally exhausted. "I'm sorry for everything I did," she whispered, her voice the clearest it had been all night. "Please forgive me; I need you to forgive me."

I cleared away the hairs stuck to her temples before lifting her eyes to mine via her chin. "Why did you leave?" I asked my question more sincerely than I did earlier.

This time, her eyes didn't dart away. She maintained eye contact by staring firmly into mine. "I did it for you. Everything I did, I did for you." Her voice was as pained as the heartache etched on her face. "Please forgive me, Slater."

Although she didn't give me an actual answer, I always struggled to say no to her in general, especially when she stared at me like she did last night.

"Please, Slat—"

"I forgive you," I interrupted.

Three little words and the burden of anger I had been carrying the past two years lifted from my shoulders in an instant. Her face scrunched up as she battled to hold back more tears. My thumbs cleared away the ones her eyes couldn't contain. Within minutes, I saw enough tears leak from her eyes to last me a lifetime, and her stomach could no longer ignore its churning.

"I'm going to be sick." She clamped her hand over her mouth as her pupils dilated. I barely got her to the bathroom in time. I'm fairly sure she didn't have any food in her stomach because nothing but smelly bourbon was expelled from her body over the next several hours.

Kylie is tall for a girl, but she's tiny in size. I was shocked how much she vomited throughout the night, but it had nothing on the shock of discovering her flawless skin still bears my name. It's on a place not many men have seen, but I saw it while replacing her vomit-stained shirt with one I carried on the bus. When she lifted her arms to assist me, the black ink peeked out of her panties. It was as surprising to see as the day she got it. . .

Kylie's wary eyes stray to mine. "No eye contact, don't mention the word 'dog,' and only eat food directly out of the packet?"

"Yes." It's the fight of my life not to laugh. I thought Kylie would be too smart to believe the bullshit spilling from my lips, but she's gobbling up every word like it's gospel. *"And don't drink the water."*

Her brows furrow. We're about to do the dreaded meet the parents routine. Kylie requested to meet my family first, then I'll meet hers next weekend. We've been dating for nearly three months, so we felt the timing was right to introduce each other to our family and friends. We've pulled into a truck stop halfway between her college and my parents' house to give our legs a bit of a stretch. Kylie's college is seven hours away from her parents' ranch, but mercifully, it's only three hours from my hometown.

Her brows are still drawn together when I lower her purple helmet over her head before wrangling the straps into submission. I don't wear a helmet while riding, but I always ensure Kylie does, especially since she lacks concern for her own safety.

"Do they even have a dog?"

I chuckle over the confusion in her tone. *"Come on, let's get this over and done with."*

I throw my leg over my bike before offering her my hand to assist her on the back. Kylie is a daredevil wrapped in a wholesome country girl facade. She lives her life to the fullest, and even though she loves being on the back of my bike, she molds her body as close to mine any time we ride. It has nothing to do with safety, and everything to do with not wanting an ounce of air between us.

Once her arms are curled around my waist, and her cheek is leaning against my back, I kick over my bike then finish our trip to our family home.

"No, thank you." Kylie's lower lip drops when she declines my mom's third offer for one of her famous red velvet cupcakes.

After placing them back on the tabletop, my mom's confused gaze floats to me. I shrug, acting innocent. It isn't an easy feat for me to pull *off. We're sitting at the wood table in my parents' rustic kitchen. The cupcakes were the third home-baked goodie my mom tried to entice Kylie with. It was also the third time Kylie declined her offer.*

"Are you celiac?" When my mom strolls toward the walk-in pantry to hunt for a gluten-free product, I lose the ability to hold in my laughter. The instant my chuckles boom around the kitchen, my mom realizes the ruse I'm playing. "What did you tell her?" She throws a packet of wheat-free biscuits at my head. A grin curls her lips when she hits her mark.

With her nervous eyes darting between me and my mom, Kylie says, "No eye contact, don't mention the word 'dog,' and only eat packaged food."

"Did you forget about not drinking the water?" My mom's voice is so panicked, it steals the color from Kylie's cheeks and forces her eyes back to the table she's been staring at the past hour.

My mom and I laugh, loving that Kylie fell for the prank my sister and I pulled on our friends years ago. Most of my friends grew up convinced my mom was the worst cook in the world, which suited me just fine. That meant there were plenty of cupcakes and cookies left over for Serena and me when they returned home.

My mom looks like a hardcore biker chick. She has as many tattoos as I do. She wears fifties-style dresses, and her dirty blonde hair is always pulled up with a bandana. I call her a biker chick. She calls herself a rockabilly housewife with attitude. The funny thing about my mom is she looks hard-core, but her insides are as soft as they come. I always joke that Martha Stewart somehow got trapped inside her body. She loves to bake; she's the best friend anyone could ever ask for, and she's one kick ass mom.

But picture being in the sixth grade and your friend's parents arriving to drop off their children for a sleepover. We had a few who left before they even walked in the front door. My mom says tattoos are a perfect way to remove judgmental people from your life. The older I've become, the more her statement rings true.

My laughter dies down when Kylie grabs a red velvet cupcake off the table and shoves it into my face. The white frosting smears all over my cheek, and some even lodges up my nose. With my mouth open wide, I glare at her. My cock stands to attention when she runs her index finger down my cheek, coating it in frosting before popping it into her mouth.

"Yummy." Her reply is only for my ears.

I'm about to pull her sugary mouth to mine when my dad strolls into the kitchen. My dad is the very definition of a biker. His short dark hair is clipped close to the side, and the top is longer in length. I joke that he has Elvis Presley hair. He hates when I say that, but my mom loves it. He wears a black leather jacket and jeans every day, and rides a custom-made chopper. He also owns a tattoo parlor in town. Every tattoo that adorns my body was placed there by him. He's a gifted artist who uses people's bodies as canvases instead of paper.

"Kylie, this is my dad, Elvis. Elvis, this is Kylie," I introduce while removing the frosting from my face with a tea towel.

My dad's dark brows shoot up high into his hairline. "Ryder. Nice to meet you, Kylie." He offers his hand to Kylie to shake.

I shrug. "Ryder, Elvis, same thing."

Kylie giggles before accepting my dad's handshake. "It's nice to meet you, Ryder."

We spend the rest of the afternoon with my parents. Kylie soon learns she can be herself around them. They're the most laidback parents you could ever meet. After dinner, my mom tells Kylie the story of how they met. Dad was the boy from the wrong side of the tracks; my mom was the preacher's daughter. They met when my dad was doing community service at her family's church. He was there to paint over the graffiti he placed on the side wall weeks earlier.

Most people expected him to paint it back to its original white coloring, but my dad upped the ante by doing a mural of Noah's ark.

The church officials were so impressed with his painting, it still adorns its wall today.

My mom got pregnant with me just shy of her eighteenth birthday. She was shunned by her parents and the church she spent her whole life growing up in. My dad knew there was nobody else for him but my mom, so he stopped his rebellious ways and got a job.

To start with, he was hired as a cleaner at the local tattoo parlor. Then, as the months went on, his artistic talent was unearthed. Now his client base is filled by elite members of the public privileged enough to be tattooed by him. He's so popular, even I have to make an appointment.

With my parents going to bed hours ago, and my make-out session with Kylie on the sofa getting hot and heavy, I carry Kylie to my childhood bedroom. Her giggles echo around my room when she notices my Hello Kitty bedspread and lamp on my bedside table.

"Thanks, Mom," I shout down the hallway, laughing.

My mom's laughter overtakes mine. "You're welcome, honey."

I don't know how many times I've come home to find a girly bedspread on my bed. My mom uses the excuse that she hasn't done any laundry, but I'm reasonably sure she does it for a laugh. She is who I get my sense of humor from.

I lower Kylie onto my pretty pink bedspread so I can ravage her beautiful body. When I lay on top of her, preparing to start my feast at her sinful mouth, she grimaces. I'm holding my weight off her with my arms, so I'm a little perplexed as to why she's hissing like she's in pain.

When I glance into her pretty eyes to seek answers to my unasked questions, they dart away. I rock my hips forward, rubbing my erection along the seam of her jeans. Her eyes snap to mine in an instant, the delicious friction between us too hot to ignore. Now that I have her eye contact back, I cock my brow, demanding she tell me why she grimaced.

"Don't get angry."

My teeth grit. I don't know what it is about that statement, but any time someone says it, I get angry.

I roll off her and lean on my hip, my jaw quivering as I battle to hold in my anger. The furious cloud in my eyes is replaced with lust when Kylie stands from the bed to shimmy out of her blue jeans. Her eyes remain fixed on me as she yanks her shirt over her head.

As her mousy brown locks spring down her shoulders, I drink in every inch of her tight little body. My cock stiffens more with every inch I travel, only softening when I spot blue gauze poking out of the waistband of her lace panties. I recognize the bandage covering her skin—very much so.

My curious eyes rocket up to Kylie, peeved as fuck she'd ruin her perfect skin with the buzz of a tattoo gun. "You have flawless skin, so why would you mark it?"

Smiling a grin that will forever highlight my dreams, she lowers the waistband of her panties. When she carefully pulls back the gauze, my heart sinks into my gut. Most guys would be stoked their girl got their name inked on them, but she broke the ultimate tattoo rule. You never get another person's name tattooed on you—ever! I learned that the hard way. It took my dad hours to cover Nikki's name on my wrist, and even now, I swear I can still see its outline.

Ready to cause physical harm to my dad, I dive off my bed. Kylie jumps in front of me before I reach my bedroom door. "I begged him to do it."

"I don't fucking care! He knows what I think about this." My angry voice booms around my room. I'm not mad at Kylie. I'm fucking ropeable at my dad. I only left him alone with Kylie for an hour this afternoon to get some groceries with my mom, and this is what he fucking does.

I side-step Kylie and am about to open my bedroom door when her voice, which is barely a whisper, says, "I'll get Tommy to cover it up."

My hasty exit halts. Tommy is my dad's rival in the tattooing industry. He's also the most sleaziest guy you could ever meet. The number of women he's slept with puts Nick's "Player" title to shame. There's no way in hell I'd let a guy like Tommy anywhere near Kylie's skin, let alone skin hidden inside her panties, and she knows that— that's why she's using it against me.

I turn around to face her, my heart freezing when I see tears in her eyes. This is the first time I've seen her upset, and I don't fuckin' like it.

"When it heals, you're getting it covered." I close my door before joining her beside my bed. "By my dad."

She smiles and nods as the tears in her eyes dry from the lust burning through her body. . .

Obviously, she never got it covered, and for reasons unbeknownst to me, I get an immense amount of satisfaction knowing it's still there.

CHAPTER FOURTEEN

KYLIE

When I turn into the entrance of the hallway my room is in, I'm scared to death by a high-pitched scream. Once I gather my heart from the floor, my eyes lift from the hotel room key I've just collected. I'm thrust toward coronary failure for the second time in under a second when I spot Melanie at the end of the hall. The lowlights bouncing off her platinum blonde locks halo her in an angelic glow someone as devious as her could never pull off, but I'm certain it's her.

After returning her squeal with one loud enough to shatter glass, I bridge the gap between us. When I reach her, I throw myself into her arms so fiercely, we topple to the ground while cackling like two crazies in a psych ward.

"It's only been a week." She's making fun of me, but she returns my embrace as if it's been years as well. "Have you been a naughty girl?"

I'm about to tell her nothing I could ever do would seem wicked by her standards, but a pair of boots moving into my vision stuffs my words into the back of my throat. When I raise my eyes, I spot the smiling face of Slater. He peers down at us, amused we're wrestling in the middle of the hallway without the mud he's used to seeing.

"I should have guessed it was you." When he offers to assist me from the floor. I tuck away the flare of jealousy my inner monologue caused before accepting his offer. "When I heard high-pitched screaming, I knew it was either you or Jenni."

His witty comment wipes the last bit of hesitation off my weary face. Today, he's acting more like the Slater I remember instead of the grumpy, brooding one I've been dealing with the past week.

"Hello again." Melanie scampers up off the floor before locking her big blue eyes on Slater. Her hands are clasped behind her back, and she's teetering from left to right. If she's trying to portray innocence, she needs to sign up for acting classes. Innocence is a look she'll never pull off.

"Hi." Slater's brisk response prompts me to offer them an official introduction. They've met previously, but more in passing than a face to face greeting.

"Slater this is my best friend, Melanie. Melanie, this is Slater, my..."

Their handshake is as awkward as the abrupt ending of my introduction, but thankfully, Slater sidesteps it like he's a baller sidestepping the defensive line. After removing my hotel keycard from my hand, he slides it into the door we're standing next to. When he walks into the room, Melanie and I follow closely behind him. Melanie's eyes bug, and my mouth gapes. This is not a hotel room. It's a house!

A large black marble kitchen is hidden behind a wall on our left. The sunken living area in the middle looks like it seats at least a dozen people, and there's a full-size dining room. The baby grand piano and three black leather sofas should make the space look squashed, but it doesn't. There's still plenty of thick, dark carpet to give you the illusion of both space and comfort.

"The living room alone is bigger than our old apartment."

Nodding at Melanie's one hundred percent accurate analysis, I pace to Slater to remove my room card from his hand. "I think our keys got mixed up."

Studying the key doesn't lessen my confusion. It has no distinct markings to indicate which room it belongs to, but I'm still confident this room isn't mine. Destiny Records, the label in-charge of Rise Up, isn't stingy, but their generosity toward their stars doesn't extend to those at the bottom of the totem pole. My room in Seattle had a standard-size bed, attached bathroom, and a mini bar, unlike this room that has a full kitchen, a jacuzzi hot tub, and a TV that's so large, it could be confused as being a projector screen.

I stop taking in the elaborate suite when Slater scrubs his hand over the stubble on his chin. It's been two years since I've seen him do it, but he only does it when he's being sneaky.

When my arched brow doesn't get him talking, I use words. "Is this your room?"

He smiles a blistering grin before shaking his head. After pacing to the far right-hand side of the room, he opens a previously closed door. "That's my room." He hooks his thumb at the door he just opened.

"You got us interconnecting rooms?!" My walloping heart makes my question come out with a quiver. It can't be helped. Half of me is excited, whereas the other half is petrified. I'll never avoid the revolving door of groupies coming in and out of his room now.

"I don't think this is a good idea." My comment wipes the smile right off his face. "I... umm..." I try to think of a way I can explain to him that this is a bad idea without informing him I don't want to witness his man-whore lifestyle firsthand.

Before I break through even a minute portion of the cloud fogging my head, Slater moves to stand in front of me. He cups my cheek, weakening my defenses with a pair of brown eyes that are oh so familiar, yet oh so painful to peer at without seeing how much I hurt him.

Mistaking the moisture looming in my eyes as disgust about his rock star lifestyle, he says, "I don't bring groupies back to my room."

I want to say his words give me comfort, but that would be a lie.

Just because he doesn't bring groupies into his room doesn't mean he won't find other places to accommodate them—such as stage curtains at an arena.

Angry I am unable to maintain his eye contact, air whizzes out of Slater's nose before he strides to the interconnecting door separating our rooms. Upon entering, his gaze returns to mine. "This will also ensure you don't do anything stupid like you did last night."

When he slams the door shut, my pulse skyrockets. Now everything makes sense. He didn't get us side by side rooms because he wants me closer to him. He did it so he can keep an eye on me and to ensure the warning he gave Sonny and the rest of the road crew stays enforced.

Growling, I march to the door, my angry strides only stopping when Melanie steps in my way. "Let's think about this first." When I try to sidestep her, she steps back into my path. "You wanted proof he still has feelings for you. Here's your proof. Look around, Kylie. You can't get any more obvious than this." She waves her hand around our opulent surroundings.

"He doesn't have feelings for me. He just doesn't want *anyone else* having them."

Melanie rolls her eyes. "Oh, that's right. Only guys who don't want us pay thousands of dollars for a hotel room per night."

"Thousands?"

Nodding, she enters the sunken living area. I follow after her, equally shocked and a smidge excited. When I join her on one of the three black leather sofas, I take in our surroundings with more diligence. There's no doubt it's a top-of-the-range suite. It has all the bells and whistles you'd expect for a rock star, except it isn't for a rock star. It's for me, the rock star's publicist's personal assistant.

Noticing my grimace, Melanie laughs. "No amount of jealousy has a man forking out this much money. He's into you. He's just a stubborn little fuck... like someone else I know."

"Shut up." I slap her arm since I can't slap the sarcasm off her face, even though I have an inkling she's right. I'm sure it's costing

Slater a fortune for me to stay here, so maybe there's more than jealousy at play. "What are you doing here anyway? Miss me enough to brave rush hour traffic for a visit?"

Melanie's parents live an hour from San Francisco, so a pop in visit isn't implausible, but I have a feeling she's been missing me as much as I've missed her. We were together twenty-four-seven the past two years, so it's been a huge adjustment not having her attached to my hip.

Melanie munches on her bottom lip as her mischievous eyes turn to me. "Slater brought me here." Her voice is more mature than her twenty-three years, so it's more shocking than her confession. "He thought I'd be a good influence on you." Her lips twitch into a mischievous grin. "He picked the wrong friend!"

Her laugh is infectious. I should be mad Slater thinks I need a babysitter, but it's the last emotion I'm feeling. If Slater thinks Melanie will settle me down, he's starkly underestimated Melanie. She's hell on wheels and creates havoc everywhere she goes, and she has no qualms about it either.

Melanie jumps onto the leather sofa like Tom Cruise did during his Oprah interview. With her arms thrown above her head, she squeals, "Let's show these fuckers how to party!"

Jumping off the sofa, she heads to the bar at the side of the living room. The glass shelves are full to the brim with liquor. When she opens a bottle without checking how much it cost, I rush toward her.

"You can't drink anything you want! A mini bar bottle costs a fortune, so imagine how much a whole bottle costs?"

When I attempt to snatch the bottle from her grasp, she yanks it out of my reach. With a roll of her eyes, she sashays to the door that connects my room with Slater's. After three brisk knocks, Slater opens the door. His eyes are still holding their earlier anger, but it's dimmed—somewhat.

"Can we drink this?" Melanie shoves her beverage of choice into his face.

My pulse beeps in my neck when he peers past her shoulder to me standing dumbfounded in the living room. "You can drink anything you want." I nearly smile until he adds on, "As long as you do it in this room."

I snarl at him, baring teeth, but before I can issue one of the many derogatory words filtering through my head, Melanie slams the door in his face.

CHAPTER FIFTEEN

SLATER

When blaring music thuds from next door for the third night in a row, it dawns on me that I picked the wrong friend to watch Kylie. I tracked down Melanie after collecting my bike from Sonny. He made it pretty fucking obvious he has no intention of backing down on his pursuit of Kylie, so drastic action had to be taken.

There's no chance in hell I'll ever allow Kylie to be with a douchebag like him. People think drummers are bad, but we're nothing compared to the scum of the roadies crew. Sonny is lucky he's still employed after the stunt he pulled Sunday night. If our tour wasn't plagued with useless crew members previously, I wouldn't have hesitated to fire him. But, as much as it sucks to admit, he's good at his job. He just needs to learn to back the fuck off when instructed.

Jenni supplied me with Melanie's contact details because she added her and Kylie as friends on Facebook. I didn't miss the curious sparkle in her eyes when she handed me her personal information. When I called Melanie, she thought I was pranking her. It was only after I recited the entire playlist from our current CD did she finally believe it was me.

That girl has a mouth like a sailor. I've heard soft curse words come out of girls' mouths many times before, but they're soft, as in "shit, ass, crap," etc. But the ones that came out of Melanie's mouth when I asked her to come on tour with Rise Up made me blush.

I guess that should have been my first hint I picked the wrong friend to keep Kylie in line.

I shouldn't say "in line." I just want someone to keep an eye on her while I'm performing. I know the games the roadies play every time Rise Up starts a set, and I didn't want to be worried about them plying Kylie with drinks—*or anything else*—while I'm on stage. Just the thought of anyone touching her makes the veins in my neck bulge. The only gratification I get is the fact my name is still marked on her skin. No guy she's slept with since me could have missed it. It makes me glad she didn't get it covered.

When Kylie's confused eyes locked with mine three days ago, I knew she was worried about seeing me with groupies. Her eyes darted away when I said, "I don't bring groupies to my room." I probably should have said, "I will *no longer* bring groupies to my room," and then she may have believed me.

I didn't get us interconnecting rooms just to keep my eye on her, though. I also wanted to have her close to me. Ever since our confrontation on the tour bus, I can't get her out of my fucking head. She's never left my thoughts. Not even when she destroyed me.

When glass being smashed sounds from the room next door, I can no longer rein in my curiosity. I need to know what Kylie and Melanie are up to. When I crank open the interconnecting door, music blasts my eardrums, and smoke filters through my nose. I'm not talking about cigarette smoke, either.

I run my eyes over the room, seeking Kylie. Fuck me, I swear half of San Francisco is in their room. The place is so crammed with people, the sofas are pushed against the outer walls to free up the living room for a mosh pit. Several couples are in various stages of making out, and a DJ is set up in the far back corner.

I walk the entire span of the living area, but I don't spot Kylie anywhere. Just as I'm about to enter one of the three bedrooms, Melanie saunters out. Her hair is ruffled, and her lips are swollen.

"Where's Kylie?"

My eyes dart past Melanie's shoulder, ensuring Kylie isn't in the room. I swear to God, if I find her making out with some random guy, I'll lose my shit.

"She's in the kitchen." Melanie's gag has me wanting to step sideways. "Where she *always* is during our parties." I shouldn't love the disdain in her voice, but I do.

I spot Kylie the instant I enter the kitchen. She's stretching up to reach a bowl in an overhead cupboard, her top riding high enough that the two little dimples in her lower back sneakily peek out. If her jeans were a little lower, I'd also see the waistband of her panties.

When I move to assist her in retrieving the bowl, I'm cut off. Sonny leans over her to seize the bowl she's after. Kylie darts under his arm before strolling to the island counter, which is covered with unopened bags of chips and pretzels. When she notices me standing in the doorway, she breaks out a smile that has me wanting to fall to my knees.

"Hey." She empties two bags of chips into an empty bowl before sauntering past me. My cock twitches when her breasts rub my arm when she slides by. There's enough space between us she could have scooted past without touching me, so I'm confident her innocent brush wasn't an accident.

I take a moment to relish her wildflower scent before helping myself to a bottle of beer in the fridge. I crack it open on the expensive black granite countertop, not the least bit worried by the large chip it creates. The clean-up bill for this suite will already cost me a fortune, so what's another expense?

After winking at Sonny, I go search for Kylie. "Game on, motherfucker."

Kylie had plenty of space to move past me without needing to touch me, but she made sure some part of our bodies connected, but when Sonny got close to her, she fled from him like he has cooties. If that doesn't tell him he's out of the game, nothing will.

Upon entering the living area, I see a handful of people sitting in a circle. When I spot an empty bottle of beer spinning in the middle of the group, I can't help but chuckle. Most of the people playing would easily be over the age of twenty-one.

"And you thought she'd keep me in line." Kylie is standing so close to me, her hot breaths tickle my earlobe. "How silly were you?"

After taking a swig of my beer, I pivot around to face her. I balk when she's nowhere in sight. *Where the fuck did she go?*

I catch the tail end of her just before she darts back into the kitchen. I could wait for her to come back out, but tell me one guy who doesn't enjoy the chase?

This time, when I enter the kitchen, Kylie is alone. "How often do you play spin the bottle?"

She continues replenishing the snack bowls as a grin curls on her lips. "As often as possible." She watches the shit-eating grin on my face drop to a frown before finishing her reply, "When I was in the fifth grade." She winks, her mood super playful. "Do you want to play?"

"Are we still talking about spin the bottle?" I give her a look, one I'm praying she still knows how to read. When she prances my way, I think I have all my ducks in a row... until the strong scent of cranberries fills my nostrils. "How many drinks have you had?"

If her drink of choice tonight has reverted to her all-time favorite, I won't be able to smell vodka on her breath. I held myself back three nights ago when she was drunk, but with how she's looking at me now, I doubt I can do it for the second time.

"A few."

Ignoring the growl rolling up my chest, she curls her hand around mine before attempting to drag me into the living room. I say attempt because I slow her down before we're even halfway there. "A few as in a handful? Or a few as in you've lost count?"

When she doesn't answer me, I tug her back, stopping her from joining the twenty-plus people playing spin the bottle. "Are you drunk?"

She waggles her brows. "Just a little bit tipsy."

She hits me with another flirty wink before plopping her backside on the ground in the middle of the circle and folding her legs underneath herself. When Kylie says she's "just a little bit tipsy," it means she's full-on drunk.

When she nudges her head to the only empty space left on the dark gray carpet, I contemplate what to do. The right thing would be to walk away, or better yet, carry her out of here over my shoulder like I did three nights ago, but when her tongue darts out to lick her top lip, like she's prepping to kiss me, those thoughts turn to dust. I'm not going anywhere. If she wants to play, we're going to play.

While taking a seat across from Kylie, I scan my opponents. The only face I can put a name to is Melanie's. She's sitting three spaces up from me, glaring at Kylie, shocked by her sudden decision to join the festivities.

One of the road crew—I think his name is Scott—takes his turn. I release the breath I'm holding in when his spin narrowly misses Kylie, landing on the girl next to her. After her eyes snap to mine, Kylie wipes her brow. I chuckle against the rim of my beer. *Yep, she's definitely drunk!*

A blonde sitting next to Scott goes next. When the neck of the bottle lands on me, my eyes missile to Kylie. Her brows are furrowed, and she has a concerned look tainting her face. With a shrug, she adjusts the bottle so it points to the guy sitting next to me.

"Hey, that's cheating!"

Kylie acts ignorant to the blonde's roar by plopping back into her seat before lifting her glazed-over eyes to mine. She's hungry. But it's not food she wants to devour. It's me.

"She can't do that. I'm kissing the drummer." The disgruntled player crosses her arms in front of her chest before locking her narrowed eyes with Melanie as if she's the keeper of the kingdom.

"Kiss him or get out." Melanie hooks her thumb to the guy sitting next to me before thrusting her hand to the entryway. "Those are your only choices."

The blonde huffs before doing as instructed without further protest. It's not all bad. The guy seated next to me isn't hideous-looking. He just doesn't have millions of dollars in his bank account. Well, I assume he doesn't. We're in San Francisco. It has more billionaires per capita than anywhere else in the world.

The next three turns pass without incident. Neither Kylie or I get picked by the spinning bottle. Now, it's Kylie's turn. She licks her red-painted lips before spinning the bottle. I watch it twirl with my heart in my throat, praying it lands on me. My palms slick with sweat when it slows to a snail's pace before it narrowly misses me by stopping on the guy sitting next to me—the same guy the blonde kissed earlier.

Kylie's bottom lip drops into a pout before she crawls toward the man the bottle landed on. Without any hesitation, I fist the scruff of his shirt, yank him across my body, then take his place. Melanie giggles loudly, but I can barely hear it over the mad thump of my heart. It's beating so fast because Kylie didn't flinch at my aggression. She smiled.

Once she's close enough I can reach her, I push my index finger against her lips, stopping her from moving any closer. Rejection sparks in her eyes, but it doesn't linger for long. After licking my thumb, I drag it across her lips, removing the thick coating of lipstick ruining her perfectly plump mouth. I want her lips bare like they were the first time we kissed.

Eager to get the show started, Kylie scrubs her lips with the back of her hand. Once all traces of her lipstick have been removed, she inches closer to me, her pace teasingly slow.

"Kiss him already!"

Melanie's demand is closely followed by the hollering chants of the players surrounding us. My fingers thread through her silky smooth locks as Kylie sucks in hearty breaths, her shoulders rising and falling. We share the same air for several moments before the urge to taste her grows too great. As her thumb traces the throb in my jaw, I push my head forward. The instant our lips brush, I know I made the right decision in enforcing my one and only groupie rule.

I am forever ruined by her lips.

CHAPTER SIXTEEN

KYLIE

"Holy shit, that party was crazy."

Melanie's baby pink silk chemise flutters against her milky white thighs when she saunters into the main bedroom of our hotel suite. I giggle when her dive onto the bed causes the morning newspapers to fly into the air. Part of my job is to gather any articles published about the band in print and online to present to Emily in bullet point format.

Today, things are pretty quiet on the gossip front. Noah and Emily had dinner at Michael Mina, and Marcus was spotted driving a convertible over the Golden Gate Bridge. Other than that, there are no huge new stories involving the band.

I glance at Melanie curiously when she sniffs the sheets on my bed. "What are you doing?"

She inhales a whiff of my spare pillow before dumping it next to her thigh with a roll of her eyes. "I thought your room would be reeking of hot, raunchy sex." She purrs out the part about "hot, raunchy sex." "I should have known better. Spin the bottle is practically a blowjob for someone as innocent as you."

When I smack her upside the head with my pillow, she flops onto the bed, laughing. "Come on, that kiss was hot!" She throws the pillow back at me, missing my face, instead hitting my chest. "Even my panties got moist watching it."

Bile burns the back of my throat. That's the last image I want in my head right now. When Melanie notices the disgusted expression on my face, she rolls her eyes. "Don't deny it. His kiss made you all wet and horny."

I'm not denying it. My kiss with Slater last night was heart-stopping, knee-wobbling, pussy-clenching good. It was the highest-rated kiss I've ever had. He tasted clean and fresh with a slight hint of the beer he was consuming. I completely forgot we were in a house full of strangers until their rowdy cheers bellowed around us. Their comments were so crude, I either had to pull back or be seen as a harlot for the rest of my life. I chose to pull back. It wasn't easy.

When I inched back, I locked my eyes with Slater's. Not even an eclipse could compete with the lusty glint in his eyes. It was as if the last two years never happened. We were once again the up-and-coming rock god and the country girl too afraid to sing in front of an audience to show off her talents.

I'd give anything to go back and fix all the mistakes I made with him, but I can't. Instead of letting the past haunt me, I jumped to my feet, declaring the snacks table needed to be replenished before making a beeline to the kitchen.

Usually, that's the only task I do when Melanie throws one of her infamous parties. I make sure the snack table is stacked and that we don't run out of alcohol. Last night was the first time I participated in any of the games she organizes. I'm glad I downed a few glasses of liquid courage before Slater arrived. Otherwise, I might have missed experiencing one of his heart-stopping kisses again.

I felt Slater's eyes on me the rest of the night, but he kept his distance. It was only when I informed Melanie at 3 AM that I was going to bed because I had to work the next day did he walk back toward the interconnecting door. When he stopped halfway through, our gazes met and held for several moments. If he had jerked up his chin, requesting for me to join him, I would have, but he didn't. He merely offered me an uneasy grin before he darted into his room, closing the door behind him.

"What's that saying?" Melanie taps her kiss-swollen lips as she stares into space. "You can take the girl out of the country, but you can't take the country out of the girl." Her eyes drift to me. "That saying applies to you. Two years and you still smell country."

It's been two years and three months since I've been back to the ranch. The last time I was there was the first time Slater met my family. . .

Slater places his duffle bag onto the twin wrought iron bed in the guest bedroom of my family home before his confused and slightly amused face turns to me. "You're on top." He motions his head to the single bed.

"Actually... I'll be sleeping in my room."

A deliriously wicked smirk forms on his mouth as his hooded gaze absorbs my body. When he takes a giant step toward me, I take a step back. My silent denial doesn't faze him in the slightest. With his brow cocked and his dick pressed against the zipper in his jeans, he takes another step forward.

I splay my hand across his chest, stopping him. "My parents are old-fashioned. They don't allow anyone to sleep in the same room until they're married."

I cross my legs, praying it will weaken the tingling sensation stealing my smarts. My excitement can't be helped. You can't see the smirk Slater is wearing. He didn't hear a word I spoke. All he knows is that we're in a room with a bed—alone.

When he takes another step closer to me, I crash into the drawers sitting next to the open bedroom door. My breath comes out in ragged pants when he moves forward until only an inch of air is between us. "I haven't had you in a week." His warm, minty breath fans my hungry lips. "Do you think I can wait another night?"

I lean in close to him—so close, our noses touch. "Then maybe we should get married?"

Panic slashes across his features as his pupils dilate. The longer I maintain my calm, cool composure, the more his panic settles in. Once I believe he's suffered enough, I dart under the arm he's bracing against the wall and enter the hallway.

"Or we could just have sex in the barn later?" I award him a flirty wink before dashing down the stairs, not missing his frustrated groan halfway down.

My parents couldn't be more different than Slater's if they tried. My dad was raised on this very ranch. My mom lived next door. They've been together nearly as long as Slater's parents, except I wasn't conceived until after they got married at the local church. Five years after I was born, I was followed by my little brother, Teddy. His real name is Theodore, but we all call him Teddy.

After Slater joins me downstairs, I introduce him to my mom and dad. They stand frozen in the entryway of the kitchen. My mom's mouth gapes as her eyes roam over Slater's body, whereas my dad's eyes zoom straight in on the tattoos snaking around his thick arms and stacked shoulders. Even Slater offering his hand to shake doesn't register with my dad. If Teddy didn't walk into the kitchen to declare Slater's tattoos are "totally sick," I don't think my parents' hypnotic state would ever end.

I sign in relief when Teddy accepts the hand my dad left hanging. When his eyes turn to mine, I offer him my thanks with a smile. Teddy is only sixteen. He's usually too wrapped up in teenage issues to bother with anyone else, but even he can't miss the awkwardness in the room.

"You have to come and meet Misty." I grab ahold of Slater's hand before dragging him out the front door, eager to be anywhere but in the kitchen that's so stuffy I feel like I'm about to die of heatstroke.

"Dinner is in an hour, Kylie," Dad informs me sternly when we reach the front porch. "Don't be late."

Once we are safe from prying eyes, I raise mine to Slater. "I'm sorry about my parents." I had no clue my parents were such judgmental people until now.

"It's fine." Slater waves away my concern with his hand. "But I take it they don't know about your tattoo?"

I slap my hand over his mouth before my eyes dart to the house, praying we're far enough away my parents didn't hear what Slater said. When the coast is clear, I drop my hand from his face, wiping it down my jeans to clear away the spit he covered it with while licking my hand.

"I'll take that as a no?"

He chuckles when I grumble, "Shut up."

The closer we get to the barn, the larger Slater's smile becomes. Still sour about his tease, I mumble, "This isn't the barn I mentioned earlier."

I giggle at his pout as I walk him up to one of my greatest loves. "Slater, meet Misty; Misty, this is Slater."

Misty runs her beautiful nose down the side of my face, sucking in the scent of Slater's aftershave on my skin. She's my beautiful light gray mare I've been the proud owner of since I was ten. She's the only thing I miss about not living on the ranch. I still ride her every opportunity, but with my schedule so jam-packed, it's lucky to be once or twice a month.

"Hey, Misty. It's nice to meet you." When Slater runs his hand down Misty's nose, she bucks up and rears.

"She has some jealousy issues." I smile when a brilliant idea pops into my head. "Do you want to go for a ride?"

If we leave now, we could ride out to the old barn and back before dinner. I just need to convince Greg to help me saddle up Misty and another horse. Greg is the lead hand on the ranch. He's been working with my dad since the day I was born. He's like an uncle to me. He's also Dylan's dad.

When Slater fails to respond to my question, I turn to face him. He's shaking his head, his face more panicked now than it was when I jokingly suggested we get married. "I'm not getting on a horse."

"Why not?"

Before he can answer me, Greg enters the barn from the other end.

I race for him, too excited to take Slater's denial as a firm no. "Can you please saddle up Charlie for me?"

Charlie is a few years older than Misty, and he's timid, so he's perfect for a first-time rider. While Greg moves to Charlie, I make my way to the storeroom to grab chaps and riding helmets for Slater and me.

When I amble out of the storeroom, the panic on Slater's face switches to mischief. "I've seen those before." His eyes drop to the chaps. "Just not in any movies you've watched."

Air hisses between his teeth when I throw a large pair of chaps and a helmet into his stomach before clipping a lead to Misty's bridle. I lay a rug on her back then fix her saddle into place. When I've tightened the straps under her belly, she rears up and kicks.

"Gentle, girl. It's okay." When Slater steps back with his hands held in the air, I shoot him a wry look. "She gets cranky when she hasn't been ridden in a while."

A huge grin spreads across Slater's face. "Sounds like someone I know."

Just as I finish saddling Misty, Greg enters the barn with Charlie. "Slater, this is Charlie." I give Charlie a firm rub on his nose. He likes things a little rougher than Misty. Charlie is all black in color except for his snow-white nose. "Charlie, this is Slater. You need to be nice to him because it's his first time on a horse."

Charlie neighs like he understands me. When I pivot to face Slater, he is once again shaking his head. I walk toward him, nodding.

"I'm not getting on a fucking horse."

Greg coughs, mortified about his explicit language. Greg has three sons, but I'm reasonably sure none of them swear in front of him. If they did, they'd get a whooping.

"It's just like riding your bike—"

"No, it's fucking not," Slater replies as his eyes flick between Charlie and me. "My bike isn't that high off the ground."

I can't help but giggle. Slater, the big bad biker, is scared of an innocent little horse. When he hears my quiet rumblings, his unamused eyes snap down to mine. He looks a cross between wanting to kiss me for my sass and spank me for laughing at him. I'll be happy with either.

When he leaves me hanging, I fist his shirt with my left hand before pulling his mouth to mine with my right. His lips are stern to start with, but as our kiss intensifies, they become smooth and silky.

After pulling back from our embrace, I whisper, "We're going to the barn I told you about earlier."

He remains quiet, silently contemplating my request. His eyes dance between mine while occasionally lowering to my lips. When my tongue darts out to moisten my top lip, a sly smirk morphs onto his face. He snatches up the chaps and helmet I tossed at him earlier to hand them back to me.

"I don't wear protection." His tone has me wondering if he's talking about the riding equipment.

With a wink that makes me wish we were alone, he heads for Greg and Charlie awkwardly lingering at the side. Greg lowers down to assist him in throwing his leg over Charlie. Remarkably, he mounts him on the first try. After using the stirrups to straddle Misty, I turn her to face Slater and Charlie. Seeing Slater on a horse is like witnessing two worlds colliding. Country and Rock N Roll all rolled into one. It's a mighty spectacular sight. . .

A pillow slapping my right cheek breaks me from my memories. "Stop fantasizing about him." Melanie thrusts her hand at the door she sashayed through only minutes ago. "He's right next door if you want to go jump his bones."

She scampers off my bed and walks back toward the door she pointed at. Just before she exits, she turns to face me. "Do you still love him?"

I nod without pause for thought. "I've never stopped."

"Then go and get him," she pleads, as if it's the simplest thing in the world to do.

If only it were that easy.

CHAPTER SEVENTEEN

SLATER

Nick slips into the empty seat next to me. "What did you do this time?" He jerks his head to Kylie, who just finished setting up the conference room for our press junket before our concert.

Grinning, I shake my head. I don't kiss and tell—anymore. Today, Kylie is back to wearing a light purple cotton dress and little black cowboy boots. She's still donning makeup, but it isn't as heavy as it's been the past week, and her hair is pulled back into a ponytail. She looks full-on country, the hottest I've ever seen her.

Not even a freezing cold shower could touch the piercing erection I had after our kiss last night. It was warm, sweet, and one hundred percent Kylie. Her kisses demand nothing but perfection, and that's exactly what you're given in return. When she pulled back from our embrace, her eyes floated between mine, reflecting a mixture of confusion, lust, and sadness. I hated the fact our kiss made her sad, where all I was feeling was euphoria.

After declaring she forgot to put out the pretzels, she leaped onto her feet and darted into the kitchen. I sank low into the carpet pile, dumbfounded she was fleeing me—again. At least it was only to the kitchen this time. When Melanie nudged her head to the kitchen, encouraging me to go after Kylie, I shook my head. I was scared shitless that the instant I let Kylie back in, she'd run again.

As I watched her from the corner of the room, my internal battle continued. She could feel my gaze on her as our eyes constantly met, but neither of us took it further than a prolonged glance across the room. When she advised Melanie she was going to bed, I made my way to my room. The reason I was hanging around like a leacher without a life was calling it a night, so I had no reason to stay.

I stopped halfway through the entrance, needing one final glance at Kylie before slipping between the sheets, alone for the seventh time this week. The first pair of eyes I spotted were Kylie's. She'd never been shy about making the first move, so I stared at her, praying she'd walk toward me, to take the first leap, to prove she's planning to stay this time around. She didn't move. She just stood still, staring at me.

Disappointed, I smirked at her before I crawled between the sheets of my empty bed, where for the first time in years, I dreamed about hay-filled barns and a girl who smells like wildflowers. . .

The instant I hoist my leg over a large black horse, I feel the most out of place I've ever felt, and I've handled displacement issues on many occasions. It's even more awkward than meeting Kylie's parents a few minutes ago. When my gaze lifts from the brown leather straps the unnamed man is handing me to Kylie, I'd straddle a horse time and time again. A beautiful smile is plastered on her face, and her eyes are crammed with lust.

After winking at me, she pulls on the reins, turning her horse around so we can exit the barn from the other end. Misty follows Kylie's prompts without so much of a neigh. Charlie doesn't follow suit. He stays standing firm.

"Go." I feel like an idiot talking to a horse, but how else do I make him go? "Move."

The guy who assisted me onto Charlie chuckles before slapping the horse's hindquarters. My eyes bulge out of my head when Charlie charges for Kylie at a pace faster than I expected. Kylie said riding a horse is no different than riding a bike. She's full of shit. My ass is bouncing all over the place, making me confident I'll have bruises in the morning.

"Gently kick him with your boots," Kylie instructs me when Charlie finally catches up to Misty.

I glare at her, mortified. "I'm not kicking a fucking horse."

Kylie laughs before demonstrating what she means. When she gives Misty a little nudge with her boots, she gallops faster. "It doesn't hurt them. I promise."

Grimacing, I give Charlie a mellow tap with my boots. When he maintains his grandma pace, I nudge him a little harder. This time, he moves closer to a trot.

"You've got it." A beautiful smile fattens up Kylie's praise.

Charlie sluggishly follows Misty up the hill, occasionally stopping to eat grass on the way. Kylie says I need to teach him who's the boss, but I'm happy for him to eat the occasional blade of grass if it guarantees me he won't buck me off.

By the time we make it to an old wooden barn, the sun is setting. I somehow manage to dismount Charlie without breaking my leg in the process. Kylie guides him and Misty into a stall inside the barn. The barn is massive in size, and when I stroll inside, I understand why Kylie always smells like hay. The outer walls of the wooden barn are full to the brim with bales of green hay.

When I massage my ass since it went numb over half an hour ago, Kylie's giggles boom around the barn. "Come on."

She gestures for me to follow her. Like a puppy hoping for a treat, I do. I adjust the front of my jeans when she climbs a ladder attached to the side wall. It appears to go into a secret room in the roof. She's wearing jeans, but her ass is too sexy for my cock not to react.

The room at the top of the ladder reminds me of a kid's tree house, except it's three times larger and has a bedding of hay on the ground. Kylie opens a window to rid the room of the musty smell lingering in the air before lighting a handful of scented candles. I wander around the space taking it in. Halfway around, my eyes zoom in on several pencil drawings of a little girl riding a horse taped to the wall.

"Did you draw these?" It's the fight of my life not to laugh during my question. If Kylie did these, she must not have an artistic bone in her entire body. I'm not joking when I say her pictures are hideous.

She slaps my bicep before pulling me away from her Van Gogh-inspired disaster pieces. After snagging a picnic blanket off a hay bale, she shakes it out until it covers a large section of the floor. She toes off her boots before lying on one side of the blanket. My cock stiffens when she taps the blanket, inviting me to join her.

When I nearly break my neck removing my boots and shirt, her laughter makes me even more eager. I haven't had her in a week. I can't wait any longer. I kneel next to her before gliding my body along hers, only stopping when our eyes meet. The friction between us is tortuous, but oh so fucking worth it.

Just as I'm about to seal my mouth over hers, she pushes on my shoulder, sending me toppling off her. Giggling, she turns her eyes to the ceiling. "Stars first."

Following her gaze, I see millions of stars in the blackened sky. It's mesmerizing.

I lie down next to Kylie then clasp her hand in mine. The only audible noise for the next several minutes is our shallow breaths as we look out at the sparkling sky through a giant hole in the roof. It's the most peaceful I've ever felt, and it makes me understand why Kylie loves the ranch so much.

After repositioning myself so I'm leaning on my hip, my eyes absorb Kylie's beautiful profile. She smiles before slanting her head my way. "You're supposed to be looking at the sky."

I drag my finger down her blooming cheek. "I found something more beautiful to look at."

Grinning, she rolls onto her hip before giving me a soft, gentle peck. "You were supposed to be a bit of fun, an adventure. I wasn't meant to fall in love," she whispers against my mouth.

I inch back, shocked but fucking ecstatic about her declaration of *love. We've only been together for three months, but we've created a lifetime of memories.*

Our next kiss is more heated than our first. I weave my fingers through her hair all caveman-style, yank her head back, then kiss her with everything I have. It's a hard, brutal kiss that reveals how happy I am that we crossed paths at the most unexpected time. It's almost our hottest kiss ever, only second to the one she gave me on my bike when we roared down the freeway at a speed too unsafe to be making out.

It takes all my strength to pull away from her delicious mouth, but a very good reason backs up my campaign. "Hand it over." When I hold out my hand palm side up, Kylie peers at me, blinking and confused. "The list."

Her lips tug into a vast smile, but her hands remain fisted at her side.

"Don't act like you don't have it. I know you carry it on you."

With a laugh that makes me want to kiss her all over again, she rolls over before delving her hand into her jeans pocket. While biting down on her bottom lip, trying to hold in her smile, she hands me an old, tattered piece of yellow lined paper.

When I sit up, Kylie copies my movements. After carefully prying open the folded-up piece of paper, ensuring I don't rip it, my eyes stray to Kylie. "Do you have a pen?"

She dives up from the blanket to snag a pencil from the table housing her hideous drawings. Once I have the paper open, I brace it against my thigh, then raise my eyes to Kylie. "Cross it off."

In the silence of the night, the crazy beat of her heart can't be missed. She kneels next to me while chewing on the end of the pencil. Her nervous, scared eyes stare into mine for several heart-thrashing seconds before they drop to the paper balancing on my thigh.

With one hand on my thigh and the other clutching a red pencil, she crosses out the very first item on her list.

1. Fall in love.

Kylie has had this list for years. She wrote it after watching a movie called The Bucket List. *She explained she wanted to have a list of things to achieve to ensure she lived a full, adventurous life. We've crossed a few items off her list the past three months, but scratching this one off is by far the most rewarding one for me.*

After folding the paper back together, I hand it to Kylie. "That's not fair," she whispers, placing her list back in her pocket. "You don't have a list."

Hiding my smirk, I pull her down onto the blanket, then glide my body along hers. This time, she doesn't push me off. Her shallow, excited breaths fan my cheeks as she glances up at me with needy, hungry eyes.

"I... l-l-like you too."

She pushes me off her for the second time. . .

My eyes float up to Kylie when she hands me the paperwork for today's press conference. "Do you still have your list?"

Smiling, she taps her pen on a hidden pocket in her dress. Now I'm curious, and somewhat petrified, to discover what items she's crossed off without me.

CHAPTER EIGHTEEN

KYLIE

I freeze halfway out of the bathroom when I notice Melanie sitting at the desk in my room with my bucket list and a black pen. "What are you doing?"

"It was all so boring." She pulls a face like she's in the process of dying. "I just added a little more sparkle to your list."

Her eyes flick up from the tattered paper to me when I murmur, "I was only fourteen at the time."

"That's no excuse." She lifts the well-used paper off the desk so she can see it without the reading glasses she swears she doesn't need. "Number twenty-four, kiss a guy with tongue." She gags, mortified I hadn't achieved that by the time I made my list. "Number thirty-three, cut one class at school. *One!*"

Her overdramatic eye roll forces a ghost of a smile to crack on my lips. Her tone alters from playful to disgusted as she reads another three items off my list. When giggles bellow out of her so rampantly, her body shakes, I snatch my list out of her hand. Panic clutches my gut when I hear paper tearing. A sob rips from my throat when my eyes drop to half of my list still in my hand. The other half is in Melanie's. I've had this list for years. This is its first tear.

Melanie's wide eyes dart between the two fragments of torn paper before she yanks open the drawer under the desk. She groans something about the hotel being useless for not having the right accessories in every desk before she bolts into her room.

Within seconds, she returns with a roll of scotch tape. Carefully, she removes the paper from my tight grip before placing the two torn pieces side by side. With her nose screwed up and sweat beading on her brow, she matches up the rips so they appear almost like one piece again.

"It'll get worse if you get it wet."

I use the towel curled around my body to wipe away my tears before they drip onto my list. Once I have my tears at bay, I hold together the two pieces as requested by Melanie. When she's confident they're methodically joined, she places a large piece of scotch tape down the middle.

"There you go, just like new."

I gently lift the paper to inspect her handy-work. Other than the shininess of the scotch tape, it looks like my well-worn and much-loved bucket list. It's only a list, but this piece of paper means the world to me.

Once my heart rate settles down, I flip over the paper to read the items Melanie added.

153. *Fuck a drummer backstage at a concert.*

154. *Fuck a drummer in the shower.*

155. *Fuck a drummer in a stretch limo.*

156. *Thank your best friend when you cross the above three items off your list!*

"You're welcome," she says, hearing the giggle erupting from my mouth without warning. "And just for future reference, I said 'drummer.' You can pick any drummer you like."

Before I met Slater, I had only crossed a few minor items off my list. I really shouldn't say minor. Losing your virginity isn't minor, but it wasn't that eventful either. But now my list is nearly three-quarters done. Even the scary things like skydiving and bungee jumping are crossed off.

I always wondered what I would do with myself once it was finished. After running my eyes over the items I've yet to cross off, I realize some things I'll never achieve.

I barely get a moment to wallow in self-pity before Melanie asks, "When did you cross number fifty-three off the list?" She waggles her brows, informing me what item is at number fifty-three without me needing to check my list.

53. Make love under the stars with the man I love...

I didn't mean to tell Slater I've fallen in love with him. I was just thinking it in my head, and it flooded out of my mouth without warning. Only once he smiled was I glad I have no control over my mouth. Although him telling me he likes *me too wasn't quite what I was hoping for, it's better than the awkward silence I was anticipating.*

Once Slater finishes chuckling, he stares deeply into my eyes. "There's another item we can cross off your list."

When he peers at the star-filled night, I know the exact number he's referring to. Because he lacked confidence on Charlie, it took us double the amount of time to reach the barn than usual. We've already missed the dinner deadline my dad set earlier, so what's another hour or two going to hurt?

Slater's chuckles die altogether when I straddle his lap. He gets heavy beneath me when I unbutton my plaid shirt. With his teeth raking his lower lip, he leans back before placing his hands behind his head to enjoy the show. Once I have the final button undone, I teasingly fan open my shirt to show him the new purple lace bra I purchased earlier this week. Purple is my new favorite color since Slater bought me a purple helmet for when he takes me on his bike. My bra is nearly an exact match to the color of my helmet.

When my shirt slips off one shoulder, exposing a generous portion of my beige skin, Slater bucks his hips. As his cock hardens more, his eyes flick to my other shoulder, soundlessly requesting for me to remove my whole shirt. While licking my lips, I run my hands up my stomach, over my breasts, and through my hair. My heart beats double time when his cock twitches underneath me. So much energy is bristling in the air, it feels like we're in the middle of summer. It's hot and sticky, which makes what I'm about to do ten times harder.

Not giving him the chance to protest, I roll off him and do up the buttons of my shirt. Slater hates being teased, so this will teach him a lesson on how it isn't nice to tease others either.

Before I even have the first button done up, his body pins mine to the blanket. His stubble scratches my chin when he presses his lips to my ear, and his erection creates panty-wetting friction with the seam in my jeans. My ruse is undone in under ten seconds, and I'm not the least bit worried. I've got a hot, tattooed man lying on top of me while staring down at me in admiration. What the hell do I have to be worried about?

"I know what you're doing." He bites down on the fleshy skin on my ear before sucking it into his mouth. "Your list says 'make love under the stars with the man I love.' Not make love with a man who loves me too."

My earlier excitement flies out the window. I was only teasing him, but his statement has me reconsidering crossing any item off my list with him.

After marking me with a love bite on my neck, he leans on his elbow so he can peer down at my face. With my ego still burning from his unexpected slap, I glance past his shoulder, preferring to stare at the star-filled sky instead of the face responsible for my naughty dreams. I hate that I'm letting a bruised ego dampen our time together, but he's the first man I've ever loved, and I always thought when I declared that, he'd automatically say it back.

How stupid am I?

When Slater notices I'm not looking at him, he rolls his hips. With the friction too great to ignore, my eyes snap back to his. Once he has my undivided attention, and he sees the disappointment in my eyes, he breathes out harshly before moving to a kneeling position. Even feeling rejected, my pussy protests from the loss of his contact.

With a yank on my arm, he pulls me up until I am kneeling in front of him, mirroring his position. "Feel this." He flattens my palm over his chest. His heart is racing so fast, it feels seconds from breaking out of his chest cavity. "Now feel this." He guides my right hand down his rock-hard six-pack before placing it on top of his equally stacked cock. "You don't need words to know what you do to me, Kylie. The proof is right in front of you. You can feel it and touch it. You don't need to hear it."

His eyes show his love and vulnerability, and it's the first time I've seen him so raw. I hate that I've made him feel this way, but I now have a better understanding of what he means. His actions prove I'm special to him, so why do I need words?

He growls into my mouth when I seal my lips over his. He inches closer so his erection presses into my hand. Desire heats my skin when I rub his cock through his jeans. I match the strokes his tongue is doing along the roof of my mouth. It's a teasing pace full of promise and excitement.

After kissing long enough I feel dizzy, I pull back. With my gaze held by his, I undo the button of his jeans before sliding down the zipper. The hiss of metal is barely heard over the frantic beat of my heart. I whimper like I did the first time I saw his cock freed from its tight constraints. It's covered with bulging veins, and the tip is glistening.

I gather the bead of pre-cum with my thumb to use it as lubricant when I wrap my hand around his twitching shaft. Slater's mouth tugs into a smirk when I slide my hand all the way down to the base before gliding it back up. I follow the same routine for another four pumps before my mouth gets in on the action.

After flattening my stomach onto the blanket, I prop myself on my elbows then circle my lips around his sensitive skin. He hisses out a curse word when I glide my lips down his twitching shaft. The sting of his fingers clutching my hair has me drawing him in deeper with every suck. I suck, lick and graze him with my teeth, shuddering when drop after drop of tangy pre-cum pumps onto my tongue. He tastes so good.

"See, Kylie? Why do you need words? Not only can you see what you do to me. You can taste it too."

He rocks his hips, serving me his cock at a speed that's both wicked and nice. His mouth gets in on the action as well. He doesn't put his lips on my body. He serenades me with his teasingly dirty thoughts. He has a filthy mouth, and it makes me suck him so far down my throat, I'm sure my neck will wear the outline of his cock for days to come. He stretches my throat with his frantic pumps while telling me it's the best head he's ever been given, how he'll never want another pair of lips on him but mine.

When I swivel my tongue around his pulsating knob, his whole body jerks. "Fuck, Kylie."

I swallow him whole, needing the quiver of his words to descend to his thighs. I suck, stroke, and lick before nibbling on the sweet spot I know will get him off. Slater loves having his balls sucked almost as much as he does his dick.

When I draw his balls deep into my mouth, the shake I'm aiming for hits his thighs. His knees pull together as he grinds his cock against my face. It's the most awkward position you can think of, but oh so hot.

Just as I prepare my face for the onslaught of his cum, Slater seizes my wrist, halting my frantic pumps. Any protests are left for dust when he rolls me over so my back is braced on the blanket. The hay under the blanket scratches my skin when he tugs down my jeans before removing my shirt and bra.

Even though my bucket list item is to make love under the stars, I can't tear my eyes away from Slater's dedication to my body to drink in the sight. He's peppering kisses across my chest and down my stomach.

My eyes snap shut when the tip of his nose grazes my throbbing-with-need clit. I fist the blanket, struggling to maintain a sense of normality when he blows hot air on my already overheated pussy. The combination of his warm, minty breath and the lust surging through my veins has my coil tightening so firmly, it snaps the instant his tongue lashes my pulsating clit. I buck against him like an out-of-

control wild horse while riding the most orgasmic, soul-shattering climax I've ever experienced.

After guiding me down from climactic bliss with long slithers of his tongue and gentle sucks, Slater crawls up my body. So my thighs can straddle his without anything in the way, he yanks his boxer shorts down before snagging a condom out of his jeans pocket. My earlier orgasm is forgotten when I watch him roll it down his cock, pushed aside for a more blinding, needy pulse.

He coats the tip of his cock with my juices before gripping my hair in a determined hold. He knows I like it a little rougher in the bedroom. With his fingers stinging my scalp and his eyes locked on mine, he lunches forward, impaling me with one quick thrust of his hips. He seals his mouth over mine, stealing the whimpers ripping from my throat. I'm wet, but it still hurts. His cock is too thick and long not to.

He pumps into me on repeat, taking as much as he's giving. It's a wonderous exchange that proves my list is as important to him as it is to me. He's not fucking me. He's making love, as per the stipulation on my list. His slower, more controlled pace doesn't weaken the intensity bristling between us. It's as intense as ever, like fireworks in a dark sky. It was like this the first time we fooled around as well—a mere week after we met. I didn't want him to think less of me, but I couldn't help acting on the energy teeming between us. That's why I kissed him like I did the night we met. It was either kiss him or forever wonder if the purrs of his engine were solely responsible for the frantic quiver of my pulse.

In case you're wondering, his engine had nothing to do with it. It was all him—the stranger I met outside a rundown old pub.

Over the next forty-five minutes, Slater relays what I mean to him without a word seeping from his lips. He may fuck like a god, but he has no issues showing his emotions while doing it. He screws me until I'm beginning to wonder if he's my penance for the years of suffering I endured when I was a teen. They say every storm ends in a rainbow— perhaps he's mine?

Slater's heart is racing more now than it was previously. Or maybe it just sounds that way because I have my ear squashed against his chest. I'm snuggled in close to his side as his callused hand smooths my frizzed hair that's years overdue for a trim.

His hands stop their smoothing motion when we hear a male voice outside the room. "She'll be here; she always comes here when she's home."

When the ladder creaks in the silence of our panic, Slater and I spring to our feet to gather our clothes dumped haphazardly around the room. Before I have all my items gathered, a door opening causes me to freeze in panic. Slater stands in front of me, sheltering my naked body with his when the person enters the room without knocking.

As Slater takes on a defensive stance, the room falls into silence. Even a pin dropping would be heard. "Yeah, she's in here, Dad. We'll be down in a minute," shouts an angry male voice I immediately recognize.

With heated cheeks, I balance on my tippy toes to peer past Slater's shoulder, wanting my suspicions confirmed. There, staring back at me, are the furious green eyes of Dylan Tucker, the one man who'll happily tell me he loves me, even knowing I'll never say it back.

After his eyes burn into mine for several heart-clutching seconds, his gaze strays to Slater. His face is hot with pure, unbridled anger. When his eyes snap down, it dawns on me that Slater has his arms crossed in front of his chest, not bothering to cover himself from Dylan's infuriating glare.

I plaster my torso to Slater's back before lowering my hands to cover his impressive package. "You're not helping." Slater's taunt is a cross between cheeky and stern.

I attempt to muffle my giggles in Slater's back, but I'm shuddering so hard, Slater shudders right along with me.

Dylan doesn't see the humor in our situation. "Get dressed, then join me in my truck. I'll drive you home."

Just as I'm about to protest that I have to take Misty and Charlie back, Dylan says, "Dad will take care of the horses."

When Dylan climbs down the ladder with a clatter, Slater chuckles. I slap his bicep before shimmying into my jeans. Once they're up my quaking thighs, I scan the room, seeking the bra Slater removed earlier.

"Are you looking for this?" Slater swings my bra around his index finger. When I attempt to snatch it out of his hand, he yanks it out of my reach. "I might need to add this to my collection."

I fold my arms in front of my chest, covering my breasts from his perving eyes. He pouts before handing my bra back to me. "Maybe next time?" he asks with a wink.

"I thought rock stars collected panties?"

He laughs even louder than before. "Not drummers, baby. We're all about the beat."

He taps my breasts with his hands while mimicking drumming noises. "Perfect rhythm. If only Dylan wasn't waiting for us outside, then I could test out more of your sexual rhythms."

Now he's sulking right alongside me.

Once we're presentable, we walk hand in hand to Dylan's truck. I hop in first. While sliding across the red bench seat, I keep my gaze low so I don't catch Dylan's furious eyes. Even if he hadn't busted us butt-naked, he'd still know what we were doing when he arrived. There's no denying the unique mix of wildflowers and motor oil slicking my skin.

When Slater slides in next to me, he places his hand on my thigh. My eyes lift to his when he taps something on my leg. For the first time the past three months, it isn't his index finger. He isn't a holding hands type of guy, but he has no issues curling his hand around my thigh when we ride. When I notice he's tapping my leg with the red pencil I used earlier tonight, I can't stop the smile that forms on my face.

"You have to use this pencil every time we cross an item off your list."

I nod, praying the quick bob of my head doesn't release the moisture flooding my eyes. "I will."

After handing me the pencil, he presses his lips to my temple before pulling me close to his chest. . .

I dart to my suitcase in the corner of my suite, pulling out every article of clothing I own before I remember I placed my pencil in the front pocket of my carry-on baggage. It hasn't been sharpened in years, but I carry it with me everywhere I go with the hope that one day I'll use my trusty red pencil again.

If last night is anything to go by, it may occur sooner than I thought.

CHAPTER NINETEEN

SLATER

"**D**o you want me to go get them?"

I shake my head at Marcus's question. Although we're once again waiting around for our band members to arrive, this time, I don't mind waiting. Why, you ask? Because the beautiful specimen known as Kylie is seated across from me. I haven't been able to get her out of my head since our kiss, and when she isn't in my thoughts, she's in my dreams every night.

My recently rediscovered fascination has me pulling out all my best moves, and tonight, I intend to collect my reward. We've been flirting so relentlessly the past few days, I'm constantly adjusting my crotch. Some of the stage crew are worried I have crabs. I don't. I just can't get Kylie alone to push our flirting to the next level. If I'm not with Marcus, she's with Emily... *or Sonny.*

He still hasn't gotten the fucking hint, but my chest puffed high when Kylie sidestepped him earlier tonight. She hasn't forgiven him for plying her with drinks with the intention of taking her home drunk. Rightfully so. I haven't forgiven him either. It's why he's been handed every shit task I can find. I even made him scrub the urinal in my dressing room earlier this week. It was a fucking glorious afternoon, but it had nothing on feeling Kylie's eyes on me the entire two hours of Rise Up's performance tonight.

Once the lights on the stage dimmed, I could also see her. She was covering her ears from the deafening chants of the crowd requesting an encore, and her fall-to-your-knees smile was plastered over her adorable face. When I walked offstage, I invited her and Melanie to the after party. Melanie squealed when I asked them to meet me in the limo in an hour. Kylie nodded as a shy smile curled her lips. She heard the innuendo in my tone. She knew what was coming next.

When she entered the limo, I once again had the urgent need to adjust myself. Her dark purple strapless dress has the middle section cut out in a crisscross design, exposing inches of the silky smooth skin on her stomach. The color of her dress matches the purple streak in her straightened hair to perfection, and her makeup is a little heavier than I like, but her lips only have the slightest amount of sheen— making them ready to be devoured. Kissed. Wholly consumed.

As Jenni climbs into the limousine, her eyes bounce between Kylie and me. Her lips twitch as a blush creeps across her cheeks. When she fills the vacant seat next to me, she nudges me. "Did you invite them?" she interrogates me quietly, ensuring Kylie and Melanie don't overhear our conversation.

A giddy flare blazes through her eyes when I nod. "I like her."

I roll my eyes. "I know." She's told me that exact thing on many occasions the past week. I'm seriously considering recording her to save her some breath.

"And so do you," she teases me with a giggle.

I bump her with my shoulder before my eyes stray to Nick, silently begging him to save me from his loved-up fiancée. The fucker hangs me out to dry. He just smirks and shakes his head, leaving me defenseless. When I flip him the bird, Jenni giggles before sliding across the bench seat to snuggle into his side.

Emily's eyes also dart between Kylie and me when she climbs into the limo on Noah's heel, but she doesn't smile like Jenni did. Her brows pull together as she fights the moisture filling her eyes. I stare at her curiously, confused as fuck as to why she's reacting like she is. Emily is an old romantic. She watches black and white movies if something in the title gives away its sappiness, so her response isn't just odd, it has me sitting on a knife's edge.

My eyes drift to Jenni. The odd expression on her face reveals she's also noticed Emily's screwball response. "*I don't know,*" Jenni mouths to my questioning stare. She's never lied to me, so I take her confession at face value.

I spend the twenty-minute trip to the club our pre-concert event is being held at with my eyes darting between Emily and Kylie. Any time Kylie catches Emily's stare, she smiles at her. Emily smiles back, but it isn't the large, heart-warming smile she usually gives people.

By the time we make it to the club, my curiosity is so piqued, I plan on staying in the limo to ask Emily what the fuck her problem is. My plans falter when Kylie forgets she's traveling with men who need a dozen security personnel just to catch a flight in a domestic terminal. It's why we use private jets now instead of a regular aircraft. When Kylie is blinded by the paparazzi lights, her hands fly up to shield her eyes. It comes too late. Her impeded vision nearly has her stumbling onto the concrete sidewalk.

Hawke moves for her, but I beat him to her. While shielding my eyes with one arm, I curl the other one around Kylie's tiny waist. She stiffens when she's suddenly grabbed from the side, but she quickly realizes who has her.

"Keep your eyes on my boots," I shout to ensure my voice is projected over the paparazzi screaming a range of questions at me.

After taking a handful of steps, the lights dancing in front of my eyes fade from the paps moving behind us to capture Noah, Marcus, and Nick entering the club. When I walk into the club, I move us to the side so I can make sure Kylie is okay.

"If you're looking at me, I can't see you. There's nothing but white blobs in front of me." My laughter joins hers, but it doesn't linger for long. "Oh my god, where's Melanie?"

My eyes missile to the door, mortified I forgot about her friend. My panic subsides when I see Melanie is being ushered inside by Marcus. She's clinging to his chest, happy to use the swarming paparazzi as an excuse to get close to him. She just needs to dull down her smile to authenticate her ruse.

"She's okay. She's with Marcus."

Smiling, Kylie locks her eyes with mine, indicating she can see again, but just like Melanie, I'll use the situation to my advantage. I keep my arms wrapped around her waist and my eyes fixated on hers. We're standing so close, we share the same air. Another inch and I'll be able to taste her lips again, and I'm not the only one noticing. The longer we stay in our little cocoon, the more wild the vein in Kylie's neck thuds. It beats out a funky tune, its rhythm similar to the pulse inflating my cock.

Noise ceases to exist when Kylie inches her mouth toward mine. When her tongue delves out to moisten her lips in preparation for our kiss, she doubles the wetness on mine—that's how close we are to kissing.

"Oh my god, that was fucking crazy!" Melanie's scream is so loud, Kylie headbutts me when she jumps in fright. I wouldn't have minded the interruption if our collision had her lips landing on mine. Unfortunately, they smack into the side of my mouth instead of on my lips as I hoped.

Melanie smirks as Kylie rubs her head. "Did I interrupt something?" When neither of us answer her, she hits me with a teasing wink before replacing my arms curled around Kylie's waist with her own. "We're not at a concert, in a limo, or in the shower."

I'm left hanging at the side of the dance floor looking like a freak with a raging hard on. What the fuck just happened? Melanie has been practically throwing Kylie at me the past week, but just as things get interesting, she drags her away from me.

"Don't try to understand them. You'll only end up more confused." Marcus curls his arm around my shoulders before guiding me to the VIP section of the club.

Tonight's venue is huge compared to the last one we visited. It has three levels, giving us the choice of either a VIP booth, a VIP room, or an entire floor dedicated to VIP clientele. We decide on the booth when we discover it has the best view of the dance floor one level below.

After ordering a double shot of whiskey, I move to the balcony to peer down at the massive group of cavorting people. It doesn't take long to spot Kylie and Melanie in the middle of the packed space. Kylie's beaming grin is obvious enough, not to mention Melanie's fire engine red dress.

When the waitress stops next to me, I accept the glass of whiskey from her tray. "Thanks."

She saunters back to the bar, acting as if her bright fluorescent yellow shorts and hot pink crop top cover more than they do. At first glance, you'd think the waiters' outfits are painted on because they leave nothing to the imagination. It's only after taking in the male version of the outfit do I realize my error. The shorts are just as skimpy and tight, but the waiters are wearing muscle shirts instead of crop tops.

With how snug their pants are, I'll have to remain standing all night just to make sure I don't have a Fluor-covered crotch shoved in my peripheral vision. I won't want to have sex for a year if I'm subjected to *that* type of torture.

When I gag, Noah's chuckle blasts my eardrums. "They're killing me." He tugs on the collar of his shirt while joining me at the balcony. "Fluorescent yellow was my favorite color. I'll never look at it in the same light now."

I throw back my head and laugh. Noah was so obsessed with the color, he coordinated it into his wedding. Thankfully, it was only wrapped around the girls' bouquet stems so the groomsmen weren't subjected to it. Although it was sappier than I'm used to, I have fond memories of the night Noah and Emily got married. I was released from rehab the week before, so with my veins needing to be clear of *any* mind-altering substances, I made sure Noah's best friend Jacob got rip-roaring drunk instead. I'd never seen him intoxicated, so I made it my mission to unravel the mystery of a drunken Jacob.

I didn't discover much more than I already knew. He's a giant teddy with the biggest fucking heart you'll ever find. His heart matches his size. Doesn't come close to his career choice, though. Out of all the careers in the world, you'd never guess Jacob is a professional fighter. Brutal too. I've watched him fight a few times the past year. He was banned for over two years for almost beating a guy to death with his bare hands. Can't say I blame him. If anyone touched Kylie like Lola's ex did her, they wouldn't be breathing like Callum is.

"Have you heard from Jacob lately?"

Noah smiles a beaming grin as his dark eyes shift to me. "Yeah, I was talking to him earlier." He shuffles foot to foot like he's about to pee his pants. "He's doing good. Has a few tricks up his sleeve."

Jacob is dating Emily's sister Lola. I thought Kylie and I were opposites, but we've got nothing on those two. Lola is small and feisty, and she has a very firm grasp on Jacob's balls. The funnier part is, Jacob loves being under her thumb.

"Jacob and Lola will be at Maddie's birthday next month," Noah shares while accepting a bottle of beer from the waitress.

When her hankering gaze roams over Noah's face, he doesn't pay her any attention. If I've learned anything the past three years, it's that Noah's attention never diverts from Emily, whether she's in the room or not.

He peers at me over the rim of his beer. "You can invite Kylie, if you want."

"Yeah, maybe." I down my double shot of whiskey in one hit before signaling for the waitress to bring me another. "Do you know what the deal is between Emily and Kylie? Things seem tense between them."

Noah rests his beer bottle against his lips before his eyes drop to the dance floor. After taking a swig of his beer, he smiles. "They seem okay to me." He motions his head to Emily and Kylie dancing side by side, both with large smiles etched on their faces. "The better question would be, what's going on between you and Kylie?"

"Good question."

I can't get her out of my head. Not just the past few days, but the past two years as well. I gave Kylie my heart fully, and when she left, she took it with her.

Noah chuckles at the grave expression on my face before squeezing my shoulder.

"I'm fucked, aren't I?" I question while accepting my whiskey from the waitress, noticing the napkin attached to the glass has her name and cellphone number scribbled across it.

"I get off in ten minutes," she purrs into my ear before prancing back to the bar.

Noah reads the message on the napkin before returning his eyes to mine. "That *all* depends on you." During the "all" part of his comment, he nudges his head to the napkin I'm clutching for dear life.

CHAPTER TWENTY

KYLIE

With each step I take, my heart thrashes more. *One step at a time,* I chant to myself. Breathe and walk; breathe and walk. It really shouldn't be that hard, but I'm petrified. The last time I entered the VIP section of a Rise Up after party, I found myself face to face with the lifestyle Slater now lives. Because I was busting to use the bathroom, I become separated from the pack, which means I'm now entering hell's gates alone.

I hear Slater's deep rumbling laugh before I spot him. He's sitting on a high-backed barstool at the end of the bar, talking to a beautiful brunette whose long tan legs aren't hidden by her short black sequined dress.

My heart drops into my stomach as disappointment smacks into me. Ever since our drunken kiss, Slater ramped up his effort to woo me back into his bedroom. I've tried to keep our relationship platonic. Not because I don't want to be with him – believe me, I want him more than anything in the world – but because nothing changed from two years ago. The reason I left him pops into the forefront of my mind every time he looks at me. But every smile, wink and playful comment weakens my defenses. Then, as each day passes, my excuses for not being with him lessen.

When he invited me to the after party tonight, I decided I can no longer deny what my heart wants. It wants him. Except now, it looks like I'm too late. At least I can take comfort in the fact that this time around, he's clothed, and she isn't on her knees.

After a final glance at Slater, I scan the room in an attempt to locate Melanie. Emily and Noah are sitting in a black booth, talking in hushed whispers. Jenni and Nick are making out like teens at the prom, and behind them is Melanie. She's participating in a deep and meaningful with Marcus.

When I make my way toward them, Melanie inconspicuously shakes her head, warning me to stay away. I narrow my eyes and huff. She can't leave me stranded like the odd man out when everyone else is paired up. I'll look like a loser.

She rolls her eyes before waving her hand to Slater. I shake my head, mortified. I am *not* interrupting him while he's talking to a lady who looks like she belongs in the centerfold of *Sports Illustrated's Swimsuit Edition.*

I silently beg Melanie from across the room. I drop my bottom lip before thinking of the saddest thing I can imagine to force tears into my eyes. She smirks before shaking her head, not buying the bullshit I'm selling. When I stomp my feet, doing my best impersonation of her famous tantrums, her smirk shifts to a grin, but she skips the headshake.

I must be getting through to her.

It's time to bring out the big guns. I drop my bottom lip again, but this time, I recall how long it's been since I've seen Misty. That brings more than a tear to my eye. It sends one rolling down my cheek. When Melanie spots my tear, her face constricts before she raises her manicured finger in the air, requesting a minute. I nod before doing a victory jig. Today is the first time I've won a standoff against her, and the feeling is euphoric.

"It was the stomping that won her over."

My immature dance moves stop at the same time as my heart. Biting on my lip, I spin around. Slater grins before freeing my lip from my menacing teeth. As he scrubs his thumb over the grooves my teeth made, my eyes rocket to the bar. His brunette friend is seated there, watching us with amusement slashed across her features. When she notices my gawk, she waves and smiles. I can't help but groan. No one should be that beautiful.

Slater chuckles, making me realize I groaned loud enough for him to hear. My unusual boldness probably has something to do with the shots Melanie handed me left, right and center earlier tonight. I was nervous, so I was hopeful a little buzz would settle the butterflies in my stomach. It was great at the start, but now that it's fading, my confidence is draining right along with it.

I'm hit with an entirely different set of nerves when Slater curls his hand around mine. His touch is warm and comforting, but it makes me as giddy as hell. I only stumble slightly when he walks us toward the beautiful brunette. Once we get close enough I don't have to squint, I realize I've seen her before. She's the bassist of Big Halo, but her name has slipped my mind.

Her eyes roam over my face before wandering down my body. My steps falter when they return to mine and I see the undeniable spark of lust brightening in them. *Huh?*

"Miranda, this is Kylie. Kylie, this is Miranda." Slater's brow cocks when he notices the expression on Miranda's face. "This one is off limits."

Miranda's brow shoots up high when Slater nudges his head to me during his last sentence. I'm just as shocked as her. "No dibs, Slater. You know the rules." Miranda's voice is as seductive as she looks, but it has no callousness behind it.

"Fuck the rules." When Slater tugs me into his side, Miranda smiles. Mercifully, I'm in too much of a lust haze from the possessiveness in Slater's tone to care that her smile doubles her attractiveness.

"Then we better celebrate while we can." When Miranda rings a gold bell on the side of the bar, three bar staff cover the wooden bar with a line of shot glasses. In sync, they lift crystal bottles high into the air to fill the glasses with clear, aroma-free liquid.

After gathering two of the sticky shot glasses, Miranda hands one each to Slater and me. I watch her in confusion when she raises my free hand to her mouth. When her tongue licks the skin between my thumb and index finger, my eyes bulge before flicking to Slater. His expression is unreadable, but he's watching Miranda with as much interest as me. When she shakes a chunk of salt onto my hand, the worried groove between his brows smooths.

"To the girls worth breaking the rules for." After clinking her shot glass against Slater's, Miranda's tongue laps up the salt from my hand before she downs her shot of tequila in one swift hit. As her tongue wiggles around the glass to make sure she gets every drop, she winks at Slater. "Your turn."

As she sucks on a slice of lemon, Slater's tongue laps up the salt Miranda missed from my hand before throwing back his serving of tequila. My pussy tingles as much as his mouth probably is when he chews on a large wedge of lemon.

After returning Miranda's cheeky wink, he shifts on his feet to face me. "Your turn." His voice is thick and rugged, making my knees join. I swallow the lump his intense gaze lodged in my throat before replacing the salt they licked off. Then, in one quick motion, I lick and sip. My face scrunches up when the disgusting liquid slides down my throat. I've always hated the taste of tequila.

When I grab for a chunk of lemon, praying it will soothe the ghastly taste, the bowl is yanked out of my reach, and I'm bombarded by a pair of warm lips. Their skillful tongue, laced with lemon, soothes the tequila burn. I'm also reasonably sure it's the cause of the buzzing sensation dancing through my body. When my hair is fisted, allowing my kisser to deepen our kiss, a moan rolls up my throat. This man knows how to kiss, and yes, I'm one hundred percent confident the person kissing me is a man, because I'd never forget the taste of his lips.

"All right, all right, you win." Miranda's yank on my shoulders pulls me away from Slater's deliciously fruity mouth. "But you cheated." She pokes her nail into Slater's chest as her brow arches. "She's supposed to pick her savior, not you choose for her."

Slater licks his lips as his grin ramps up. "Your chances of kissing her are *almost* as good as Sonny's. Neither of you have a fucking chance."

Miranda's laugh gains her the attention of several men in the room. "One night with me will be all she needs to jump that fence."

My eyes snap to hers. When she winks, the penny finally drops. *She likes girls.*

Slater's brisk shake of his head draws my focus back to him. "No fucking chance. It'll never happen—"

"We could share." Miranda shrugs like sharing is something they often do.

"No. Fucking. Chance."

Slater sucks in big, heaving breaths between each word, but it has nothing on the workload of my lungs when he sits on the barstool then tugs me until I'm sitting half on his lap and half-standing. Once he has me where he wants me, he spreads an open hand possessively on my right hip, splaying his fingers just above the area where his name is inked on my skin.

Miranda's big lips drop into a pout. "I'm going to miss my wingman."

When Slater chuckles, she gives me one last wink before joining a group of guys and girls at the other end of the bar. I spin around to face Slater so I can absorb his knee-weakening face. His eyes are beaming with lust, but they're also glossed over. "Are you drunk?"

He smiles so wide, the corners of his eyes get a small gathering of lines. "I'm just a little bit tipsy."

I slap his chest, pretending to hate the mirth in his tone. In reality, I love it. "Slater tipsy or Kylie tipsy?"

He tugs me in even closer so we share the same air. "Does it matter?"

No, no it doesn't. That's what I want to say. Instead, I return his intense lust-filled gaze while ignoring the glares being directed at me when women from all walks of life notice my crotch balancing against Slater's. They know I'm possessively staking my claim, and they're not happy about it.

CHAPTER TWENTY-ONE

SLATER

I'm not even close to being tipsy, much less drunk, but I'll never tell Kylie that. I love that she has her claws out, ready to pounce on anyone if they get too close. She's never been shy at making the first move, and I'm ecstatic she's putting steps in place to stake her claim. I didn't think she would after witnessing her grim expression when she walked into the VIP section of the club.

Her face paled when she saw me sitting next to Miranda. I sat with Miranda because she was the safe option. Her interest in men is as lacking as mine. The waitress was disappointed when I returned the personalized napkin, declining her offer. There's only one girl I'm interested in taking home, and a romp in the bathroom isn't enough incentive to risk getting her back between my sheets.

I could have put Kylie out of her misery when it dawned on me she was unaware Miranda is gay, but her interaction with Melanie was too entertaining to interrupt. She was stomping her feet in true Maddie form, yet she still had the hungry eyes of over a dozen men.

When I approached her, she was biting her lip so hard, I was surprised she hadn't drawn blood. As I pulled her lip away from her teeth, I wished I was biting it. I laughed again when she responded to

Miranda's wave with a groan. Miranda is gorgeous, but she has a manufactured look. You know the look you can get from any plastic surgeon's office? Kylie is also gorgeous, but her beauty is natural and completely unique to her. No one could replicate her exactly, and it's that uniqueness that makes her even more appealing.

When Miranda rang the bell, I knew she wanted to play the tequila game we've played many times before. Our stats are mostly even. It's the experimenting college girls who keep Miranda's numbers high. You know the ones who can use "I was young and in college" as their excuse when they wake up in a girl's bed the following morning.

I did cheat when I kissed Kylie. You're supposed to remove the lemons from their reach and make them choose which lemon-flavored mouth they want to kiss the tequila burn away. I didn't kiss Kylie because I had doubts she'd pick me. I kissed her because I couldn't wait any longer. My cock was already hard from licking the salt off her hand. I haven't tasted her skin in years, so I was dying for a little nibble.

Her mouth was laced with tequila, but she tasted like heaven. I've gone two years without kissing anyone, and her kiss made it worthwhile. Kissing Kylie is more satisfying than any groupie fuck I've had.

Miranda's suggestion we share Kylie, though. I've got plenty of words to say about that. I couldn't believe her gall. I don't share in general, but there's no chance in hell I'd ever share Kylie with her. That's why I placed my hand on Kylie's hip. I was telling Miranda to back the fuck off. Unlike Sonny, she respected my request. She's good like that.

After Kylie orders a drink from the bartender, I can't help but smile when she returns to stand between my legs, especially considering there's an empty bar stool next to me. Her eyes study my face for several long seconds before they lower to the tattoos on the bottom half of my arms.

"You've got some I haven't seen."

"Yeah, a few." I twist my arm to show her my latest creation. It's a replica of my bike my dad inked on my lower right forearm three months ago.

"Oh my God, it's Gertie!"

I gag. She nicknamed my bike the week we started dating. I fucking hate the name she chose. For one, if my bike had a name, it'd be one as tough as she is—not a pansy old lady's name.

"I was planning on taking you for a ride tomorrow, but you lost your chance now—"

"She's here?" Kylie's voice is so loud, Jenni and Emily peer over at us. They smile when they see how comfortable we look. It's as if we're back at the cabin Noah and Emily now call home. I'm not surprised. When I forgave Kylie, I forgave her. I can't put it any simpler than that. "In San Francisco?"

When I nod, Kylie snatches my beer out of my hand, slams it down so roughly she nearly cracks it, then drags me out of my seat. "Come on," she pleads when her tugs on my arm are unsuccessful. When she quietly murmurs, *"Please,"* I know I'll never say no. I can't deny her pleading eyes.

"Go tell Melanie you're leaving with me, then meet me at the top of the stairs."

With a squeal, she sprints to Melanie. While she hugs her good-bye, I send a message to our driver, asking him to bring the limo around the front. I've just placed my phone back into my jeans when Kylie arrives at my side. She practically gallops down the stairs since she's so excited.

After wrangling through a human jungle of overzealous fans, I tuck Kylie under my arm before tackling a much more challenging side of my job. Fortunately, we catch the paparazzi by surprise since they're not expecting the band to leave so early.

The only photo they capture is my rear end when I dive into the limo on Kylie's heel. She sits across from me as our transport pulls away from the curb, her chest rising and falling in rhythm with mine. The paparazzi push their cameras close to the windows, trying in vain to snap a shot, but once we merge with traffic, the flashes illuminating the inside of the limo fade.

When Kylie's lust-crammed eyes scan my body, my cock leaps in my jeans. This is the first time we've been alone, and although her eyes show she's tipsy, she most certainly isn't drunk. Add that fact to the sexual tension crackling between us, and my dick has gotten super chummy with my zipper.

"Come here."

I want her to come to me, to take the first step needed to fix the errors we've both made. My heart slithers into my gut when she shakes her head. Rejection hits me full force, like a Mack truck slamming into a brick wall. When she notices my reaction, she smiles before nudging her head to the open partition window behind her. The energy teeming between us heightens when I push a button on the dashboard to close the partition. The smile she breaks out when the driver's head is no longer visible is one of the most dazzling I've seen.

"Come here," I request again, my voice scratchy.

This time, she doesn't shake her head. She just falls to her knees before seductively prowling toward me. When her intense, heated gaze runs down my body, my cock hardens. She's licking her lips while staring at my crotch, revealing her intentions without a word spilling from her lips.

When she reaches me, she yanks my black leather belt out of its loops and cranks open my belt buckle. I'm dying for her to suck my dick, but I stop her hurried movements by plucking her off the floor and having her straddle my lap. I want her lips on my mouth even more than I want them circling my cock.

I kiss her hard, lapping up every whimper tearing from her throat with my tongue. Our kiss is fire-sparking, spurring a new type of excitement. I thought performing on stage was electrifying, but it's nothing compared to Kylie's kisses. Her kisses alone could send me to the brink.

We kiss until our lips feel bruised; I'm hard enough to burst my zipper, and we've reached our destination. I'd keep kissing her if the driver didn't tap on the partition, signaling that we've arrived at the hotel. When I inch back from Kylie's tempting lips, she wails. I almost tell the driver to circle the block so we can finish what we've started, but Kylie slips off my lap before I have the chance. She's realized we're back at the hotel—the same hotel where my bike is stored.

After running her fingers through her hair, she checks her face in the mirror behind me before her glowing eyes drift to me. "Are you ready?" She surprises me that she can go from horny to calm in a matter of seconds. When I adjust my crotch, she giggles. "I'll take care of *that* after we've gone for a ride."

I walk awkwardly through the hotel lobby, praying none of the paparazzi or fans snapping my photo will notice my cock is pressed against my zipper. I breathe a sigh of relief when we enter the elevator to start our descent to the garage.

Excitement beams out of Kylie when we enter the basement garage of the hotel. She loves riding on the back of my bike as much as I love riding it. When my hand lunges into my saddlebag, I hesitate, afraid I'm showing my hand too early. Call me a soft cock, but I still carry her purple helmet with me everywhere I go.

When Kylie spots her helmet, her eyes dart up to mine. I no longer care how soft I look when she smiles her knee-dropping grin. My name is still inked on her skin, showing she wasn't ready to let go of our time together either.

The tears in her eyes sizzle when I nervously clean out the cobwebs inside her helmet. One of my biggest fears is spiders, and she knows this. She quickly brushes it away, but I don't miss the salty blob that falls down her cheek when I place her helmet on her head and tie the straps under her chin.

When I hand her a pair of sunglasses, she looks at me curiously. That's expected, considering it's pitch black outside. "The paps," I explain. "I've been caught without glasses before. I nearly sideswiped a parked car."

While she laughs, I throw my leg over my bike before offering her a hand to help her on the back. When my bike kicks over, her squeal shreds through my ears. After curling her arms around my waist, her cheek balances against my back. Just like that, in a matter of seconds, two years vanish. It's once again me and two of my favorite girls.

The flashing of the paparazzi lights starts the instant they hear my rumbling engine coming up the garage exit ramp. As they scream out a range of questions, I glide my bike between them. Most of their requests are for my date to lift her head so they can capture her face. They're surprised I'm on a date because it's the first time they've seen a girl on the back of my bike.

Once it's safe, I pull back on the throttle. We zoom through the heavy traffic surrounding our hotel, leaving the paparazzi on foot for dust. I can't see Kylie, but I know she's smiling. Her cheekbones lifted against my back the instant my back tire skidded across the pavement.

The traffic around Fisherman's Wharf is always heavy, but that's the advantage of having a bike. I can maneuver through the cars without any hassle, meaning I quickly lose the paparazzi tailing us in cars. We race past cars so fast, they become nothing but blurs. I could slow down, but there's no greater sound in the world than the purr of my engine combined with Kylie's giggles.

CHAPTER TWENTY-TWO

KYLIE

The warm wind whipping past my face as Slater weaves in and out of traffic dries the tears streaming down my cheeks. So many memories filtered through my head when I hopped on the back of his bike. It's as if the last two years never happened, and my bursting-at-the-seams happiness can only escape via my eyes.

After loosening my hold on his waist, I wipe away the wetness the wind missed before reattaching my grip. When Slater gives my tear-soaked hand a squeeze, I seek his gaze in the bike's mirror. Like he can read my thoughts, he adjusts the mirror so we can see each other. When he notices my tears, his speed slows, and his head darts side to side, trying to find somewhere safe to pull over. I plaster a massive grin on my face, wordlessly conveying that my tears are happy ones. I squeeze his hips with my thighs before tightening my grip around his waist, molding my body as close to his as possible. I can tell the exact moment he reads my silent reassurance because the hugest smile spreads across his face a mere second before his bike lunges forward so fast, I can no longer hold back my excited screams.

When we hit the entrance of the Golden Gate Bridge, I throw

my arms in the air and release the loudest squeal ever, stoked that number ninety-six is officially being crossed off my list, and even more exciting than that is the fact I'll cross it off with my trusty red pencil.

Once we reach the end of the iconic bridge, Slater does an illegal U-turn and goes over it again. As we get toward the end for the second time, he yells, "Again?"

Squealing, I nod. His smile reflecting in the side mirror makes me want to ride over it a hundred times.

This time, when we reach the end, Slater weaves his bike through the small roads of Sausalito. Within minutes, he pulls into a deserted café on the water's edge. The lights from San Francisco reflect off the bay's waters. It's one of the most spectacular sights I've seen.

"I hope you still have your red pencil?" Slater questions while assisting me off his bike.

When I nod, his kiss-swollen lips curve into a broad grin. Now the San Francisco skyline is the second most spectacular sight I've ever seen. After clasping my hand within his, Slater walks us toward the closed café. I could imagine how beautiful the view is during the day, considering the outside deck butts up against the water.

When he opens the door and walks inside the café, my eyes nervously dart around the spotlessly clean space. "We can't go inside; it's closed." I point to the closed sign swinging in the door he just opened.

He presses his index finger to his lips, silently requesting I be quiet before pacing deeper into the empty café. "Oh fuck!" he yells when he crashes into a table.

I try to mask my giggles, but when he turns around and runs straight into another table, I can't help but laugh.

My chuckles die down when a light in the stairwell switches on. "Who's there?"

I can see half of Slater's face. His eyes are opened wide, and his face is rattled. "Run!"

The panic in his voice has me bolting out the door we just

entered in under a second. My legs move surprisingly fast considering I'm wearing a tight mini dress. My heart almost leaps out of my chest when I realize Slater isn't following me. He's still in the cafe—alone and without protection.

I yank his baseball bat out of the saddlebag on his bike before raising it above my head, ready to attack. The shake making my arms flap like chicken wings slackens when Slater's deep chuckle rumbles out of the café. He's leaning on the doorframe with his arms folded in front of his chest and a shit-eating grin on his face. I throw the bat to the ground before resting my arms on top of my head, hoping a stretch will tell my lungs they can start breathing again.

As my body fights hard to replenish with oxygen, Slater sexily struts my way, picking up his bat on the way. "I'm glad to see you were coming back to save me."

When I punch him in the arm, he laughs even louder. After placing his bat in his saddlebag, he bands his thick arm around my shoulders to guide me back into the café.

A middle-aged lady has taken up Slater's position in the doorway. She has a large smile and welcoming eyes. "You gave the poor girl a heart attack."

Slater chuckles but doesn't deny her claims, because even a stranger knows I'm seconds from coronary failure. "Kylie, I'd like you to meet a very dear friend of mine." He stops just in front of the pretty, gray-haired, blue-eyed lady. "Maggie, this is Kylie. Kylie, this is Maggie, the official mother hen of the band."

I accept the handshake Maggie is offering. "Hi."

After ushering us into the café, Maggie switches on the main lights. My eyes drift over the space, eagerly absorbing all its quirky details. It's a standard-looking retro café, except for one wall near the front counter. It has a selection of photos proudly on display. The pictures are a timeline of Rise Up's rise to fame. The very first photo appears to have been taken quite a few years ago. Slater's dreads are only two inches long, and his arms are draped over Marcus's and Noah's shoulders. He's smiling brightly at the camera. Nick is standing to the right of them, awkwardly out of place.

As I follow the timeline of photos, Nick's inclusion in the band becomes more apparent. The very last photo is on a much larger stage than the first. A smile carves on my mouth when I notice Slater has his arm wrapped around Nick's shoulders. I thought I misunderstood Slater's dislike of Nick the weekend we stayed at the cabin, but from looking at the photos, I'm reasonably sure Slater was not a fan of Nick's a few years ago. I'm glad they worked through whatever issues they had.

"The first photo was taken the at Rise Up's first gig at Mavericks. The last one was when they performed at the Staples Center in Los Angeles." Maggie's voice is full of admiration. "I'd love to take a photo of them at every arena they've performed at, but they travel too far and wide for me to keep up with them now."

"I offered for you to travel with us." Slater pulls down some chairs from a tabletop before gesturing for us to sit. "But for some reason, this was more appealing to you." He waves his hand around the café.

Maggie smiles before pacing into the kitchen at the back of the café. When I take a seat in one of the chairs Slater pulled down, he drags my chair closer to his, sending a shrieking noise bouncing around the room. I press my lips to his just as Maggie reenters the room. The three bottles of beer she's holding clang together when she notices our joined lips.

When Slater drapes his arm over my shoulders, the confusion in her eyes disappears. "You got your heart back?" She asks her question so quietly, I'm shocked when Slater nods. I didn't think he would have heard her.

"Finally." He clinks his bottle against Maggie's before using the rim to conceal his mammoth grin. "And I'll never let her go again."

My heart melts when Maggie tells me the boys from the band bought her the café as a retirement gift. She was reluctant to accept it, but the boys soon made it apparent they wouldn't take no for an answer. She explains how Lola, Emily's sister, asked her about a poster of the San Francisco skyline she had hanging in her office at Mavericks one afternoon. Her dream had always been to open a B&B in Sausalito, but after encountering a few bumps in the road, her dreams were never fulfilled. Before she knew it, thirty years had flown by.

When Lola told Jacob about Maggie's dream, Jacob shared the news with Noah. Once Noah told the rest of the band members, they all chipped in to purchase the café for Maggie.

"There are four small cabins attached to the back of the café, and Maggie has plans to extend the floor space in here to add another three rooms." The pride in Slater's voice makes me misty-eyed. "I tried to convince her to travel with us, you know, to ensure the beer was the coldest it could be, but for some reason, a B&B sounded more appealing to her."

He laughs when Maggie throws a red dishcloth at him. Once the redness on his face fades, Maggie fills me in on everything I missed the past two years. I'm surprised when she informs me about Noah's accident. By looking at him, you'd never know he was so severely injured. She shares photos of Emily and Noah's wedding she clipped from magazines, and a few private ones she took herself, and she gushes like a proud grandmother when she shows me photos of Maddie and Jasper as newborn babies.

I'm having such a fun time, I'm not even bothered to discover the sun is beginning to rise by the time Slater and I head back to his bike. After ensuring my helmet is on tight, Slater straddles his bike before assisting me on the back. I wave goodbye to Maggie before banding my arms around his waist and resting my cheek on his back. His heart is thumping so hard, it's audible over the healthy rumble of his engine. Although it's summer, a dense layer of fog covers the bay, giving it an eerie effect. It's still outstandingly beautiful, just in its own unique way—much like the man I'm cozying up to.

Due to the early morning hour, we miss the paparazzi who were at the hotel when we exited last night. Slater helps me off his bike before removing my helmet. I scan his gorgeous face as he stores it in his saddlebag. I was shocked when he pulled my helmet out. I tried to brush it away before he noticed it, but I'm reasonably sure he saw the tear that fell from my eye. I've never stopped loving him, and the fact he still carried my helmet with him two years after I left him reveals he still cares for me too. That's why I've decided to tell him why I left. He deserves to know he did nothing wrong. I need to make sure he understands that, so it's time for me to be honest. Then, hopefully, he can forgive me and we can move past this.

When Slater curls his hand around mine in an attempt to walk us toward the elevator bank, I plant my feet on the ground, halting his retreat. "Can we talk?"

His face mars with worry, but he nods nonetheless. After leaning his glorious backside against his bike, he tugs me close to his side. "What did you want to talk about?"

I suck in a quick whiff of his manly scent before blurting out words I hope to never say again. "I want to tell you why I left."

He stiffens as his grip on my waist tightens.

"You didn't do anything wrong. It was because—"

My words are stolen by a delicious pair of lips. I try to pull away, but Slater's skills are too wonderous. Although my brain is demanding I yank back, my heart encourages me to return his kiss. We kiss furiously, like an electrical storm after a hot, humid day. It's beautiful and heart-stopping, making my brain turn to mush by the time he withdraws from our embrace.

"Don't.... you.... Umm. Weren't we..." He smiles, loving the effect he has on me. "What were we talking about?" I know what I'm trying to say. My mouth just won't cooperate with my brain.

When Slater's grin widens, I slap him on his chest before shaking my head. It helps to clear some of the fog burrowed deep inside. "Don't you want to know?"

His eyes dance between mine for several heart-clenching seconds before he shakes his head.

My brows furrow. I hadn't expected him to say no. "Why?"

As panic makes itself known with my gut, my gaze lingers on his torso. Perhaps he doesn't want me anymore, and that's why he doesn't care?

He returns my eyes to his by lifting my downcast head. "It's in the past. Can't we leave it there?"

I stare into his darkened eyes that show how vulnerable he's feeling. He has a tough exterior, but when you look closely, you'll see he wears his heart on his sleeve. His massive heart is the main reason I left him.

"But I need you to promise me something, Kylie."

I nod without pause for consideration. I'll promise him anything if it means he'll be in my life again.

"Promise me you'll never leave again without saying goodbye. No matter what happens, no matter how bad it seems, I need you to promise that you won't leave without saying goodbye." He stares into my eyes, his hurt unmissable. "I barely survived it the first time; I won't survive it a second time."

My eyes burn from the sudden rush of moisture forming in them. Nothing but hurt is reflecting in his beautiful eyes. Hurt I placed there. Hurt that'll take me years to repair. Hurt I promise will never mark his face again.

"I promise."

CHAPTER TWENTY-THREE

SLATER

Instant relief. That's what I feel when Kylie promises she won't leave again without saying goodbye. She never makes a promise she can't keep, so I can take her vow at face value—thank fuck. I wasn't joking when I said I barely survived it the first time. When she left, she took my heart with her. You can't function without your heart. Believe me, I tried. It wasn't fucking pretty.

I'm not saying being heartless is my excuse for the poor choices I've made the past two years, but have you ever tried to live without your heart? Trust me, it's hard to live with morals when you don't have a heart. I truly became heartless without her.

Call me a coward, but I shut down Kylie's confession because I'm cautious about bringing up the past. I've done some shit I'm not proud of, and although Kylie would never judge me, I don't want her to look at me differently than how she is now. Her eyes aren't just beaming with lust, but also love.

Furthermore, nothing she could say would change how I feel about her, so why bring all that anger back to the surface? Even without her telling me, I'm reasonably sure I know the reason she left.

When Nick removes my baseball bat from the saddlebag of my bike to smash Jenni's car with it, the theories I've been suspicious of the past few months ring true. Jenni and Nick are a couple. Fuck. Me. I thought Jenni was smart.

Noah motions his head to Nick, requesting my assistance, but I shake my head. When Kylie spots my gesture, her eyes narrow before her head jerks like Noah's. Her eyes thin even more when I shake my head for the second time.

"Jenni needs to see him for who he really is. This might be the final push she needs to stay away from him."

"What about Nick?" Kylie locks her eyes with mine. They're steaming with anger. "Isn't he your friend? Shouldn't you help him too?"

I shake my head once more. Nick isn't my friend. I can't stand the guy, but since I've never told Kylie what happened between us, she's unaware I caught him sleeping with my fiancée in my fucking bed.

"You're better than this." With a disappointed sigh, Kylie paces toward Nick and Noah, who are lying on the ground next to Jenni's demolished BMW. I'm shocked when the moonlight glistens on Nick's cheeks. I've never seen him cry, not even when I knocked him out after the whole Nikki incident.

I was having doubts about Nikki for a few months, but I promised her my hand in marriage and had every intention of keeping my promise. My parents were together from a young age, and I wanted to emulate their relationship. I tried to convince myself that every relationship, even the best ones, have rough patches, but the instant I walked in on her with Nick, I knew that was one bump we'd never smooth out.

Cutting Nikki out of my life was easy. Nick was a lot fucking harder. Noah was adamant we needed him in our group. He stupidly believes he's the final piece of the puzzle that makes our group whole. I fought tooth and nail to have him kicked out of Rise Up. I even quit at one stage. If it hadn't been for Noah saying he'd do anything to make me stay, anything at all, I'd still be laying down bricks at all the housing developments popping up around Ravenshoe.

After a night of drinking, an agreement was reached. Ten percent of Rise Up's profits for the rest of our musical career would be donated to the Serena Scott Foundation, and I was allowed to punch Nick once. Marcus agreed to the charity donation without a second thought but refused my second request. After a few beers and numerous whispers in his ear, he finally relented—on one condition: I wasn't allowed to knock Nick out.

He was pissed when Nick lay unconscious on his grandma's garage floor for twenty minutes after I hit him. It wasn't my fault. I thought he'd take more than he did. His fighting skills certainly lacked at that time, but with how hard he swung my bat at Jenni's car, I'd say he's rectified that now.

"Noah is taking Nick to a hotel." Kylie slides back next to me before resting her head on my shoulder. "Maybe you should go with them?"

She gasps when I shake my head. Hating that I've disappointed her, I pull her to sit on my lap. I'm about to head on the road for three weeks, so I don't want to spend my final weekend with her worrying about Nick. Another gasp seeps from her lips when she feels my cock jabbing into her curvy backside. With the vein in her neck throbbing, her eyes shoot to Marcus and Nicole, who are seated across from us. Satisfied they're not paying us any attention, her lust-filled gaze returns to mine.

"Pool in ten minutes." She fakes a yawn before slipping off my lap and darting toward the infinity pool at the front of the property.

I wait approximately five seconds before taking off after her. What? I'm impatient as fuck when it comes to anything Kylie-related. I muffle her squeals with my hand when I catch up with her. She's screaming so loud, she'll wake up Noah's neighbors, and I'm barely touching her—yet.

When we reach the pool, Kylie steps away from me before slipping her cotton dress over her head. Her pale beige skin illuminates in the full moon. After peering past my shoulder, she unclasps her bra and slides her panties down her legs. Fuck, she's gorgeous. Her body is pure perfection: lush curves, pert tits, and a slit that tastes sweeter than honey. My cock aches to be inside her.

She winks before diving into the pool without so much of a splash. By the time her head surfaces out of the water, I've removed my boots and shirt and am in the process of removing my jeans. She watches me with needy, hungry eyes when I slide my jeans all the way down my legs. She's seen my cock a hundred times already, but she can't get enough.

I fuckin' love that.

My entrance into the pool isn't as elegant as Kylie's. I run up to the edge and dive-bomb into the water. Her giggles boom around the pool area, only dissipating when I lower my mouth over hers. I'm glad the pool is heated, but even if it weren't, nothing would dampen the hotness. I've never seen a more beautiful sight than Kylie's lust-filled eyes glistening in the moonlit ocean.

After swimming us to the edge of the pool, I nudge Kylie's thighs apart until her pretty waxed pussy shimmers with more wetness than just water. I cup her breast before sucking one of her pert nipples into my mouth and sliding my other hand down the smooth planes of her stomach. Her hot breaths are visible in the cool night air when two of my fingers break through the folds of her pussy. I scissor them slowly, encouraging her to open up for me before seeking the sweet spot inside her.

When I find it, she arches her back, which mashes her glorious tits into my face. I release her nipple with a pop before paying the same dedication to her other one. After my tongue treks across it, I blow on it, urging it to stiffen as effectively as my cock. It follows along nicely.

As my tongue worships her tits, my fingers pump in and out of her pussy at a frantic pace. I finger fuck her brutally, needing her to come before I can step up to the home plate. I want to take my time with her, to taste every inch of her, but with my bandmates' voices echoing in the distance, I can't. We're going to fuck, and we're going to fuck hard... as soon as I figure out how I can fetch a condom from my wallet that's all the way over there.

When my eyes stray to my jeans, Kylie's glossed-over eyes follow their direction. "Shit." She knows I don't fuck if my cock doesn't have a raincoat. Never have. Never will. "It's okay. We'll take this back to our room. It's dry and warm there, so it'll be better anyway."

She doesn't try to fool me with smoke or mirrors. She's just straight up honest. It makes me reckless. "Are you on the Pill?"

Her eyes rocket to mine. My fingers are still in her pussy, but her dilated pupils have nothing to do with that. She's shocked. "Yeah, but—"

"Then we're good to go."

When I attempt to pull my fingers out of her slick canal, more than eager to replace them with my cock, she clamps the walls of her vagina around me, halting my retreat. Although it's a tactic to stop me from reaching my ultimate goal, it's also the biggest fucking turn on. The strength she has in her pussy is mesmerizing.

"You don't fuck without a condom."

I smile at her cute stumble over the word "fuck."

"Then maybe we ain't fucking. Maybe we're making love." I'm stirring, but the stupid ass sentiment in my voice doesn't make it sound like that—neither does the loved-up flare blazing through Kylie's eyes. "Don't look at me like that, Kylie. I'm not a man you should look at like that."

"Like what?" The look I'm referencing ramps up on her face as she bobs down so low in the water that not only do my fingers get super friendly with her crotch, so does my cock. "I'm just over here, waiting to be ravished. You're the one delaying things." She takes in a big gulp of water before squirting it in my face. "What's the matter? Afraid you'll come within two seconds of touching me without protection?"

Yes! "No." I remove my fingers from her pussy, spread her thighs even wider, then line up my cock. "I'm just trying to work out how long my swimmers will last in heated water. Wouldn't want anyone I haven't fucked claiming I fathered their baby."

She tries to respond to my rile, but I slam home before she can. Fuck. Me. If I had any idea this is how good she felt unwrapped, I would have ditched condoms months ago.

"Slater..." She says only my name, purring both syllables.

I crowd her against the pool wall before drawing my cock back out. I've never been a fan of the disco lights they put in pools, but I'm fucking loving it now. One is right between Kylie's legs, meaning I can watch my cock pump in and out of her even with the moon behind my back.

"We've got to be quick, alright? I'll make it up to you later."

She doesn't reply. Unless you count moaning as words.

After adjusting one of her legs so it sits higher on my hips, I place one hand behind her back to protect it from being scratched by the pool edging before the other clutches the lip of the pavers so I can use it as leverage for my pumps. I slam into her on repeat, using the waves crashing to shore as coverage for our loud splashes. My mouth handles Kylie's moans. Her pussy ripples around me, sucking at me. I thrust harder, giving her everything I have. She didn't come earlier, so I sure as fuck ain't coming until she does.

I'm fucking her so roughly, I'm sure I'm going to bruise her. She doesn't seem to mind. Kylie likes things rough. She's usually the one demanding I pull her hair before digging her heels into my ass to urge me to go faster. My dad was right. It is the quiet ones you need to watch the closest.

"Oh.. Ohh... Ohhh..."

Here they come, the screams I'd give anything to hear.

She tightens around me, then trembles. "Slater, oh, God, Jesus." Her squeaky clean words don't match the expression on her face. She's flushed with ecstasy and biting her bottom lip. "I'm... I'm—"

"Right there with you, so hurry the hell up."

She smiles, but it doesn't stop a freight train from crashing into her. She claws and screams, and her whole body shakes when the heat of my cum adds to the sensation roaring through her body.

Fuck yes. Here it is. I've hit the fucking jackpot.

Once her pussy finishes milking my cock of my spawn, Kylie's blitzed eyes lock with mine. "I love you."

I drag my lips down her cheek, across her chin and over her collarbone, expressing what she means to me without words. My lips only stop their devotion when murmured voices move closer to us.

Cackling, we jump out and dry ourselves with the towels the best we can with Jell-O legs before hiding in the shadows of the pool room. I don't know how many times I have to muffle Kylie's giggles with my mouth while we're getting dressed. Even whipping her with the towel doesn't stop her happy chuckles. Anyone would swear she wants me to be caught with my pants down.

All playfulness is snuffed when I murmur, "I hope they don't go swimming with my swimmers."

She whacks me in the gut just as Marcus and Nicole enter the pool area via the front gate. "We're the only ones stupid enough to go skinny dipping with an audience."

If it were anyone but Marcus and Nicole approaching us, I would have argued. However, Marcus is as stiff as the ties he dons most days, and putting it nicely, Nicole is a prude.

"On the count of three, we'll make a run for it. Are you ready?"

Kylie finishes slipping her dress over her head before nodding.

"One... two..." I start running, leaving her to face the wrath alone.

She's on my heel in under a second, years of track helping her overtake me just as we reach the edge of the cabin. I don't think Marcus and Nicole saw us, but I'm reasonably sure they can hear the heavy clomps of our feet as we bolt across the wooden deck.

We stumble into the living room, laughing at our close call. "Holy fucking shit. I'm dead. Running like that after what we just did—"

My words are cut off by Kylie's hand getting friendly with my stomach for the second time in two minutes. When she nudges her head to the right, I shift to face the direction she's gesturing. Jenni is sitting on the sofa, her pale face amplifying the bright red streaks teeming from her eyes. Fuck!

I slant my head to Kylie. "Can you give us a minute?"

After running her hand down my arm in a supportive manner, she nods. I wait for her to enter the hallway of our room before going to comfort Jenni. As I've said previously, she's not my sister, but I can't help but treat her like she is.

It takes nearly thirty minutes for Jenni's tears to subside, then another ten to confess she's pregnant with Nick's baby. My first thought is to kill Nick, because that's the only way I can cut the rope Jenni just lassoed around his waist. No matter what happens, he's tied to her until the day she dies. Their baby guarantees that.

I'm proven wrong when Jenni murmurs, "My mom wants me to get an abortion."

"What. Why?"

I'm devastated for her when she explains everything that's happening with her family. I don't know what I could possibly say to make it easier on her, so I just comfort her the best I can. I tell her she'll always have Emily and me to support her and her baby if she decides to keep it, and that she isn't alone, and that we'll never stop loving her.

My promise doesn't have the effect I was aiming for. It causes even more tears to trickle down her face.

By the time they've settled, nearly two hours have ticked by. While rubbing a kink in my neck, I head to the room I'm sharing with Kylie, emotionally and physically drained. I'm surprised to find Kylie still awake. It isn't a good surprise. Her beautiful face is stained with tears, and her bag is packed and sitting on the floor.

Ignoring the mad beat of my heart, I finish entering the room, closing the door behind me. "Are you going somewhere?"

"Yes." Her head barely bobs, but it sends fresh tears spilling down her cheeks. "I'm going home."

"Why?" Our entire weekend has been perfect, so I'm at a loss as to what's suddenly changed.

"Do you love me, Slater?"

I nod without pause for thought. I've loved her since the day I saw her at the Bar N Barrel.

"Then say it." She stares at me with tear-filled, begging eyes. "Tell me you love me."

"You don't need to hear—"

"Yes I do!" she interrupts as moisture floods her cheeks. "Say it! Just say it!"

I'm too shocked to form words. She's never voiced anger about me not saying it the prior six months, so why is she so worked up now? I show her what she means to me. I express it every fucking day, so I don't need to tell her as well.

When I fail to reply, she snags her bag off the floor. "Goodbye, Slater."

When she rushes for the door, I move faster, slamming it shut before she can exit. When I brace my back against it, blocking her only exit, she digs her nails into my arm so deeply, she draws blood.

"What the fuck, Kylie?" I'm yelling, but it can't be helped. I'm pissed as fuck. First Jenni, now this.

"You won't tell me you love me, but you'll tell her!" Kylie thrusts her hand to the door like whomever she is talking about is standing behind it.

"Who?"

When she steps back with a growl, I step forward. "Who?" I question again, louder this time. "Who has you so fucking worked up, you're acting like a mental patient?"

"Jenni!" She angrily wipes at the tears careening down her face. "You told her you love her, but you won't say it to me!"

I balk, confused. I didn't tell Jenni I love her, did I?

Oh, fuck, yes I did.

"I didn't mean it like that." My raging heart is heard in my reply. "I was trying to comfort her. I don't see her like that. I swear to you, I didn't mean it how you're thinking."

I clutch the top of her arms to coerce her eyes to mine, needing her to see the truth in mine. She's not seeing things clearly, and it's making her unhinged.

When I get her eyes, I wish I hadn't. They're so broken. "I tell you

I love you every day for months, and not once have you said it back." She bites down on her lower lip so fiercely, I'm certain my arm won't be the only body part sporting wounds tonight. "But I just heard you say it to her."

"Kylie..." I have no words. The pain on her face is too much—it's all too fucking much.

I love her with all my heart, but the last girl I said those words to broke me, so I swore I'd never say them to anyone ever again. They're just useless words. They don't mean anything. I only said them to Jenni because I think of her as a sister. I didn't mean it in the manner Kylie thinks I did.

"I lo—"

Kylie slaps her hand over my mouth. "I don't want to hear it now."

Desperate for her to see through the jealousy clouding her, I place her hand on my chest. My heart is racing, panicked as fuck I'm losing her. "This belongs to you. Everywhere you go, it goes with you. It belongs only to you."

My eyes plead with her to believe me, to see what I've tried to show her for months: I love her.

When she remains quiet, I yank my wallet out of my jeans to remove the photo I carry of Serena. Kylie chokes back a sob when I hold the picture out in front of her. I never told her about Serena's death because she passed nearly eleven years before we met, so the conversation never came up. Kylie and I talk, but it's never overly serious.

"Jenni is like a sister to me, nothing more."

Over the next hour, I explain everything to Kylie about Serena and how I can't help but treat Jenni as if she is my sister. Kylie apologizes for overreacting before begging for forgiveness. No matter how many times I tell her she has nothing to be sorry for, she apologizes over and over again until exhaustion overtakes her, and she falls asleep in my arms. . .

I thought we had worked everything out...until she vanished the very next day. Maybe now seeing firsthand how much Jenni loves Nick, she'll realize Jenni was never a threat to our relationship.

"I need to tell you one day, though, Slater." Kylie's crackling voice exposes she's on the verge of crying. "Otherwise guilt will eat me alive."

"One day." I draw her into my chest, needing her as close to me as possible so she'll stop the memories of that night re-cracking my heart. "Just not today."

CHAPTER TWENTY-FOUR

SLATER

I don't know if she realizes she's doing it, but every two seconds, Kylie's tongue darts out to moisten her lips. It's driving me fucking crazy, because we're not alone. The fancy ass hotel Rise Up is occupying this week is so elegant, it has an elevator attendant—and attendant whose funky smell can't weaken the throb of my cock. I'm so fucking hard it hurts.

While glancing up at the elevator dashboard, praying it will hurry the fuck up and get to the forty-eighth floor, I adjust my crotch for the third time the past minute. Just as I stop my zipper from biting my cock, I spot the curve in Kylie's lips. She's smirking but trying to keep it on the down low by slanting her head to the side so her hair shelters her face.

Like a freight train crashing into me, clarity forms. She's teasing me—on purpose.

Two can play that game.

After drinking in every inch of her enticing body, I crowd her against the mirrored wall of the elevator car. I stand close enough my every intention can be revealed without speaking a word, but not close enough her budded nipples can scratch my chest.

She stares at me with lust-filled eyes, her chest rising and falling in sync with mine, her hope just as high. "What are you doing?"

I don't answer her. I merely increase her breathlessness by running my thumb over her plump, bare lips. I can see the back of the elevator attendant's head in her massively dilated eyes, but I no longer care that we're not alone. My lips are on hers before any of the objections in her eyes can be articulated.

When I drag my tongue along the roof of her mouth, her moan is felt all the way to my cock. I push in closer, not wanting an ounce of air between us. The hem of her dress inches high on her smooth, beige thighs when she curls her legs around my waist. I rock my hips, rubbing my stiffened shaft against the heat between her legs. Her kiss shouldn't make me so hard, but considering it's Kylie, I'm not surprised. Her kisses aren't ordinary. They're the all-encompassing, will *never forget them in a million years* kisses. They're as sweet as her face and as wicked as the sex fiend she brings out in the bedroom.

A stern cough attempts to interrupt our kiss. I ignore it. I've been dying for this for years, so I refuse to let anything stop me from ravishing her mouth right now.

"Floor forty-eight."

The deep grumbling voice has Kylie attempting to unwrap her legs from my hips. I hold on tight, denying her soundless request to be set down. After securing her in place—as close to my crotch as possible—I walk out of the elevator with one eye open to ensure we don't crash into anything. My cock rubs the seam of her panties with every step I take. If we weren't being eyeballed by two old biddies monitoring the corridor like we don't have a hall pass, I'd slip her panties to the side and drive home. Alas, lewd acts in public are more Jacob's specialty. Unless a pool is involved, Kylie and I keep our rendezvous behind closed doors.

When I make it to the alcove of our rooms, I brace Kylie's back on her bedroom door before digging my wallet out of my jeans, silently fucking praying my room key is readily available. The alcove amplifies Kylie's moans, making me even stiffer. If I don't get her inside soon, I might have to take a page out of Jacob's book. The entrance of our room is close enough, isn't it?

Just as I pull the keycard out of my wallet, Kylie's hotel room door swings open and we tumble inside, all legs and arms. When I land on top of Kylie, she releases a deep *oomph*. It's barely audible over Melanie's hysterical giggles.

Although I'm most likely crushing her to death, Kylie stares up at me with a huge smile plastered on her beautiful face. It's so captivating, if we weren't being bombarded by several questions at once, I'd return to making out with her on the hard hotel room floor.

"Where have you been?"

"Why didn't you answer your phone?"

"You scared us half to death."

"You shouldn't be going anywhere without a bodyguard."

When my eyes lift from Kylie's blooming face, I'm confronted by the members of my band, their partners, Melanie, Hawke, and even Cormack has joined the party. My bandmates' faces are crammed with amusement. Jenni and Emily look panicked. Melanie is laughing so hard, she's bent over holding her stomach. Cormack looks pissed, and Hawke, well, he still looks like Hawke.

After scrambling to my feet, I assist Kylie off the floor. Once she's back on her feet, she stays facing the hallway, too embarrassed to face the circus head-on. It's unfortunate for her that Emily and Jenni have no tact. They fuss over her like we just went three rounds in the ring instead of me pinning her to the floor with my hips.

When they walk her toward the living room, Kylie soundlessly pleads for me to save her. Most of her friends growing up were boys, so she finds this type of stuff daunting. I could save her, but since I want her to feel she's a part of the Rise Up dynamic, I wink at her instead.

I see the quickest roll of her eyes before Marcus blocks her from my view. "Cormack is going to ban you from riding your bike."

"Like fuck he is." Although pissed at Cormack's assumption I can't take care of myself, I slant my head to the side so I can reconnect my eyes with Kylie, praying everyone will get the hell out of her room so we can finish what we started in the elevator.

"A quick message wouldn't have killed you. Emily and Jenni were panicked out of their minds since you've been gone all night." The expression on Noah's face doesn't match his stern tone. He's loving standing between me and the woman I'm eyeing like she's dessert. "I'm just glad you still had it in your pants."

"It wouldn't be if you'd all get out of my damn room—"

"This isn't *your* room." Nick's voice drips with sarcasm. "It's Kylie's." He moves to stand in front of me, blocking my view of Kylie. "How many months of cock blocking did you do to me with Jenni?"

An enormous shit-eating grin etches onto my face. I get great pleasure knowing my attempts to keep him away from Jenni gave him blue balls.

When he notices my smile, Nick steps closer to me. "Maybe I should hang out in your room a little longer." His amused eyes flick between mine as his lips furl high. "You're not busy, are you? You don't have any plans I'm interrupting—surely?"

"Slater!" is yelled out in stereo when my knuckles connect with Nick's nose.

I return the stare I'm being hit with. "What? I restrained myself." I only backhanded him instead of punching him like I really wanted to.

With Nick's chuckles ringing in my ears, I stride toward Kylie, my steps fast and impatient. A squeak pops from her lips when I pluck her from the sofa. Once she's thrown over my shoulder like I did a week ago, I make a beeline to the interconnecting door between our rooms. I've never been patient, so you can sure as hell be guaranteed I'm not waiting a second longer to taste her again.

Kylie's giggles are barely audible over the laughter erupting in her room, but it picks up when I kick the door shut. After setting her on her feet, I spin around to ensure the door is locked. I don't want any more interruptions. I've waited years for this.

By the time I pivot back around, Kylie has already unzipped her dress. When I take a step toward her, hungry and unrepentant, she takes one back. While gazing into my eyes, she releases her clutch on her dress. It slips off her body with a soundless whoosh, landing in a heap around her feet. As my eyes absorb her enticing body, my cock stiffens painfully fast. Her body is a temple I plan to worship for the next several hours. Inches of luscious curves, generous, mouthwatering tits, and a glistening slit her sheer panties are poorly concealing.

A growl rumbles in my chest when I notice her dark purple panties are so tiny, my name is visible on her smooth hip. Seeing my name on her skin flips a switch inside me. I've always been a little dominant in the bedroom, but it'll take on a new meaning today.

"Come here," I command, my voice deep and rugged.

Kylie bites down on her bottom lip then shakes her head. I slant my head to the side and arch my brow, warning her my patience is stretched thin. She smiles, loving the macho idiot I'm portraying. She loves being chased, and I'm pleased to see our separation didn't change that.

After unclasping her bra, she discards it on the floor alongside her dress. My teeth grit when she covers her perfect tits from my view with her arm, but since I've caught on to her ruse, I don't let her see my disappointment. I'd hate for her to know I'm coming for her before I have the advantage.

It's a pity for all involved that Kylie knows me as well as she did years ago. With a frisky wink, she darts toward the main bedroom. I'm on her heels in under a second, my hunger too dire to let something minute like my boots failing to gain traction with the ground deter me.

After banding my arms around her waist, I attach my lips to her neck. Her laughter switches to a moan when I bite, lash, and suck on her delicious skin. As her head lolls to the side, one of my hands slithers up the smooth planes of her stomach to grope her more-than-a-handful breasts. Her breathing becomes urgent, almost needy when I roll her budded nipple between my index finger and thumb, tweaking it until it's so firm, it could cut through diamonds.

As I guide her toward the bed in the master suite, I grind my cock against the silky curves of her ass, fighting the urge to shred her panties off her body and drive home. Unlike our last foray in the pool at Noah's cabin, I have no reason not to take my time with her. I'll just fuck her first then move on to foreplay. I'm too impatient. I need her heat wrapped around me more than my lungs need air.

When Kylie's knees hit the duvet, I push her forward and arch her back so her ass sits at the height of my crotch and her tits splay across the bed. Forever impatient, I release my cock from my jeans, slide her panties to the side, then grind my cock's head up and down her glistening slit. The moans emitting from her lips add to my impatience. Even knowing I should prepare her to take all of me, my patience is stretched too thin.

Kylie rolls her hips, enticing my eagerness even more. "Please, Slater."

I guide my cock through her wet folds with one hand while the other fists her hair. She purrs more, loving my determined hold. She always liked things a little rough in the bedroom. After ensuring my cock is coated in her juices, hoping to ease the friction, I shift my eyes down, eager to watch our fire-sparking connection.

"Fuck." My growl comes out rough, pissed my cock isn't wearing a raincoat. "Hold on, I need a condom."

I release my grip on her hair before snagging my wallet out of my jeans, which are gathered around my ankles. Another curse word seeps from my lips when I fail to locate a condom in the compartment of my wallet I store them in.

When Kylie hears my haggard groan, she cranks her neck back to peer at me. "In my clutch in the living room." Her voice is riddled with nerves, like she's worried I'll be pissed she's carrying a condom in her purse. Am I concerned? You'll have to ask when my brain isn't mush from all the blood in my body being transferred to my cock.

After snagging a condom out of Kylie's purse, I walk back into the master suite, rolling protection down my stiffened shaft on the way. My eager steps falter when my eyes lift to Kylie. She appears to be in the position I left her, but I know she's moved, because her meager pair of panties have been ditched, erotically exposing her gorgeous ass and bare slit to my fervent eyes. Let me tell you, it's a glorious fucking visual. My cock stands to attention, as if to say, *play time, motherfucker!*

I prowl the last few steps, too delighted by the visual to rush things as I was earlier. God, she's beautiful—almost too perfect for me to touch, but I must. I'm starved of her taste, dying to be reacquainted with every inch of her. I need to fuck her hard and fast, then, once she says my name in a husky whisper, my focus will shift to reestablishing the connection we once had.

Kylie fists the sheets in a white-knuckled hold when I rub my cock through the folds of her drenched pussy, swiping its head over her throbbing nub three times for good measure. My cock throbs with need when her sexy purr vibrates all the way to the base. I push in the first inch, eager to feel her squeezes more profoundly. Her pussy sucks at me, a ravenous, greedy suck that reveals I'm not the only one eager to get the party started.

With that in mind, I thrust my fat cock inside of her in one quick pump. She calls out, her husky moan nearly enough to set me off. Fuck I've missed that noise. The grunts. The moans. *Her.*

I bury myself inside her so deeply, if I were to put my hand on her stomach, my dick would poke it. Pain is most likely sparking across her womb from my engorged knob ramming into it, but her moans give no indication that she's in pain. They beg for me to go harder, faster, riskier.

I give her what she wants and then some. While rocking into her on repeat, I brush my fingertips over the silky skin of her inner thighs.

"Oh...," she moans, her back arching when I find the nub

patiently waiting for stimulation. I grind my thumb down on her clit before circling it, ramping her moans up even more. If my bandmates didn't get the hint to leave, they'll have no doubt what we're doing. Kylie is practically screaming, her shouts as vocal as the grunts bubbling in my chest when I feel how swollen she is from taking my cock. Her pussy lips are puffy and red, but also glistening with arousal.

"You hurting, baby? Do you need me to go slower?"

Kylie shakes her head. "No. Don't stop. It's just been a while. I need time to adjust."

Lust-hazed head or not, nothing will stop my chest from swelling with smugness. She said "a while" like it's been a lot longer than a couple of weeks. I'd even go as far as saying months. If that doesn't make me as happy as a pig in mud, I don't know what will.

"This will help." Not giving her the chance to protest, I pull out my cock, fall to my knees, then bury my head between her legs. Even my odd angle can't deny the tightness of her pussy. She's as clenched now as the first time we fucked. I made her bleed that night. I'm not doing that again.

I drag my tongue along her sore lips before dipping it right down low on the sensitive skin between her ass and slick canal. I stretch her with a tenderness that amplifies the wetness glistening between her legs, but with the hunger of a man who can't get enough of her taste. She stiffens when I get close to the puckered hole she never let me near we when dated, but I'm pleased to say her knees don't creep across the sheets like they usually did.

Forever willing to test the waters, I give her ass a quick swipe with my tongue. I smile when I hear her shudders in her moan before I return my devotion to her pussy. We've got hours, so untouched orifices can wait. My cock can't.

I eat her pussy without restraint, loving that her tight body doesn't put up a single barrier between us. Her glorious ass is in my face, her pussy on my mouth, and her clit is buzzing between my thumb and index finger. The only way this could get hotter was if she had my cock in her mouth.

Now there's a brilliant idea.

"Scoot up."

Kylie groans when my mouth leaves her pussy, but before an objection can be fired off her tongue, I snap off my condom, almost castrating myself in the process, then lie beside her, but reversed. When my cock almost gouges out her eye, she figures out what I'm attempting to achieve, and I swear to God, she has my cock in her mouth even faster than that.

"Jesus, baby. Hungry much?"

She gabbles out a reply, but I can't hear a fucking thing she's saying since my cock is stuffed into the back of her throat. Any talking is left for dust when I curl her thighs around my ears before chowing down. Her ass is no longer in view, but for what I miss visually, I make up for with sneaky fingers. I drag my thumb over her clenched hole at the same steady pace my tongue devours her slick pussy. It's a fast, hungry embrace that has me fucking her face as if it's her slit.

After ramming my hips forward so fast, she gags, I press my thumb against her back entrance, loving that it opens for me with only the slightest protest. I suck her clit into my mouth before slipping my thumb inside her deeper, my boldness encouraged by her scent that grows muskier with each millimeter I notch inside her.

"I'm going to fuck you here, Kylie. It's as hungry for my cum as your throat." Her hopeful moan vibrates my knob. "First your mouth, then your pussy, then your ass. I'm going to claim every inch of you —*today*." Her entire body quakes at my last word.

I suck on her clit so hard, her ass accepts all of my thumb as my name tears from her throat. Her screams are so loud, I'm sure every guest on our floor can hear them—my bandmates included. I shouldn't love the idea of them hearing Kylie in the throes of ecstasy, but I do. It has me eating her faster, almost brutally. I drag my tongue up and down her damped slit while my thumb pumps in and out of her no-longer virginal ass at the same pace my cock fucks her mouth.

I lick, pump, and graze my teeth over her thrumming nub on repeat until she climaxes for the second time, but this time, her screams are muffled by the cum jetting out of my cock.

Mouth down. Pussy and ass to go.

CHAPTER TWENTY-FIVE

SLATER

Kylie's head lifts from my sweat-slicked chest to peer into my eyes. Hers are beaming with lust, her lips are swollen, and her hair looks like a bird is trying to nest in it, but she's still incredibly beautiful. She looks so quaint, I almost have a heart attack when she asks, "Do you want kids?"

The idea of being a father freaks me the fuck out—so much, if it were any other girl asking, I'd be halfway out the door by now, running so fast she'd never catch me. The only reason my naked ass remains in my bed is because the woman who asked often has me craving things I never knew I wanted, so perhaps one day I may add rugrats into the mix. One day far far *far* away. I've just got Kylie back, so I plan to hog her time for at least the next three years. I don't want to share her just yet—not even with a mini version of myself.

When Kylie arches her brow, prompting me to answer her, I drag my hand over my dreads. "Maybe one day."

I thought I expressed my statement with positivity, but Kylie's expression reveals I desperately need acting classes. Tears cloud her eyes as her pupils widen. Anyone would swear I told her I've been sterilized for years with how oddly she's reacting.

"You want kids that bad?"

Her face screws up as she struggles to hold back her tears. "No. It's not what I want. It's—"

Her confession is cut off when I catch sight of the alarm clock on the bedside table. *We're late!*

"Can we continue our conversation later? I've got somewhere really important to be."

Kylie muffles a yawn with her hand before snuggling into her pillow with a nod.

"*We've* got somewhere important to be," I correct.

When I stoop down to lift her out of bed, her beautiful naked body makes me hesitant in my pursuit. We only finished fucking an hour ago, but my cock is acting as if he hasn't sought release three times already today.

After reminding myself for the hundredth time this week that she isn't going anywhere, so I have plenty of time to explore her body later, I hand her the dress she was wearing last night, urging her to hurry up.

Her brows shoot into her hairline. "I can't wear a clubbing dress during the day."

Desperate to continue the plans I organized days ago, I place the shirt I was wearing earlier over Kylie's head before pulling her hair out of the collar. It barely covers the generous curves of her backside, but it'll stop any man who may be in her room with Melanie from seeing a piece of her only I've touched.

When I guide her to the interconnecting door between our rooms, she winces with every step we take. I take a mental note to be a little gentler with her tonight. I want her to feel me for days after we've fucked, but I hate the idea of her being in *actual* pain. I took care of her after claiming her like no one else has, but she's still feeling sore all over. Some kinks can't be rubbed out no matter how hard you try. Believe me, I tried to fake it for years. Gave me nothing but disappointment.

After unlocking the door between our rooms, I plant a peck on

Kylie's kiss-swollen lips, then gently nudge her into her room. "You have ten minutes to get ready."

"For?" She stands in the doorway, watching me curiously.

The confusion on her face clears when I ask, "Do you want to cross off number seventy?"

Her eyes flicker as she recalls what item number seventy is on her bucket list. I can tell the exact moment recognition dawns as she smiles the most dazzling grin. With a nod, she dashes into the main bedroom of her suite, cringing.

By the time I've replaced my shirt and jeans with clean ones, brushed my teeth, and gathered our tickets Emily got for me yesterday, Kylie is back leaning against the door of her room, looking as ravishing as ever.

As our elevator car descends to the lobby, her excitement is as obvious as the panic on her face when I notched the first inch of my cock into her ass. It's a flighty expression that can only truly be understood by the words it's delivered with. "I'm so excited, I could pee my pants."

Thank fuck, the remarks she vocalizes in the bedroom are ten times dirtier than that, and one hundred percent hotter. Anal sex isn't easy in general, let alone with a virginal, untouched hole, but Kylie handled it like a pro. She trusted me with her body, and her trust was reciprocated tenfold. Our exchange was blistering, and I can't wait for round two.

I feel the excitement thrumming through Kylie's body when I interlock our hands just as the elevator arrives at the lobby. When we exit, I spot Hawke standing to the side, snarling at me since we're late. I don't usually take a bodyguard with me when I go out, but we're about to enter the twilight hours, and we're walking, so additional protection isn't just smart. It's necessary.

While shadowing Hawke outside, I lower a knitted beanie over my head before tucking my dreads inside, hoping the loss of my distinctive trademark will make me less obvious to my fans.

Hawke opens the usually locked side entrance door of the hotel before nudging his head to the alleyway. "I'll stay a few feet behind you, but if you become concerned about anyone, signal, then I'll move in."

I jerk up my chin, advising I understand his instructions before re-clasping Kylie's hand in mine. When we exit the hotel, we're blinded by paparazzi lights. I'm so unprepared, I don't have time to shelter my eyes, meaning I can't see two fucking feet in front of me. I'm pissed as fuck but praying the paps annoying me are men of their words when they pledge, "Give us a handful of useable shots, then we'll leave you alone."

I tug Kylie into my side before raising my eyes in the direction the voices came from. "Smile, baby. If they get a decent photo, they may leave us alone."

Kylie smiles, but she directs it at me, not the paparazzi begging for a more scandalous shot.

"Slater, this way."

"Over here."

"Can you kiss?"

"Who's the mystery girl?"

"Are you in love?"

I wait approximately thirty seconds before I start walking again. Since my arm is curled around Kylie's waist, she follows right along with me. When we make it to the sidewalk without incident, my brows furrow, shocked the paparazzi are doing as promised. They continue snapping us, but they leave a decent amount of distance between us, happy to utilize their long range zoom.

Halfway out of the alley, my eyes drop to my watch. "We've have ten minutes to make it all the way down to Pier 33 before our ferry leaves without us."

Kylie swoops down to remove her shoes. Once they're clutched in her hands, her glowing eyes lock with mine. "Catch me if you can."

With a cheeky wink that has me wanting to fall to my knees, she hightails it onto the sidewalk, her fast speed gaining a fair amount of distance between us in an extremely short period. Grinning, I take off after her, but not before cranking my neck back to make sure Hawke is following us. He is, but he doesn't appear happy about it.

When I catch up to Kylie, I grasp her other hand in mine before increasing my speed. Our weaves through the swarm of tourists mingling around Fisherman's Wharf soon lose the paparazzi tailing us, but it gains us over a dozen curious gawks. They're most likely gawking in glee, because none of my fans have seen me smile like I am right now. I love what I do, but I wasn't *in* love with it. If that makes any sense? But this... I could get use to this.

By the time we make it to Pier 33, I'm gasping for air, and Kylie is giggling loudly. I thought I missed her lips the most, but her laugh is making a quick liar out of me. Once I get my breathing under control, I hand our tickets to the attendant, and they usher us straight onto the boat.

"Are you okay?" Kylie questions, still giggling.

I haven't exercised in years because all the workout I need to stay fit is done behind my drum kit—or in the bedroom—so every muscle in my body is feeling our sprint.

Nodding, I suck in some big breaths while making a mental note to add leg reps into my workout sessions. Once my normal breathing returns, we move to the bow of the boat, wanting the best view of Alcatraz as it comes into sight. Even though it's nearly summer, a thick blanket of fog covers most of the Bay. It gives it an eerie feeling that matches the marvel peeking out from behind it. It's glorious, but nowhere near as compelling as having my body wrapped around Kylie's. We snuggled together the entire thirty-minute trip, happy to use the fog as an excuse to get cozy.

Kylie's excitement beams out of her when I snap her photo next to the "Welcome to Alcatraz" sign, then it leaps onto mine when our private host motions for us to climb onto the back of a golf cart so they can drive us up a steep hill. I would have died if I had to slum it with the regular visitors.

After being greeted at the main entrance by a second hostess, we're ushered into a small death trap of an elevator to take us to the third level to collect a set of headphones for our audio tour. Our hostess offered to give us a guided tour, but I'd rather experience it like everyone else. From the reviews online, the audio tour isn't as dorky as it sounds.

When I put on my headphones, I turn the volume down, preferring to pay attention to Kylie's reactions. I don't need to hear what they're saying to know what's happening. Kylie's face tells the whole story. Sometimes her brows pull together tightly or her eyes gloss with tears. A handful of times, she jumps in fright before her eyes dart to shrapnel marks on the concrete floors. But my favorite moments are when I see her happiness at crossing another item off her beloved bucket list in her smile.

It wouldn't matter if we're touring Alcatraz or eating grilled pickled sandwiches, the smile on her face when she crosses an item off her bucket list is the most rewarding part for me.

CHAPTER TWENTY-SIX

KYLIE

"Are you sure you don't want to stay?" I glance into Melanie's blue eyes, mine pleading. "Slater said you can stay as long as you like."

The elation I felt visiting Alcatraz was replaced with sadness when Slater and I walked into my hotel room to find Melanie had her bags packed and was ready to go home.

After briefly considering my request, Melanie shakes her head. "You two need privacy." She bumps me with her hip. "Besides, I achieved what I came here for, so now it's time for me to go home."

"You didn't do what you were supposed to do. You were *meant* to keep me in line." I give her a fake stern look. "You didn't do that. Since you arrived here, I've been forced to do many *hideous* activities against my wishes. Like playing spin the bottle, and I stayed out all night last night. I haven't slept for over thirty hours." My voice is dramatic. "Oh, and I may even fuck a drummer in the shower tonight."

She slaps my arm while giggling. "See, proof my work here is done."

"What about Marcus?" I keep my interrogation on the down low, ensuring Marcus and Slater won't overhear our conversation since they're in the living room.

When Melanie's eyes stray to Marcus, I smile. She's still got the lost puppy dog look her eyes held the night they met, but it's not as woeful now. It's got more grit behind it—like she's finally got a grip on her obsession. I doubt it, but she's certainly upped the caliber of her acting skills the past month.

"It's complicated." She bends down to pick up her suitcase before nudging her head to Marcus. "*He's* complicated. In a totally wicked way, but there's only so much a girl can do in a short amount of time."

When they notice Melanie has collected her suitcase, Slater and Marcus head our way. Marcus removes her bursting-at-the-seams suitcase from her grasp and walks toward the door while Slater lingers awkwardly at the side. He knows how much I'm hurting, but he doesn't have a clue how to fix it, and neither do I.

Deciding to use actions instead of words, I sling my arms around her tiny body and hug her fiercely.

"I love you too," she whispers in my ear, proving she understood my embrace. After dragging her finger down my crinkled nose, she shifts on her feet to face Slater. "Thanks for everything." She waves her hand around the room we've occupied the past week. "It's been a lot of fun."

Slater jerks up his chin before giving her a quick, friendly hug. When she whispers something in his ear, the worried expression on his face clears for a smile. "I will. I promise."

When Slater joins Marcus in the foyer to show Melanie the way out, I swear my heart cracks. This is even harder than it was the first time we said goodbye. I don't know why. I'm just stating what I'm feeling.

"Bye."

Our fingers lock and hold for her first three steps before my hand is left suspended in mid-air without my friend's touch to ease the flood filling my eyes. I lose the ability to hold back my tears when Slater closes the door with Melanie on the other side. They barely dribble onto my chin when Slater wraps me in his arms then walks us into the living room. He cradles me on his lap while running his thumbs under my eyes, battling to slow the torrent pouring out of them.

When his endeavor triples, he locks his nurturing brown eyes with mine. "I can tie her to the bed if you want?" His tone exposes he isn't joking. He'd do anything for me—even risk kidnapping charges.

I drag my hand under my nose to gather the contents before shaking my head. "It's okay. She wouldn't have left unless it were important."

"Then why are you crying?" He's not upset about my tears. He just hates them.

"She's really important to me. She's the only family I have."

Slater's brows furrow, but he remains quiet, suspicious the first time he visited the ranch was my last. He's right. I haven't spoken to my family in years. . .

To say my parents weren't impressed we missed dinner would be a major understatement. They were furious. My mom barely speaks a word to me, and my dad glares at me from across the table. Any time Slater attempts to spark a conversation with him, his responses are short and clipped. A few times, he doesn't even attempt a response.

When my parents announce they're going to bed, my dad's eyes lock with mine before he nudges his head to the stairwell, demanding I follow him. With reluctance and my anger at an all-time high, I kiss Slater on the cheek before following my parents to bed. I hate that they're treating me like a child when I'm an adult.

I'm lying in my bed for nearly an hour when someone taps on my bedroom door. "Come in." I keep my voice at a whisper, my intuition knowing it's Slater.

Two seconds later, he walks into my room, closing the door behind him. His bare feet are barely audible, but I lift my hand, signaling for him to stop. I know every creak my floor makes since it's been my room the prior twenty-one years.

"Step left," I say in a hushed whisper.

Slater smiles before taking a step to his left.

"Now two paces forward."

After five minutes, I guide him to my bed without a single creak of a floorboard. When I scoot over and lift my comforter, inviting him to join me, he unbuttons his jeans and removes his shirt.

My pussy tingles when he slides between the sheets, but it has nothing on the loud thump of my heart. "If my dad finds you in my bed, he'll shoot you."

I muffle his chuckles with my hand, mortified he's laughing. I'm not joking.

"I'm not going to do anything. I just want to snuggle with you." He bumps me with his shoulder, wordlessly demanding I roll over. When I do, he melds his back to mine, and I die a thousand deaths. Sweet Slater is just as tempting as the dominant alpha he unleashes in the bedroom.

When I wake the next morning, my sheets are still warm, but Slater has left my bed. We planned an early start since it's a seven-hour trip back to my college. I take a quick shower before going downstairs to discover him sitting in the kitchen, talking to my mom. I smile when she cautions him to be careful as the scrambled eggs she's serving him may be hot.

"Morning, Mom." I press a kiss on Slater's cheek before dropping my lips to his ear. "Good morning."

His lips curl into a lusty grin before he shovels a forkful of eggs into his mouth. When he moans, my mom smiles, loving his wordless praise.

For the next hour, the three of us sit in the kitchen, talking and eating the breakfast my mom prepares every morning for the boys once they've finished their morning chores. She makes bacon, eggs, fresh-baked bread, hash browns, and freshly cut fruit. You can survive days without eating after one of her famous breakfasts.

When Slater goes to collect his overnight bag from his room, my mom cozies up to my side. "I like him. Things got off on the wrong foot yesterday, but just the way he speaks of you shows he really respects you."

My heart rate soars as I hug her tight. I knew with time she'd see the huge heart Slater hides with his rough exterior. "He's a great guy, Mom. I..." My sentence falls short when I detect another presence in the room. Slater has returned from gathering his things.

After thanking my mom for her hospitality, his gaze turns to mine. "Meet you outside?"

I nod before dashing into my room to put on my boots and collect my helmet. I've just slipped my feet into my riding boots when a shadow darkens the doorway of my room that smells like Slater and me combined. It's an odd blend, but undeniably addictive.

"I'll drive you to school later today," states a male voice from the doorway.

When I lift my gaze, I spot Dylan leaning against my doorjamb. "It's okay. Slater is taking me back."

Once I finish tying the laces on my boots, I jump off my bed and attempt to skirt past Dylan. I say "attempt" because he steps to the side, blocking my exit from the room.

"I know why you're doing this. Why you're with someone like him." He spits out "him" as if it's a batch of fresh vomit. "But enough is enough. We get you don't want to be a rancher's wife, but you're taking this shit too far."

When I attempt to sidestep him, he grabs my wrist hard enough to leave a bruise. "Let me go!"

After yanking my wrist out of his grip, I gallop down the stairs. When I hop off the bottom step, I crash into the solid chest of my teeming-with-anger father. "Dylan will take you back to school."

I shake my head so fiercely, tears fall down my face. Slater is outside on his bike waiting for me.

"If you walk out that door, you walk out it for good," my dad warns, his voice a deep snarl.

My eyes snap to his, certain he's bluffing. He's my father, my own flesh and blood, yet he wants me to pick between him and the man I love.

"Peter." My mom strolls toward us, her eyes pleading. "She's our daughter; please don't do this."

"No, Mary. I will not allow someone like that to be a part of our family." He nudges his head to Slater during the "that" part of his comment.

My eyes rocket to my mom. Hers expose her devastation. She's as upset as me.

"I love him."

She nods, understanding I have no choice but also disappointed it's come to this. Tears slip down her cheeks when I throw my arms around her neck. "I love you. I will always love you."

Ignoring my dad's warning for me to choose wisely, I hug my mom for the final time, spin on my heels, then bolt out of the house as quickly as my quivering legs can take me. Slater's brows furrow when he notices me rushing toward him. No amount of fake smiling will hide the wetness careening down my face.

"Are you okay?" Unlike my father's vicious words, Slater's are crammed with worry.

I nod before hooking my leg over his bike. I curl my arms around his waist, then brace my cheek on his back, signaling for him to go. He squeezes my hand before kicking over his bike and slowly gliding it down my parents' long, dusty driveway. My mom's tear-stained face watches us the entire time.

Once we're on the main road, Slater adjusts his mirror so he can see my face. When he spots the tears still streaming down my pale cheeks, he pulls over. I lie and tell him I'm crying about leaving Misty, and that I'm upset I won't see her again for weeks. He chuckles before offering to bring me back to see her every weekend. That in itself proves I made the right decision choosing him. I'd always chose him, even knowing it might be the last time I'd speak to my family. . .

"I haven't seen my family since the day we left the ranch."

Slater remains quiet as his eyes drift over my face. I don't need to tell him why. He's been judged enough in his life, he already understands.

"When I left the cabin, Melanie took me in when I had nowhere else to go."

I'll be forever grateful to her for the day I turned up on her doorstep with nothing but an overnight bag and a bucket load of guilt. Even though we'd never met in person, she welcomed me into her home with open arms. We faced our darkest days together, and I truly don't believe I'd be here today if she hadn't been at my side.

CHAPTER TWENTY-SEVEN

KYLIE

Los Angeles

"Are you okay?" Emily rushes into the bathroom to pull down the wad of toilet paper stuffed under my nose. When she notices the blood gushing out, she grabs a roll of toilet paper out of the stall so I can replace my soaked-through one. "What happened?"

"Just some excited fans."

I could give her a more detailed explanation, but she doesn't need one. She knows how eager the fans get when the band is in the vicinity. When Marcus and Noah walked by the holding room, and a group of twenty women got frazzled by their presence, they charged for them. I tried to stop them. I received a harsh elbow to my nose for my efforts. I nearly retaliated with an equal amount of violence, but the blood pouring from my nose stopped me.

Emily waits for my bleeding to taper before pacing to the bathroom door she only entered five minutes ago. "I'll arrange for someone to take you to the hospital—"

"No, it's fine; I'm fine." The last expense I want added to my already vast collection is a hospital bill.

Emily's shoulders rise and fall twice before she spins around to face me. When I see the tears welling in her eyes, I take a step back. She looks truly devastated.

"It's not as bad as it looks," I assure her, trying to dampen the guilt tainting her beautiful face. "Although it hurts like a son of a bitch, I'm fairly sure my nose isn't broken."

She giggles at the mirth in my tone, but it does little to subdue her panic. "I'd feel better if you had someone look at it. You need an x-ray to ensure it isn't broken."

"It's not broken. I'm fine." When my assurance doesn't smooth the groove between her brows, I suck in a big breath before forcing out words I'd rather not speak. "I can't afford to go to the hospital." My shaky voice relays my embarrassment. "I don't have adequate health insurance."

My eyes dart away from hers, my pride severely beaten. Emily is already aware I'm not covered by Destiny Records' health insurance policy. It was the urgent matter she needed to discuss with me when we arrived in San Francisco. They sent her an email advising my claim for premium health insurance had been denied and that they were requesting I sign a waiver stating I understood I was not covered through their insurance company, and if I wished to stay employed, I'd have to seek my own personal protection within the next thirty days.

I've only had basic health coverage the past two years. It was one of the reasons I had so much trouble securing a job. Anytime I was successful, my premium health insurance was denied, then not long later, my position was made redundant. I've tried a few different options the past two weeks to get adequate coverage, but I've not yet been successful.

"You do have full health benefits." Emily's eyes float up from the ground to me before she whispers, "Noah is paying for it."

"Why?" My short reply can't conceal my thrashing heart.

After brushing away a tear that has fallen from her eye, she stares at me tenderly. "The insurance company sent your medical history records with the reason why they denied your claim."

I gasp, equally shocked and pissed off. Generally, they just deny my claims; they don't inform potential employees the reason why they rejected it. Now I understand why Emily has been looking at me differently the past few weeks, and why tears form in her eyes when they shift between Slater and me. She knows my secret.

She all but confirms it by asking, "Does Slater know?"

When I shake my head, an annoying tear topples down my cheek.

"Is it the reason you left him?"

My lips tremble as I jerk up my chin, answering her without words.

"Oh, Kylie, you need to tell him. He deserves to know."

"I've tried." My voice is as weak as my efforts the past two weeks. "He keeps telling me to leave the past in the past."

When more frustrating tears fall from my eyes, Emily engulfs me in her tiny arms. She rubs my back in a soothing manner while whispering her apologies in my ear.

Not even two seconds later, the bathroom door shoots open so fast, it nearly comes off the hinges. Slater charges inside, his face marred with panic. "Kylie, are you okay? Noah just told me what happened."

When he tugs me back so he can inspect my damaged nose, Emily glides her hand down my arm before stealthily making her way to the exit.

I stop eyeballing her departure when Slater sucks in a sharp breath "What the fuck?" His eyes rocket in the direction I was just peering. "You need to hire more security. This shit isn't acceptable."

Understanding Slater's anger isn't really for her, Emily nods before walking through the door, closing it behind her. Not speaking a word, Slater lifts me to sit on the counter before carefully pulling away the tissues stuffed under my nose. My nose went numb ages ago, but I'm confident it's still bleeding. It isn't just the slightest trickle running over my lips that gives it away. It's the devastated look on Slater's face.

"I'm fine. It doesn't hurt."

He rolls his eyes before wetting two paper towels. Once they're damp, he drags them across the blood that has dried under my nose. The harshness of the gritty material running across my top lip reminds me how his stubble scratches me when he kisses me. The last two weeks have been a fairytale. It's as if the last two years never happened. Our relationship has returned to how it was before we spent the weekend at the cabin.

We spend every waking moment together, ensuring we make up for the time we lost. I rode with Slater on his bike to Los Angeles, denying Emily's pleas to go in the tour bus with the girls. We took advantage of the beautiful ocean views along the way by stopping to snap numerous candid shots. We had lunch at Nepenthe. The views of the ocean stretched for miles. It was truly breathtaking.

When we arrived in Los Angeles, Slater asked if I wanted my own room or if I'd like to bunk with him. It was mean of me to contemplate his question for as long as I did, but I couldn't help but tease him. He loves riling people up, but he hates when they return the favor.

After putting him out of his misery by agreeing to share his room, we settled into a routine rather quickly. It's been perfect, everything I could have ever wished for, but no matter how many times I try to bring up the past, he shoots me down by saying he wants to leave the past in the past.

My focus shifts back to Slater when he grumbles, "Did she have an elbow the size of a truck?"

Once he has the blood cleared away, he pushes his thumbs on each side of my nose.

"Sorry," he apologizes when I grimace. "It's going to bruise, but I don't think it's broken."

I nod. "I told Emily it wasn't broken." I sound extra throaty since my nostrils are blocked from swelling.

"I thought you would have learned by now not to get in the way of fans and their idols." Although his voice is still laced with anger, it isn't as strong as earlier.

When I giggle, the cheeky glimmer that usually fires in his eyes returns. After gathering the bloodied tissues to dump them into the trash, he helps me down from the countertop. Warmth blooms across my chest when he cocoons me with his thick, tattooed arms. I feel so loved and protected, my earlier confession to Emily isn't the only one I'm professing today.

"I love you, Slater."

I never stopped loving him, but this is the first time I've said it since we've been back together. He stiffens before he inches back so he can lower his eyes to mine. I'm panicked... until I see the mammoth grin he's wearing.

"I love you too," he replies.

I balk, shocked. He never said it back. Not once. Not even when I begged him to the night at the cabin.

I'm bitch-slapped for the second time when the reason for his backflip smacks into me. I've often wondered if he thought I left him because of the fight we had over Jenni. That isn't why I left him—it isn't even close.

"I didn't leave you because of Jenni."

When he attempts to render me speechless with his sinful lips, I step back. What I need to say should have been said years ago, so I can't hold it back for a second longer. I don't want to hurt him, but it's time for him to learn the truth. I want him to know. I *need* him to know.

"I didn't leave you because of Jenni," I say again, my voice quivering when I see the panic in his eyes. "I left because of Serena."

His brows pull together as confusion clusters in his eyes. . .

My heart beats at an unnatural rhythm when I assess the photo Slater is holding in front of me. It's faded and looks dated, but the girl smiling in the picture looks so similar to Jenni, it's spookily eerie.

I remove the photo from his tight grip so I can scrutinize it more diligently. The girl appears to be in her early teens. Her light blue eyes shine just as brightly as her smile, and her lips and nose are identical to Jenni's in every way, but instead of having Jenni's strawberry blonde hair, she has a satin scarf wrapped around her head.

"That's my sister Serena." Slater's tone is off. He sounds both upset and proud. I discover why when he adds on, "She died nearly eleven years ago."

"I'm so sorry." My eyes fill with tears as guilt slams into me. "I should have never accused you. I'm truly sorry for the way I reacted."

I've been apprehensive about Slater's relationship with Jenni the past few months. The messages they shared don't seem more than two friends talking, but they're constant, usually two to three times a day. Then when I overheard him say he loves her and that he'd look after her, I overreacted. I'm already afraid of losing him, and his declaration created more doubt for my stupid theory. I've told him for months that I love him, but he's never said it back. Just from looking at his photo I have a better understanding of his relationship with Jenni.

"Don't apologize; you didn't know. I should have told you about her months ago." He presses his lips to my temple, relief that I believe him all over his face.

"What happened to her?" I sit on the end of the bed, unable to tear my eyes away from Serena's photo. She's incredibly beautiful, but so young, and I hate that her life was cut so short.

After sitting next to me, Slater curls his arm around my waist before glancing down at her photo. "She had ALL, Acute Lymphoblastic—"

"Leukemia," we say at the same time.

As my lungs fight for air, I struggle to keep my emotions under control. It's a woeful waste of time. Tears fall down my face so hard and fast, my hands can't keep up with them.

"She died six days after her thirteenth birthday. That photo was taken on her birthday," Slater informs me. "I know Jenni isn't Serena, but I can't help but treat her like she is. She looks so much like her, I struggle remembering she's not."

"I'm so sorry," I say again, except this time I'm not just apologizing for his loss, I'm apologizing for my appalling behavior. "Please forgive me; I'm truly sorry."

My heart aches so much, it feels like someone is squeezing it tightly. As my lungs continue to fight for air, my breathing becomes shallow and panicked. When Slater hears my wheezy breaths, he removes Serena's photo from my grasp and places it on the bedspread. He then tugs me onto his lap before encouraging me to take in some deep breaths.

"You're alright. Just keep breathing, baby."

He rubs one hand down my back, while the other wipes away my tears. I try to form words, to say something that would express to him how sorry I am for everything I've done, but I can't form any words. The only sounds I can make are my gasps as I fight to fill my lungs with oxygen. I know he loves me, but it hurt hearing him say it to Jenni. Even though he shows me every day that he cares for me, I selfishly wanted to hear it as well. Now I just feel terrible.

Since the only word I can form is "sorry," I say it to him over and over again until exhaustion overtakes me, and I fall asleep in Slater's arms.

A few hours later, I wake up startled. Slater's back is braced against the headboard, and I'm still cradled in his arms. The steady rhythm of his breathing indicates he's asleep. It's restless but still undeniable. I sit quietly, staring at his face for nearly an hour before I finally work up the courage to slip out of his embrace.

He murmurs something in his sleep when I press a kiss on his plump, warm lips. "Goodbye, Slater."

After gathering my bag, I make my way out of the cabin, my heart breaking more with every step I take. . .

Slater releases a deep, harsh breath, like someone just punched him in the stomach when I confess, "I was first diagnosed with ALL when I was thirteen." My scratchy voice reveals the barrage of emotions I was hammered with while reflecting back on my memories. "The second time was two months before we went to the cabin."

When Slater's fists clench so fast, the air ripples, I drop my eyes to his chest, unable to maintain his eye contact. I don't need to see him to feel his anger, though. I hear it in his hissed words. "Why didn't you tell me?!"

He doesn't wait for me to answer him. It's for the best. He's too worked up to process facts over fear right now anyway. He paces back and forth while struggling to figure out if he's pissed or devastated. He could possibly be a bit of both.

"I would have been there for you!" The veins in his fists bulge with every word he speaks. "I *could* have been there for you!"

He stops pacing when I murmur, "That's why I didn't tell you. I loved you, and I was reasonably sure you loved me too, but our relationship was about fun and adventure. It wasn't about hospital visits and doctor's appointments. And it most certainly wasn't about death. I was petrified, Slater. Not just about dying, but losing you as well. Every week I convinced myself I either had to tell you the truth or give you up, and every weekend, my heart overruled my head. You can't deny what your heart wants, and my heart wanted you more than anything in the world."

When I lock my eyes with Slater's, the pain darkening his breaks my heart. I hate seeing him so vulnerable, but it doesn't change my viewpoint. There are so many things I wish I could go back and change, but this isn't one of them. I'm disgusted at myself for the cowardly way I left, but I'll never regret my decision. Slater deserved the world—even if it meant I couldn't be a part of it.

"When I found out about Serena, I realized how selfish I had been keeping my sickness from you, but I also knew I couldn't put you through that type of heartache again."

"That wasn't your choice to make, Kylie." He clenches and

unclenches his fists as he fights to ignore the moisture teeming in his eyes. "That wasn't your fucking choice."

"You would have given it all away. Everything you and the band had worked for, you would have left it all behind." He shakes his head, denying my claims, but I don't back down. "Yes, you would have! But I refused to do that to you, Slater. I loved you too much to make you face that type of heartache again."

The pain in his eyes when he talked about his sister was all the proof I needed that he would have given up everything to stay with me while I battled through my illness, but I couldn't do that to him. I loved him too much. It killed me walking away from him how I did, but it was the right thing to do. He had worked too hard for too long to give up his dreams, so I made a decision for the both of us—the right decision.

"You can hate me for what I did, for how I walked away, but don't *ever* believe I intentionally set out to hurt you. That was *never* my intention."

"I don't hate you." His voice is less brittle than it was earlier, but ten times more gravelly. "I love you, Kylie. I have since the day you walked into the Bar N Barrel."

"Then you know why I had to do what I did? Why I had to put you above me?"

I choke back a sob when he nods. It isn't a confident nod, but it's still a nod nonetheless.

CHAPTER TWENTY-EIGHT

SLATER

I swear my cock notices Kylie entering the room before my brain registers it. When I adjust my crotch, wordlessly warning him to calm the fuck down, Kylie friskily winks before following Emily to the far back corner of the meet and greet room. This meet and greet has been going for nearly three hours, and I'm dying to get out of here. My hands aren't just sore from drumming for two hours straight, they're aching from signing so many autographs. I need someone to invent some sort of contraption that can sign on my behalf because this shit is getting old real quick. I'll forever love our fans, but I'm a drummer, not a writer, so I'm more than happy to leave the writer's cramp to them.

Things have been great between Kylie and me the past few weeks. Actually, it's better than great. It's fucking perfect. *She's perfect.* The only low point was when she told me she had ALL—not once, but twice.

It killed me knowing she kept that from me. The night she confessed gutted me so much, I struggled to hold in my tears. I don't cry; I never cry, not even when my sister died, but when Kylie said she had the same disease that snatched Serena from my family way too early, I couldn't stop tears from forming. Just the thought of losing Kylie scared the shit out of me. *It still does.*

I was deceitful when I said I wouldn't have given everything up. I would have given it all away in an instant when I found out she was sick. There was no way I would have gone on the road for weeks at a time, leaving her at home sick and alone. I would have never done that to her. I fell in love with her from the moment I saw her. She was all I ever wanted, and she would have always been my number one priority. So as much as it hurt that she made the decision for me, I understand why she did it. She did it to save me, so even though I really wish she would have saved us, I also understand how different my life would be if she had done that.

Some good came from our heart to heart. I got to tell Kylie that I love her. She was shocked but aware I didn't say it because I felt forced. I said it because I truly mean it. After she left me, I realized how stupid I had been letting my ex control my feelings. I didn't know what love truly meant until I met Kylie, so I won't go another day without telling her what she means to me. I'll tell her I love her until she's sick of hearing it, then I'll tell her some more.

Kylie was open and honest with me last week, so I've been trying to do the same ever since. She's being sly by using the trick I used on her against me. Any time I try to bring up the past, she sexually tortures me until my cock overrules my head.

"It's in the past; can't we just leave it there?" she continues to quote.

One day my cock won't be so mesmerized by her, and I'll have the chance to explain all the shit I've done the past few years.

Ha! Who the fuck am I kidding? My cock will never get enough of her.

I chuckle to myself while signing a final concert poster for a fan. After handing it back to her, I stand from my seat, eager to stretch my legs since I've been sitting for the past several hours.

She squeals loud enough for three states over to hear before hugging the poster close to her barely covered chest. "Thank you so much! I'm a huge fan—your number one fan."

"That's great to hear. Thanks for coming to our show."

The blonde flutters her eyelashes as she twirls a piece of hair around her index finger.

Here it comes. The same thing that happens at the end of every concert.

"Do you want to get out of here?" She licks her top lip as her lust-filled eyes bore into mine. "I have a hotel room one block over."

Just as I am about to reply, a stern cough sounds over my shoulder. I don't need to turn around to know who's there, I can sense her a mile away, but I do because I love when she gets riled up with jealousy.

When I crank my neck back, my suspicions are confirmed. Kylie is standing firmly with her tiny hands on her cocked hips, and her narrowed eyes are shooting daggers at the blonde. Let me tell you, jealousy has never looked so fucking good.

I don't need to decline the blonde's invitation. Even someone with air for brains has no trouble deciphering the tension bristling between Kylie and me. It's so fucking hot, the blonde's annoyed huff when she storms away makes it feel like I'm sitting on a furnace.

When I take a step in Kylie's direction, she stops monitoring the blonde's departure to lock her eyes with mine. Now instead of being narrowed, they're wide with desire. I arch my brow, wondering if she'll make me chase her like she usually does, or if she'll stand firm. When I spot the corners of her mouth lifting, I know she's going to run. *Yee-fuckin'-ha!*

She makes it all the way to the stage before my long strides catch up with her. When I band my arms around her waist and hoist her off the ground, her squeals echo around the empty stadium, startling a few of the stagehands. She loves being chased, and I love nothing more than chasing her.

After pinning her to a wall at the side of the stage, I seal my mouth over hers. Our kiss starts slow, but when she parts her lips to let my tongue slip inside, it ramps up in intensity. I kiss her with everything I have, certain I'll never get enough of her delicious taste.

While my zipper bites my cock, I move us into the wings of the stage, not wanting any spectators to see our hot and heavy make out session. I love making Kylie quiver and shake, but I sure as fuck ain't letting any other man get in on the action—even if he keeps his hands to himself. If he wants to jerk off, he better go watch porn, because that's the only guarantee he'll end the night without my baseball bat rammed up his ass.

When I break through the thick curtains at the side of the stage, Kylie yanks her lips away from mine. Anyone would swear it was me pulling back from how loud she whimpers. She doesn't need to speak for me to hear her torment. I can see it in her eyes. I'm also aware any time I try to coerce her into going further backstage, she shoots me down like getting hot and heavy with a drummer backstage at a concert isn't on her bucket list.

I showered Melanie with thankful texts when Kylie showed me the items she had added to her list. When we crossed off number one hundred fifty-five—*the best limo ride I've ever had in my life!*—I sent her the hugest bouquet of flowers I could order, but any time I encourage Kylie to cross off number one hundred fifty-three, she denies my advances. I have no clue why, but it's giving me a severe case of blue balls.

"I'd never let anyone see you." There's no chance in hell I'd ever let that happen. I'd *never* let another man see skin that belongs to me.

"I know that." Kylie drags her teeth over her bottom lip, amplifying their plumpness. "I just don't want to do anything *here*." She emphasizes the "here" part of her statement with a hint of bitterness.

"Why?" I question, curious as to why her eyes are clouded with more jealousy now than they had when the blonde propositioned me. "It's on your list, so why don't you want to cross it off?" I smile a grin that reveals the cocky bastard I am under the tattoos and dreadlocked hair. "You've also never been shy, so out with it, spill the *real* reason you don't want to get frisky in public."

When her eyes stray to my chest, I roll my hips. As my cock becomes friendly with the heat between her legs, her eyes snap back to mine. They reveal what I'm saying is true—she isn't shy by any means—but they also expose that she's hesitant.

"It has something to do with me, doesn't it?"

She wiggles, trying to lower her legs. I hold on tightly, denying her request. She huffs and attempts to cross her arms in front of her chest. Her efforts are fruitless. We're standing so close to one another, even her scrawny arms can't fit between us.

When her eyes drift back down to my chest, I lift her chin, forcing her eyes back to mine before cocking my brow, wordlessly demanding an explanation. She rolls her eyes, ignoring my request. I rock my hips upward four times. She groans and snaps her eyes back to mine, pissed I'm using her attraction to me against her but having no defense against it.

I arch my brow again, implying I'll tease her until she tells me what I want to know. "I've got nowhere to be and enough adrenaline surging through my blood to last three nights, Kylie, so either confess now, or when you're so fucking tired, we won't be able to put your jealousy to good use."

"Fine!" she drawls out the one word as if it's an entire sentence. "I saw the whole... *stage curtain* incident." She air quotes the words "stage curtain."

Although I'm smug as fuck she took my threat as literal, I'm still stumped as to what she means. "What stage curtain incident?"

She takes in numerous deep breaths, her breasts thrusting out with every inhalation before she breathes out, "In San Diego."

I give her a look, indicating I don't have a fucking clue what she's talking about. "You're going to need to spell it out for me, because I'm fucking lost on where you're going. That's not surprising; you're shit at giving directions."

She nearly smiles until the reason for our conversation crashes back into her. "I saw you with a groupie in San Diego." Her words are barely whispers but crammed with palpable anger.

"What groupie?" I cringe when my question comes out snappier than I expected. I'm not angry at her, just still clueless as to why she's so riled up.

She wiggles her hips, once again requesting to be put down. I reluctantly set her back on her feet before pressing my palms against the wall behind her head, trapping her in front of me. "What groupie?"

She glares at me while snarling, "I didn't think to get her name." My jaw muscle quivers when she bobs under my arm before making a beeline toward my dressing room. "You probably didn't either."

I seize her wrist and pull her back to me. She huffs again while folding her arms in front of her chest. My eyes dart down to her cleavage. I can't help it. I'm a guy, and she has fantastic tits.

When she notices the direction of my gaze, she tries to hold in her smile. She fails miserably. She loves the effect her body has on mine.

I give her a few moments to gather her composure before confessing, "I haven't fucked a groupie in weeks." I'd like to say months, but unfortunately, I can't.

My brows furrow when Kylie mutters, "You weren't fucking," under her breath.

"I haven't *touched* a groupie in weeks," I clarify.

She murmurs something under her breath again, except this time, it isn't loud enough for me to hear.

"What?"

When her eyes dart away, I growl before warning her I won't hesitate to pin her to the wall and punish her with my cock until she tells me every damn secret I see hiding in her eyes.

Finally catching the drift on how things are about to go down, Kylie's eyes snap to mine before waving her hand at the lower half of my body. "I saw a groupie attached to.... *that.*"

My eyes widen. "When?"

I hate even admitting this, but excluding Kylie, no one but the waitress in the San Diego nightclub has sucked my dick the past two months.

When Kylie whispers, "Opening night," I shake my head.

Her nostrils flare. "I saw you, Slater—"

"It wasn't me." I crowd her against the wall, ensuring she can feel my pulse racing through my body when I say, "I haven't touched or fucked a groupie since I saw tears in your eyes when I walked out of the bathroom in the nightclub in San Diego. Seeing you on the verge of crying gutted me, Kylie. I'd never felt dirty, but I did that night." When she peers up at me with big, glistening eyes, I finalize my assurance. "I've never lied to you, so why would I start now? There hasn't been anyone since then, I swear to you."

"What about the lipstick on your shirt? It was the same night." Her words aren't as bitter as they were earlier. They're more curious than anything.

"If I had to change my shirt every time a fan got a little excited, I'd have a million shirts. You know what they're like. The elbow your nose got hit with last week is a prime example of the people I handle at the end of every show."

"But he said... You had lipstick... They were your boots, weren't they?"

Since she appears to be interrogating herself, I don't offer answers to her blubbered questions. I just wait for the truth to dawn in her eyes. It's a very short three seconds.

"Sonny!"

With her fist clenched into balls, she storms through the stage curtains. I quickly follow behind her. She's not responding like I hoped, but a feisty Kylie is just as seductive as the Kylie I was trying to convince to get freaky with me backstage.

Her angry strides are so long, it doesn't take her much time to reach the makeshift table the roadies circle at the end of every concert. Sonny spots her the instant she walks into the room. That pisses me off more than the concerned glint his eyes gets when he sees the angry red streaks lining her face.

"You okay?" He gets within two feet of Kylie when she rears back her hand to slap him hard across the face. The crack of her hand connecting with his cheek booms around the room. It's closely followed by the roar of a drunken road crew.

Sonny recoils, shocked by Kylie's brutality, but the confusion in his eyes clears way when she sneers, "It wasn't Slater behind the curtain, was it?"

Sonny shrugs, acting innocent. It's a pity for him Kylie wasn't born last week. "Who did you use to fool me into believing it was Slater?"

Sonny's throat works hard to swallow but he remains as quiet as a church mouse. It's a shame his minions didn't understand his vow of silence was meant to extend to them.

"That was me." Mark's slur exposes the level of his intoxication.

"Shut up!" Sonny glares at Mark like he's seconds from dissecting his nuts via his throat.

"What?" Mark sounds confused. "You told me to get Slater's boots out of his dressing room, then you found that hot groupie, remember?"

When his eyes gloss over like he's recalling a fond memory, my jaw tenses. I'm not pissed he got a blowjob from a groupie—that's a perk of the entertainment industry—it's the fact Sonny set me up, no doubt in the hope it would have Kylie warming his sheets.

As Kylie slaps Sonny again, hard enough to leave a mark, I storm toward him, ready to unleash my own form of punishment. Just as I grab the scruff of his shirt, Kylie slips between us, suspending my fist midair. "I've handled it."

Her eyes dance between mine. They're fired by a unique mix of panic and happiness. I know where her panic resides from—I'm seconds from beating the living shit out of Sonny—but I'm stumped by her gleeful glint. I honestly can't tell if she's happy she taught Sonny a lesson or because Mark's confession proves I haven't had *any* contact with *any* groupies since she arrived back in the picture. I guess it doesn't really matter. Either way, I love the brightness her eyes hold.

After curling one hand over my fist sitting mere inches from

Sonny's cheek, she flattens her other one over my heart. "I think it's time for us to cross number one hundred fifty-three off my list, don't you agree?"

My cock stiffens when the worry in her eyes switches to hunger. She's panting so hard, her breasts thrust up and down with every breath she takes, and her cheeks are flushed, exposing her arousal. She's the hottest I've ever seen her.

"Let it go, Slater. He isn't worth it. You, though, are worth every minute of every day."

She weakens me, but in a way I don't mind.

After lowering my fist, I lock my eyes with Sonny over Kylie's shoulder. "You're lucky I have more pressing things to handle right now." I nudge my head to the exit sign illuminated in the far right of the space. "Pack your shit. You're fucking done."

I throw Kylie over my shoulder before charging for my dressing room, taking a mental note to send Melanie Marcus for a week after crossing this one off.

CHAPTER TWENTY-NINE

KYLIE

"Stop it."

I slap Slater's arm, simmering his chuckles from Jacob getting busted teaching Noah's daughter, Maddie, how to flip the bird. We're gathered in Noah and Emily's cabin for Maddison's first birthday. The rest of the band traveled back to their hometown two days ago, but Slater and I stayed in Los Angeles so we could cross a few more items off my list. We flew in this morning and headed straight to the cabin.

My return to this side of the country was a stark contrast to my trip two years ago. When I traveled to Melanie's condo, I caught the bus. It was an exhausting forty-eight-hour trip, but it was the only way I could afford to get to the other side of the country. I used a majority of my savings having the windows on Jenni's BMW replaced after Nick took to them with Slater's baseball bat. I felt incredibly guilty for the way I behaved the night before, but since I couldn't offer my apologies in person, I had to get inventive. It was an expensive apology, but the relief it came with lightened my shoulders.

I arrived at the bus station preparing to buy a ticket to travel back to the ranch. I had nowhere else to go and figured my dad would welcome me home if I turned up with my tail firmly planted between my legs. Just as I strolled up to the ticket counter, Melanie called me. The odd hour of her call wasn't unusual. Even now she forgets the time difference between our states. When I answered, she squealed so loud, even the homeless beggar outside the bus station heard her. She was drunk dialing me—again! She had done it at least a hundred times since our friendship started.

When I burst into tears, her happy slurs stopped. There's nothing more sobering than the gut-wrenching sobs of a heartbroken woman. After telling her everything that had happened, minus the detail that I was leaving an up-and-coming rock god, Melanie invited me to stay with her.

I originally declined her invitation. "I can't travel across the country on a whim."

"Why not?" she asked.

I went silent for a few minutes, trying to think of a legitimate excuse.

"What have you got to lose?"

"Nothing—"

"Exactly!" she said.

And just like that, the decision was made. I turned up on her doorstep two days later wearing the same clothes I left the cabin in.

Melanie and I met on an online forum for people diagnosed with ALL. She was diagnosed just shy of her twenty-first birthday and went into remission two years later. We were in Seattle celebrating her remission, and it was our final hurrah before we had to reenter the daunting world known as "life."

Even via an internet connection, Melanie and I had an instant bond—just like I did with Slater. When we met face to face for the first time, I realized why we clicked so well. Melanie is a female version of Slater down to the most minute details.

Slater tried to brush off my confession with a laugh when I told him about their similarities last week, but after hitting him with evidence after evidence after evidence, not even he could deny their likeness. I hate that Melanie became my crutch right at the time I had to leave Slater without a leg to stand on, but I'm also grateful. I honestly don't know what I would have done if she hadn't offered me a place to stay and a shoulder to cry on.

My thoughts are pulled back into the present when Slater bands his arms around my waist and draws me close. "Do you wanna go for a swim?"

My eyes snap up to his. "Isn't that the pool they got married on?" I keep my volume on the down low, praying Emily and Noah won't overhear our conversation. How was I to know when we were christening a random pool, they'd buy the cabin and get married on it?

"It's a bit late to be worried about that now, isn't it?"

When Slater pulls me back so I can feel his erection straining against his zipper, I scan the room. Noah is talking to Jacob on the sofa; Emily and Lola are replenishing the snack tables, and Jenni and Nick are playing with Jasper on the ground. A handful of people are hanging around the large living area, but I only recognize Maggie, and she's too busy taking photos to notice us slipping out the side entrance to relive memories that kept me warm two winters in a row.

"Five minutes." After spinning in his arms the best I can since he's holding on tight, I press a quick kiss on Slater's smiling lips. "And I mean five minutes this time."

His lips curl against mine before he jerks up his chin. After a final scan of the room, I slip outside unnoticed. Within seconds, Slater is on my tail.

He's forever impatient.

"What?" When he drags his lips down my neck, goosebumps rise in their wake. "You have no idea how many times I've stroked my cock to this very memory."

I groan. "I may have flicked the bean on an occasion or two."

"Fuck me, Kylie." He grinds against my ass almost brutally as a growl rumbles in his chest. "Do you want me to come in my pants?"

"I'd rather you do it in my pussy, but whatever floats your boat."

He growls again, but this one is more painful than his first.

I slant my head back to peer up at him. He looks seconds from being sick. "What is it?"

"I don't have any condoms left. We used the last one on the plane."

I shouldn't smirk, but I do. Joining the mile high club is as riveting as it sounds. Most likely because we had access to the business class bathrooms, but either way, it was a fun task to cross off my list.

"Then we'll fool around like naughty teens whose parents are sleeping only one room over." I open the pool gate before steering him toward the double cabana at one side. They're an addition the pool room didn't have the last time I was here.

"Or I could just fuck you without one—"

"Slater, don't. You have rules, and I'm fine with that."

He sits on the padded cabana seat before pulling me down so I'm straddling his lap. "My rules don't apply to you."

"Why, because I'm the reason you made them?"

I gasp in a sharp breath when he nods. "I originally made them for these." He runs his index finger over my lips. "But these will need their own set of rules as well." His hand drops to the buds straining against my thin shirt. "Then we'll throw an entire fucking book at the area getting warmer the more I speak."

"It's always hot and slippery around you. I can't help it. You make me want to be all types of naughty."

He drags his teeth over his lower lip in a totally sexy way. "Show me."

The way he makes me feel invincible is displayed in the most glorious way when I slip off his lap and scoot back until my back is flush with the thick material of the cabana. With my eyes locked on his, I sweep open my thighs. Mere years ago, I would have never been bold enough to do something so wickedly deviant. Now, I'd do anything to keep the spark his eyes are holding. They may be brimming with lust, but I'm paying more attention to the glint hiding deep beneath their hungry haze.

I shiver at the growl that rolls up Slater's chest when I slip my panties to the side. I could take them off entirely, but this feels more risqué, like we're seconds from being busted. The thrill adds to the heat pumping through my veins.

His tongue slides across his lips, following the trail my finger makes down the nude lips of my pussy. I waxed mere days ago, meaning every glistening inch of me is exposed to his ravenous eyes.

"Do it," he whispers when the tip of my finger breaks through the seal of my throbbing sex. "Fuck yourself there."

We moan in sync when I slip my finger inside myself. My finger is nowhere near as girthy as Slater's but it still feels phenomenal. That probably has more to do with Slater's cock springing out of his jeans than anything else. He's the thickest I've seen him, his head as purple as my helmet.

"Keep going," he encourages, inching closer to me. "But also do this." My back arches when he adjusts my hand so my palm grinds down on my clit with every pump my finger does. "Feel good?"

"Uh-huh."

I thrust my finger in deeper when he fists his big, thick cock. He strokes it at a speed matching my pumps, a brutal fucking pace that leaves no doubt to how unhinged we are for one another. We're still fully clothed, with only the most intimate parts of our bodies on display, but the energy is electrifying. I can imagine how the hard bumps in his stomach are contracting as he rocks his hips like he does while fucking me, and how he always adds an extra flick to his pumps to ensure he hits the sweet spot inside of me.

My fingertip doesn't come close to the reach his cock gets, but my imagination is wonderous, and it soon has me racing toward climax. My leisurely jog breaks into a sprint when the scruff on Slater's chin scratches my inner thigh. He knows I'm close, and he's not willing to let an orgasm slip away without getting a taste of the sweetness he's consumed a minimum of once a day the past five weeks. The thought alone sets me off.

With my fingers stilled and my ass lifted off the cabana, I thrust my quivering sex into his face, mashing it with his mouth. As I call his name into the warm night air, Slater drags his tongue up my glistening slit and around my stationary digit before flicking it over the bud, sending delicious zaps over every inch of my body.

CHAPTER THIRTY

KYLIE

"I don't know what I find sexier." My eyes turn to Slater sitting in the passenger seat of his car. "You on your bike or in this car."

Grinning, he revs his engine, sending a nice purr through my seat. The tingling sensation mimics the ones my pussy was hit with when he slid behind the steering wheel of his sexy dark gray car. I don't know much about cars, but this one is nearly as gorgeous as its driver.

I keep my eyes on Slater's profile the entire thirty-minute trip from Noah's cabin to Slater's condo. I'm not the only one gawking. His eyes continually flash over to mine as well. Once I bust his perverted gaze, he awards me a quick smirk before returning his focus to the road. I'm glad he hasn't been treating me differently since he found out my secret. Most people act awkward, like I'm breakable or something. Dylan did. My friends did. Even my parents did. The only ones who haven't are Melanie and Slater. They still treat me as if I am me, not someone who was dying. Just me.

My eyes go crazy when we pull into an apartment building near the docks. The building is a warehouse conversion with exposed brickwork and black steel features. It suits Slater to a T: tough, rugged, and gorgeous.

After jabbing a button inside his glove compartment, his hand brushing my thigh on the way by, a black roller door cranks open, exposing an underground garage. Upon entering, I scan a handful of top-of-the-line cars and bikes in the garage. Only extremely wealthy people must live in this building because their rides scream money.

Slater pulls into an empty space before jogging around the car to assist me out. I'd comment on his chivalry if I didn't know the underhanded reason for it. He knows how weak my legs are, because he made them that way.

He grasps my hand in his before guiding me into an idling elevator at our right. Its car is so small in size, the sexual energy bouncing between us is even more prominent than normal. My nape beads with sweat while my thighs wobble. I love that even weeks of constant contact haven't dampen our eagerness. He wants me now as much as I craved him every day for the past two years. We have zero self-control.

The vision of him driving his sexy car is enough to have the air crackling with energy, much less the wicked event we undertook a mere hour ago. Both mind-hazing deeds are in the forefront of my mind when I whisper, "At least there's no elevator attendant this time around."

When his eyes snap to mine, my pulse quickens. His gaze is predatory and reveals he has his target locked. Within seconds, I'm pushed up against the elevator wall, and his delicious lips are exploring my mouth as if it's the first time he's sampled it. This kiss goes against all the other kisses we've shared. He didn't just steal the land from beneath my feet at the Bar N Barrel all those months ago, he confiscated my heart as well.

When he inches back, I whimper. While mumbling a curse word under his breath, his eyes drift to a security camera dome mounted in the corner of the elevator. He stares at it for several heart-thrashing seconds before his eyes return to me. When my tongue delves out to moisten my lips, he groans. I'm not meaning to tease him. My mouth just dried up from the way he's staring at me with hungry, hankering eyes.

My heart rate jumps up when he smirks a sinfully delicious smile. After tugging his shirt over his head, he hooks it over the camera, grinning when it covers the dome with only one throw. My giggle shifts to a moan as his lips become friendly with my collarbone.

I'm just as eager, but I'm not sure if my heart can take another risqué adventure this afternoon. "Your shirt took care of the camera, but what about your neighbors?" I don't want to make things awkward for him if other tenants walk in on us.

His hand slips up the back of my shirt to undo my bra with one quick flick. "There are no other occupants. I own the building."

My jaw falls open. Not just because his confession means every pricey car I just absorbed is his, but because he undid my bra so quickly.

His lips lift against my skin when he feels my pulse fluttering in my neck. "I'm all about the beats, baby."

He taps his hands on the curves of my breasts in a beat that matches Rise Up's very first chart-topping hit, "Surrender Me."

"Except now. This is going to be hard and fast so we're done before my security guy figures out he has x-ray vision." He drops his jeans to his knees, slips my panties to the side as I did only an hour ago, braces his forehead against mine, then drives home. "Fuck me, Kylie. I swear it gets better every time I take you."

After adjusting my hips, he picks up his pace, pounding into me on repeat until I scream his name during a blinding, terrifying orgasm fifteen minutes later. It shreds me of everything I have, leaving no doubt I've never exploded like I am now. I'm quivering all over. My mouth is dry, and my body is drenched with sweat.

Just when I think I've got ahold of myself, his cock pulsates as he reaches release. I tighten around him, milking him of every drop of his cum. His grinds slow to a pace that steadies the arrhythmia of my heart.

I feel his lips rising against my skin once more before he drags them down my cheek. "Only you can make me crave another round while I'm still inside you." His twitching cock exposes the truth of his statement. He just came, yet he's still hard as a rock.

"How about a tour first, then we'll see where the evening takes us?"

He nips at my lips, my neck, and my collarbone before sliding his cock out of me. My panties slip back into place when he sets me on my feet, but the clench of my thighs from seeing our joint arousal on his cock makes a quick mess out of them. The first time we had unprotected sex was when we were in a pool, so it didn't have this same messy all-encompassing feeling. When I left Slater, I never thought I'd experience this type of happiness again, so I'm eternally grateful.

Slater tucks his cock back into his jeans before locking his eyes with mine. "You good?"

I jerk up my chin. I'm more than good. I feel fantastic.

With a smile that reveals he heard my thoughts, he snags his shirt from the camera dome before guiding me out of the sex-scented elevator car. My erratic heart I've just settled down beeps at a new pace when we enter his massive loft. The inside matches the exterior, with exposed brick and black steel in abundance. The kitchen is done in black marble and sits in the far right-hand corner, and the windows looking over the bay are floor-to-ceiling. All the furniture is very masculine and black. Leather sofas, a dining room table, custom drum kit, and a slate billiard table fills the space. It screams bachelor pad, but in a sexy *I'm a man* type of way.

"How many rooms do you have?" His loft is massive, but it's very open with only two doors on the far left-hand side.

Slater grins while holding up his index finger.

"How many girls have you brought here?" Praying he didn't hear the nerves in my voice, I pad closer to the windows that look out at the docks. The view is spectacular while also private. Only a handful of unused boats are anchored near the marina.

In the reflection of the glass, I see Slater's grin enlarge before he holds his index finger in the air again. I keep my back to him so he won't see the mammoth smile stretching across my face. I'm beyond ecstatic I'm the only girl he's brought here.

I stop hiding my smile when he curls his arms around my waist and draws me back. He'll feel the excitement dashing through my veins, so why hide my happiness? We watch the sun set over the water in silence. It's a breathtakingly beautiful sight that strengthens the love I have for this man. I broke his heart; there's no denying this, so things could be a lot murkier than they are.

Once the sun disappears from the horizon, Slater angles his head so he can see my eyes. "The sunsets are one of the reasons I wanted this place, but do you want to see what sealed the deal?"

When I nod, he clasps his hand around mine before walking us to the elevator we exited only minutes ago. I hadn't noticed when we entered, but there's a much larger industrial-sized elevator next to the one we used.

I rib him with my elbow, assuming his thoughts are as dirty as mine. "Don't you need a few more minutes?"

He throws his head back and laughs but says nothing to alleviate my curiosity.

The carefree smile he's wearing turns blistering when the elevator dings, announcing its arrival. I can't help but giggle when its doors pop open. Standing proudly in the middle of the commercial-sized space is Slater's bike, Gertie. He had it shipped back here three days ago. I knew he was missing her, but I didn't realize just how much until now.

He waggles his brows before strolling to his beloved bike. I eye him curiously when he kicks up the stand to push her into the living room. Once he has her in a prime position, easily viewable throughout the loft, he lowers the stand and steps back.

"You can't have a bike in your living room."

"Why not?" His eyes roam over Gertie in admiration. "She likes sleeping inside; don't you, girl?"

When my loud giggle rumbles through the quietness surrounding us, Slater's eyes snap to mine. His glare should have me walking away with my hands held in the air, but this is too hilarious not to tease him about.

"Now I understand why you've only had one girl in your loft," I choke out between spouts of laughter.

My laughter cools when he replies, "I've only had one girl in my loft because there's only one girl I want to *fuck* in my bed."

The crudeness of his words can't stop excitement thrumming between my legs. Slater is a little rough in the bedroom, but I wouldn't have him any other way. I love his arrogance. It's almost as sexy as his handsome face.

"And what girl is that?" My words are strangled through the excitement clutching every inch of me. "Gertie?"

I flash him a flirty wink before spinning on my heels and sprinting toward one of the two doors on the other side of his loft. He's on my heels in under a second, catching me before I'm even halfway across the room.

CHAPTER THIRTY-ONE

SLATER

I thought playing drums for two hours solid is hard work. It's nothing compared to keeping up with Kylie's insatiable appetite. I'm no better. Every time I have her, I crave another hit. I swear, she's worse than any addiction I've had. Would I change it for anything in the world? Fuck no. I'll never get enough of her.

While sluggishly opening my eyes, I stretch out my arm in an attempt to pull Kylie closer to me. When my hand comes up empty, I lift my head from my pillow and peer at the bathroom. The steam coming out the bottom of the door indicates she's in the shower. I'd love to join her, but with the side effects of only having three hours sleep last night crashing into me, I flop onto the mattress, praying for a few more hours.

"Alright, calm down," I instruct my cock when he digs into the mattress, announcing he knows Kylie is most likely naked since she's in the shower.

I roll off the bed and stagger to the bathroom. I don't have to shred off my clothes as I go since I sleep naked. Just before I enter the steam-filled space, I hear a faint murmur. I reduce my speed before carefully prying open the bathroom door. I smile when I discover what the murmuring is. Kylie is singing, and her voice is... *unbelievable.* I don't know the song she's singing. It's from a few years back and way too country for me, but holy shit, she sings it well.

When she reaches the chorus, I recognize the song. It's by the country singer who turned pop. What's her name? Taylor someone? Taylor Swift. Yeah, her. It's her song about Romeo and Juliet. It's not my style of music, but the way Kylie sings it has me frozen in shock like I was over ten years ago when I heard Noah sing for the first time.

Once her performance ends, I can't help but clap and holler. I'm in complete fucking awe. I'm only through my second wolf whistle when Kylie's shampoo-covered head pops out of the marble shower. "What are you doing?"

"Listening to you sing!" I make a *duh* face. "Hot damn, Kylie, you're so fucking talented."

My praise should raise her chin, not see it balancing on her gorgeous tits. When I step closer to her, preparing to raise her head back where it should be, the low hang of her eyes starts an avalanche. She's just realized I'm naked, and I fuckin' love the quick inhale she does to announce her fascination with my dick.

After stepping into the shower, I turn on the second shower head so I can get some water since she is hogging hers before spinning around to face her. "Why haven't I heard you sing before?"

She returns her eyes to my face before wetting her lips with saliva. When her hand moves for my rapidly stiffening cock, I swat it away. I know what she's doing, and although my insides friggin' love her attempts to steer our conversation into much dirtier waters, I'm genuinely interested in her reply. She has talent—*real talent*—so why the fuck isn't she exploiting it for all it's worth?

When she pouts, I fight my hardest battle to keep my cock flaccid. I miserably fail. "Answer my question—*then* we'll fool around."

Her eyes linger on my chest while she deliberates. Just when I think she'll never answer me, she murmurs, "I get stage fright."

"Why? You have *nothing* to fear. You have a gift that needs to be shared."

I'm not stroking her ego because I want her tonsils to stroke my cock. Her talent blew me away. I can't believe she hides it from people.

"That's real sweet of you to say." Her country twang fills my head with naughty thoughts.

"I'm not saying it to be sweet—there's nothing sweet about me. I'm being honest."

When she sees that honesty in my eyes, she smiles a broad grin. Her beautiful smile causes me to lose the ability to control my cock. I'm shocked I've kept him contained this long. She's naked and smiling. This is way above my level of expertise.

After pulling her lips to mine, I plunge my tongue into her wet, inviting mouth. As my tongue guides her to a manic state, her soap-covered hand works my cock into a frenzy. The silkiness of her hand combined with the wetness of the body wash coating it has my chase to climax hitting fruition faster than I'd like.

I could come now if her needs weren't always on the forefront of my mind when we fuck. Instead, I drag my lips away from her sinful mouth, yank her hand off my cock, then nudge her back a step. She stares up at me with wild, famished eyes as a wave of water glides down her bubble-covered locks.

Once all traces of shampoo have been removed from her hair, I nudge my head to the bottle of conditioner near her left ankle. "Time to condition." My words come out rugged, like I dragged them through gravel before spitting them out. Stopping her almost killed me, and my throat is still harboring the wounds.

When Kylie bends down to collect the conditioner, a groan tears from my throat. "Hasn't anyone ever told you to bend with your knees?" Her ass is in prime position for me to plunge my cock inside her.

"And where's the fun in that?"

When she giggles, I spank her ass. "Always a tease."

Any chance of maintaining a rational head slips down the shower drain when she stands from her crouched position then spins to face me. Her eyes are beaming with lust, and her teeth are grazing her bottom lip, but she's not just horny. She's in love.

Her lips twitch, preparing to speak, but I'm on her before a word can escape her mouth. While kissing the living shit out of her, I guide her legs around my waist before bracing her back on the tiles. My mouth captures every breathless moan parting her lips when I grind my stiffened shaft against the silky smoothness between her thighs. Her heat alone could set me off.

When her impatience gets the better of her, she lines up my cock with the entrance of her slit before notching in the first inch. I rest my head on her sweat-beaded forehead before spearing the last eight inches with one quick thrust.

Her eyes bulge when I take her to the very base, but her moan tells me she loves it. I love seeing her like this too. Taken. Whole. Overwhelmed. No matter how many times I see the spark only our connection ignites in her eyes, it'll never be enough.

"What?" I question when Kylie peers at me over the screen of her iPhone. Her brows are pulled together; she looks genuinely confused.

After shaking her head, she returns her eyes to her phone's screen. We were in the process of having breakfast when her phone dinged with a hundred text messages. She's been weird ever since.

I set down my piece of toast before shuffling my chair closer to hers. When my eyes drop to her phone, I spot Google Alert after Google Alert for my band. That's not uncommon. When we're on home turf, we're bombarded by the paparazzi. Fans love seeing us in our natural environment, so the paps' pestering is worse when we're not on tour.

"You may want to alter your specs, or you'll add an additional thousand alerts to your pile by the end of the week."

"This is part of my job..." Confusion juts her words as a wrinkle pops between her brows. "... A job I'm not sure I have anymore. I was employed to help Emily during the tour, but it's over now, so does that mean my position is also redundant?"

I chuckle before striding into the kitchen. "You don't need to worry about working. I'm more than capable of taking care of us both."

"Uh-uh. No. It's not happening." She shadows me into the kitchen, her steps faster than the ones she uses when she wants me to chase her. "I'm not being *kept*." She spits out her last word like it scorched her throat with bile.

"Then how about we make a deal?"

I dump my plate into the dishwasher before spinning around to face her. When my eyes leisurely glide down her body, she folds her arms in front of her ample chest. She knows what I'm about to say, but she wants me to showcase my pigheadedness in all its glory.

"If you keep me sexually satisfied, I'll keep you fed—"

My sentence is cut short from her grabbing an apple out of the fruit bowl and pegging it at my head. I catch it mid-air, take an enormous bite like I didn't just feast like a king, then prowl toward her. With each step I take forward, she takes a step back, her wish to flee thwarted when she crashes into the kitchen counter. Once I'm close enough she can reach me, she cups my jaw before inclining her mouth toward mine.

Just as her cinnamon-scented lips brush mine, she bobs under my arm and dashes out of the kitchen murmuring, "No deal," on the way.

Assuming she wants to be chased, I give her a five-second head start before taking off after her. I'm taken aback when my arrival in the dining room has me stumbling upon her at the table, glancing down at her phone again.

This time when I peer at her screen, I notice it's showing a job search website. Growling, I yank her phone out of her hand, toss it onto one of my black leather couches, plant my ass in the seat next to hers, then drag her until she's sitting in my lap.

I know she hates the idea of being kept—Noah faced the same issues with Emily—but things in our industry are different. I can't risk having her out in public. There are too many fucking lunatics who'd harm her just to get back at me. The lengths some groupies go to are scary. Look at Megan as a prime example. Things could have ended a lot worse for Nick and Jenni if Isaac hadn't stepped in—not that Jenni is aware of that. Nick kept it from her, and for the first time in forever, I agree with his decision. She had enough on her plate with Noah's accident and a newborn baby. She didn't need more stress.

When I explain my reasoning to Kylie, she listens intently while adding an occasional nod to our conversation. Once I've given her every example I can think of, I sweeten the sauce. "It's only six weeks until we go back on the road anyway. Then you'll be back to earning your own money."

"Okay." She doesn't sound convinced, but it's better than a straight-up denial. "I'll bunk with you for six weeks, then once I get paid, I'll pay you back."

I try my hardest to hold in my chuckles. Only the smallest sound escapes my lips, but it's enough for Kylie's eyes to narrow into thin slits.

"We'll keep a tally of your expenses on your phone, then you'll know how much you owe me." I have no intention of taking her money, but if it makes her happy to keep a tally, then that's what we'll do.

After agreeing to my terms with a handshake, we spend the rest of the day hanging around my loft, eating, watching movies, and making out like crazy teens. I had no clue how much I've missed the simple things in life until I can only do them a couple of weeks out of the year. I haven't sat down and watched a movie in the past six months, but today, Kylie and I have watched three. Mercifully, she enjoys action and comedy movies as much as I do. We save the steamier stuff for when we're in front of the camera instead of behind it.

CHAPTER THIRTY-TWO

SLATER

While scooting up my mattress to lean against the headboard after our third romp of the day, my tired eyes scan my room. Halfway across, I spot a sliver of yellow sticking out of Kylie's jeans. I smile, loving that she still carries her bucket list with her everywhere she goes.

When I pace to her jeans to carefully remove the list from her pocket, my weary muscles scream in disgust. The paper has been so extensively used over the years, it's veined with brittle creases. When I unfold it, I notice a large piece of scotch tape is holding it together. It looks recent, like its surgery was only performed a few weeks ago. If Kylie loves her list as much as she did years ago, I'm confident its repairs weren't done without a truckload of tears. She loves this list —*almost as much as I love her.*

My veins thicken with euphoria when I discover how many we crossed off with the red pencil I gave her, then my heart sinks when I notice she's also crossed off number three. I've barely worked through my confusion when Kylie exits the steam-filled bathroom. A tiny towel is covering her delectable curves from my view, and another is drying her hair.

When she notices I have her bucket list in my hand, her lips tug into a vast grin. "It's nearly done."

I nod. It is, but not in the way I was hoping.

"Why did you cross off number three?" I already know her answer, but I want to hear it directly from her.

She stops drying her hair, her eyes welling with tears. "I can't..."

I can tell she wants to say more, but it's taking everything she has to hold in her tears, so she can't produce words. When a single tear careens down her cheek, I brush it away before pulling her into my chest. She smells freshly showered, the body wash and shampoo she used masking her wildflower smell.

"You need to add it back onto your list."

Her wet hair clings to my chest when she shakes her head. "I want to finish my list. I can't if it stays on there."

I'm certain she can hear my racing heart, but I don't give a shit. It's early in our re-established relationship, but she's always been *it* for me, so this isn't a hard decision for me to make.

"We will find a way to cross it off your list."

Kylie intakes a sharp breath before her head pops up from my chest. She stares at me in shock, equally pleased and scared. She's not the only one frightened. I'm suddenly fretful she means we'll cross it off right now.

"I'm not saying this year, or even next year, but one day."

She smiles a heart-stopping grin. "That's A-Okay with me. I just got you back, so I'm not willing to share you just yet."

After pressing my lips to her wet temple, I snag a black permanent marker off my bedside table then hold it out for Kylie. She smiles like I lassoed the moon for her before accepting both the pen and her list. She carefully flattens it onto the bedside table before using her teeth to pry open the marker. The world fades into the background as I watch her return item number three to her bucket list.

There, in thick black ink for the world to see is an event that should scare me more than it does: *Have a baby.*

CHAPTER THIRTY-THREE

KYLIE

"It's just you and me, baby."

I swallow, battling to keep the bile in my stomach while returning Slater's stare. After watching my throat work through its dryness, he smiles a wide, full-hearted grin. He can smile. He's not the one on the verge of having a panic attack. That's all on my shoulders—regrettably!

"You have nothing to fear," Slater continues to encourage me, his eyes never leaving mine. "It's just you and me in the living room of our loft." The way he says "our" quickens my pulse, much less when he stands so close to me, we almost become one. "Close your eyes." When I do as instructed, I feel his smile instead of seeing it. "Block out everything but my voice."

Noise ceases to exist when he whispers encouraging words in my ear. He tells me I'm brave, beautiful, and smart, before adding a thick slathering of naughty thoughts into the mix. His pep talk spikes my confidence so much, this time when I reach for the mic, my hand only slightly shakes.

When rustling sounds around me, my eyes pop open. My heart launches into my throat when I notice Slater is strolling back to his barstool. I seize his wrist, stopping his hasty retreat. "Stay with me." He couldn't have missed the plea in my voice, but just in case, I add begging eyes into the mix.

After dragging his index finger down my screwed-up nose, he nods. "Are you ready?"

I nod, eager to get this over and done with. "Do it. Rip the Band-Aid off in one quick motion."

When Slater signals to the gentleman next to us that I'm ready, a smile tugs on my lips. Slater selected the first song he heard me perform. It's Taylor Swift's "Love Story."

With nerves clutching my throat, my first few lines come out shaky, but one glance into Slater's eyes soon takes care of them. He's watching me with nothing but love and admiration all over his face. After a big breath to cool the blood roaring through my body, I give my performance everything I have, pretending it is just Slater and me sitting in the living room of *our* loft.

Although he's been encouraging me the past four weeks to sing in front of him, I always find it difficult. I hate performing in front of anyone—even my parents. In an attempt to curb my panic, Slater stood behind me, acting as if he wasn't even in the room. As each day went on, he slowly moved to stand in front of me. I've been able to sing in front of him the past two weeks, but tonight is different. For one, we're in a karaoke bar, and two, we're here with his bandmates. Noah included.

I have my back facing the stage. Slater thought my nerves would be kept at bay if I couldn't see the faces of those surrounding me. It appears to have worked. It's as if it is just a country girl belting out a tune to the man she knows without a doubt is her Romeo.

When the song finishes, the bar plunges into awkward silence, and my heart plummets into my gut. *Silence isn't good, is it?* Slater smirks at my pale face before he motions for me to turn around. I crank only my head, fearful of what the crowd's reaction might be. I'm surprised when I spot numerous smiling faces. Even a handful have gaping mouths. When they erupt into a huge, roaring chant, I jump out of my skin. Their claps are as thunderous as my heart colliding with my ribs.

"You did it," Slater mutters into my ear, his pride unmissable. "Do you want to sing another song?"

I shake my head. "I'm so nervous, I can't guarantee I won't pass out, or even worse, hurl on the shiny, polished stage."

Slater makes a disappointed face before curling his hand around mine. As he walks us back to the booth his band members are seated in, several strangers offer up words of encouragement. Noah stares at me with wide eyes when I slide into the black leather booth across from him but remains quiet.

When Nick dumps an array of shot glasses down in front of us, I pick up the closest one and slam it down, needing some more liquid courage to hear the words I see in Noah's eyes. He's the main reason I was so nervous. Having an amateur watch me sing is bad enough, let alone a professional. When Noah sings—my god, I get goose bumps. His voice is one of the most talented I've ever heard.

"Fuck, Kylie. You can really sing."

My eyes rocket to Noah's, shock marring my face. Those were not the words I expected to hear.

Slater squeezes my thigh as if to say *I told you you're good.*

"You have a gift." Noah smiles a big beaming grin. "Unless you want it exploited, you better hide that fact from Cormack."

Slater laughs off his worry. "If Kylie wants to sing, I'll support her all the way." His eyes stray to me, full of unvoiced pride. "Is that something you want, baby?"

I shake my head, more than happy to have one musician in our relationship. I only performed tonight because Slater handed me shots, left, right, and center since we arrived, knowing I'd never have the courage to go on stage without being tipsy.

Slater squeezes my thigh again. "If you change your mind, let me know."

With a wink that says way more than his words ever could, he plucks two shots of tequila from a pile of many before raising my hand to his mouth. "Now where were we before you fuckin' killed it on stage?"

The next morning, I'm awoken by a deliciously sugary scent. While groaning, I sluggishly open my eyes. The wetness in my mouth triples when I drink in every inch of the glorious visual in front of me. Slater is barefoot, shirtless, and smirking. The top button of his jeans is undone, revealing the most spectacular V muscle I've ever seen, and his shoulder is propped against the doorframe, meaning his sexy tattooed biceps are exposed for my ravenous eyes to devour.

I'd take a few more minutes to drink in the stimulating visual if I hadn't spotted the article responsible for the sugary scent lingering in the air. He's holding a large glazed jam donut. It's a standard donut you'd pick up at any donut shop, but it has a lit candle in the middle of it.

"Happy birthday, baby." Slater pushes off the doorjamb and sexily saunters my way. When he lowers the donut so I can blow out the candle, I do, albeit hesitantly. Today isn't my birthday, so I'm a little lost on how to reply.

With my head still woozy from the shots we shared last night— some directly from the ridge I was admiring earlier—I gingerly murmur, "It's not my birthday until next month."

I hate hurting his feelings. He has the date right; he just mixed up the month I was born, but wouldn't it be more awkward if I left him believing he had the right date?

"I know that." His chuckle makes me hot all over. "But we'll be on the road by then, so I won't be able to give your gift until we returned. I figured you'd rather have it early than late."

I nod, agreeing with him. He's not the only impatient one in our duo. When he pops a large chunk of donut in my mouth, a long, salivating moan vibrates from my lips. The glaze is delicious. "Holy fuck."

While Slater adjusts his crotch, I help myself to another large chunk, moaning even louder this time around. As I lick the sugary goodness from my lips, my eyes float up to Slater's heavy-hooded gaze. "Do you want a taste?"

When he nods, I move to a kneeling position, tear off a generous portion, then arrow it toward his scrumptious lips. He opens his mouth in preparation for a taste, but he's left hanging when I issue him a cheeky wink before shoving his share of the donut into my mouth.

"Hey—"

His protest is cut off when I press my lips to his. When my tongue delves into his mouth, which tastes delicious with a hint of coffee and toothpaste, my knees scrape along the sheets. I thought I was laying a trap, not getting snared by one.

When I tug Slater forward by his unbuttoned waistband, he pulls back. "We can't." He licks his lips, getting every drop of glaze I missed before heading to the walk-in closet. Like it could get any worse, he covers his chest by throwing on a shirt.

He grins, loving my whine, while handing me a pair of my jeans and a shirt from my side of the closet. I nearly toss them to the side, but the excited delivery of his next set of words stops me. "Time for presents."

I bound out of bed, throw on the clothes he supplied me, then rush into the bathroom to brush my teeth, grimacing when I catch my reflection in the mirror. My hair is a ragged mess, and my eyes have dark circles from a lack of sleep, but thankfully, the love sparkling in them offers a distraction from their tired appearance.

After pulling my hair up into a high ponytail, I walk back into our bedroom. Slater is nowhere to be found. When I enter the living room, I scan the space, hunting anything that resembles a present. My shoulders slump when my search comes up empty for gifts, but my heart kicks out a healthy tune when I find Slater in the kitchen drinking coffee.

I steal a quick sip out of his mug, gagging when the horrid taste hits my tongue before snuggling into his chest. I just brushed my teeth. Toothpaste and coffee don't mix... unless you're sampling it straight out of Slater's mouth.

When a vibrating sensation rattles my hip, my eyes rocket down. While waggling his brows, Slater digs his phone out of the front pocket of his jeans. He keeps the screen out of my view while reading the message he received, his smile doubling the longer his eyes shift left to right.

"It's here."

The excitement in his words jumps onto my face when he guides me to the elevator.

"Is my gift outside?"

Remaining quiet, he gestures for me to enter the elevator car before him. Once we're inside, he hits the B button for the basement.

"If you bought me a car, I'll shoot you. I already have nearly one thousand dollars in expenses to pay back once I start working again, and that doesn't include rent, so there's no way I can pay back a car."

My rambling tapers off when our exit from the elevator coincides with him hitting the button to raise the roller door. When hot, stuffy air whips up my hair, my eyes shoot down to my jeans, wondering if I should change into a pair of shorts since it's so hot.

I lose the chance when Slater tugs me to his side. His body heat makes me even warmer, but in a good, *I can't wait to get him alone* type of way.

As we round the corner of his building, the sound of his heart smashing into his ribs overtakes my pulse shrilling in my ears. I'm so panicked he's seconds from coronary failure, I stop walking to peer up at him. For a man with a racing heart, his smile gives no indication to the battering his insides are facing. He appears happy, perhaps even a little misty-eyed—even more so when he nudges his head for me to look forward.

When I do, moisture burns my eyes as a sob rips from my throat. My response frightens Misty, but not enough for her not to run her nose down my cheek, as thrilled by our reunion as me.

CHAPTER THIRTY-FOUR

SLATER

Kylie's face when Misty dries her wet cheeks with a neigh makes the effort it took to get her here worthwhile. I'd go to hell and back if it created the same response.

After giving them a few minutes to become reacquainted, I join them at the side of the docks, eager to give Kylie her next gift. When Misty rears up like she did when we met, Kylie giggles. "Easy, girl. He's one of the good ones."

Once she settles her down, she throws her arms around my neck to hug me fiercely. Her wildflower smell is even more dominant now. "How did you do this?"

I clear away the tears Misty missed before turning her around to face the other side of the docks. "I may have had some help."

She gasps even more loudly than she did when she noticed Misty as her eyes snap to mine. So many words are said without one escaping her lips, and they're more beautiful than the ones she sang last night.

"I love you."

After squashing her lips against mine, she sprints to her mom, who's leaning on the horse trailer that brought Misty and Charlie to

Ravenshoe. When Mary notices Kylie's tears of joy streaming down her face, she matches her speed stride for stride. They meet halfway, crashing into each other's arms with tears streaking their faces and a string of words that don't make any sense.

At one stage, I was panicked my plan would backfire. The first few times I called the ranch, Kylie's dad answered the phone. He didn't give me a chance to speak. He just hung up the instant I announced who was calling. Kylie had been photographed with me constantly the past six weeks, and her name was plastered in several articles as the girl who finally tamed Rise Up's bad boy, so he assumed Kylie had been with me the past two years, which only we know isn't true.

When I recalled Kylie saying the ranch doesn't have a Monday to Friday routine, I switched tactics. I rose early one morning, before the sun was even up, to try her home phone again. That time, I got her mom. She sobbed when I informed her who was calling, and her voice was barely a whisper when she asked if Kylie was okay. She was just as surprised as I was when I informed her Kylie had been living in Orange County the past two years.

I talked to Mary for nearly an hour while Kylie slept. When I told Mary I wanted to buy Misty from her, she blatantly refused my request. I was about to beg when she said, "Misty is Kylie's horse. I gave her to Kylie on her tenth birthday. She belongs to her. You don't have to buy her."

Two more early morning phone calls, and a few hours of begging Jacob and everything was set. Mary would bring Misty and Charlie to my loft to surprise Kylie before carting them to Jacob's dad's property where they'll stay until I find somewhere more suitable for them to go. Nick's dad, Harrison, offered for the horses to stay at his farm in Petersburg, but Jacob's house is only five miles from my condo, so Kylie will be able to visit them there more often.

The mad beat of my heart kicks up when Kylie and Mary walk back to me with their arms twisted around each other. When they're a few paces away, Kylie loosens her grip around her mom's waist before charging for me. I chuckle when she smashes our lips together so firmly, our teeth clang.

Mom watching or not, if she keeps kissing me this way, I'll take her against the wall of my building.

When she notices my body's reaction to her kiss, she smiles against my lips before inching back. "You brought Charlie too?"

I wait for her to clear away the wetness she left on my lips before nodding. "We have a mutual agreement. If I let him eat all the grass he wants, he guarantees he won't kick me off." Her smile makes what I say next ten times harder, "So what do you say? Wanna go for a ride?"

Squealing, she nods before wiggling her hips, requesting I set her down. While she aids Mary with loading Misty back into the horse trailer, I go fetch her a change of clothes before spending the remainder of our day riding around Thomas's expansive paddocks.

By the time we arrive back at our loft, my ass is the deadest it's ever been. I offered for Mary to stay with us, but only now is it dawning on me that it may be a little awkward, considering I only have one room. I had the penthouse and garage converted, but the remainder of the building is in its original warehouse condition. I didn't need the room nor the money, so I was happy for it to stay vacant, but now I'm putting some serious thought into having them converted into apartments so Mary can visit Kylie as often as she likes. I'm sure even Melanie would be up for an all-expenses-paid trip across the country.

While Mary, Kylie and I ride the elevator, I take a mental note to call my builder. With the right amount of coin on offer, I'm confident he'll get to work the instant Rise Up goes back on the road.

When we exit the elevator, the living fucking daylights are scared out of me from a massive "Surprise!" roaring through my loft. After gathering my heart from the floor, I raise my eyes. My bandmates, their partners, Jacob, Lola, and my parents are standing in my living room, smiling broadly.

While Emily gives Kylie her birthday greetings, Jenni joins me at my side. "I know her birthday isn't until next month, but we didn't want to miss the opportunity to eat your mom's famous triple-layer chocolate cake." As she rubs the little bump in her stomach, her mouth salivates.

Like my mom can read Jenni's pregnancy cravings, she walks out of the kitchen with her famous cake covered in several candles. When everyone breaks into a surprisingly well-tuned version of "Happy Birthday," Kylie's smile competes with the twenty-four candles on her cake, only disappearing when she blows them out with one large breath.

———

My mom's cake is as good as I remember, but that doesn't mean she'll go easy on me when I enter the kitchen hoping for another slice.

"What? It's fucking delicious."

I grin like a loon when she cuts me a super large piece. Give my mom the slightest compliment, and watch how well-rewarded you'll be for it.

After polishing off my third slice today, using my tongue to get every last drop of frosting, I hand my sparkling clean plate to my mom. She laughs before dunking it into the suds in the sink. "I don't even need to wash it."

Before I can reply, Jacob's deep, rumbling laugh bounces around my loft. I don't know what Kylie is telling him, but she's had him in stitches most of the afternoon.

"She gets along well with your friends."

My eyes stray back to my mom before I jerk up my chin. "Yeah, she does."

Everyone loves Kylie the instant they meet her. That's why I haven't told them she was sick. I know what Serena went through when everyone found out. They treated her differently. The kids at school avoided her like she had the plague, worried leukemia might be contagious, and even her pathetic boyfriend she should have never had vanished. I hated how she was treated, so I'll do everything in my power to ensure Kylie is never treated the same way.

"Can I ask you something?"

My mom finishes drying a dish before turning around to face me. Her eyes are glossed with sheen, revealing she heard the panic in my question, but she nods all the same.

I swish my tongue around my mouth, praying a bit of moisture will ease out my words. "What are the chances of being diagnosed with ALL for a third time?"

Kylie is well now, but I'm terrified she'll get sick again. Although I could google statistics, my mom is a chairperson on the Serena Scott Foundation, so she's very knowledgeable about this type of stuff.

"Kylie had ALL twice?"

"You knew about the first time?"

Nodding, her eyes shift from Kylie to me. They're brimming with tears. "I had an inkling just from looking in her eyes. They have the same fighting spirit Serena's had; I just didn't know what caused it. Then when you said you met her on the anniversary of Serena's death, I knew she was brought into your life for a reason." Her throat works hard to swallow before she continues. "How old was she the second time?"

I cross my arms in front of my chest to hide the shake of my hands. "Twenty-one. It's why she left me."

My mom exhales a big breath that rattles my dreads. "I don't know what the odds are of her getting it again, but the fact she survived a second bout shows how truly strong she is. Usually adult patients who relapse only have a ten percent survival rate past five years."

Her confession sucker-punches me. It steals the air from my lungs before threatening to bring up the three slices of cake I gobbled down.

Upon spotting my pale cheeks, my mom tries to coerce me off the ledge. "She's strong, Slater. Look at her."

When she thrusts her hand at Kylie, I follow the direction of its swing. She's smiling and laughing with our friends—happiness is beaming out of her.

"Serena wouldn't have brought her into your life to have her taken away. You have to believe that. Don't treat her like a porcelain doll that might break. She'll never forgive you if you do."

After squeezing my hand in support, she takes Kylie a large piece of her birthday cake. Even with her eyes revealing she is stuffed to the brim, Kylie thanks my mom with a smile before shoveling a fork full of frosting into her mouth. When she moans, our eyes collide. Her smile is for everyone else, but the glint in her eyes is solely for me.

When she uses the fork to summon me into the living room, I muster up my best fake grin before following her demand to a T. Kylie is a fighter. The fact she made it this far proves how strong she is. I'll never stop worrying, but for now, I'll enjoy having her back in my life and treat every day as a fucking blessing.

CHAPTER THIRTY-FIVE

KYILE

Three months later...

Jenni and Emily gasp in sync when I step out of the bathroom. Emily's eyes fill with tears as Jenni rushes for me as fast as her seven-months-pregnant belly will allow. She fusses over me, ensuring the purple satin dress she designed specifically for me is sitting right. Once she's finished fussing, I pivot to face the full-length mirror. I squeal before I can stop myself.

My ball gown gathers in all the right places, giving me the illusion of an hourglass figure. When you first look at my face, you'd assume I'm not wearing any makeup. The only reason I know I am is because my freckles have been blended into the background. My hair is back to the original length it was when I met Slater two and a half years ago. No, it didn't grow that much the past five months. It's the work of hair extensions. The hairdresser Jenni hired is so talented, I can't tell where my real hair ends and the extensions start.

Overcome with glee, I throw my arms around Jenni's shoulders, startling her. It's taken me a few months to get used to the affection Jenni and Emily lavish me with every day. Dylan and his two brothers were my best friends growing up. I had a handful of female friends at school, but the distance between our ranches meant we didn't see each other outside of school hours. Once I left for college, all my female friends ceased to exist, until I stumbled upon Melanie.

"Can you please take a photo so I can send it to Melanie?"

"I could." Emily shrugs as if she's not really into the idea. "Or you could show her yourself."

My eyes snap down to hers. My height already gains me three inches on Emily, but the altitude-daring heels I'm wearing means I tower over her.

When Emily fails to extinguish my confusion, my eyes turn to Jenni. Her cheeks are flushed, and she has a huge smile etched on her face. "She's in the living room—"

I'm halfway out of the master suite before the entire sentence leaves her mouth.

"Melanie!" I squeal when I spot the back of her in the living room.

As I rush for her, my body perspires in an attempt to lower my erratic pulse. I haven't seen her in person for nearly five months. Text messages, phone calls, and FaceTime can't compare to seeing someone in the flesh. I can't hug someone over the phone, and I've missed hugging her so much it hurts.

With a smile as bright as the sun, Melanie spins around to face me. After squealing an ear-piercing scream, she races across the room, causing her short black ball gown to swish around her white thighs.

"What are you doing here?"

"Oh my god, where did you get your dress?"

"Your hair, I love it."

"Your hair, I love it!"

We continue throwing questions at each other until we become breathless. Emily and Jenni watch us from the doorway of the master suite with amused looks on their faces, most likely realizing this is what they look like every time they greet each other.

"You look beautiful," I tell Melanie.

I'm not lying. She's the most dazzling I've ever seen her. Her platinum blonde bob has been changed to a very short pixie haircut, making her blue eyes sparkle even more. She's wearing a black strapless dress with a fitted bodice, and her skirt fans out just below her navel. Her killer high heels add a few extra inches to her tiny five-foot-four height, and although she appears to have lost a bit of weight the past five months, she's undeniably beautiful.

"Thank you." She twirls so I can see the complete package before holding me back at arm's length. "You look smoking hot too! What have you got under there? Because I swear your boobs weren't that big the last time I saw them."

When she yanks down the front of my dress, exposing one of my naked breasts being held in place with Hollywood tape, I slap her hand away. "Now I'm certain you're Slater's twin."

She flashes me a frisky wink. "I guess that's why he brought me here. He thought I'd be a good influence on you." She battles to hide her smile but miserably fails. "But he—"

"Picked the wrong friend!" we scream in sync.

Our laughter bellows around the room, only stopping when someone knocks on the main door of my suite. Certain it's Slater, I rush to the door, eager to reacquaint our lips since it's been over four hours since we've kissed. I may also be dying to thank him. He's been spoiling me rotten the past four months, but seeing Melanie again tops any gift he's given me.

I swing open the door before throwing my arms in the air. "I love you more than the moon and the stars and the ocean. I love you more than anyone!"

Marcus's plump lips curve into a broad grin. "I love you too?" he says hesitantly, as if it's more a question than a statement.

With a roll of my eyes, I tug Marcus into my room before popping my head into the hall, seeking Slater.

"Slater will meet us in the ballroom," Marcus informs me when he notices my dropped lip. "He had some *loose ends* he needed to tie up." His smirk switches to a genuine smile. "His time got *cut* short, leaving him *trimmed* of time."

He chuckles to himself, seemingly entertained by an inside joke we're not privy to. Before I can ask him what the hell he is talking about, Melanie kisses him hard on the mouth. My mouth gapes over her audacity; Marcus freezes in surprise, and Emily and Jenni gasp. I don't know where to look, so my eyes bounce between Emily and Jenni, the empty hallway, and occasionally to Melanie and Marcus.

After what feels like minutes, Melanie pulls away from their embrace. After fixing her dress into place, she wipes her index finger over her lipstick-smeared mouth before snagging our masks off the entranceway table and hotfooting it into the corridor. "Now that's been taken care of, let's go party!"

She saunters down the hall like kissing a world-famous bassist is an everyday occurrence for her. I wave goodbye to Jenni and Emily before taking off after her. Marcus follows me, but he maintains an amicable, yet curious distance.

Melanie remains quiet as we ride the elevator, but her eyes continually stray to Marcus, who's standing in the corner, soundlessly summarizing. When the elevator dashboard signals we're about to arrive at the second floor, Melanie hands me my mask. The Serena Scott Annual Gala Fundraiser is being held in the ballroom of our hotel. It's a masquerade ball, so all attendees are expected to be dressed in formal attire with a mask covering their faces. The ticket sales alone raise millions of dollars for people suffering from ALL.

Slater explained Serena's foundation was set up to assist people like me with poor medical insurance. It pays for their medical bills and assists in accommodating the family members supporting their child or partner going through such a horrendous illness. I'm so proud of Slater and his family for starting this organization. Anything that helps lessen the burden on those families is the greatest gift you could possibly give them.

My treatment was aggressive and painful, not just physically but emotionally as well. Because I was so young when diagnosed, I didn't have the option of storing my eggs before treatment began. When you're thirteen, you're not worried about future children; you just want to live. Seeing how much happiness Maddie and Jasper bring to Emily and Jenni's lives made me feel torn. I was angry and heartbroken when I crossed number three off my list. Not because I couldn't have children, but because I knew I'd never finish my list with it on there.

The chances of conceiving naturally after chemotherapy are low in general, so my chances are basically non-existent. When Slater said we'd find a way to add it back to my list, my heart nearly burst. He's never been too shy to admit that having kids scares the living shit out of him, so the fact he encouraged me to add it back proves how much he loves me.

Melanie and I follow Marcus to the registration table to sign up to become bidders for tonight's auction. Several exclusive items supplied by Rise Up will be auctioned along with other elaborate items. All the profits raised from the auction will go directly to researching if there are any links between ALL sufferers and certain pesticides. With an increase in ALL patients coming from rural and remote areas, they believe some patients may have been overexposed to certain chemicals, which may have contributed to their diagnosis.

"You need to show your paddle when you bid on any item," the lady behind the desk explains.

I giggle when she tells me my paddle number is sixty-nine. When she narrows her eyes, I laugh even louder. You'd think since I'm twenty-four I'd be more mature, but I'm not. When you've been through what I've been through, you never want to grow up. A majority of my teen years were spent in the hospital, so I have a lot of teenage rebellion left to be unleashed. Lucky for me, Slater is one of the biggest kids I know.

"Are you ready?"

Melanie almost faints when Marcus offers her the nook of his arm to guide her down the stairs. When she accepts after a flabber-gasted response, I follow them down the wrought iron stairwell. The ballroom is full to the brim with people. All the ladies are dressed in figure-hugging ball gowns. Some are full-length like mine, and others are short and sexy like Melanie's. The men are wearing tuxedos. Most are black in color, but a handful of the more extravagant gentlemen are decked out in bright yellow, red, and blue tuxes.

As I finalize the last few steps, my eyes shift around the space seeking Slater. We've been so inseparable the past six months, the four hours we've been apart today is the longest we've been sepa-rated, and it's honestly killing me.

When I jump down the last step, my heart leaps into my chest. My smile is so wide, my cheeks hurt from the sudden incline. The quartet assembled on the stage just began performing "Love Story" by Taylor Swift. That can't be a coincidence—surely!

My intuition is proven right when a sexy voice behind me says, "You're more beautiful every time I see you."

I turn around so fast, dizziness clusters in my head, and a handful of tears drop down my face. I take my time drinking Slater in, starting at his black polished dress shoes before my eyes float over his perfectly tailored black tuxedo pants and fitted jacket worn over a white dress shirt. I smile when I notice his wonky bowtie. It's sitting just to the left, matching the natural flow of his lips when he smirks at my giggle. His silk mask makes his piercing brown eyes darker than normal, and his chin is void of a single bit of stubble.

He's gorgeous, yet oh so different than the man I saw only hours ago.

When Kylie scrubs her hand over my scalp, her expression is a cross between amused and panicked. "Your dreads," she whispers, like she's dreaming. "They're gone."

I nod, confirming what her eyes can't believe. My dreads are gone. My head is bare and cold from the crew cut the hairdresser gave me earlier today, but my heart is full of pride—although it's nothing on the pride I felt when I spotted Kylie gliding down the stairs. Her beautiful face was covered by a mask, and her hair was several inches longer than it was when I left her hours ago, but I've memorized every inch of her face and body, so I'd recognize her whether she's wearing a fancy ball gown or a burlap sack.

We've been inseparable the past six months, and today is the longest we've been apart. You'd think I'd hate being tied down, but I've loved every minute of it. Being tied to Kylie is the best thing that's ever happened to me, and I'm not just talking about those times in the bedroom.

I'd originally planned to meet Kylie back at our hotel room, but decided to surprise her here instead. The song I arranged for the quartet to play is one of the corniest songs I've ever heard, but it's *our* song. Kylie told me she sang it that morning because she was deliriously happy, and for some reason unbeknownst to me, I made her that way. She believes meeting me saved her, even though I know without a doubt she's the one doing the saving. Although I hate country music with a passion, and you'll never catch me listening to it on a regular day, I'll happily play our song on repeat just to witness the smile that graces Kylie's face every time she hears it.

I'm drawn from my thoughts when Kylie giggles. When I arch a brow, demanding an explanation for her laughter, her cheeks flush pink. That's a shock. I've never seen her blush before. "You kind of look like Brad Pitt."

I roll my eyes and gag. Kylie, Emily and Jenni are fucking obsessed with that guy. I don't get it—seriously! He's more than double their age.

I stop whining when she adds on, "But at least ten times hotter."

Smiling, I attempt to tug her close by her tiny waist. My plans are thwarted when her hand shoots up to scrub my scalp again, making me worried she likes my crewcut more than my dreads. This is the third time the past minute she's rubbed the bristles on my head. I don't mind. Her nails scratching my scalp feel nice; I just don't want her to get used to my new 'do.

"Don't get used to it. I'm growing my dreads back."

She smiles so broadly my cock stiffens painfully fast. "Good, because I love your dreads." Her voice is throaty, as if she too is struggling to ignore the tension bristling between us. "That's why I'm so shocked you shaved them off. They're a part of who you are."

"It did it for Serena's foundation."

It killed me watching the hairdresser cut off the dreads I've been growing since I was thirteen. It was even more painful than getting me into this tuxedo, but when an anonymous bidder offers three million dollars to cut them off, I'll cut them off. I can grow back my dreads, and that amount of money will greatly benefit families suffering through what my family went through. It also means people won't have to struggle like Kylie did when she went into remission.

With my approval, my mom made some changes to Serena's foundation the past three months. Now we don't just help people suffering from ALL, we also support the survivors, the people like Kylie, who are left unemployable because they can't get adequate health coverage.

It pissed me off when I found out what happened to Kylie. She still faced the fight of her life after she went into remission. That's fucking bullshit. No one should endure that, so when I had an opportunity to add an additional three million dollars to the ten million Rise Up contributes each year, I jumped at the chance. That amount of money will give our new campaign a massive boost.

"Someone placed a bid of three million dollars for me to cut them off."

Kylie's mouth pops open. "Holy crap. I don't think the measly four hundred dollars I saved for the auction will cut it."

Her amount is only skimpy because last week she paid me back the one thousand, seven hundred, and twenty-three dollars my phone said she owed me. When she forced me to take her money, I donated it to Serena's foundation in her name. She then requested to know how much rent an apartment like mine would fetch, so she could pay her share. I probably shouldn't have laughed at her expression when I said her half would cost over fifteen thousand a month, but her shock was too adorable to ignore.

After calming her down the best way I know how—sexually—we negotiated terms that suited us both.

"Bid on anything you want, then you can pay me back." I press my lips to the shell of her ear. "You just have to pay me like you do for your rent. Deal?"

Her breath turns ragged as her glowing eyes dance between mine. After not even two seconds of deliberating, she nods. I may have negotiated to add extra items to her bucket list in exchange for free rent. My requests were eerily similar to the ones Melanie added seven months ago.

"Then let's get this party over with so I can see what you look like underneath that dress."

Kylie giggles before slipping her hand into the one I'm holding open for her. As we weave through the dense crowd, we gain the admiring eyes of many.

"They're all as shocked by your haircut as I was," Kylie murmurs halfway across the ballroom, wrongly believing people are gawking at me because they recognize me.

That isn't what is happening. They're staring at us because she's so incredibly beautiful, they can't help but look. How do I know this? Kylie didn't recognize me with my new haircut, so there's no chance in hell a bunch of snooty millionaires would recognize me. My dreads made me easily recognizable, but now they're gone, and I'm wearing a tuxedo and a mask—I'm completely incognito. I'd love the anonymity if I didn't feel so naked without my dreads.

I tug Kylie to my side, wordlessly warning every guy in this room that she's taken. A few get the hint and look away, but a good handful need a stern finger point to get the hint. I really wish she'd wear the diamond engagement ring I bought her. We're not engaged. I just want her to wear it so the roadies will back the fuck off. They still see her as bait since she doesn't have a ring on her finger, but she refuses to wear the ring I purchased. She said until we're engaged she won't wear any ring, not even one that cost me millions of dollars.

By the time the auction starts, Kylie has a few glasses of wine under her belt, making her bids more daring than normal. "Four thousand dollars."

She stops waving her number sixty-nine paddle in the air when the gentleman bidding against her raises his bid to five thousand dollars.

"Ten thousand dollars," Kylie announces without hesitation.

I'm not bothered by her high bid. All the money raised from the sale of my signed drum kit goes to Serena's foundation, and I'm more than happy for Kylie to owe me a fortune in sexual favors. I'm secretly hoping to add a few more digits to her tally.

When the man fails to immediately counterbid, Kylie arches her brow at him, goading him to bid again. From this distance, I have no clue who he is, but his pricy dark blue tuxedo and black feathered mask scream money.

The crowd gasps when the gentleman counterbids to twenty thousand dollars. When Kylie turns to face me, people think she's discussing a possible bid increase. In reality, she's scheming. "I think I can get him to go higher."

"Then do what you need to do."

I trust her. She can read people a mile away, so I'm confident she has this sucker by the throat.

With a wide smile, loving my lack of worry, Kylie shifts on her feet to face the auctioneer. "One hundred thousand dollars."

I choke on my spit. I wasn't expecting for her to bid *that* high, but I'm so fucking glad she did. My cock stiffens just thinking about all the fun things I can add to her list for that amount of money.

As Kylie stares down the man across the room, she fans her cheeks with her bidding paddle, acting nonchalant. Her cool, calm composure cracks the more the room falls into silence. It appears as if her sucker radar is a little askew tonight—*thank fuck!*

My cock softens when the tuxedo-clad gent counterbids, "One hundred ten thousand dollars."

Kylie tries to mask her excitement. She does a terrible job. "I love you, but I don't love you *that* much."

The auction attendees eyeballing us from afar chuckle loudly, believing I've been left disappointed. I have been, but not in the way they're thinking.

When the auctioneer taps his gavel on the podium, Kylie pouts before slinging her arms around my neck. "Sucker."

After placing a chaste kiss on my lips, she scans the crowd, looking for another attendee she can swindle for a donation. With her attention rapt on that, she fails to notice the gentleman she just siphoned one hundred ten thousand dollars from is crossing the room. Only once he stops to stand in front of me do I realize who he is. It's Cormack. The man who gave Rise Up our start. He also owns our record label.

"Hopefully, this will make up for my lack of judgment." He keeps his voice at a whisper, ensuring Kylie won't overhear him. "From now, any employee Destiny Records hires will be covered by the company's insurance, no matter what their medical history may be."

I jerk up my chin, grateful he heard the words Noah and I spoke to him when we discovered he was planning to terminate Kylie's employment since she couldn't get adequate health coverage.

"It's a good start."

After we shake hands, I join Kylie at the side of the auctioneer's podium. I plan to bid on a trip to Fiji coming up next. A tropical holiday on a secluded beach sounds ideal right now.

It might also be the perfect place for a romantic proposal.

CHAPTER THIRTY-SEVEN

KYLIE

"I can't believe we're going to Fiji!"

I rock on my heels, stoked tonight was a raving success all round. The auction alone raised nearly five million dollars for sufferers of ALL, and I used four hundred dollars to buy a personally signed drumstick from the world's best drummer, Slater Scott. As if that isn't already exciting, Slater was the successful bidder for an all expenses trip to Fiji.

"I'll need to get a passport. I've never traveled out of the country before."

Slater peers at me with weighed down eyes. "You have plenty of time. We can't go for at least another six months."

That's a mood killer. When he won, all I could imagine was him in nothing but a pair of board shorts, or even better – swim trunks! I've never seen him in shorts. He has a few pairs of boxers stuffed in the back of his drawers, but he doesn't wear them. He usually goes commando under his jeans, so I either get him in jeans or buck naked. I guess I shouldn't complain. The visual is glorious—nearly as tempting as he looks now.

The glands in my mouth have been overworked tonight from the amount of drooling I've done, and don't get me started on his new haircut. Seriously, I love Slater's dreads because they're one of his unique qualities, but his shorter 'do doesn't hide his gorgeous face. I had no clue how defined his cheekbones were until he removed his mask earlier tonight, and his brown eyes appear larger in size. Tonight, it'll be me chasing him around our room, not the other way around.

"Jesus Christ, Kylie." A shiver runs through my body when Slater brushes his lips on my earlobe. "If you keep looking at me like that, I'll fuck you in this elevator." When my eyes rocket to Melanie and Marcus standing to our right, Slater adds to his warning, "Yes, even with them in here with us."

My pussy throbs in anticipation, but it feels like a bucket of cold water is thrown over me when Melanie murmurs, "We can hear you, you know, but please don't let us stop you. I'm dying to see your *drumstick*."

Slater isn't deterred by her tease—not in the slightest. When the elevator arrives at our floor, he steps closer to me, looking like a man who was abandoned in a desert for a week without water. He's staring at me like I'm his salvation, like I'm his bottle of water.

"Since you're wearing heels, I'm going to play nice." His eyes glide over my body, stopping at my four-inch black pumps. "I'll give you a ten-second head start."

I cock a brow, calling out his deceit without words. He has no patience whatsoever. Ten seconds feels like a lifetime to him—except when he's in the bedroom.

"Ten... nine... eight," he slowly counts in his deep, seductive voice. "Seven... six..."

I kick off my heels, throw them into his chest, then sprint out of the elevator before five is close to leaving his lips.

"Five, four, three, two, one. Ready or not, here I come!"

I make it all the way into the entryway of our hotel room before he's on my heels, but because I'm too busy glancing over my shoulder,

I run straight into the entryway table, sending the large vase of flowers sitting on the top tumbling to the floor.

Slater scoops me in his arms to carry me over the shards of glass like a husband would carry his wife over the threshold. "Anyone would swear you're the rock star. You're always trashing hotel rooms."

I attempt to rebut, but the instant his lips land on mine, I'm rendered speechless. His smooth chin is missing the stubble that usually scratches my chin and neck, but his mouth has the same wickedly delicious taste it always has.

After laying me on our bed, he raises the skirt of my dress until it sits around my waist like a belt, then he slides my panties down my legs. One zipper, and I'd be fully exposed, but he's too impatient for that. My breaths grow needy when his thumb circles my clit a mere second before he slides two fingers inside me. The sensation is already overwhelming, so imagine how catastrophic it gets when he drops his mouth to my pussy to replace his thumb with his tongue. He's still fully clothed, wearing a tuxedo, for crying out loud, and the thought makes the naughtiness more palpable.

"Grind against me, baby. Fuck my face how I plan to fuck your pussy."

I wait for his hot breaths to stop fanning my clit before raising my ass off the bed and rocking against him as requested. His hands come up to my hips, his fingers gripping me roughly as he devours me with both his mouth, fingers, and his heart. There's such a primitive rawness to our lovemaking that I fall in love with him more after every embrace. He's not a tender lover, but there's a tenderness in the way he makes me feel that more than makes up for a lack of flowery words. He has my back, and I'll always have his—forever.

When he feels me tightening around his fingers, his lips skim lower and lower until he's lapping up the goodness his tongue missed the first time around.

"Mmm..." His lips vibrate against my drenched flesh.

Knowing I'm close, he increases the speed of his pumps, grinding them in and out of me in the pattern matching the rock of my hips.

When his tongue slips over the puckered hole in my rear, fireworks explode in front of my eyes. I quiver beneath him, my back falling into the mattress with a moan. My eyes close as an orgasmic wave overwhelms me. It's a beautifully terrifying two minutes.

He guides me back to earth with gentle licks and timed thrusts before climbing up my body, unclipping his wonky bow tie on the way. While he shrugs off his jacket, I set to work on the buttons concealing his magnificent torso from my avid eyes. It's been over twelve hours since I've absorbed the artwork covering his pecs. It's been way too long.

Once we have his jacket and shirt removed, and his pants huddled around his knees, Slater pulls down the front of my dress like Melanie did earlier. His brows pull together when he sees the Hollywood tape maintaining my modesty.

"Better to be safe than sorry," I say with a shrug.

"Mmm-hmm."

His moan hits every one of my hot buttons. It also has my eyes straying to the unopened box of condoms on the nightstand. We've gotten a little careless with protection the past few weeks. Slater says it's because he's had me bare, and he can't go back, but I don't hear it like that. He knows the odds of me getting pregnant are about the same as me inviting a woman into our bed—neither are likely to happen.

"If you're worried, I can always fuck you here instead." My face mashes with the mattress when he flips me over without warning. He grinds his thick cock head against my ass, eliciting a hearty moan that reverberated through my chest. "No worries then."

I silently pull my knees together. I'm not shy when it comes to this man. I just don't want him to know how much his crudeness turns me on. I shouldn't bother. If the glistening between my legs doesn't tell him how much I'm into him, the moan I release when he spanks my ass with his big, manly hand is a sure-fire indication.

CHAPTER THIRTY-EIGHT

KYLIE

Slater's head pops up from a document he's reading when I enter the room. "Thank you for bringing Melanie here last week. I just realized while showering that I never thanked you. I was somewhat preoccupied, but that shouldn't excuse my manners."

The big groove between Slater's blond brows smooths when he notices I'm wearing nothing but a towel. "It was my pleasure."

I'm not sure if he's talking about Melanie or our strenuous activities on the night in question. If his smirk is anything to go by, I'd say it's a bit of both.

With my Saturday night filled by a ravenous Slater, Melanie and I spent Sunday hanging out in her room eating and talking for hours like we used to. I filled her in on everything that's happened in my life the past several months. She seemed happy, but surprisingly quiet for Melanie. The only time her eyes sparked was when our conversation veered toward Marcus. She has it bad for him. He walked her to her hotel room after the gala, but she wouldn't share any more details on what happened after he dropped her off, which is so unlike her. Not even a ball gag keeps her quiet when it comes to sexual endeavors.

"What are you looking at?"

After plopping my backside next to Slater's, I peer down at my passport application and photos I took earlier this week. When Slater won the trip to Fiji, he said we couldn't go for another six months, but the very next day, he said he was planning for us to go within the next month. I don't know what caused the sudden change in dates, but I'm so excited about going to Fiji, I don't care when we go.

"Cormack arranged for someone to pick up your paperwork. They'll take it to the courthouse to get a rush order on your passport."

My brows pull together as my confused eyes lift to his. "Why do I need a rush order?"

Normal passport applications are processed within weeks, so mine should be here in plenty of time.

He sucks in a big breath before he swivels his body to face me. "I thought maybe we could go to Fiji next week."

I stare at him in shock. It isn't a good shock. I don't know what's going on with him, but I have noticed a drastic change in his personality the past few days. He's treating me differently, similar to how I was treated when people found out I was sick. He's been walking on eggshells, and he's even been more cautious in the bedroom.

"I've arranged for us to go to the doctor's today so we can get the vaccinations we need for our trip." As his eyes dart down to the documents in his hand, he mutters, "They'll also do a full check-up on you while we're there."

My heart plummets into my stomach. "No." I stand from the sofa and pace away from him, needing distance before I say something I'll regret.

"Please Kylie, I need you to do this—"

"Do what exactly?" I rapidly blink, praying a rush of air will keep my tears at bay. I knew he was treating me differently, and this is the icing on the cake.

With his hands held out in front of himself, urging me to calm down, he steps closer to me. "The earlier we find out, the better your chances will be."

"I'm not sick!"

When I attempt to skirt past him, he grabs ahold of my wrist, halting my angry retreat. I keep my eyes fixed on the ugly Persian rug in the living room. If I look at him and see the devastation his words are holding, I'll break. If I break, I'll cry.

"Baby, look at me."

I shake my head.

"Please, Kylie."

The pain in his voice cuts me to pieces. With my heart hanging as low as my head, I sheepishly raise my eyes to his. The hurt in his voice has nothing on the pain in his eyes.

"You had a bloody nose on Sunday—"

"Everyone gets bloody noses, Slater; it doesn't mean anything."

"I know that, I do, but you also have a bruise on your thigh that isn't getting any better."

His eyes dart down to the big circular bruise on my thigh. I got it when I ran into the entryway table in our hotel room the night we returned from the gala. At the time, it didn't hurt. I was too busy enjoying being lavished with Slater's affection.

When I woke up the following day, the little bump had turned into an extremely angry bruise. I iced it, took some pain pills, and forgot about it. That same afternoon, I had a bloody nose. To me, it was no big deal, but Slater was mortified when blood trickled over my lips.

"I know me. I know my body. I'm not sick."

My words don't offer him any comfort. His face reveals he's grieving me, even though I'm standing right in front of him.

His glossed-over eyes stare into mine as he hauntingly whispers, "Please do this for me. *Please*, Kylie."

I hate doctors. Hate is a strong word, but I really do hate them. I spent the equivalent of months with them the past two years, and the entire time, they poked and prodded me. But I want to ease Slater's panic—almost as much as I want him to look at me like he did last week.

After sucking in a deep breath, I slowly breathe out, "Okay."

He wraps me up in a firm hug. "Thank you, baby, thank you."

An hour later, we're sitting in a super fancy waiting room. The furniture in this doctor's office looks like it cost more than my last doctor made in a year. Slater is sitting next to me. He hasn't spoken a word since we walked in, but his bouncing knee ensures I can't mistake his worry.

I place my hand on his knee, stopping his fidgeting movements just as the nurse calls my name. She introduces us to Dr. Webster, a short, stubby man with a gentle smile. He gestures for us to sit in the chairs opposite him before taking down my medical history and vitals. Once he knows me with nearly as much intimacy as Slater, he inspects the bruise on my thigh. I won't lie. I'm jittering like a kid walking into school for the first time. I'm a bundle of nerves.

After lowering my skirt, Dr. Webster requests for me to rejoin Slater behind his impressive mahogany desk. "Considering your history, it is commendable you came in today. I highly doubt you're a fan of me and/or anyone in my profession."

Slater's grip on my hand tightens as I smile. I like Dr. Webster. He knows I don't like him, and he's fine with that.

"I'm sure you're acutely aware of the signs of ALL, but I also want to assure you these types of symptoms can be anything from a common cold to simply being just a bruise."

I squeeze Slater's hand back, attempting to lessen his panic.

"I'll arrange for a nurse to come in and take some blood for testing."

I breathe out sharply before nodding. I'm not a fan of needles either.

"If the test comes back with an elevated blood count, I'll order a bone marrow biopsy for later in the week."

"I would like the biopsy done today—if Kylie is okay with that?"

When Slater's fearful eyes turn to mine, seeking permission, I nod. Needles scare the shit out of me, but the fear in his eyes is more daunting than any medical procedure I've faced.

Dr. Webster flicks through the planner on his desk. He turns the pages back and forth several times, seeking an opening. "I'm fully booked," he replies, not looking up from his planner. "I can do—"

"I want it done today."

I peer back at Slater, taking in his ticking jaw and narrowed eyes on the way. He stops shooting daggers at Dr. Webster when he realizes he's secured my attention, but no amount of fake smiling can remove the cloud of fear hindering his usually bright eyes.

After a big breath, he says more politely, "I'll pay anything you want if you can get it done today. *Please.*"

Dr. Webster's eyes dance between Slater and me for several long seconds before they eventually settle on me. "Okay. I'll get the nurse to prepare the outpatient surgery room now."

Slater holds my hand during the procedure, his eyes never leaving mine. He brushes away the tears that drip down my face when the needle is inserted into my back and drags his thumb over my hand when I grimace about the weird pulling sensation from the marrow being drawn out. The procedure only takes fifteen minutes, so I chose not to have a sedative. They always make me drowsy, and I would have been required to stay at the office for several hours after the procedure. Slater only has the next two days off before a week of concerts, so I don't want to spend half of our day hanging around a doctor's office.

"Make sure you take these pain pills every four hours for the next two days," Dr. Webster instructs while handing me a prescription for pain relief. "I should have your results back in a week. If it's sooner, I'll call you."

Slater and I thank Dr. Webster with a shake of our hands before walking to the town car waiting for us downstairs. Slater remains quiet the entire trip back to our hotel. He doesn't even flinch when the paparazzi asks him crude questions in an attempt to pry a reaction out of him.

The ride in the elevator is the quietest we've ever made. Electricity is still crackling between us, but it isn't the only thing cracking —so is my heart. When we enter our suite, Slater releases my hand so he can hightail it to the liquor cabinet to pour a double shot of whiskey. He downs the generous helping in one gulp before pouring another.

No longer able to hold in my tears, they freely stream down my face. "Please don't do this." My voice is as pained as my heart feels.

When Slater pivots to face me, fear clutches my chest. His eyes are full to the brim with salty moisture.

"You know what it was like for Serena, so please don't treat me how everyone treated her."

The past few months have been perfect. Not once did he treat me like I was a fragile flower that might break at any moment. I loved that about him, but when I look at him now, all I see is fear reflecting back at me. I promised him I wouldn't run without saying goodbye, but I never promised I'd stand by and watch a disease destroy the man I love. I'm no longer concerned about what this disease could do to me; I'm concerned about what it will do to him.

After watching a tear careen down my cheek, Slater sets his glass down so roughly, it nearly cracks. He murmurs a curse word under his breath before he strides to me so quickly, he creates a ripple in the air. He engulfs me in his arms, lifting me off the ground in one fluid movement. When his delicious mouth encloses over mine, his tongue delves inside, sampling and tasting every inch. The intoxicating mix of whiskey with the salt of my tears flavors our kiss. It fuses my heart back together before lowering its pulse to a much lower region.

By the time he finishes devouring my mouth, my tears have dried, and my panties are soaked. He pulls back from our embrace with a curse word similar to the one he used to start it, his eyes wide with panic. "Shit, did I hurt you?"

His kiss was so intoxicating, I didn't endure even the slightest ping of the pain I felt earlier. It was too scrumptious to be painful. When I shake my head, he kisses the corner of my mouth before sitting on the sofa. A moan topples from my lips as I straddle his lap. His erection is straining against his zipper, proving he finds me as attractive now as he did last week—thank goodness!

He tucks a strand of my hair behind my ear before raising his eyes to mine. "I'm sorry, baby." The painful glint in his eyes shifts to forgiveness. "I'm just... *scared.*" His last word is barely a whisper.

"I know. So am I." I'm not scared of being sick again. I'm scared of hurting him. "But I'm still me. I'm still the same Kylie who went skydiving with you last month." The corners of his mouth tug higher. "I'm still the same Kylie you had sex with in your elevator." His lips curve into a full grin as he bucks his hips like a wild stallion. "And I'm still the same Kylie who's planning to get you into a pair of the tiniest swim trunks you've ever seen on a beach in Fiji."

When he chuckles a full, boisterous laugh, it proves without a doubt, even if I am sick again, I'll do everything in my power to stay with him.

I'll fight until my very last breath.

CHAPTER THIRTY-NINE

SLATER

I did exactly what I said I wouldn't do when I suspected Kylie was sick again. I treated her differently, like she's fragile and could break at any moment. I remember how much Serena hated being coddled, yet I still did it to Kylie. I panicked, and I fucked up, but in my defense, I'm scared out of my fucking mind I'm about to lose her. The fear is real. It keeps me awake because I can't stop thinking about the next steps we will have to take if her tests come back against us.

To everyone, it seems as if my fear has diminished the past few days. Only I know it hasn't. I've just hidden it. I mask my feelings by acting like everything is okay, even though I'm dying on the inside. I've called Dr. Webster every day the past three days requesting Kylie's results. Every day he assures me they should be arriving soon. I really hope they do because I'm not sure how much longer I can keep up with this charade.

I don't think Kylie has noticed, but every time I make love to her, my eyes aren't just roaming over her body in appreciation, they're actively seeking additional bruises. Serena's first symptom was a large bruise she got on her forearm from me. We were playing catch in the yard, and when she missed one of my curve balls, it hit her in her arm. The bruise was huge and lasted for days. Mom took her to the doctor the following week when it didn't go down. That started the process of her diagnosis.

Serena was taken from our family so quickly because it had formed in her liver and spleen by the time she was diagnosed. She did chemotherapy and radiation, even knowing she was only delaying the inevitable, but it gave her additional weeks to say her goodbyes. It wasn't enough as far as I'm concerned.

"Fifteen minutes until show time."

When Kylie's head pops into the dressing room I share with Marcus, I try to mask the look of worry on my face. My endeavor comes too late; she's already seen it.

She hesitantly walks into the room, passing Marcus as he exits. After straddling my lap, she undoes the top three buttons on her dress. I shake my head, horrified she's been using sex to subdue my panic the past three days but aware my cock will never be able to refuse her.

"If we had longer than fifteen minutes, I'd cross number 199 off our list. But since we only have fifteen minutes, repayment number 183 will have to do."

As she slips off my lap to kneel before me, I stroke her jaw, preparing it for the stretch it's about to endure. "Are you sure you'll be able to fully cross it off in *only* fifteen minutes?" The cheekiness in my tone hides the hammering of my heart.

She giggles while locking her eyes with mine. Fuck, she's gorgeous. And she's not the faintest bit scared about having ALL again. She amazes me every day with how unbelievably strong she is.

"I think I'll have you done with a few minutes to spare."

From the fire in her eyes, I'm certain she'll meet her target.

Kylie hit her target. I was on stage at the scheduled time feeling more relaxed than I was the night before. The road crew has been leaving the lights on at the side of the stage at my request. That way I can keep my eye on Kylie during our performances. It's lucky I've performed these songs hundreds of times before, so my eyes can continually dart to Kylie without ever losing the tempo of the song.

I'm three-quarters through our current set when I notice one of the stage assistants approaching Kylie. When she hands her a large white envelope, my breathing lowers to shallow pants even though I'm exhausted from playing the drums for the past hour and a half.

Time slows to a snail's pace as I watch Kylie read the document inside the envelope. Her face pales mere seconds before she yanks her phone out of her pocket. Even from a distance, I swear I can see tears shining in her eyes as her fingers fumble over the screen.

Three seconds after she squashes her phone to her ear, her hand shoots up to cover her mouth. My heart sinks into my stomach when she flees away from the stage. When I freeze with my drumsticks mid-air, unable to move out of fear, Nick stands next to me, still strumming his guitar. He says something, but my mind doesn't register a single word coming out of his mouth. All I can see is the devastated look on Kylie's face before she darted away.

Nick nudges me with his knee before jerking his head to the curtains Kylie just fled from. "Go, Slater!"

I stand from my drum kit so quickly, the cymbals topple over. You know the feeling you get when you're so drunk everything around you is a blur? That's how I feel right now. I stumble and trip over my own feet, even though I haven't touched a drop of alcohol in days.

I somehow manage to get to the side of the stage, although I'm disoriented and confused.

"She's in your dressing room."

The tears streaming down Jenni's face cause my eyes to water, but they also kickstart my feet. I race to my dressing room, scanning it five times before my brain clicks that Kylie isn't inside. Just as I'm about to exit, a loud sob comes out of the bathroom. It's the cry of someone who sounds truly heartbroken. It rips through my chest and maims my heart.

I rush to Kylie, wanting to comfort her. After a frantic search, I find her huddled on the ground in the shower. She's cradling her legs in her arms, and her cheek is resting on her knees. She's gripping a white sheet of paper so tightly it has a large crease down the middle. As she rocks back and forth, horrifying sobs rack her body so hard, she shudders with every one.

I sit on the wet tiled floor before pulling her into my arms. I comfort her the best I can while fighting to keep my own tears at bay. Now I don't just feel like I'm dying. I'm certain I am. My heart feels like it's being torn in two. I can't fucking lose her.

Please god, don't take her away from me.

Why didn't I force her to go to the doctor's the instant I saw the bruise? Why didn't I make her have blood tests every month? If only I'd been more diligent, we could have avoided all this heartbreak.

It takes several long, heartbreaking minutes before Kylie's head lifts off my chest. Despair marks her beautiful face. As my eyes dart between hers, I silently beg for her to tell me everything is okay. I don't want to hear any other words come out of her mouth, other than she's okay.

She tries to form words, but every time she moves her lips, only a painful whimper escapes. After a beat, she hands me the piece of paper she's gripping to near death. After scrubbing the back of my hand over my moisture-filled eyes, I read the handwritten letter.

Dear Kylie,

I never understood why you left the man you loved when you found out you were sick. Why sacrifice your own happiness for another? Why put anyone's happiness above your own? Now I fully understand why you did what you did. You did it because you love him even more than you love yourself.

Please remember that when you read the next part of my letter. Everything I did, I did for you, because I love you more than I love myself.

I never went into remission. I was informed at my last appointment that my condition had become terminal. I wanted to tell you, but I didn't want to see your devastation when you found out, so I lied instead. The happy glint in your eyes when you thought I was in remission was worth betraying you, even though I knew it would eventually break your heart.

I went through the stages of grief. The very first step was denial, then I was angry, then I was sad, then I finally came to terms with what was going to happen. I was going to die. I just refused to leave until you got the life you deserved.

You thought I didn't know about Slater until after you got back together. You were very wrong. You've always been a loved-up drunk, and you mentioned him a few times the past two years. I knew it would only take him seeing your beautiful face one more time for him to fall head over heels in love with you again.

Well, that was my plan. I just didn't realize he was as stubborn as you are. With a little pushing, you got there in the end, and I'm so incredibly happy for you. The joy on your face last week made me realize I made the right decision to keep this from you.

A few times, I wanted to tell you what was happening. I really wanted my best friend by my side, but just like Slater, I knew you would have given it all away in an instant to be with me. I loved you too much to force you to do that, so, just like you, I sacrificed my happiness for the person I love.

You have the most beautiful soul, and it was my absolute plea-sure to call you my best friend. I love you; I believe in you, and I know one day you'll find it in your heart to forgive me. I lived the fullest life I could by squeezing eighty years into twenty-four. Out of those twenty-four years, my best ones were with you.

Please don't cry for me. Please don't grieve. Live! Live the best life you can live and live it for both of us. But more than anything, remember everything I did, I did for you. I'll be waiting for you in heaven in another eighty plus years. Look for the sexy angel with two margaritas in her hands.

I love you, and I'll miss you every single day.

Your very best friend in the world,

Melanie xx

This will make me the biggest fucking asshole in the world, but I sigh while reading Melanie's letter. I'm devastated for Kylie—truly, I am—but I thought I was coming in here to console her over her diagnosis. I thought I was losing *her,* so my first thought was relief, which is rapidly changing to guilt.

Don't act like you wouldn't have done the same thing. If you were in my situation, you would have reacted the exact same way.

"She died last night," Kylie whimpers into my chest, her voice a painful whisper.

The dam in my eyes nearly spills over when I snap them shut. Now I *am* the biggest asshole in the world.

"I'm so sorry, baby. I'm so fucking sorry."

CHAPTER FORTY

SLATER

Melanie's funeral is being held today in her hometown of San Jose. The band canceled the last two shows so I could support Kylie through her grief. She's truly devastated over losing her friend. I know the process of grief, and most of the guys in our band do as well, so we're all supporting her the best we can.

The first day, she spent the entire day in bed. I held her and wiped away her tears while offering her silent support. The second day, she was angry. Not just at the disease that stole her friend from her, but she was also angry at Melanie for not giving her the chance to say goodbye. I tried to force her to read Melanie's letter again. When she refused, I read it to her, and I'll continue reading it to her until she understands why Melanie did what she did.

She loved Kylie, so she sacrificed her happiness for her, just like Kylie did for me. Kylie can't be mad at her for that. Melanie loved her enough to save her from months of pain.

"Are you two ready to go?" Marcus asks.

I peer over at Kylie, who's standing at the hotel window looking outside. She's wearing a mid-length black dress with red pumps, and her long hair has been pulled back in a braid.

"Yeah, just give me five minutes."

Marcus nods before moving into the hallway of our hotel. The whole band is in San Jose to attend Melanie's funeral. With the exception of Marcus, the rest of the band didn't really know her, but they're here supporting Kylie and me. They're my brothers, and they'll support me while I support Kylie.

Kylie's eyes lift to mine when I stand next to her. They're the clearest I've seen them the past three days. It's the first time I've seen them without tears. After roaming her eyes over my black suit, a faint grin etches on her face.

"Are you ready to go?"

When she nods, I clasp her hand in mine, then guide her to the town cars idling downstairs. When we exit our room, Jenni and Emily's eyes lift to Kylie, where they relay their sympathies without words.

Kylie remains quiet in the elevator, and she doesn't make a sound the entire trip to the funeral home. The only noise that escapes her lips is a giggle when we enter the funeral home. It's so quiet, I barely hear it, but it forces the first smile on my face in days.

When I raise my eyes, I discover what Kylie is laughing at. The funeral parlor is decked out like one of Melanie's extravagant parties. Streamers and helium balloons are on every available surface, large poster-sized photos of Melanie in various poses cover the walls, and several of the guests are decked out in bright fluorescent colors. Anyone would swear we've turned up to a nightclub instead of a funeral.

"She always loved to party," Kylie whispers, smiling.

While we head to the front pew, my bandmates slip into the back row. Kylie greets people I assume are Melanie's parents. Melanie got her platinum blonde hair from her mom and her blue eyes from her dad. She was a mixture of them both.

When Kylie takes a seat next to Melanie's mom, I sit next to her before gripping her hand in mine. Her pulse is still thrumming through her body, but it doesn't have the pause that freaked me out so much the past three days.

Halfway through the service, Kylie makes her way to the podium. Her strength surprises me when she completes her eulogy without a single tear escaping her eyes. "You better make my margarita a double." When she presses two fingers to her mouth then raises them to the sky, several of the attendees copy her.

As Kylie retakes her seat, a projection screen lowers from the ceiling. A handful of tears slip down her cheeks when Melanie's grinning face lights up the screen. She's sitting crossed-legged on a bed that appears to be in her childhood bedroom. Her message must have been recorded within the last week because she's sporting the same pixie-style haircut she had at the gala, and Marcus's signed bass guitar she won in the auction is sitting behind her.

"Hi guys!" The speakers are up so loud, Kylie jumps in fright. "I know you're supposed to be grieving, but where is the fun in that?" Melanie rolls her eyes in an unsophisticated but cute way. "If there's one thing I did right in my life, it was partying. I was the queen! So my final gift to all you people down there..." She points her fingers in all directions like she's pointing out her little minions. "...is an invitation to one of the most elaborate, elegant, invigorating—hold on, that starts with an 'I,' *whatever*—all-expenses-paid party of your life. No crying is allowed, so get those tears out now."

When she gives the crowd at her funeral a death stare, my eyes shift to Kylie. She's smiling while peering up at Melanie in awe. Her eyes have a slight sheen glossing them, but she's fighting to keep her tears at bay.

"Raise your glasses and have a drink for me. I love you all, especially you." Melanie squashes two fingers to her lips and holds them into the air like Kylie did earlier. Half of the room copies her movement.

Melanie leaps up from her bed and pads toward the screen like she's about to turn off her video recorder, but just before she does, her head pops back into the picture. "I wasn't going to say anything, but I can't leave without telling someone. This is too *huge* not to be shared."

While Melanie squats down in front of the camera so only her face is visible, Kylie giggles again.

"Marcus..... *oh, Marcus,*" When Melanie's moan vibrates through the speakers, my eyes snap back to Marcus, who's seated in the last pew. He smiles before gently shaking his head. "That kiss—my goodness... That kiss was..." She goes quiet, her expression the most serious I've seen. "... It was perfect. Everything I'd ever dreamt of. *You* are perfect, a true gift from God, so don't let anyone tell you any different."

She brushes a tear off her cheek before peering at something in the distance. "Please remember the promise you made last week, and I'll be sure to remember mine." In less than a second, her expression switches back to her normal cheeky demeanor. "Now let's get out of this boring funeral home, and go party!"

She blows a final kiss to the camera before the screen goes black.

CHAPTER FORTY-ONE

SLATER

Melanie wasn't joking when she said an elaborate, all-expenses-paid party. Her wake is being held at a local nightclub, and she even hired a DJ. She knew she was dying, and she wanted her friends to send her off in style.

An hour into the wake, I head to the bathroom. After doing my business, I exit the stall, spotting Marcus standing in the middle of the lemon-scented space. His eyes track me as I make my way to the sink to wash my hands, but he remains quiet.

Once I've dried my hands with a paper towel, he hands me a USB stick. "This is part of the promise I made with Melanie." His voice is scratchy—somewhat hesitant. "She doesn't want Kylie to watch it until she's over her grief process. She believes you're the best person to know when that will be."

Nodding, I place the USB stick into my pocket. It will be a good few weeks before Kylie will be ready to see whatever is on there.

"This is the other half of my promise."

He hands me his phone. It's playing a video of one of Melanie's parties. Kylie appears in several scenes, replenishing the snacks and restacking the beer in the fridge. Occasionally the screen turns to

Melanie, who sticks her finger down her throat, appalled by Kylie's "attempt" at partying.

"Every party she does the same thing." Melanie twists her phone to a guy I'd guess to be in his mid-twenties. "This is Trent. He's been eye-fucking Kylie all night long—"

"I totally have," Trent interrupts, smirking like a smug fuck.

His smile doesn't linger for long when Melanie confesses, "But Kylie shoots down *every* move he makes." After twanging Trent's lower hanging lip, she walks through a massive group of partygoers, stopping at a gent who's around the size of Jacob. "This is Paul. He's tried numerous times to get into Kylie's panties." On closer inspection, I realize Paul is more a white version of Marcus. "But, nope, no action for Paul either."

My jaw ticks when Melanie adds on, "I've lost count of the number of guys I've tried to hook her up with the past year, but she hasn't touched a single one, so I've made it my mission to find out why."

A ghost of a smile cracks onto my lips when the video jumps to Kylie sitting in a small, poorly furnished living room. She's holding a large glass of pink-colored liquid—you know those oversized wine glasses they pour cocktails into—and slurring so badly, I can hardly understand her.

"What about Tyler?" questions a voice behind the camera I recognize as Melanie.

"Nope," Kylie replies, shaking her head.

"Paul? He wanted to kiss you last week."

"No." Kylie dramatically draws out the short word. "Not Tyler, not Paul, not Jarrod, not anyone." She places her drink on the coffee table before stumbling to Melanie. "There's nobody else but him. I will *not* touch a man who isn't him."

"Who?" Melanie's tone is spiked with eagerness.

The screen goes blurry when Melanie aids Kylie back onto her feet since she tripped over the ottoman. Once their giggles die down,

Kylie peers straight down the camera before murmuring, "Slater Scott. I love him more than I love myself."

As Melanie's loud squeal bellows out of the speakers, my heart clutches. Even thinking she broke my heart didn't stop me from loving her, so I'm glad to discover she felt the same.

The camera shifts, then Melanie's grinning face takes up the screen. Her hair is in the original bob she had when I met her after our concert in San Diego. "I've been trying to get a name out of her for months, and I finally got it. Prepare yourself, Slater, because we're coming to get you," she warns a mere second before the video freezes.

I hesitantly hand Marcus's phone back to him before dragging my hand over my head, feeling its tremor as it runs over my clipped hair. Two years Kylie waited for me—two whole goddamn motherfucking years. Now I know without a doubt I am the world's biggest asshole. She sacrificed everything for me, and I thanked her by being an idiot who ended up in rehab and fucked anyone with two legs. Although confident she deserves someone much better than me, I can't give her up. I love her too much.

Marcus squeezes my shoulder before handing me a white piece of paper. Some of the weight on my chest eases when I read the hand-written letter.

Hey, Drummer Boy,

I didn't show you my video to make you feel bad. I showed you it to prove how much Kylie loves you. You're probably feeling like the biggest ass in the world. Rightfully so. You should. I read every article about you I could get my hands on when Kylie spilled your name, and I have to say, your list of accomplishments is impressive.

You rightfully earned the title of Rise Up's Bad Boy, but do you know what? Even if Kylie unearths everything you did the two years you were separated, she'll still love you until her very last breath. She'll love you even when you're no longer famous; she'll love you even when you're old and gray, and she'll love you even when you piss her off, and she refuses to talk to you for a week.

She loves you, Slater, warts and all, so my final wish is for you to love her back the same way. Fulfill her every wish and desire; make sure she finishes her bucket list, and love her as much as she loves you.

Until we meet again.

Melanie xx

P.S - If you maintain your side of the bargain, I promise I won't haunt you! I also promise to only sneak the occasional peek of your drumstick while you're in the shower (wink wink.)

My chuckle booms around the bathroom, even knowing Melanie wouldn't hesitate to haunt my ass if I ever stepped out of line with Kylie. But even before I read her letter, I already planned to do what she requested. I'll love and cherish Kylie until my very last breath, even when she doesn't talk to me for a week.

CHAPTER FORTY-TWO

KYLIE

As I scan my surroundings, a smile curves on my lips. I should have known Melanie would have thrown the most extravagant party you could imagine for her wake. She would never settle for anything less. Every weekend our apartment was bursting at the seams with people attending her regularly staged events. We didn't have any money, but that didn't stop us from throwing the best parties Orange County had ever seen.

Most of our friends arrived with the alcohol and snacks, and we supplied the venue and the music. Although I never participated in the games Melanie organized at her parties, I still looked forward to them. Her parties kept our minds occupied on something other than the aggressive treatment we were going through. It gave us something to look forward to during our shitty weekly hospital stays.

I love Melanie, but I was so angry with her the day after I got her letter. I was mad she didn't give me the chance to say goodbye. She could have told me she was sick when she attended the gala last week, but she didn't, and I was furious with her for that.

It was only when Slater read her letter out loud did I realize I had no right to be angry. I did the same thing to him, and I loved him more than anything in the world. Although I'll never get over losing her, I've already forgiven her. What she did was the most selfless thing she'd ever did, so I can't fault her for that. She saved me, just like I chose to save Slater.

Speaking of Slater, he's just stepped out of the men's room. While standing frozen in the doorway, his eyes glide over my body. Excitement dashes through me. He hasn't looked at me like that in over a week—not since the day he discovered the bruise on my thigh.

He makes his way across the crowded room, weaving in and out of the hundreds of people attending Melanie's wake. Today is the second time I've seen him in anything but jeans and boots. He's wearing a black suit with a dark gray dress shirt underneath. He looks so incredibly alluring, if I weren't attending the funeral of my best friend, I wouldn't be able to keep my hands off him.

When he stops in front of me, he tucks a stray piece of hair behind my ear. "Are you ready to go?"

I nod. I said my final goodbye, so now I'd like to grieve in private.

After clasping my hand in his and saying goodbye to his band members, he guides me to a town car waiting out front for us. The instant we exit the nightclub, I'm blinded by paparazzi lights. Slater growls before tugging me into his side. He shelters our eyes from the blinding flashes with his arm before breaking us through the human jungle separating us from our mode of transport.

I climb inside the idling Escalade before scooting across its warm leather seats. Slater promptly shadows me. When he tries to close the door, the paparazzi block his attempts. He kicks the cameras out of the way with his boots before slamming the door closed.

"They're fucking crazy," he grumbles, his voice doused with anger.

A giggle rumbles in my chest, startling even me. The more I try to hold in my laughter, the more it erupts from my mouth.

Slater peers at me in shock before a smile tugs his lips high. "That time in San Francisco?" His grin enlarges as he recalls the memory I'm reminiscing.

A few days after she left San Francisco, Melanie FaceTimed me when I was lying in bed with Slater. When I answered her call, she talked so fast, neither of us could understand a word she was speaking. It was only when she held up a gossip magazine did it dawn on us what she was talking about. The magazine had a two-page spread about the after party Rise Up attended. There were several photos scattered throughout the article.

I was mortified when she zoomed in on a photo of me. It was from when I stepped out of the limo. I looked like a deer trapped in headlights. My eyes were the size of dinner plates, and my mouth was open wide. I laughed when I noticed they also had a photo of Slater's backside when we snuck into the limo only an hour later.

Right down the very bottom of the two-page spread was a photo of Melanie and Marcus. It certainly wasn't the biggest picture; it also wasn't the most glamorous, but it was her and Marcus together, and she was ecstatic. She bought every magazine in her hometown so she could send copies to her family and friends. Even Slater and I got an autographed copy.

"She loved her five minutes of fame."

"She sure did," I reply quietly. "I'm going to miss her so much."

When my tear-welling eyes lift to Slater, he slides me across the seat until I'm sitting in his lap. Once I'm where he wants me, he runs his callused hand down my back soothingly. He doesn't say anything. He doesn't need to. His comfort is all I need.

A few minutes later, our car arrives at our destination. I pop my head off Slater's chest to gaze into his piercing brown eyes. "Where are we going?"

"Home."

He slides out of the car, taking me with him. When he places me back on my feet, I scan our surroundings. Other than a private jet on my left, the airport appears abandoned, so I'm not so sure we should trust any plane stored here.

Slater chuckles at my reaction before accepting the handshake of a gentleman dressed in a crisp pilot's uniform. "I'm Captain Davis.

It's a pleasure to have you aboard, Mr. Scott." His kind green eyes drift to me. "And you too, Mrs. Scott."

Before I can correct him, Slater presses his index finger to my lips, halting my response. "We'll board in a few minutes."

Captain Davis nods before entering the small plane. Once he's out of view, Slater shifts his focus to me. "Do you want to go home?" His voice is packed with sincerity.

I want to nod. The band has been on the road the past two months, so I'd love nothing more than to go back to the loft I now call home with Slater, but I also understand the band has another two weeks of scheduled concerts to perform, so we can't go home just yet.

"We postponed the next two weeks of concerts."

I smile, loving that he can read my thoughts.

"I'll take you anywhere you want to go, Kylie, just name the destination."

His eyes alone reveal the honesty in his statement, much less the promise in his words.

"Even Fiji?"

He chuckles his loud, boisterous laugh. "Even Fiji. Although I may need to get a bigger plane."

Not thinking, I press my lips against his. I've missed his mouth on mine the past three days, and if the deep moan escaping his throat is any indication, he's been missing mine as well.

Our kiss starts slow but soon progresses to needy. The past three days is the longest we haven't been sexually active since we've been back together. I went two years without any form of sexual contact, so I had a lot of missed opportunities to make up for, but it doesn't feel right enjoying life when my best friend just lost hers, so I inch back away before I've gotten my fill.

As his fingers brush the heat on my cheeks, Slater's eyes drop to mine. "Where do you want to go, baby?"

"Take me home."

He nods before placing a final kiss to my lips, then he walks us toward the impressive-looking plane. Just as we're about to board, his phone vibrates in his pocket. His smile vanishes when he glances at the screen. I understand why. My heart skids into my stomach when I see who is calling. It's Dr. Webster.

"Hello." Slater's short greeting can't hide the tremble of his voice. "Uh huh, yep."

His brows scrunch before his watering eyes snap to me. After he releases my hand from his sweaty grip, he scrubs the bristly hair on his head. The vein working overtime in his neck hits me with a severe bout of nausea. Feeling my knees buckle, I sit on the ground, believing it's the safest option. I don't want to faint on the hard asphalt.

After disconnecting his call, Slater gathers me in his arms, then walks us into the plane without a word leaving his mouth. He sits us in a large white leather recliner before drawing me close to his chest. The rapid beat of his heart indicates how panicked he is.

I thought I knew my body better than this. I was so certain I wasn't sick again; I only agreed to the tests to relieve Slater's stress, not increase it. I pant, unable to fill my lungs with air. I think I'm in shock—and perhaps even on the verge of a panic attack.

"Breathe, baby, breathe."

Slater snags a bottle of water off the table next to us, undoes the lid, then lifts it to my lips. The water trickling into my mouth is heavenly to my dry throat, but it adds to the queasiness of my stomach, and don't get me started on my screaming lungs.

"I'm sorry. I'm so sorry." My watering eyes float up from Slater's chest to his eyes. "I can't put you through this again. You don't deserve to go through this again—"

He presses his index finger against my mouth. "You don't have ALL."

"What?" I'm certain I heard him wrong.

I didn't. "You don't have ALL."

He chuckles while scrubbing his hand down his face. When his eyes return to mine, his laughter gets so loud, it vibrates through both his body and mine. A smile tugs at my lips. Not because I don't have ALL, but because of his infectious laugh.

He exhales so deeply it dries the tears on my cheeks. "I love you, baby."

"I love you too." My reply is hesitant, unsure why his mood shifted from panicked to manic in a matter of seconds.

He balances his forehead against mine, its clamminess undeniable. "It's lucky we added number three back onto your list."

I yank back as my heart rate soars. "I'm pregnant?"

As a blistering smile stretches across his face, he nods.

Holy shit!

CHAPTER FORTY-THREE

SLATER

Four Weeks Later...

I won't lie; when Dr. Webster told me Kylie was pregnant, I crapped my pants. I was so convinced her results would come back negative, I didn't stop to consider that they could be positive. Kylie's chances of getting pregnant naturally were around five percent, so we got a little lax using protection. I should have known my sperm are stronger than that. There's no stopping the Scott men's spawn.

Because Kylie is still grieving, she hasn't acknowledged her pregnancy just yet. She feels wrong expressing happiness when she just lost her best friend. I understand her apprehension, so I'll continue supporting her through her grief without mentioning her pregnancy until she's ready.

She's still grieving, but I've seen sparks of the old Kylie returning the past few days, so I've decided now is the right time to give her the USB from Melanie. When I hand it to her, she peers at me curiously before plugging it into her laptop. When I realize it's a video like the one I saw in the bathroom in San Jose, I remove the USB from her laptop and place it in the flat screen on the wall in our loft.

The movie is a timeline of Kylie and Melanie's friendship the past two and a half years. It's similar to the one Marcus showed me last month, but more based on them, instead of the men Kylie rejected. It even has the day Kylie arrived at Melanie's apartment wearing the clothes she left the cabin in.

Kylie squeezes my hand several times throughout the movie. Just from watching the hour-long clip, I can see how important Melanie was to Kylie, and I finally understand why her grieving process is taking longer than initially expected. I also understand why Kylie previously stated Melanie is a female version of me. We were two peas in a pod. We just had different bits between our legs.

By the time the movie ends, Kylie has the most beautiful smile plastered on her face. It grows when I click on a second file on the USB. It's a similar video to the one shown at Melanie's funeral. She's sitting on her bed, crossed-legged and smiling brightly.

"Hi, gorgeous. I couldn't tell you everything I wanted to say in the video at the funeral so I made you your own special edition. I have one last gift I'd like you to help me give." Melanie rubs her hands together as her throat works hard to swallow. "Because I was diagnosed with ALL at twenty-one, I had the opportunity to store my eggs. Even having no intention of using them, for some strange reason, I had them gathered and stored. When I met you, I initially thought I did it for you. But after meeting your boyfriend, I highly doubt you'll need them."

My hope soars when Kylie's hand covers the tiny bump low in her belly. This is the first time she's acknowledged her pregnancy in the past four weeks.

"What Serena's foundation is doing is very admirable, and it will help a lot of people, but I think we can go one step further. Maybe we can help out the young girls like you who were too young to have their eggs stored?" Melanie stops talking to wipe a tear off her cheek.

As she struggles to rein in her composure, her eyes dart around her room.

Several seconds pass in silence before she gains the courage to continue. "I want to donate the eggs I have stored to women who have been through what we've been through. Can you do that for me?"

Kylie nods, even knowing Melanie can't see her.

"Great!" Melanie beams, aware Kylie would never deny her request. "I love you, Kylie, and I miss you loads and loads. I'll see you on the flip side."

After squashing two fingers to her lips, she raises them to the sky. Kylie copies her movement just as the screen goes black. In silence, I watch her profile. I never know what to say to help her, so I just comfort her the only way I know how. I pull her into my lap then run my hand down her back.

"I miss her," she murmurs into my chest a short time later.

"I know you do, baby."

I see how much she misses her every time I glance into her eyes. Part of her soul vanished the day Melanie died.

Her head pops off my chest so she can peer into my eyes. "I miss you too."

A broad smile etches on my face. I've missed her too, but I understand this is part of the process of grieving her friend. "I know you do, baby."

When she rolls her eyes, I see sparks of the old Kylie reigniting in them. "Do you think you could ask your mom about Melanie's suggestion?"

I nod without pause for thought. I accidentally let it slip to my mom last week that Kylie is pregnant when she dropped off some home-baked goodies. She was beyond ecstatic. She would have never said anything to Kylie or me, but she was worried she'd never become a grandmother because she knew the statistics on infertility for chemotherapy patients. After I shared our news, she's even more convinced Kylie is a gift from Serena. The more I think about it, the more I believe it too.

"It's a great idea, but I don't think we should do it under Serena's name."

Kylie's brows furrow. She appears utterly confused.

"We should do it under Melanie's name. It was her idea, so she deserves the credit."

A huge smile carves on Kylie's face. "I love you."

"I know you do, baby," I repeat, laughing.

It isn't that I don't want to say it back. I love her more than life itself, but I want to keep the mood light because it's the first time I've seen the true Kylie emerging from the shadows the past four weeks.

When she grabs one of the cushions off the sofa to smack me upside the head, my loud chuckle echoes around our loft. Then my eyes bug when she stands before pulling her long-sleeve shirt over her head. We haven't done anything more than kiss the past month, so you can imagine how much I've missed seeing her beautiful body.

Her hesitation is all part of her grieving process, so I'd never push her into doing anything she wasn't ready to do, even if my body craves her more than air.

When she saunters backward, the swing of her hips gains the attention of my cock. Once she has a few feet between us, she removes her bra and drops it to the ground. My teeth grit when her forearm covers her perfect tits from my view, but I have no chance in hell of stopping my raging hard on. Her body is fucking dynamite.

After sliding her panties down her mouthwatering thighs, she winks before darting for our bedroom. I'm on her heels before she's even halfway across our living room. The instant my lips brush her neck, her giggles switch to a moan.

There's my girl. Back stronger than ever.

Around an hour later, we're snuggled in bed, panting from the exhaustion of ecstasy.

Kylie's breath ruffles the fine hairs on my chest when she murmurs, "I can't believe we're having a baby."

I chuckle. I'm still shocked.

She balances her chin on my tattooed pec before locking her big beautiful eyes with mine. "Are you okay with this?"

I nod. I'm fine with it, because it's happening with her. If it were anyone else, I'd be running right now. It also helps knowing she'll be tied to me forever. Even if I royally fuck everything up, she can't get rid of me, no matter how hard she tries.

"Don't even think about screwing up, Slater." Her voice has an edge of wittiness to it. "Because if you do anything wrong, Melanie will follow through with her threat."

I chuckle. I have no doubt Melanie will haunt my ass if...

Hold on, how does she know about Melanie's threat? No one but Marcus knows about that.

When I arch a brow, demanding Kylie spill the beans, she bites down on her bottom lip. "You left her note in your suit pants that have been lying on the floor in our walk-in closet the past four weeks." She slaps my chest. It's more playful than intended to hurt. "You do know what a laundry basket looks like, don't you?"

"I've seen one a few times in my life, but laundry has never held my interest for long. Besides, isn't that what I have you for?"

I laugh when she socks me in the gut. This one was to maim.

Once my chuckles settle down, she rests her head back on my chest, where she remains quiet for the next several minutes. "It is true, you know."

"I know." I run my hand down her hair. "I won't give Melanie a reason to haunt me. I'll behave—"

"I'm not talking about that." She lifts her head so her eyes can roam over my face. She's lost a little bit of weight the past four weeks, but she's still the most gorgeous girl I've ever seen. "I know everything that happened when we were apart. I googled everything I could find about you after the stage curtain incident."

She sounds embarrassed. I don't know why. She didn't do anything wrong. I'm the one who should be ashamed. I made a fool out of myself during those two years, and I'd give anything to go back and change every fucked up thing I did.

I attempt to comment on her statement, wanting to apologize for the stupid things I did, but she presses her index finger on my mouth, halting my words. "And in spite of all that, I still love you, and I continue to fall in love with you more every single day. I love you, Slater—warts and all."

CHAPTER FORTY-FOUR

SLATER

Four Months Later...

"A re you sure this looks okay?"

"Fuck yes," I reply without hesitation.

Kylie is wearing a teeny tiny black string bikini. She looks as hot as... I don't have a word to explain how hot she looks right now. The most gorgeous part is her beautiful round belly proudly on display.

"I feel ridiculous."

I grimace while peering down at the floral print board shorts Kylie purchased for me. At first, I refused to wear the hideous, ball-busting, penis-shrinking monstrosity she bought for me. But once her eyes pleaded into mine, and she promised I'd be thoroughly rewarded for wearing them, I would have *never* denied her request. My cock and I will do anything for her.

Giggling, Kylie paces to the overflowing suitcases we haven't bothered to unpack. "It was either those or these." She swings a pair of red speedos in the air.

I gag. Just seeing them hanging from her finger is enough to make me want to vomit. "I'll stick with these, but what's wrong with wearing jeans to the beach? I have no intentions of going in the water, so why do I need swim trunks?"

Kylie and I have finally arrived in Fiji. It took us longer to get here than we would have liked. Kylie needed time to grieve, and the band has been in the studio recording our third album the past two months, so life got away from us.

"I could go naked? We do have the entire beach to ourselves, so technically clothing could be optional." *Although it would make it hard to hide the engagement ring I have in my pocket.*

"Don't worry. I fully plan on getting you naked on that beach." Kylie rakes her nails over my pecs before cranking open the double white doors of our suite, showcasing the beautiful beach that's solely ours, while also blasting our room with stuffy, humid air. "But you'll be on the bottom."

I chuckle while shadowing her outside.

By the time we head back to our private bungalow, I'm thoroughly satisfied and exhausted. Kylie's sexual appetite has always been impressive, but now that she's pregnant, she's even more demanding —and I fucking love it.

"I thought you said you weren't going swimming?" Kylie questions as we walk hand in hand into the blissful comfort of our air-conditioned bungalow.

I had no intentions of swimming, but have you ever been to Fiji? It's fuckin' hot. I've been guzzling down water all day just to stay hydrated. I swear someone inserted a leaking tap into my armpit—that's how much I'm sweating.

"Fuck," I curse under my breath when it dawns on me I went swimming with Kylie's engagement ring in my pocket.

When my hands dart into the pockets of my board shorts, I groan loudly. My pockets are empty.

"You okay?" Kylie questions, concerned.

No. I swallow a brick in my throat before jerking up my chin. "Yep!"

Her ring cost me a fucking fortune. The jeweler said you're supposed to spend ten percent of your yearly salary. I don't know if he was full of shit or not, but forever wanting to be better than anyone else, I jacked it up to twenty percent. Between you and me, that's a fuck ton of money.

"Are you sure you're okay?" Kylie bridges the gap between us. "Because you don't look very well."

I'm not surprised. I feel sick. How could I have been so stupid to go swimming with her ring in my shorts? You'd think I'd feel a diamond of that size falling out of my pocket.

Kylie places her hand on my cheek, checking if I have a fever. I don't have a fever. I'm just fuming at my own stupidity. When she flips her hand over, coolness encroaches my cheeks. *Maybe I do have a fever?*

After pulling her hand away, Kylie makes a face. "Maybe you're not sick; perhaps you're scared?"

My eyes roll. I'm not scared of anything except spiders. Those hairy-legged bastards are gross. And I'm petrified of losing Kylie. I couldn't live without her. People think I'm overreacting, but they don't know the hell I went through that week waiting for Kylie's results. I couldn't eat or sleep because I was so worried I was about to lose her.

To lessen my panic, I now make Kylie have monthly blood tests. That way, if her blood count rises by even the slightest increment, additional tests can be ordered. Kylie thinks I'm a worrywart, but she complies with my demands just to give me peace of mind.

When my eyes turn to Kylie's, I sigh loudly. The ring I'm

panicked about is sitting exactly where it belongs—on her ring finger that she's wiggling in front of my face. My wild heart rate decelerates just from seeing the ring that cost me more than my entire loft. Thank fuck she found it.

"It fell out of your pocket before we went to the beach."

When she giggles, I glare at her. I'm glad she can see the humor in the situation. I can't. I'm on the verge of a fucking heart attack.

Hold on just one dang minute. Since she's already wearing my ring, do I still need to propose?

Kylie must be able to read my thoughts. "Get on your knees, Slater."

I drop to the ground and crawl toward her, like a slave begging his master for forgiveness. I've been practicing the perfect grovel the past few months, just in case I need it during our marriage. I'm far from perfect, but Kylie assures me she loves me for me, so I'll continue being who I am. That means the occasional bout of groveling will be required at some stage in the future.

Once I reach her feet, I peer up at her, leaning sideways so I can see her face past her seven-month-pregnant belly. I raise myself onto my knees and end up face-to-face with her well-rounded tummy. I love her belly—seriously I do—but just like Charlie, the baby and I have an agreement. It's not to move at any stage during sexual activities. If he or she complies with my request, I supply it with an unlimited amount of glazed jam donuts, which Kylie assures me the baby loves. Thankfully, our agreement is working well for both parties at this stage.

I place a quick peck on Kylie's belly before raising my eyes. Here it is, right here and right now, four words I assumed would never seep from my lips. "Will you—"

"Yes!" she squeals before I even get the whole question out.

And everyone says I'm the impatient one.

EPILOGUE
SLATER

Four years later...

No matter how many times I visit her, it never gets any easier.

While sucking in a big breath, I scan the cemetery, seeking the paparazzi hiding in wait. They never cut me any slack, even while visiting a cemetery.

Penelope wiggles in her car seat. "Come on, Daddy."

I unbuckle her, prop her on my hip, then lean back in to grab the tulips I purchased at the florist this morning. The instant I place Penelope on the ground, the sound of clicking cameras rises from the bushes at the entrance of the cemetery.

After raising my middle finger in the air, I turn it in the direction the noise is coming from, smirking arrogantly about how they won't be able to sell any of the pictures they're snapping. I've learned the past few years that no magazine will print a picture of me flipping the bird, so that's exactly what I give the paparazzi anytime they hassle me. I don't mind posing for photos during events, or when I'm on tour with the band, but once I'm home, I expect a little bit of respect, and, God forbid, privacy.

Penelope's beautiful giggle bellows out of her when she notices my finger. "Unky Jacob said that's not a nice finger."

"Uncle Jacob doesn't know what he's talking about." I return her to my hip before quickening my pace. Because the cemetery is gated, they can only capture us while we're in the parking lot.

Once we're far enough away they'll no longer get any photos of Penelope, I place her back on her feet. "They're pretty flowers, Daddy." The country twang in her voice makes me smile.

"Thank you, darling," I reply in my best fake country accent.

Penelope is our little blessing, the baby Kylie and I thought we'd never have. She's turning four in six weeks and three days. Yes, I know the exact number of days because she updates me first thing every morning. She's been counting down the past three months.

Penelope is named after both Serena and Melanie. Her full name is Penelope Rae. Penelope was my sister's middle name, and Rae was Melanie's. Her face is as beautiful as her mother's, and she even has a small gathering of freckles across her button nose. Her hair is a cross between Kylie's and mine, making it dark blonde in color. It's so flawlessly straight, I often joke it would be perfect for dreads.

I haven't been able to grow my dreads back since I cut them off for charity years ago. I've tried, but getting past that annoying fuzz stage in your late twenties and early thirties is fucking annoying. I could get away with it when I was a teenager, but I'm a dad now, and I look fucking ridiculous with a ball of fuzz on the top of my head, so I have my hair clipped all the time.

Once I reach her gravestone, I place the tulips on top before squatting down to clear away the leaves fallen over her plaque. A ghost of a smile stretches across my face when Penelope gathers the leaves to place them in a pile underneath a tree. She's a bit of a tree hugger.

When the gravesite is back in presentable condition, I sit on the ground before offering up my lap for Penelope. I don't say anything. I don't need to. She knows I'm here, quietly reflecting on our memories.

Around five minutes later, Penelope grunts. She's as impatient as I am. I'm surprised she even lasted five minutes. "I miss Mommy."

"I know you do, baby girl. So do I."

When I adjust her position so she's sitting sideways, her dazzling hazel eyes lock with mine. My heart clenches when I see her little tears. Wanting to ensure her tears don't fall, I pretend to steal her nose. "I've got your nose." I stick part of my thumb out between two fingers.

Penelope's mouth gapes open as her hands shoot up to her nose. "Give it back, Daddy."

I don't believe her anger. There's too much of her smile peeking out from beneath her hands for her ruse to be plausible.

"I'm going to eat it."

When I raise my hand to my mouth, Penelope leaps out of my lap, squealing. "You can't eat my nose, Daddy," she protests, mortified. "You can eat my boogers, but not my nose."

I throw my head back and laugh. How was I ever scared of having kids? Penelope ensures I never have to grow up. I even have the privilege of testing out her toys for "safety" before she's allowed to use them.

"I've already had breakfast today, but thanks for the offer."

Her smile competes with the sun. "You're welcome."

She has wonderful manners. I have no clue who she gets them from.

After popping her nose back on her face, I stand, taking her with me. "Did you want to go and visit Nevaeh?"

Penelope's pupils widen as she nods, excitement beaming out of her.

I lean over and kiss the top of the gravestone. "I'll come back in a couple of days," I promise before walking hand in hand out of the cemetery with one of my most precious gifts.

As I buckle Penelope in her car seat, she lets out a little yawn. She's been waking early the past few mornings, and it's catching up with her.

She's asleep long before we reach our destination, and continues napping even with me removing her from her car seat and wrangling through a swarm of paparazzi who always know how to find me.

When I enter Nevaeh's room, I try to wake Penelope up. "Penelope..."

She mumbles incoherently while turning her head in the other direction.

"Penelope, Nevaeh is here."

The instant Nevaeh's name escapes my lips, Penelope's head darts up off my shoulder. "Nevie?" she questions, half-asleep.

When she spots my nod, she squirms in my arms, requesting to be put down. As I set her on her feet, her eager eyes bounce around the room. They stop when someone at the side of the room greets her, "Hi, Penelope."

"Mommy!" Penelope charges for Kylie, who's sitting in a reclining chair, nursing our newborn daughter Nevaeh in her arms.

It took nearly a year of IVF to add Nevaeh to our family. We used a similar service now offered to sufferers of ALL through the Melanie Greystone Foundation, but instead of using a donated egg, we harvested a small number of eggs from Kylie's one remaining working ovary. Since Nevaeh completes our family, Kylie donated her remaining eggs to Melanie's foundation.

There was a heap of legal bureaucracy the foundation had to wade through to legally give away Melanie's eggs as she requested. But with the help of Jenni's dad, Michael, we jumped through the hoops, and the foundation has been going strong the past two years. It not only receives donations from previous ALL sufferers, but they also accept egg donations from the general public as well. It can claim credit for eighteen children being born to ALL sufferers since its inaugural year.

Nevaeh was born four days ago via an emergency C-section. The last four nights are the longest I've been separated from Kylie in the past nearly five years. It's also the only time Penelope hasn't had her mom and grandma at her beck and call twenty-four-seven. She's been missing Kylie just as much as I have. We visit Kylie and Nevaeh every day, but it's not the same as seeing her for every minute of the day. I really hope the doctors will give me permission to take my girls home today, because I'm missing them like crazy.

Our home is a rustic farmhouse on the outskirts of town. I never thought I'd live on a ranch, but the instant I saw the for sale sign swinging at the front of a property neighboring Jacob's dad's house, I knew I had to buy it. It's the perfect place to raise our family.

It needed a lot of work, but I had contacts in the construction industry since I worked in it before I became famous. My old crew was more than happy to work on our property from sun up to sun down, meaning the rebuild was completed just before Penelope was born.

We originally planned to divide our time between the farm and our loft, but once Penelope started crawling, it became apparent the loft wasn't baby-friendly, so our time at the farmhouse lengthened until we stayed there full time.

The warehouse conversion of my building was completed nearly three years ago. It makes a neat profit for Penelope's, and now Nevaeh's trust funds. The loft is still in its original bachelor pad condition, but now instead of it being a bachelor pad, it's where Kylie and I spend our dirty weekends. Either Kylie's mom looks after Penelope at our ranch, or my mom takes her for overnight visits at her house, then Kylie and I spend the weekend naked in our loft. Even after five years, I can't get enough of my girl, so you can imagine how often I plan weekend getaways.

Has my panic about Kylie getting sick diminished at all the past four years? No, it hasn't. But I'm confident even if she does get ALL again, she'll give it her hardest fight to ensure our girls aren't left without a mother. She'll fight until her very last breath, and I have no doubt she's strong enough to overcome any obstacles thrown at her.

"We went and saw Aunty Rena," Penelope informs Kylie.

"Did you?"

Kylie's empty hand runs down Penelope's hair, smoothing the bird's nest her car seat made. Once she has it all straightened, her eyes lift to me, questioning if I'm okay. I nod. Today is the anniversary of my sister's death, but taking Penelope to her gravesite eased the pain I usually experience.

"Oh no." Penelope's bottom lip drops into a pout. "I forgot to give Aunt Rena her horsey."

Penelope is obsessed with horses just like her mother was at her age. She has a large collection of toy horses she displays on purposely built shelves in her room. This morning, she picked out her favorite horse to give to Serena. When she told me she was giving her favorite horse to Serena, a tear formed in my eye. I felt like the biggest fucking pussy in the world, but I was so proud of my baby girl, I wore my tear with pride.

Penelope never had the privilege to meet her Aunt Serena or Aunt Melanie, but she undoubtedly loves them. She asks questions about them all the time and proudly tells her playmates about the two guardian angels watching over her.

"It's okay, baby girl."

I gently remove Nevaeh from Kylie's arms so she can comfort Penelope. She hates seeing tears in her eyes nearly as much as I do. When I glance down at the bundle of pink in my arms, so many memories of Serena smash into me. Nevaeh has strawberry blonde hair and tiny little facial features just like Serena did. The only difference between them is their eye color. Nevaeh's are brown. We called her Nevaeh because it is "heaven" spelled backwards, and she's our own little slice of heaven.

"Maybe we can go give Aunt Serena your horsey on our way home today?" Kylie suggests, halting Penelope's tears while forcing a mammoth grin onto my face.

"You're coming home?"

When Kylie nods, I holler and jump in the air. I've missed her so fucking much the past four days, I never plan on being away from her this long ever again.

Kylie giggles when Penelope joins me in jumping around in euphoria. Nevaeh continues sleeping peacefully in my arms, unfazed by my reaction.

If you'd asked me five years ago where I'd be today, I would have said at a strip club or on stage performing with my band. If you told me I'd be happily married to the love of my life and a father to two little princesses, I would have laughed in your face, told you to stop taking drugs, then run away from you scared out of my mind that a lunatic was talking to me.

Back then, I had no clue how much I needed my girls in my life.

Our band is still one of the world's most successful bands. We sell out concert halls within minutes of the tickets going on sale, and our albums are always multi-platinum. My bandmates are my brothers, and their children are my nieces and nephews, but at the end of the day, my girls are, and always will be, my number one priorities.

They're my life, my soul, and the sole owners of my heart, and I wouldn't have it any other way.

The next book in the **Perception Series** is Isaac's story. It's already released and available to download. It is called Enigma. books2read.com/Isaac1

Don't fret — Marcus's story is already published. It's under the **Bound Series**. Please note, this series is HOT HOT HOT! You can find book one here: <u>Chains</u>

Facebook: facebook.com/authorshandi

Instagram: instagram.com/authorshandi

Email: authorshandi@gmail.com

Reader's Group: bit.ly/ShandiBookBabes

Website: authorshandi.com

Newsletter: https://www.subscribepage.com/AuthorShandi

If you enjoyed this book - please leave a review.

ALSO BY SHANDI BOYES

Denotes Standalone Books

Perception Series

Saving Noah *

Fighting Jacob *

Taming Nick *

Redeeming Slater *

Saving Emily

Wrapped Up with Rise Up

Protecting Nicole *

Enigma

Enigma

Unraveling an Enigma

Enigma The Mystery Unmasked

Enigma: The Final Chapter

Beneath The Secrets

Beneath The Sheets

Spy Thy Neighbor *

The Opposite Effect *

I Married a Mob Boss *

Second Shot *

The Way We Are

The Way We Were

Sugar and Spice *

Lady In Waiting

Man in Queue

Couple on Hold

Enigma: The Wedding

Silent Vigilante

Hushed Guardian

Quiet Protector

Enigma: An Isaac Retelling

Twisted Lies *

Bound Series

Chains

Links

Bound

Restrain

The Misfits *

Nanny Dispute *

Russian Mob Chronicles

Nikolai: A Mafia Prince Romance

Nikolai: Taking Back What's Mine

Nikolai: What's Left of Me

Nikolai: Mine to Protect

Asher: My Russian Revenge *

Nikolai: Through the Devil's Eyes

<u>Trey</u> *

The Italian Cartel

Dimitri

Roxanne

Reign

Mafia Ties (Novella)

Maddox

Demi

Ox

Rocco *

Clover *

Smith *

RomCom Standalones

Just Playin' *

Ain't Happenin' *

The Drop Zone *

Very Unlikely *

False Start *

Short Stories - Newsletter Downloads

Christmas Trio *

Falling For A Stranger *

One Night Only Series

Hotshot Boss *

Hotshot Neighbor *

<u>The Bobrov Bratva Series</u>

Wicked Intentions *

Sinful Intentions *

Devious Intentions *

Deadly Intentions *

<u>Coming Soon</u>

Nanny Dispute *

Protecting Nicole (December 26) *

www.ingramcontent.com/pod-product-compliance
Lightning Source LLC
Chambersburg PA
CBHW071131180726
48291CB00007B/2130